A Rogue in Firelight

The Whisky Rogues, Book 1

Previously published as
LAIRD OF ROGUES

Susan King

ARE YOU SIGNED UP FOR DRAGONBLADE'S BLOG?

You'll get the latest news and information on exclusive giveaways, exclusive excerpts, coming releases, sales, free books, cover reveals and more.

Check out our complete list of authors, too!

No spam, no junk. That's a promise!

Sign Up Here

www.dragonbladepublishing.com

Dearest Reader;

Thank you for your support of a small press. At Dragonblade Publishing, we strive to bring you the highest quality Historical Romance from some of the best authors in the business. Without your support, there is no 'us', so we sincerely hope you adore these stories and find some new favorite authors along the way.

Happy Reading!

CEO, Dragonblade Publishing

Additional Dragonblade books by
Author Susan King

The Whisky Rogues Series
A Rogue in Firelight (Book 1)

Highland Secrets Series
The Scottish Bride (Book 1)
The Forest Bride (Book 2)
The Guardian's Bride (Book 3)

Celtic Hearts Series
The Hawk Laird (Book 1)
The Falcon Laird (Book 2)
The Swan Laird (Book 3)

For my amazing, wonderful,
very patient family.

Prologue

"Oh, what a tangled web we weave
When first we practice to deceive . . ."
—Sir Walter Scott, *Marmion,* 1808

Scotland, the Highlands
May 1, 1822

MOONLIGHT AND MIST gleamed over cobblestones as Ronan MacGregor approached the tavern, wary as he went, boots echoing on the dark street. The old port town of Culross, known for coal and salt exports, favored smuggling traffic too. Free traders swept down from the hills to move clandestine goods swiftly out the harbor of a night. Soon another such cargo would go out.

He had numbered briefly among those rascals, but it was time he returned to life as laird, lawyer, whisky distiller. New-minted viscount as well, dare he claim it. That could bring an estate and suspicion too; some might assume he wanted the property that much. What he wanted was justice.

Tonight, traveling north from Edinburgh to his home in Perthshire, he intended to meet friends in a tavern. He had sent a message; what he had heard in the city made it imperative he find them.

Light glowed in the tavern's crown-glass windows as he stepped into a haze of smoke, noise, and lamplight. His Highland gear—belted plaid, old jacket, tartan waistcoat—stood him in good stead here. In the city, he preferred well-tailored clothing of dark superfine, for the Courts of Session and Justiciary would look askance at a lawyer in Highland kit. Even so, he wore his hair longer than most and kept to the stubborn note of a tartan waistcoat. If a Whig eyebrow twitched here or there, so be it.

When attending to matters of whisky and transport, he and his companions kept to the tartan and the Gaelic as well. They knew the value of caution.

Entering the main room, he felt a prickle along his neck thanks to the watchful habit he had formed in war and occasional smuggling. The patrons looked ordinary enough; old men in plaids and bonnets sharing ale and playing cards, perhaps down from the hills for the cattle market; a weary family eating supper; the tavernkeeper, a maid. No excise officers here.

He pushed through a curtain into a smaller room. Two Highlanders sat at a table, one lean and fair, the other brawny and dark. They looked up.

"Glenbrae, here at last," said the tall blond fellow in Gaelic.

"Greetings, Stewart. MacInnes." He sat. The table held glasses, a squat brown crockery jug, and a plate with leftover crumbles of cheese and oatcakes.

Iain MacInnes reached for the jug and poured a dram into a small glass, handing it to Ronan. "How was the city?"

"Grand and busy. Filled with rumors of the king's visit this summer."

"His visit has been dangled and canceled for more than a year." Arthur, Viscount Linhope—simply Mr. Stewart here— broke off a bit of cheese. "He may not come at all."

"It seems likely in August."

MacInnes raised his glass, amber liquid gleaming. "To King Geordie, may he learn to love the Scots, which he does not. How was court?"

"A verdict of 'not proven' for my client, so he is free. But the lad never should have been arrested. Remember," Ronan added low, "John R. MacGregor, advocate, was never here. Nor were his friends, a doctor and an engineer. Just MacGregor, Stewart, and MacInnes. Three reprobates."

MacInnes lifted his glass. "To rogues and reprobates."

Linhope saluted too. "And here's to Will MacGregor and John, Lord Darrach, who began this sore adventure."

Ronan drew a breath against the names, the tug in his heart. His brother. His cousin. He took a sip.

MacInnes indicated the glass. "Tell us what you think."

Ronan swirled the liquid. "It is not Glenbrae whisky, I know that."

"Glenbrae has no equal," Linhope laughed. "This is new."

Ronan tasted again; malt, heather, peat, a hint of earth and stone in the water source, he decided. He cupped it on his tongue, seeking an elusive taste. Grass and wild garlic. He swallowed the sweet burn of it.

"Pitlinnie," he declared. "Over three years in the keg."

Iain butted Linhope with an elbow. "No one can tell the whisky like the laird of Glenbrae."

"Pitlinnie does not trim the burnside that runs past his still, so his whisky tastes of what grows there. This is good." Ronan turned the jug to read the handwritten label. *Pitlinnie. Fine Highland Whisky.* "It will sell."

"He is shipping this out tonight. The English pay well for Highland whisky," Linhope said. "Northern whiskies made with good barley malt are heaven's nectar compared to Lowland liquor made from cheap grains. Pitlinnie will profit."

"But we are not here to talk about Pitlinnie." Iain watched Ronan. "What news?"

"If you wonder about the Darrach estate, the matter remains unresolved since my cousin died intestate. Now it goes to the courts."

"Go to Darrach Castle and look for his will yourself," MacInnes suggested.

"I hear the housekeeper stayed on to wait for the new lord. Mairi Brodie told me," Linhope added, "when she wrote for advice in treating a tenant's persistent cough."

"Ah." Ronan had made his peace with Mairi Brodie, but he felt guarded. A deeper love he would never find, though she had married his brother instead of himself. He shrugged.

"Hugh Cameron went to Darrach Castle to search. It is his task as my solicitor. Not my place. We must keep the matter clean."

MacInnes nodded. "Something else on your mind? You sent word to us."

"Aye. The time has come to retire our concern. But you know that," Ronan said.

"We all knew the risks when we took this on after your kinsmen were killed," Linhope said. "We agreed to finish their work to honor them. It has gone well so far."

"We have completed their work, and I am grateful to you both."

"We would never abandon you to danger." MacInnes grinned.

"Both of you like a risk," Linhope said. "Not me. If Ronan says we are done, good then."

MacInnes huffed. "What then of the Wild Whisky Rogues? I like the name, and the reports of us in the news."

"It makes us seem like heroes. We are not," Ronan said.

"We provide a service. We move goods about, collect funds promised to your kinsmen, and share it with their families." MacInnes shrugged his big shoulders. "It is an honor to be called Whisky Rogues by the Bard of the North himself."

"Sir Walter Scott christened Will and Darrach the Whisky Rogues for their escapades, not us," Ronan pointed out. "He called them Highland heroes in plaid, defenders of their people, saving the ancient Celtic brew. But we all know it could all go black as the Earl o' Hell's waistcoat."

"Could. But wait. Pitlinnie wants a new arrangement," MacInnes said. "Very lucrative."

"Pitlinnie wants what benefits him. We refused him before."

"Nor is he pleased to have to move his lot this night," Mac-

Innes said.

"Better we go back to what we do best," Ronan said. "Doctoring, building, defending—and making whisky legally. The Glenbrae distillery is doing well. You are welcome to join me."

"The Whisky Rogues will soon be forgotten," Linhope said. "We finished what Will and Darrach began, saved their names and that of Glenbrae. It is done."

"They took bullets for us," Iain said grimly.

"And we wish those two brave fools were here now. But they are not. It is time to end it, just as Ronan says," Linhope replied.

Ronan glanced at the doorway, seeing nothing unusual. "I hear the laws will change in January. Highlanders will no longer benefit from free trade. Licensed distilleries will profit. We are gentlemen, not thieves. My grandfather forfeited his lands and title for loyalty to Prince Charlie, and plunged his family into poverty. But my father raised us to have manners and education, and began to rebuild that legacy. I intend to continue that, not destroy it."

"Not just a lawyer, but a war hero who never runs from risk," Linhope said to MacInnes, who nodded.

"We need to be wary, lads, with more excise officers and more arrests and penalties ahead. We did what we agreed to do," Ronan said.

"Aye, then," Linhope said, nudging MacInnes, who nodded reluctantly.

"Good. We will talk later." Ronan stood, leaving coins on the table. Heading for the door, he felt a prickle on his neck, dread in his gut. "Go. *Now*," he growled to his friends.

He stepped outside first, leery, seeing only empty tavern steps, moonlit street, and dark buildings. Down the way, two carts. Horses. Something was not right—

Footsteps, shadows, the glint of pistols as men swarmed out of the darkness. "Stop!" a man called. "His Majesty's excise officers. Which of you is Glenbrae?"

Whirling, Ronan felt a pistol poke hard in his back. He spun away, but meaty hands grabbed, yanked, punched, held him. A shot rang out and whizzed past his head. He struck out an elbow to catch a jaw, ducked to evade a clubbing. Beside him, Linhope and Iain took and gave blows as the fierce brawl escalated on the tavern steps.

"Stand fast!" Two men had MacInnes by the arms now, the big man nearly wrenching free. Others knocked Linhope to his knees. Feeling cold steel press against his temple, Ronan went still. Two men grabbed his arms from behind.

"MacGregor of Glenbrae," another man growled. "Aye, you are the one."

"Where is your warrant?" Ronan demanded. "On the very steps of this tavern, you need permission to invade its boundary or threaten its patrons."

"Talks like a long-robe! Hah! You lot are the ones we seek. Whisky Rogues, found at last!" The man spit. "MacGregor of Glenbrae, with cronies Stewart and MacInnes. We are the excise, arresting you for crimes."

Held fast, breathing hard, Ronan recognized Peter Dawson, an excise officer who had come close to catching them twice before. His late brother Will had believed that Dawson was in the pay of others set on taking down the Whisky Rogues. Suspecting Dawson was responsible for the deaths of his brother and cousin, Ronan felt sure of it now.

"Specify the crimes you witnessed," Ronan said. "We have done no wrong here."

"We had word you three are moving illicit parcels tonight. A load o' peat reek just left by secret transport. Take 'em," Dawson ordered.

Someone shoved Linhope forward. MacInnes bellowed, his arms pulled hard behind him. Ronan felt a slam to his head, cobbles lurching toward him. Blackness.

Chapter One

Edinburgh, Scotland
June 1822

THE STONE STEPS leading down to the dungeon vaults beneath Edinburgh Castle were steep and timeworn, so Ellison Graham proceeded carefully in thin slippers. In one gloved hand, she held the skirt of her gown, lavender muslin trimmed in black ribbon; with the other hand she took Lady Strathniven's arm to steady the older woman as they descended toward the ancient wooden door where a red-coated guard stood.

Ahead, Adam Corbie, nephew of the viscountess and secretary to Ellison's father, spoke to the sentry and waved a folded letter. "This letter of permission is signed by Sir Hector Graham, Deputy Lord Provost of Edinburgh, and allows us entry."

"My gracious, it is hot today," Lady Strathniven remarked, her dimpled cheeks flushed, the color creeping upward to the iron-gray curls neatly framing her face.

"It will be cooler inside, my lady," Ellison said.

"I hope so. But I trust this will prove worth the trouble." The lady fluttered a silken fan and peered impishly at Ellison, brown eyes twinkling the brim of her straw bonnet clustered with silk flowers and ribbons.

Ellison laughed affectionately. Lady Strathniven's beauty had endured, though she was the same age as Ellison's father, her longtime friend. Sir Hector had gone gray too, becoming even more stodgy and grumpy. He would strongly disapprove of their visit today if he had known.

They joined Mr. Corbie as the sentry beckoned them into the dark interior to meet a second guard. Both wore scarlet coats, white cross-bands, dark tartan trousers, and black tricorns as soldiers of the Regiment of Foot assigned to Edinburgh Castle. And both looked displeased to see the visitors.

"This is not the public entrance, sir," the sentry told Adam Corbie. "Visitors who wish to see these prisoners must purchase a ticket from the office of the Governor of the Castle and come in through the main entrance."

"This letter exempts us," Corbie said stiffly. "These ladies need not wait with the public. Miss Graham is the daughter of the deputy lord provost, who is also chief of the constabulary. And this lady is my aunt, Lady Strathniven. They wish to privately view the prisoners."

As the guards conferred, Corbie glanced back. "Ladies, I am glad I could ensure privacy for us away from the public."

"Thank you, Mr. Corbie," Ellison said. "Papa refused when I asked his permission to visit the dungeon."

"He is protective of you, Miss Ellison." They had known each other for so many years that he familiarly used her name; she had ceased to do so, wanting a bit of distance. Lately, Corbie had made it clear that he was fond of her, perhaps too fond.

"Adam, we are widowed ladies who need no escort," his aunt pointed out, "but we do appreciate it. I am very curious to see the Highland fellows the whole city is talking about, but the crowds have been so large."

"You need not wait with the common crowd, my lady. It is my pleasure to escort you and Miss Ellison."

She gave him a cool smile, trying not to encourage his interest. Knowing him since her girlhood, she understood his haughty air masked a need for praise. Wanting to be kind and polite, she also wanted to keep him at arm's length; she feared that too much familiarity might stir him to think of marriage.

She did appreciate his use of her maiden name rather than her married name, a choice many Scotswomen made. 'Mrs. Leslie' seemed like another person now, a foolish girl freed from a calamitous marriage by tragedy. She had strived to be complacent and subdued for her father's sake since the scandal, glad for the chance to start over.

Yet starting over brought a dull life, and she had let it happen. She still clung to the grays and lavenders of half-mourning, which seemed to reflect her life now. Yet today she would risk a little disobedience and adventure. She craved some excitement again.

"But sir, viewing hours have not begun today," one of the guards told Corbie.

"Read this!" The secretary poked at the letter. "Special permission to view the Whisky Rogues. Ridiculous name," he muttered. "Guard, may I remind you that I am Sir Hector Graham's secretary."

"Oh, very well." The guard beckoned them to follow.

Ellison was fascinated by the subterranean maze under Edinburgh Castle. Walls of hewn stone formed corridors that were dim and cool. The eerie light of flaming torches flickered over winding passageways cut from the living rock centuries ago.

She wanted to absorb every detail to describe it in the novel she was secretly writing. The warren of passages and dungeon cells beneath the ancient castle inspired ideas. Even more, this opportunity to see actual Highland smugglers could make all the difference to her story.

But she kept her thoughts to herself. Her family thought she still dabbled in poetry, though she had not written verses since her husband's death. Knowing her father would disapprove of novel writing, she had not shared her efforts.

They passed the iron-barred doors of cells recessed into the rock. Through the apertures she glimpsed lantern light, men moving about, heard murmurs, and smelled cooking that thankfully masked less pleasant odors.

"Are the whisky criminals here?" Lady Strathniven asked. "It is so crowded."

"They are further on, madam," the sentry replied. "These are the foreign prisoners. Some were captured after Waterloo and some have been here much longer."

"Will they be released soon?" Ellison asked. "What about the smugglers?"

"That depends on the government, Miss Graham. Prisoners of state are housed here, though most others go to the new jail on Calton Hill. The Lord Provost ordered the whisky smugglers placed here temporarily. Soon they will be sent to Calton."

"They are only here because they generate income for the city," Corbie explained.

"We sell a good number of tickets to see them, sir," the guard agreed.

"Scoundrels," Corbie said. "But the city can use the extra revenue with the king expected soon. Our office is organizing it, you see," he boasted.

"Aye, sir. This way, around this corner."

"Oh my, such a long walk," the viscountess complained. "These fellows are quite the sensation this summer. A Highland man is always a sight to admire, I think."

"So interesting," Ellison agreed, hiding her anticipation.

"I do not share the sentiment," Corbie remarked with a sniff.

"The newspaper accounts are thrilling. Ellison reads the articles aloud to us at breakfast. Dangerous rascals, *The Courant* called them this morning," the lady said.

"This whole matter is absurd," Corbie muttered.

"Adam, we are grateful for your company, but do try to be more pleasant."

"I am sorry, Aunt. But incarcerated men should not be lauded by the public."

"Just down here," the guard said, gesturing.

Ellison's heartbeat quickened. Reports of the Whisky Rogues had fired her imagination for months. Now she would see them at last. A tale of smuggling could add excitement to her novel, which she feared was progressing too slowly.

Not even Lady Strathniven, whom she adored, knew she was

devoting long hours to studying Scottish history and longer hours writing in secret. The viscountess said her poetry should be published; even Papa admitted the lines had some quality. But Ellison wanted to write adventurous tales of old Scotland like Sir Walter Scott, or Miss Jane Porter's novel *Scottish Chiefs*. She had to guard her passion fiercely and silently.

Besides, Lady Strathiven could not keep the smallest secret, and Papa would think writing a novel was just another unfortunate impulse on his daughter's part. She was careful to avoid distressing him. Her widowed father worked diligently for Scotland, though raising three daughters seemed to bewilder him. Caution created a dull existence, but Ellison had found adventure in writing and imagining stories.

When the notorious Whisky Rogues had been captured, she had read avidly about their adventures in the news journals. Once the Lord Provost decided to allow visitors to see the famous rogues for the benefit of a fee, she wanted to attend too.

She nearly trembled with anticipation. Not contrary by nature, she did possess an impulsive tendency to leap first and think later, though she tried to subdue that.

"Miss Ellison, you are wool-gathering." Corbie took her elbow. "Public hours will begin soon and we must leave here before then."

"Everyone is mad for a peek at these fellows," Lady Strathniven said. "The most interesting thing in this city for a long while."

"Until the king's visit. We expect him in August now," Corbie said.

"That does not give your office much time to prepare," Lady Strathniven said.

"We have been planning for months on the chance, but we will be even busier."

"I thought Sir Walter Scott was leading the organizing committee," Ellison said.

"Yes, and he has plenty of ideas—revues, receptions, balls,

dinners, and so on—but our office must make the arrangements. Some of his requests are outlandish."

"Adam, you promised that Ellison and I will have invitations to the royal events."

"I will do my best to arrange it, Aunt. Women are not invited to all the events."

Frowning at that, Ellison suddenly heard a plaintive melody. "Fiddle music!"

"That's one o' them playing," the guard said. "No harm in it."

At the end of a corridor stem, two sentries sat at a small table near a cave-like cell with a wide iron grate set into the rock opening. In the cave, Ellison saw three Highland men. Thin sunlight streamed through an aperture high in the rock wall, illuminating their forms and faces.

Transfixed by the music, compelled by curiosity, she walked forward. The cell's interior was simple—a straw-covered floor, bench, table, three narrow cots. The fiddle player, tall and fair-haired, stood. Two men sat on the bench. Ellison drifted closer.

The fiddler was a master, the tune a favorite she had heard at dances. His gilded hair swept over his brow, his fingers were deft and nimble. He had a fine face, she thought. Gentle. Kind. One of the seated men held a book in his hands; he was big and brawny with a swarthy dark beard and unruly black curls. The man beside him appeared asleep, chin dropped, arms crossed, long legs extended. A scruff of beard and long dark hair framed a face with handsomely shaped features, dark brows, thick eyelashes.

All three wore belted plaids of various patterns, crumpled shirts, shabby waistcoats, stockings, and worn leather shoes. Though unkempt head to foot, they looked strong and healthy, and younger than Ellison had expected, each perhaps thirty or so.

Highlanders of a rough sort, just as the newspapers claimed. The accounts claimed they spoke only Gaelic, lacked manners and education, and had a dull intelligence. Yet the fiddler played with skill, the black-haired brute was absorbed in reading, and the third fellow, though resting, possessed a banked power. He tilted an eyebrow when her shoes scuffed the floor near the cell, as if instantly alert.

"Highland scoundrels," Corbie said. Startled, Ellison turned.

"I find them intriguing," she answered. He huffed.

"Oh my," Lady Strathniven said, flapping her fan. "They are rather stunning."

Watching them from under her bonnet rim, Ellison felt a wrench of compassion. She had lived in the Highlands as a child. Life had been happy there, and she had affection and respect for the Highland people, appreciating the nobility in their character, their language and traditions, and their plight as well.

Perhaps these men had been brought low by English laws that were not always fair to Scots. She sighed, knowing something of the smuggling trade from conversations in her father's house. Highlanders who produced whisky and other goods felt forced to find ways to slip past English authorities and avoid heavy taxation just to help their families survive. She felt great sympathy for them.

Did these men have families, wives, children? The poignant fiddle music touched her heart, brought tears to her eyes. The sight of the prisoners stirred and surprised her.

"Rascals," Corbie said. She nearly jumped. "Do not fear, Miss Ellison. I am here to protect you." He touched her elbow.

"I am not afraid. It just seems wrong to intrude on their privacy."

"Criminals must give up the right to such privileges."

"Oh, my," Lady Strathniven breathed. "Hardly savages! Why, with a barber, decent clothing, and better circumstances, all three would pass for Highland gentlemen. Can you not see them as noble clan chieftains with velvet jackets and feathered bonnets?"

"No," Corbie said.

"Oh, aye! They look rather heroic," Ellison agreed. "They might have stepped out of one of Sir Walter Scott's epic poems."

"I am glad we came to see them." Lady Strathniven took Ellison's arm and smiled.

The viscountess had been Ellison's mother's dearest friend, and so took on a maternal role toward Ellison and her sisters after their mother died nearly ten years earlier. A few years ago, when Lady Strathniven had lost her husband, she became even closer to the Grahams. Ellison loved her dearly, enjoying the lady's salty and generous nature, refreshing and kind.

"We must go," Corbie said just as the fiddler began a slow, sad melody.

"Soon. I want to listen to the music," the viscountess replied.

As the music flowed, Ellison sensed dignity and intelligence in the three quiet men. Each had wildness and a sort of powerful grace. She felt strongly that none of them belonged here in prison, though she knew little about their circumstances.

The black-bearded man set down his book, flexed his big hands, and glanced up. Seeing Ellison, he smiled shyly. His size gave him a beast-like appearance, but his hands, eyes, and expression were gentle. She smiled, feeling a twist of compassion.

The sleeping man—or perhaps he was merely bored, she thought—stirred then, broad shoulders pressed against rock. He murmured in Gaelic to the larger man.

Aingeal, answered the black-haired beast. The two murmured again.

Hearing and understanding some of their words, Ellison gasped softly. *Angel.*

Gaelic had been the language of her nurse and the Highland servants, so her ear and tongue had attuned early to that lilting language. Later, she studied with a tutor in Edinburgh. For all his grousing, Papa encouraged education for his daughters and was pleased when Ellison relied on her knowledge of Gaelic when she joined an Edinburgh ladies' society that occasionally traveled to the Highlands to help poor Gaelic-speaking families.

Iain, why are you smiling? the bored one asked.

An angel has come to visit, his friend answered. *Open your eyes, lad.*

Aingeal. They meant her. Ellison felt her cheeks burn.

"Ruffians," Corbie muttered. "This is no place for ladies. We have seen enough."

The bored Highlander flashed open his eyes with a glare like a blue arrow.

"Oh, my," Lady Strathniven breathed, flapping her fan.

That piercing gaze found Ellison. She met and held it, a moth to that blue flame.

The man had the rare beauty only some possess, his face an elegant blend of angle and curve, strength and tenderness. Long-lidded eyes under dark brows, squared jaw, and firm rounded lips framed by a dark beard; hair dark as a roast chestnut waved to his shoulders. His gaze was like a lightning strike.

A chill ran through her, crown to foot. Here was the hero of the adventure she was secretly writing; here was the Highland rogue she imagined: noble, strong, beautiful.

"Fascinating," Lady Strathniven murmured.

"Oh aye," Ellison whispered.

"Rude," Corbie muttered.

The Highlander closed his eyes and leaned back. His big friend yawned. The fiddler set down the instrument.

"The one fiddles a decent Irish tune, I suppose," Corbie admitted.

"Those were Scottish tunes," Ellison pointed out.

"No matter. These rascals will go to trial soon and the city will be quit of them. Tried, sentenced, hanged. Shall we go, ladies?"

"Hanged? Mr. Corbie, you seem determined to condemn them," Ellison said.

"They are reprehensible rogues, not the noble Highlanders of Mr. Scott's writings, Miss Ellison. You must set aside such lofty ideals. It does you no good."

"Ideals are essential. They ennoble us," she said. He made a scoffing sound.

Suddenly aware of that burning blue gaze again, she glanced toward the cell. The man looked away. The fiddler spoke in

Gaelic and the others answered.

"Likely trying to plot their escape, though it is impossible," Corbie grumbled.

"They are saying," Ellison replied, "that they feel like animals in a zoo."

The bored Highlander swerved his gaze to look straight at her.

"A ZOO INDEED," Iain said.

"And you a wretched bear," Linhope said. Iain grunted.

Narrowing his eyes, Ronan watched the young woman in lavender and a straw bonnet, all golden curls and porcelain. She understood Gaelic, he was certain.

"Careful," he warned the others. "Your angel knows what we are saying."

"Oh!" said the angel, confirming it.

"What is it, dear? Did they say something wicked?" The older lady, plump and handsome, turned. The angel's mother?

Rosy color spread into the girl's cheeks. "They mentioned an angel."

"You do look quite pretty today, Ellison."

Ellison. He liked the name. Feminine, with a tenor of strength. So this young lady of apparent privilege understood Gaelic; perhaps she was Highland. Not many bothered to learn Gaelic these days, and her group was separate from the daily crowd, indicating a special position. Ronan frowned.

Iain, the beast, had a poet's heart; the lass was angelic, even enchanting. Willowy and petite, with golden hair spiraling under her bonnet, she was all creamy skin and easy blushes. Despite a china-doll prettiness, her gaze was intelligent and interested.

Pity she was just another who paid a fee to gape at the Highland prisoners.

She looked at him directly and he tilted his head to acknowledge it. Her lips quirked in a smile as she turned away. He felt a tug of attraction, but would not allow himself to show interest in a haughty society girl.

An uncomfortable thought struck. He wondered if he had met her at some occasion in the city, though he would have remembered her, of that he felt sure. Generally he avoided such events, but as a lawyer, son of a chieftain, cousin to a clan chief, and an available bachelor, Sir John Ronan MacGregor had some value in social circles. Possibly he had met both women; the older one looked familiar.

The girl turned to the others. "Mr. Corbie, Lady Strathniven. Shall we leave?"

"Of course," the young gentleman replied.

Strathniven. He had met the viscountess several years previously in a solicitor's office when he and his cousin, John MacGregor, newly Viscount Darrach, had engaged in a heated discussion with Lord Strathniven over land rights, explaining their family's legal and moral claim to the land. Ronan had nearly snapped at the lady's husband, a truculent gentleman. The Crown-awarded viscount had spouted the letter of English law and claimed a property to which Ronan and his cousin had the traditional right.

They had lost. Strathniven had prevailed. Ronan recalled the lady's apparent embarrassment at her husband's insistent and rude behavior.

Just now, he had heard the ladies' escort mention Sir Hector Graham, Deputy Lord Provost of Edinburgh. Ronan had met the man in passing on more than one occasion, and found him a terse fellow uninterested in others' viewpoints. Was the girl related to him?

Slumping, he hoped his outward aspect as a possible criminal, bearded, unkempt, unimportant, would obscure his real identity if they had seen him before.

"Fascinating. True, we should go." Lady Strathniven fanned

herself. "But I would like to see these Whisky Rogues again."

"Best not return, my lady," Corbie said. "Best call them what they are—scoundrels, ruffians, brigands, roughshod savages, Highland devils."

"That is excessive even from you, Adam," she replied haughtily.

"But accurate. Miss Ellison, do you feel well? You have gone pale."

"We must not stand here staring at them so. It is rude." She had been watching and listening in silence, and had indeed paled.

True, Ronan thought. Gawking at prisoners could only amuse for so long.

Standing, he went to the iron grate. The viscountess smiled up at him. No spark of recognition there, just curiosity. Lifting a hand, he waggled his fingers. She fluttered her fan and nearly giggled.

"My lady, come away from that rascal," said Corbie.

"Oh bother, Adam. They have nice manners and are no threat."

"My lady." Miss Graham took the woman's arm. Her glance met Ronan's.

"*Slàraich, mo aingeal,*" he murmured. *Farewell, my angel.*

She blinked, gasped, eyes wide.

"*Ah, tha i a' tuigsinn,*" he murmured. *So she understands.*

She whirled away, and the man called Corbie took her arm.

"Miss Ellison, did he insult you? I will have a word with him!"

"Do not. He was polite. We shall go."

Ronan stepped back, aware that he would never see Miss Ellison Graham again. Soon he and his friends would be sentenced and either imprisoned, banished in servitude, or hanged. Only a miracle would save them. He knew the law, and knew their poor chances.

An angel might have visited, but a miracle was unlikely.

Chapter Two

"'P EOPLE VISIT THE Castle dungeons just to see the prisoners, while ladies brave enough to venture there are alarmed, fanning themselves madly, distressed at the sight of these dangerous Highland rogues—'"

Ellison paused, reading aloud from that day's edition of *The Edinburgh Observer*. Her attention was caught by the illustration showing the smugglers in the dungeon: three bearded men in plaid. More, the article provided names.

Stewart, MacInnes. MacGregor of Glenbrae. But which was which?

"Read on," her younger sister Juliet said impatiently. Ellison glanced up to see Juliet, Lady Strathniven, and Adam Corbie all waiting expectantly.

Rain pattered at the windows as they sat together at breakfast in the dining room of the Graham home on George Street. Despite the morning's downpour, Corbie had arrived early, as usual, to work with Sir Hector in the study. Lady Strathniven had arrived soon after, eager to escape some renovation work in her home on nearby Charlotte Square.

"Go on," Corbie picked up his cup of coffee. "Distressed ladies, etcetera."

"We were not distressed in the least, Adam," his aunt replied.

"We?" Juliet squeaked. No one answered.

Corbie huffed and rose from the table to refresh his coffee at the sideboard, then heaped sausages onto a plate. He returned and sat.

"I would like to see the prisoners," Juliet said, "but Papa will not allow it."

"You are thirteen, dear," said Lady Strathniven. "None of us would allow it."

"Ellison, I nearly forgot," Juliet said. "Papa wants to speak with you this morning. I came down earlier and saw him going to his study."

"Thank you, dear." Ellison's stomach sank. Did Papa know about yesterday's visit to the Castle—or, worse, had he learned about the novel she was writing? But she kept the manuscript locked away, and Sir Hector rarely ventured into his daughters' territory.

"He seemed displeased. But Papa is hardly ever pleased," Juliet added blithely. "Do finish reading before you go."

Ellison resumed. "'Despite being rough and uneducated, the Whisky Rogues are strong, healthy, and pleasing in visage,'" she read.

"And very polite," Lady Strathniven added, then nibbled at her toast.

"Don't stop, Ellie." Juliet leaned forward. Rain sluiced against the windows, diluting the sunny cheerfulness of the floral wallpaper and golden damask curtains chosen by their mother. For a moment, Ellison wondered what Lady Graham would have thought of her visiting the dungeons. Likely she would have approved, sweetly and firmly overriding her husband. But Mama had passed just after Ellison's fourteenth birthday.

As she narrated, Corbie demolished his sausages. "Yes, yes—they fiddle, read, play cards, but they are thieves," he said then. "The noble Highlander is a myth."

"Every Highlander I have ever met was polite and intelligent," Ellison defended.

"Clearly, you have not met enough of them, Miss Ellison."

"I spent my childhood in the Highlands and we still go there often, you know that. To a one, they are considerate and kind. I am sorry you have a different opinion."

"Read!" Juliet urged.

"'Visiting the dungeon to see the prisoners is a popular outing this summer. Even notable citizens appear. Recently seen were—'" Ellison stopped.

"Who?" Juliet asked.

Corbie plucked the page away from Ellison. "Ah! 'Lady Strathniven and Miss Graham in the company of a gentleman were admitted privately—'"

Juliet squealed, leaning forward in a flurry of white muslin and red-gold curls, but missed grabbing the newspaper. "You all went there? Does Papa know?"

"In my defense, Miss Juliet, the ladies hounded me like harridans."

"Mr. Corbie! We asked nicely, and you agreed," Ellison said. Surely her father had seen the newspaper by now, she thought. "But how did *The Observer* know?"

"Journalists are busy, curious, and always interested in our sort," Corbie said.

"Our sort? Papa is of interest due to his position, but we are not."

"Papa must let me see the Highlanders too," Juliet said.

"You are too young," said Lady Strathniven. "Married ladies, especially widowed ladies, may do as they please. Your sister Deirdre is married and might have gone too if she had not chosen isolation in the north."

"The Isles are cooler in summer, and Deirdre and her husband have a beautiful estate there," Ellison said. "Besides, she is expecting a blessed arrival and should not travel. She must be disappointed to miss the royal visit."

"Deirdre invited me this summer, and asked Cousin Lucie to bring me with her this very week," Juliet said. "So I suppose I will miss seeing the famous prisoners and the king's visit too. Deirdre and Lucie will not treat me like a wee girl."

"One day you will have more privilege, my dear. You and your sisters have all grown up too quickly, I vow," Lady Strathniven said.

"My lady, Mother would have been so grateful to you for all you have done for us these years," Ellison said gently.

"Thank you, dear. I have tried to do my best. Shall we hear the rest of the article?"

"Let me read it!" Juliet reached for the paper. "'The Highland criminals may display a noble spirit, but poor actions invite poor circumstances.'"

"Indeed, they would look as noble as clan chiefs, given proper Highland dress," Lady Strathniven said dreamily.

"I hope this entire debacle ends soon," said a deep voice from the doorway.

Ellison looked up as her father entered the dining room. Tall and imposing with iron-gray hair, his broad torso encased in black with a brown damask waistcoat, Sir Hector Graham was a fine-looking man even in his late sixties. But deep lines framing his mouth had replaced the smiles Ellison remembered.

As he entered, a little dog trotted in on his heels. Sir Hector narrowly avoided stepping on the long-haired terrier that sat to look up at him.

"Ellison, your pup is always underfoot," Sir Hector muttered.

"Here, Balor!" When the dog came to her, she broke off a bit of bacon for him.

Sir Hector went to the sideboard and peered at the silver samovar as if it might magically produce coffee. Ellison rose and filled a cup, adding cream for him.

"Good morning, my lady," he told Lady Strathniven as he took a chair. "How goes the work at your house?"

"Endless, Hector," Lady Strathniven said; they had known each other since childhood. "I am heading to the Highlands for the summer and will leave them to it. Will you come up to visit as usual?"

"This summer will be too busy. We will miss seeing you, of

course." He took up a newspaper from the stack and snapped its pages open.

Ellison felt her stomach drop. "Would you like sausages and eggs, Papa?"

"I had breakfast earlier. Coffee will fortify me until luncheon. Ah, the *Observer* has another piece about the Highlanders," he said, turning a page. "The *Courant* too."

"Papa, may I see them before I leave for the summer?" Juliet asked.

"Absolutely not. I'd prefer none of you saw them, but it seems I am too late." He peeked past the page. "Juliet, you have music lessons today. I pay dearly for your tutors. Go practice."

"Yes, Papa." She rose and left the room. Ellison wished she could leave too.

"Hector, please do not be cross with us," Lady Strathniven said.

"My dear Marjorie, a widow of your standing may do as she pleases."

"Your daughter, as a widow, has that right too."

"I am sorry, Papa," Ellison blurted. "We did not want to trouble you."

He lowered the paper. "Mr. Corbie could have troubled me with this. I thought the permission I signed was for you, sir. Harangued, were you?"

"In a word," Corbie said.

"My fault, Hector. I asked Ellison to come with me. Adam obliged as our escort."

"So you could indulge in a common spectacle." He lowered bushy eyebrows over gray eyes. "Ellison, I hope it was an unpleasant lesson in the consequences of poor decisions."

"The girl is hardly planning a life of crime," Lady Strathniven said.

"I have a bigger problem regarding these whisky runners. Mr. Corbie, I will need you to compose a reply to the royal secretary. A letter was delivered to me last night."

"Yes, sir."

"And Ellison, I will see you in half an hour in my study."

She gulped. "Yes, sir. But Papa—what if those men are wrongly accused? Everyone assumes their guilt."

"Leave that to the Court of Justiciary, Miss Ellison," Corbie said.

"True, men are sometimes unfairly accused," her father replied. "But our legal system usually discovers such things. Highlanders have some hardships, but we must pursue and punish those who break our laws, whether the writ is Scots or English. The government is not so mean an institution as you may think, Ellison."

"These Whisky Rogues have captured your daughter's fancy, sir," Corbie said.

"Our Ellison is not easily dissuaded of dreams and ideals," Sir Hector agreed.

Not eager to hear a fresh analysis of her faults, Ellison set down her napkin and stood. "I must go. I have correspondence to finish."

She went to the door, Balor trotting along behind her. Stepping out of the room, she sighed. Somehow she always managed to displease her father. Deirdre lived an idyllic life with her handsome earl now, after a harrowing year; Juliet was outspoken but charming. And Ellison had made an impulsive, romantic mistake that her father would neither forget nor forgive.

As she walked away, she heard Lady Strathniven.

"Hector, leave her be. She has been through enough at twenty-six. Her dreams have given her a fine talent for writing, to her credit."

"Her poetry is good. But her dreamy nature will be her undoing. I had hoped she'd marry again, but I fear her impulsive character counts against her."

"Sir, and my lady aunt—if I may speak," Corbie said. "You may have guessed already how fond I am of Miss Ellison. I would like your approval to court her with an intent to marry. I am aware of her—foibles."

"Oh," said Lady Strathniven. "I wonder if she—"

"We can discuss it later, Adam. I must go back to my office."

Ellison hurried to her room, fighting tears. If Papa wanted her to marry stiff-necked Adam Corbie, a man with no imagination and a lofty opinion of himself, her refusal might cause strife. Corbie was sole heir to the wealthy Strathniven estate, which would be enough to decide the matter for everyone but her.

As a widow, she had earned the right to make her own decisions. But her father consistently dismissed that.

This summer, she decided, she would make sure to enjoy her independence somehow. She would ask Lady Strathniven if she could go to the Highlands with her. There, she had the freedom to write, and recover from lingering heartbreak—and perhaps she could restore her fading spirit before it was too late.

That renewed her determination and sensed of hope.

Soon she was seated at her desk, taking her manuscript from its locked drawer. She wanted to shape the story's hero, an ancient Highland lord, to resemble the Highlander she had seen yesterday.

She smoothed a fresh sheet of paper, dipped pen in ink, and began.

The Highlander's eyes, the deep blue of a lochan in summer twilight, went soft and sad as he remembered once more the hurt that had torn his heart like the sharpest blade. To see Lady Isabella again after five years was a blow to his very soul. He had immured his heart against her charms after she had dealt him a deep and unseen wound on the day that Isabella Grant had chosen the Earl of Strathearn over Ruari MacAlpin of Garslie.

Small laird by sunlight, poet by candlelight, cattle-thief by moonlight—yet Garslie's strength, cleverness, and devotion could not compete with wealth and treachery.

He scrabbled a living on rocky land, scratched heartfelt words on parchment, borrowed cattle when it was merited, and loved a lass who looked away.

She crossed out a word, scribbled a change, wrote on.

"THAT'S A MOURNFUL tune, lad," Iain MacInnes said. "Brings the ghosts out the very walls."

Linhope shifted to a livelier melody while Iain flipped cards on the bench next to Ronan. They had cards, books, even a chess set. If the backward Whisky Rogues acted like fine lords, the Castle Governor had declared, more visitors would come.

Ronan leaned back against the wall, unaccountably irritated by the joyful song and Iain's foot tapping in time. His nerves felt raw. Weeks of being trapped here threatened to break his usual reserve.

Arthur, Lord Linhope, was skilled in music as well as medicine; MacInnes was content with cards, books, sketching plans on the walls, and was annoyingly cheerful. Both were making the best of incarceration. Ronan knew he should take a lesson from them, but today he just needed a good glower.

He had no talent for whiling away the hours. Once he had aspired to bad poetry, and could cut a neat step on a dance floor. But he'd be damned if he'd dance to that fiddle to amuse the visitors here.

Cards, then. He dealt a quick hand on the bench.

"*Ach*," Iain said, tossing a card to the floor. "Nine of diamonds! Curse of Scotland, they call it. More bad luck we do not need."

Hearing footsteps and the chatter of a new group of visitors, Ronan did not look up. People often came to gawk, but the angel of a few days ago had not returned. He might show some interest if she did.

Miss Ellison Graham. Recalling her delicate loveliness, he reminded himself she had stared at them like all the onlookers before she left.

Linhope stopped playing. "The ladies enjoy the music," he said in Gaelic. "May it stir them to plead for mercy for three captive lads. And if their kinsmen are court judges, that may help too."

"Most justices are stonehearted fellows who do not give a damn what the ladies of Edinburgh think." Ronan tossed down a card. "I know many of them."

"I wonder when we will have word of a trial or a transfer," Iain said.

"Fifty-eight days since the night of our arrest, fifty-three since we came to Edinburgh," Ronan said. "I am keeping count."

"What does it matter? It is too long." Sighing heavily, Linhope sank to sit on the straw-littered floor. "Public sentiment favors us. That may help."

"Perhaps the jury of fifteen will include someone who enjoyed your fiddling," Ronan said. "Still, there may be a way out of this."

"Escape?" Iain asked hopefully.

Ronan glanced at the cluster of muttering visitors and lowered his voice, even speaking Gaelic. "That was done here long ago when a cattle reiver went out a window in a high dungeon cell on bed linens and shirts, and climbed down the castle rock. He got away."

"Huh. None of us would fit through that window, even if we could climb up there." Iain pointed to a narrow aperture high in the rock wall.

"Well, escape is punishable by further imprisonment," Ronan said. "There may be a legal way to get out of here."

"How?" Linhope asked.

"I am thinking. If I could visit the Advocates Library down the street, I could find a solution quickly."

"Not likely you'll get there. If we were in Calton jail, we might escape," Iain said. "I know the building's plan."

Ronan huffed. "Be glad we are not there."

"Horrible place," Linhope agreed. "That handsome new building is already a hellish prison. Worse than the old Tolbooth it replaced."

"It is a pretty fortress on its high hill, all towers and turrets," Iain said. "A fine design. Visitors even mistake Calton for the Castle." He threw down a couple of cards and crowed. Ronan groaned, seeing them.

"Last year I visited the Calton infirmary with a colleague," Linhope said. "We could do little for the men there. The guards are not allowed to summon medical assistance except in severe cases. The Deputy Lord Provost is in charge of the constabulary, but either he is unaware of the conditions, or does not care to improve them."

Hearing footsteps out in the corridor, Ronan glanced up as that afternoon's crop of visitors walked away. "Someone dropped a news journal."

Linhope went to the wide grate to stretch an arm through the lower bars, managing to grab the paper. Returning to sit and study the pages, he laughed.

"We are mentioned here. Smugglers, ruffians, brigands . . . Hah! A sketch of three hairy beasts in plaid." He held up the page.

"A fair description," Ronan grunted. "What's the date?"

"Thirtieth of July," Linhope said. "Have we been here that long? *Tempus fugit*. And look here. The king is expected to arrive in August."

Iain huffed. "I shall get my best Highland kit ready."

"By God," Linhope said then. "'The Duke of Atholl will be returning to Perthshire from his property on the Isle of Man. He plans to attend the funeral of a friend.'" He glanced up. "Sir John Murray MacGregor. A kinsman, Ronan? I am sorry."

Ronan felt a clench of sadness. "A cousin, aye. Chief of the Gregorach, the MacGregors. My father grew up with him. Sir John was tough as old leather but a fair man. We admired him, even as boys." Memories flew past, some happy, some tainted with regret. He scowled.

"Sir Evan is now chief of the MacGregors," Iain said. "Your second cousin, that one."

"A good man. The clan will do well by him."

"Thanks to you. He owes you his life, Ronan. A hero's stand, they say," Iain added.

Ronan shook his head. "Evan was the hero that day in India, facing the odds as he did. We fought to save him and each other. Not everyone made it out," he murmured, thinking of lost kin and friends and recalling courage and grief on a day he wished he could forget. Years ago, he had sailed to India to join his cousin, exchanging out of a Highland regiment to the dragoons to be at Evan's back. Since then, feelings had gone sour between them.

"Once the Darrach estate is yours, you will have the right to be part of the chief's tail," Linhope said. "A full chieftain of the Gregorach."

"The matter still needs sorting. And Sir Evan will not welcome a kinsman accused of smuggling. But he will be a fine leader." He threw down his cards, and now Iain groaned.

Linhope picked up his fiddle again to begin a slow tune. The music seemed to draw the sadness out of the very air, transforming the mood. Ronan leaned back, closed his eyes. Thoughts of his Highland home past with the melody—the breeze over the hills, the heather in summer, the cool drench of a stream, the honeyed fire of whisky down the throat. He imagined lying in a meadow in clear, fresh air, laughing, a woman in his arms, soft and warm. Nameless, faceless, but someday—

He frowned as the imaginary lover became the delectable Miss Graham. *No.* If he had a future at all, he would not trade a Highland life for life with a city lass, especially one whose very kinsman held the fate of prisoners.

Dreams were a long way off. For now, his concern was how to avoid a hanging.

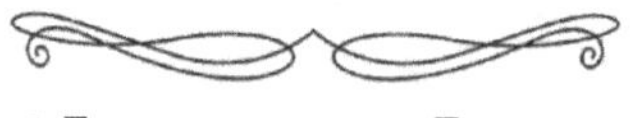

Chapter Three

"ELLISON," SIR HECTOR said, "we must discuss a delicate matter. Mr. Corbie is aware."

"Papa, I have explained and apologized for the visit to the dungeons."

He came around the desk to lean against it, crossing his arms as he scowled down at her. Adam Corbie stood nearby, frowning too, as if in imitation. Seated, Ellison straightened her posture against their intimidation. Yet her father looked troubled rather than angry.

"This is more serious," he said.

Had he found her novel? She smoothed the skirts of her gray muslin trimmed in indigo ribbon, colors reflecting the morning rain. No matter what she did, she struggled to retain her father's love and approval, once so secure.

She took a breath, prepared to defend herself. Her marriage three years ago to a viscount's son, romantic but hasty, had been followed too soon by his fatal fall from a horse. Her widowing had stirred sympathy among family and friends, but Sir Hector could not forget her lapse in judgment. Mr. Corbie echoed that opinion.

"I will need your assistance in a difficult situation," her father said.

Ellison blinked. "My—assistance?"

He picked up a letter from the desk, its royal seal broken.

"The king's secretary sends constant requests regarding the king's visit. We do our utmost to satisfy them."

"You and the Lord Provost are working diligently with Sir Walter Scott and the Celtic Society to prepare for the visit. I would be happy to help with the details."

"Only in this matter, Miss Ellison . . ." Corbie said.

"Adam, please." Sir Hector held up a hand. "The king's arrival has not been publicly confirmed, but we expect him in August. That gives us six weeks before the city turns topsy-turvy. Our office is responsible for many of the arrangements. Mr. Corbie, might I add, is proving invaluable."

"Thank you, sir. But Sir Walter is an efficient chief organizer with some excellent ideas."

Ellison pinched back a smile, remembering that Corbie previously called Scott's ideas outlandish. "Some are calling it the 'Celtification of Scotland,'" she said.

"Hmph. We hope to avoid a spectacle. But a new problem has arisen." Sir Hector tapped the letter. "King George, it seems, is very fond of Highland whisky."

"I am sure your office can provide him a good supply."

"He takes a dram or two every night, they say, and more, and is devoted to the habit. He is especially fond of two particular whiskies."

"Does he know most Highland whisky is illicit, thanks to English laws?" Ellison asked pertly. "What he enjoys may come from casks smuggled into London."

"He, ah, may not realize that," her father said. "The king prefers Glenlivet and has requested to meet George Smith, the distiller, to extend his compliments. Lord Arbuthnot's office is arranging a royal introduction."

"A nice honor. Is Glenlivet whisky considered legal or illicit?"

"Mr. Smith obtained a license recently, just in time. Now we are told the king is equally fond of Glenbrae whisky. It is equal to The Glenlivet in the king's opinion, the royal secretary says." Sir Hector cleared his throat. "Glenbrae is produced in Perthshire."

"Surely you can provide that whisky to the king too. But how could I help?"

"King George has asked to meet the Glenbrae distiller also."

"Of course. Is Glenbrae illicit or licensed?"

"Licensed, we hope. Mr. Corbie, check this year's listings." Corbie went to a bookshelf to pull a large ledger free, then set it down to flip through it. "This request will not be handled by the Lord Provost's office," Sir Hector continued. "As deputy lord provost, I oversee the constabulary and prisons."

"Prisons?" Ellison paused, then realized. "Oh! Glenbrae! I read the name in the journal—is he one of the Whisky Rogues?"

"Exactly. The Glenbrae distiller is presently incarcerated."

Ellison nearly laughed. "The king's favorite dram is produced by a smuggler?"

"It is hardly amusing, Ellison. MacGregor of Glenbrae is a crofting laird, a tenant of the landowner. He might make the brew, but whoever owns the land is legally the distiller. That presents another complication. Mr. Corbie, did you find a listing?"

"Here it is." Corbie glanced up from the ledger pages. "Glenbrae distillery in Perthshire was licensed two years ago to John R. MacGregor of Glenbrae."

"That must be Viscount Darrach. Glenbrae and Darrach make up that estate."

"Glenbrae is not far from Strathniven, sir," Corbie said. "Darrach belongs to the MacGregors, so several MacGregor families live in those glens. The land was parceled out to others. My aunt owns part of it. Many there are crofters. Tenants."

"The countryside near Strathniven is beautiful," Ellison said.

"And overrun with smugglers," Corbie said.

"The real complication is that Viscount Darrach died last year," Sir Hector said.

"Oh! Can the new viscount be introduced to the king?" she asked.

"Unfortunately," her father said, "I have heard that there is confusion over the Darrach inheritance, so there is no heir as yet.

It must go to the courts to decide."

"But Papa, if you simply supply the whisky, would that not satisfy the king's request?"

"The king expects to meet the distiller. He heard the fellow is a peer and so he insists on meeting him. Even the Glenlivet fellow is not a landed peer."

"Oh, dear. But how could I be of help?" Ellison asked.

"What we must determine," her father went on, "is if this incarcerated MacGregor is in fact the distiller. He needs to supply the whisky. Excise officers have not found it."

An odd chill trickled along her spine. "Ah, the prisoners speak Gaelic. You will need a translator."

"Exactly. A sergeant in the Regiment of Foot translates for them, but we must be discreet here. No one must know about this. A brief interview is all we need."

Her breath quickened. Here was a chance to see the smugglers again, talk with them, learn more for her novel. "Of course, Papa. I can help."

"Good. You have a grasp of the Gaelic language, since you spoke it as a child with the servants, and have put it to good use in your work with the ladies' society."

"But I do not claim fluency. That would take a lifetime."

"Lady Strathniven tells me you are very proficient."

"I adore her, Papa, but she exaggerates all our accomplishments. She thinks I am an expert in languages and an extraordinary poet." She laughed. "Juliet is the equal of Beethoven, and Deirdre draws like Raphael. And you, sir, will be Lord Provost one day."

He pursed his lips. "The lady has a good heart. We just need some translating."

"Sir, this is no task for a young lady," Corbie said. "Let me talk to the fellow."

"Do you speak the Highland tongue? I did not think so," Sir Hector barked.

"Papa, you said Viscount Darrach died. Can I ask when, and

what happened?" She was always curious about such things, and her father had included her in this.

"Shot in a hunting accident. Very unfortunate."

Corbie shut the ledger. "The excise said it was murder. The young man came upon smugglers in the hills. The housekeeper at Strathniven told us that he had just inherited the property and did not know the area, nor was he well known in the glen."

"Murder!" Ellison shuddered. "And so near Strathniven!"

"Thieving and smuggling are everywhere in the Highlands, Miss Ellison. But my lady aunt only keeps legal whisky at Strathniven. The housekeeper makes sure of it."

"Does she," Sir Hector drawled. "So they all say up there. As I recall, the excise officers reported that these so-called Whisky Rogues killed the viscount."

Astonished, Ellison sat straight. "I cannot imagine that, having seen them."

"An innocent's observation," Corbie muttered.

"If a tale of smuggling and the murder of a peer were to reach the journals, it could go poorly for us as we arrange the royal visit," her father said.

"Papa, can you simply tell the Crown there is no distiller to introduce?"

"Lord Arbuthnot, as Provost, insists that the Crown's every request be met. It is imperative that the king feel good will toward Scotland. If he is displeased, he may decide to visit France instead. Economically, politically, and personally—disastrous."

Her father's reputation might suffer; she could see the concern in his eyes. "Then I will bring your message discreetly to this Mr. MacGregor and you will have answers."

"Just a few questions about the whisky."

"Will he be paid for the whisky given to the king?"

"He is a prisoner, stripped of rights," Corbie said.

"It is a reasonable question, sir. Unless he makes it himself, other Highlanders deserve payment for it. Aye, Papa?"

"This entire affair is an infernal nuisance," Sir Hector muttered, and sat.

"Sir, we could present the whisky and say that an introduction could not be arranged," Corbie said. "Two years ago, the Lord Provost sent the king a gift of Highland whisky in honor of his succession. Sir Alasdair Drummond—the Lord Lyon, King of Arms, if you recall, brought it down to London against all odds—a supreme effort to ensure that it was presented to the king."

"Which is why the king favors Glenbrae whisky," Sir Hector said. "Besides, the king hates being refused. To be blunt, Corbie, you and I could both lose face if this does not go smoothly."

"True. Every detail of the royal visit must be successful. I will accompany Miss Ellison to interview this fellow."

Seeing her father nod, she smiled faintly. "Very well. Shall I explain the king's request? Mr. MacGregor will want to know his whisky is favored."

"No. The less he knows the better."

"Yes, Papa." She hid a rising excitement. Which prisoner was MacGregor? The man with the searing blue eyes and resonant voice came to mind. She sighed.

"Sir, if we present a prisoner amid Sir Walter's spectacle," Corbie said, "that could make us a laughingstock."

"True. Those rough Highlanders should not be seen," Sir Hector agreed.

Ellison recalled Lady Strathniven's words. *With a barber, decent clothing, and better circumstances, they could be taken for fine Highland gentlemen.*

"Papa," she said, "could you introduce MacGregor to the king as Glenbrae, the laird and the distiller? It could be done very quickly."

"Impossible!" Corbie said.

"An interesting thought." Sir Hector frowned.

"They say royal introductions last only a minute or less. But there are strict protocols for an introduction—proper etiquette, required dress, and so on," she said.

"Absurd," Corbie replied. "The assemblies in Edinburgh will be attended by hundreds, even thousands, of peers and dignitaries, even Highland chiefs with their entourages. Bringing in a prisoner into that situation is unthinkable."

"He could dress as a gentleman for the occasion," Ellison said. "Papa, as chief of the constabulary, you could arrange his release for the day."

"Unthinkable!" Corbie looked appalled.

Sir Hector frowned. "I wonder."

"If the man is kin to the deceased viscount, perhaps he is even the heir," she said.

Corbie snorted. "Even more ridiculous."

"Is this fellow presentable?" her father asked.

"No," Corbie said.

"Yes," Ellison said. "They would all look like gentlemen, given the right clothing and proper grooming."

"Next it will be lessons in manners!" Corbie waved a hand.

"Perhaps!" Ellison felt sudden excitement. She could be even more help to her father. "What if I tutored him in manners and protocol?"

"Better if we tell the Crown the fellow is dead," Corbie snapped.

"A risky proposition." Sir Hector scowled, tapped his fingers. "I suppose it is possible that he could be the heir if he is a kinsman of Darrach."

"Perhaps he could be introduced as such," Ellison said.

"Adam, find out the status of the Darrach inheritance," Sir Hector said.

"This is madness," Corbie muttered. "We would be complicit in fraud. Treason."

"Then we would claim the fellow misled us," her father said bluntly.

Astonished, Ellison looked at her father. His gray eyes were hooded like a hawk's; he might suggest it, but wanted nothing to do with it.

"Never mind," she said. "I will speak to the man and ask your questions."

"Thank you, my dear."

The little flood of enthusiasm faded. "Papa, is possible to pardon this man? Then you would not be presenting a prisoner."

"Good heavens, we can hardly do that!" he replied.

"The king's desire to meet him might warrant it," she pointed out.

Corbie huffed. "You know little of the law, Miss Ellison. Sir, your daughter is a perpetual romantic. This is not helpful."

"Mr. Corbie, since you need my help, be gracious about it," she snapped.

"Ellison," her father warned.

Twisting her fingers in her lap, she smothered her impatience. If she could prove helpful, she could win back some of her father's regard. And she could see the Highland prisoners again and satisfy her curiosity about such things. Her dull existence made her long for some small adventure, and here it was.

"That will be all, Ellison," her father said. "Arrangements will be made for you to speak with this fellow."

She stood. "Papa, if you do decide to introduce Mr. Mac-Gregor, he will need a translator then too."

Sir Hector sighed. "Another consideration. Adam, assist my daughter with whatever is needed. Now, to other business." He picked up a document in dismissal, as if she was instantly forgotten.

Ellison went to the door and opened it as the men quietly conferred.

"Preposterous, sir, to involve the prisoner. Even dangerous," Corbie said.

"We are in a precarious position and must consider all angles. The king could cancel altogether. What is this request from Scott about scaffolding?"

"Scaffold seating will be erected on Castle Hill for the crowds, and he wants blue bunting installed with it."

"Expensive and excessive!"

Ellison shut the door silently behind her.

Chapter Four

"TEA," THE GUARD called as he pushed a wooden cart, china and silverware rattling on a small tray, into the cell. Unlocking the iron grate, he entered and set the tray on a rickety table, where the tea things wobbled precariously. "Tea and visitors!"

Iain yawned; Linhope, also dozing, sat up. Ronan closed the book he was reading, not keen on tepid tea or tittering guests this afternoon. He was weary of this place and the ruse as Highland scoundrels, but the guises protected their identities, their kin, and glen folk too. With luck, one day he and his friends would return to their lives and livelihoods.

These weeks had made him more determined to push for greater justice for Highland folk, once he was free. Too often they were thought common, uneducated, simple, unworthy, and he felt it keenly here. The culture, the legacy, the loyalty and pride of the Gaels deserved appreciation and preservation. More than ever, he wanted to promote the truth to help them. But for now, this ploy must continue.

"Hey," Iain murmured. "The angel is here again."

Ronan looked toward the door. She was there, setting gentle foot on stone, crossing the straw as if floating—a vision in lavender trimmed in black lace, a little bonnet curving around her head, a few golden curls escaping. The gentleman who had accompanied her before was back as well. Corbie, he recalled.

Ronan stood, as did his friends, in expectant silence.

Her companion stepped forward. "I am Mr. Adam Corbie, secretary to the Deputy Lord Provost of Edinburgh." He was a slight man, sandy and plain in a tailored suit. The curl of his lip matched his sneering tone.

The young woman translated into Gaelic, not realizing it was not necessary.

"This is Mrs. Graham-Leslie," Corbie went on, indicating her. "She will speak with you briefly. You will show decent manners in her presence, or the guards will be on you directly." She translated, cheeks turning pink.

Corbie huffed and looked at her. "They do not have a word of proper English."

"They may understand some," she answered. "Mr. Corbie, please wait outside. I need a few minutes." She shooed him away with a gloved hand.

Ronan pinched back a smile. Corbie seemed oblivious to her subtle impatience with him. And, he noted, the young lady had a married name. Interesting.

Stepping outside, Adam Corbie stood close to the grating to watch them. The young woman smiled as if she had just arrived at a garden party. As she moved, a floral and vanilla scent wafted lightly over the dungeon's older, less pleasant odors. She was as delicate and divine as a beam of sunlight in this dank place.

"*Beannachdan, a dhaoine uaisle,*" she said. "Greetings, gentlemen." Her accent was good, but not native. "You are Mr. MacInnes, Mr. Stewart, Mr. MacGregor?"

Iain bobbed clumsily and Linhope made a proper bow. "*Fàilte,*" he said, welcoming her in Gaelic. "A pleasure to meet you."

The good doctor stopped short of kissing her hand, Ronan noted sourly. As for his turn, he only nodded in silence.

"I am pleased to meet you." Her smile was as impish as it was angelic, with fleeting dimples. Altogether a devastating sight in this sorry place, Ronan thought. She was petite, with lush curves and graceful bones, and a serene air that held a thread of steely determination. The effect took him down swiftly, though he gave nothing away.

"May we offer you tea, Mrs. Graham-Leslie?" Linhope asked in Gaelic.

"Keep your distance, sir," Corbie growled, watching like a hawk beyond the bars.

"Miss Graham will do. I am widowed and do not use my married name."

Ronan raised a brow. Some Scotswomen kept their maiden names; Mairi Brodie had done so. Yet this girl from an aristocratic family in the city had made an unusual choice; the status of widow could reap benefits in social circles. He glanced toward the disapproving, possessive fellow at the cell door. Perhaps he was courting her.

"Miss Graham—" Linhope indicated a bale of straw. "Would you care to sit?"

She tipped her bonneted head, a golden curl slipping free. Ronan savored the rare sight of beauty and grace, so extraordinary in this dreary underworld. Surprisingly, she seemed at ease, not in the least uncomfortable. It was almost as if she enjoyed it.

He narrowed his eyes. Why was she here, and what did she want?

She picked up the teapot. *"Am bu toil leat tì?* Do you want tea?"

Iain and Linhope both thanked her. She began to pour into three cracked cups.

"Cha toil leam tì," Ronan said. I do not want tea. He folded his arms petulantly, but only against the damnable effect she had on him. Her mere presence, this delicate wee widow who tossed her suitor out and bravely faced three accused criminals, softened his hard reserve. He liked tea; he disliked a breach of his emotional barricade.

Linhope shot him a dark glance. *Behave,* it said.

Ignoring Ronan, she poured tea and served cakes as if the cell were a parlor in a fine mansion. The little cakes were studded with currants. Likely stale as a rock, he thought.

Iain and Linhope accepted cups and cakes, and when the girl offered a cup to Ronan, he took it and declined the cake. What did this pretty visitor want? Instinct urged him to hide his ease with teacups and manners and lovely ladies pouring for gentlemen. The same instinct told him to keep to the Gaelic and play the simple crofter.

He glanced at his companions to remind them, but they were too besotted to notice. Linhope sipped, Iain slurped, both smiled. Ronan held his cup and scowled.

"Now," Miss Graham said, balancing her teacup in white-gloved hands, "which of you is Glenbrae?"

Startled, Ronan said nothing, but Iain pointed. "That's him."

"I am *from* Glenbrae," Ronan emphasized in Gaelic, shooting a sight-dagger toward Iain for good measure. The fellow missed it, content as a happy pup.

"Mr. MacGregor—Glenbrae—may I have a word with you?"

"Me?" His surprised retort slipped out.

"If you please," she said in all her angel brightness. She moved toward him, barely coming to his shoulder. He looked down at her. Too close. Stepped back.

"What is it, Miss Graham?"

"It is Mr. Ronan MacGregor? Of Glenbrae? Is that correct?"

He paused. His baptized name was John Ronan MacGregor; as a lawyer, he was John R. MacGregor, while Ronan was used by kin and friends—and the justiciary court.

"What do you want of me?" he asked stiffly.

"I have your welfare in mind with only good intentions. I was sent by my father."

Ah. There it was. "We do not need saving by heaven's grace. Goodbye, Miss."

"Oh! Not that!" She nearly spilled her tea. "My father is the Deputy Lord Provost of Edinburgh. Sir Hector Graham. He sent me here with a message for you."

Ronan frowned. "Why would a father send his daughter to such a place?"

"He cannot be seen here himself. I offered to translate."

"Miss Ellison, are you done?" This from Corbie at the grate.

"Not yet," she called, adding in Gaelic to Ronan, "I trust I am perfectly safe here."

He bent slightly. "You are safe, madam," he replied softly. "But do not try to change me with charitable intentions or a churchy mission—or try to convince me of your father's demands if he will not face me but sends a slip of a lass in his stead."

"Change you and convince you?" She looked up. "But Mr. MacGregor, that is precisely what I mean to do."

Her eyes were silvery gray, wide and limpid, her lips full and rosy, her gaze guileless and sparkling with intelligence. Ronan's heart succumbed in that moment to her candid, whimsical, sensual charm. He stepped back against its subtle force.

"Miss Ellison," said the fellow at the door. "Shall I come in there now?"

"I am fine, Mr. Corbie," she said in English.

Intrigued by the girl and irritated by the fellow, Ronan leaned close. "Call off Sir Hound and tell me your business here. You and I are not acquainted. I would certainly have remembered you. Go on, deliver your father's message."

She looked up at him, face tilted, eyes bright. He was as wary of her innocent appearance as her mysterious mission. "You are the distiller of Glenbrae whisky?"

"I am."

"Miss Graham." Now the pesky escort grabbed the bars. "We have been here too long. Come out, please, or I will fetch you out for your safety."

"One moment, Mr. Corbie." Her gaze stayed with Ronan.

"Is he being discourteous, Miss Graham?" Ronan murmured.

"It is just his nature."

"Since your young man is anxious, I assume your visit is unofficial and your father's request clandestine."

"Somewhat." She glanced sideways at Corbie.

"The man is about to stuff himself between the bars," Ronan said. A smile teased her soft, rosy lips.

"You there!" Corbie called. "Move away from the lady. I have my eye on you!"

Ronan thrust out an arm, palm flat, for silence. All the while he watched the Graham girl. Corbie bit off the next word and glared through the bars.

"What about my whisky?" Ronan asked.

"Do you have a supply hidden away? Do you smuggle whisky?"

"I will not answer either question. Hector Graham knows better than to ask."

"Will you reveal where your whisky is located if it was to your advantage?"

"Advantage? That depends. Why these questions?"

"We must know, you see, because—well, an important gentleman enjoys your whisky and would like to meet you."

"What nonsense is this?" he asked in a flat tone.

"It is not my place to say. You may learn more later."

"I can hardly wait," he drawled.

She watched him for a heartbeat, two. "The Whisky Rogues are folk heroes, did you know?"

"Not heroes, lass. We are fiction, courtesy of Sir Walter Scott. But if this important gentleman wants to send a key, clean clothing, and a horse, I might agree to meet him."

A tiny dimple danced beside her mouth as she smiled. That whimsical little hook drew him in like a lure for a fish. "I am sure you would."

"One favor for another." He shrugged.

"Miss Ellison, I am coming in," Corbie said. "Guard, open the door."

"I must go." Ellison Graham set down her cup and turned, nodding farewell to MacInnes and Linhope. She glanced back at Ronan. Something flickered in those silvery eyes that he could not quite read. Regret? "I am sorry, Mr. MacGregor. I wanted more time to talk."

"Not with your watchdog growling at us. Shall I have a word with him concerning his manners?"

"Manners!" She laughed, dimple flashing, eyes sparkling. "Thank you, no. I must leave. Good day, sir."

"Good day, Miss Graham." All in soft Gaelic, their private conversation thrummed through him as she turned away.

The guard opened the door and she slipped through. Corbie took her arm to squire her away, even as he sent Ronan a dark glance. Then they vanished into the shadowy corridor.

Ronan turned to see Linhope and Iain watching. "What?"

"The deputy lord provost sent her?" Linhope asked. "Why?"

He shrugged. "To ask if I distill Glenbrae whisky and if I have a secret store of it. Some important fellow wants it."

"If he could show us some favor, give it to him," Linhope said.

"I suspect she knows little about it and wanted a bit of adventure. I sensed a spot of rebellion."

"I like a lass with a spirited nature," Iain said.

"Aye." Ronan glanced toward the empty corridor. Her presence and her soft scent lingered. He breathed in, out. "If they knew where our cache is hidden, they would be quick to claim it."

"We can do little about that from here," Linhope muttered.

Chapter Five

"WHAT A PITY Juliet is not here to join us for supper," Lady Strathniven said. "I so enjoy her gift at the pianoforte after a good meal."

"She left this afternoon for the Isles to visit Deirdre." Ellison set down her fork, satisfied after the late informal supper of barley vegetable soup, cheeses, fresh-baked rolls, and good French wine. Seeing that the others were nearly done, she rang a little silver bell to signal a maidservant that they were ready for the table to be cleared for coffee and pudding.

"I am thankful Juliet will miss the madness about to descend upon Edinburgh," Sir Hector said. "It promises to be chaotic. My lady, when will you depart for the Highlands?"

"I am off to Strathniven tomorrow, although I will return in time for the glorious spectacle. Ellison, I hope you will come north with me. Do bring wee Balor, he is such good company! Sir Hector and Adam, you are welcome too, though you may be busy."

"Perhaps after the king's visit." Sir Hector sat back as two maids entered, one removing the supper dishes, the other carrying a glass bowl containing a trifle of berries, cream, and cake, which she served in small glass bowls, then poured coffee. When both maids departed, Sir Hector cleared his throat.

"I spoke with Lady Strathniven before supper and explained our dilemma. I thought she might be of some assistance," he said to those gathered around the table.

"Your scheme sounds intriguing," Lady Strathniven said. "I am excited to help."

"Scheme?" Ellison looked from one to the other. "Has something been decided?"

Corbie frowned. "Whatever we say here is in strictest confidence. It could pose a risk for all of us," he added somberly.

"I know," his aunt answered. "And I have thought about your predicament. Some say the only thing King George truly admires about the Scotch is their whisky, true?"

"We intend to show him all that is good about Scotland," Sir Hector said.

"You must please him. Yet you cannot trot a prisoner before a king, even if the man brews the best drink in the Highlands. Thus, a scheme is needed, and I can help."

"We cannot risk disappointing the king," Sir Hector said.

"Then you must send the fellow to Strathniven for the summer. He can be properly trained for a royal introduction there, and no one would be the wiser."

"Strathniven? Interesting." Sir Hector frowned thoughtfully.

"It is a good suggestion, Papa," Ellison said.

"The man is in prison!" Corbie protested.

"Let him out. Surely Sir Hector can arrange that." The lady waved a little silver spoon and dipped it into the trifle.

"It is not that easy," Sir Hector replied. "Marjorie, what do you know of Glenbrae and Darrach? Both glens are near Strathniven. Did you know the viscount?"

"There are so many MacGregors up there. But I never met the viscount, nor do I know your MacGregor. He reminded me of someone, though perhaps I was mistaken. They are a handsome people, the MacGregors. Such presence."

Sir Hector waved impatiently. "What of Viscount Darrach?"

"I never met him, as I said. Castle Darrach is a long ride from Strathniven, but I enjoy touring the countryside up there, and have ridden through the glen in my carriage. So picturesque! You must see it next time you visit! I did hear the viscount was a young man, killed while hunting, they say. Very tragic."

"They say a bit more than that," Corbie commented.

"My housekeeper mentioned talk of murder and smugglers in those hills. But there are ruffians all over the Highlands who misbehave. Every Highland glen has dozens of stills, they say. The people are clever at hiding them and carting their whisky about secretly. They have no choice if they want to survive," she added crisply.

"They are caught often enough by excise officers," Sir Hector defended.

"It is not for me to condemn what they do. But I never venture out at night unless my driver takes me to visit a friend or my sister. She has a country house not far from mine, you know."

"Mrs. Beaton is a lovely lady," Sir Hector said.

"If this viscount met with calamity, remember that some Highlanders resent members of the peerage." She pursed her lips. "When my husband's father acquired Strathniven years ago, it was part of a vast estate once held by MacGregors. A forfeited earldom, I believe. My husband was granted a title of viscount. Not everyone in the region was pleased about it. Jacobite loyalties and resentments linger there."

"Those resentments may never end, Aunt." Corbie helped himself to more trifle.

"True. Some years ago, a few MacGregors petitioned to regain their ancestral land lost in the uprising. I remember solicitors waving documents about and arguing, but my husband prevailed. It was his right through the Crown. Such handsome and nice young MacGregors, they were. I felt sorry for them. What a delicious pudding!" She dipped her spoon again. "Fresh peaches and strawberries. Wonderful. Tell me, how long will Mr. MacGregor be a guest at Strathniven?"

"I cannot promise he will be there," Sir Hector said.

"Dear Aunt, remember that he is a criminal," Corbie said.

"Ellison and I saw these men when you did, Adam. And I saw

three proud and vigorous Highland men in difficult circumstances. Since this laird of Glenbrae is a neighbor of Strathniven, I would like to be of help."

"Are you sure, Marjorie?" Sir Hector asked quietly.

"Yes. The solution to your predicament seems simple to me. The fellow must be prepared for a royal introduction. That cannot happen in prison, but we can accomplish it at Strathniven, where only we would know who he is."

"It would take time to prepare him," Ellison said.

"A fortnight or two, even longer," Lady Strathniven agreed.

"This is preposterous," Corbie said. "Sir, you cannot seriously consider this."

"If a justiciary court reviews their case soon, they could be tried and sentenced before the king arrives," Sir Hector said. "Otherwise, it may be necessary to move them."

"Move them? Where?" Ellison asked.

"Hanged," Corbie barked. "All of them."

Stunned, Ellison paused with her spoon halfway to her lips and stared at him.

"Moved out of the Castle," Sir Hector corrected sternly. "To avoid attention."

"King Geordie will want all the attention on himself," Lady Strathniven said. "He will not like being upstaged by Highland heroes. He would throw a royal tantrum."

Sir Hector coughed. "We should not express opinions on this so bluntly, my lady."

"Aging widows can say what they like." She sniffed.

"It would be horrid to hurry their sentencing for the king's convenience," Ellison said. "I hope you will not allow that."

"They should get what they deserve," Corbie said.

"Considering the uproar over the hangings that occurred here two years ago," Sir Hector said, "the courts will avoid any hue and cry. Perhaps the man could be transferred into my custody until the king departs."

"Wherever he goes, he must remain under guard," Corbie said.

"I so love our wee scheme!" Lady Strathniven exclaimed.

"My lady, this is not amusing," Sir Hector warned.

"Papa," Ellison said, "Mr. MacGregor must be informed. What if he refuses to cooperate? He may not want to meet the king."

Corbie huffed. "If he refuses, there would be consequences."

"Consequences?" She looked at her father.

"I will see what can be done," Sir Hector said.

Ellison stabbed a fat berry in her dessert bowl. "I had hoped for a reprieve."

Corbie laughed. "Unlikely!"

"The man must appear proper in every respect. *Comme il faut.* We have our work cut out for us, Ellison dear," Lady Strathniven said.

"I do not think it is decided," Corbie said.

"I think it is," Lady Strathniven said.

"It may be our best choice," Sir Hector said. "Prepare the fellow and we will see."

"I can tutor him in the etiquette required for a royal occasion," Ellison agreed. "Papa, you said Sir Walter has written a pamphlet with advice on decorum?"

"He has. I will give you a copy."

"When we are done with this Highlander," Lady Strathniven said, "he will be a gentleman anyone would be proud to present. We could try his new skills at Strathniven with a country supper or a dance!" She clapped her hands.

"We are not giving this scoundrel a holiday," Sir Hector warned.

"Sir, I do not believe your daughter should spend time with him," Corbie said.

"But I speak Gaelic," Ellison reminded him.

"She is essential for this," Lady Strathniven pointed out. "Mr. MacGregor will require proper clothing. Adam, you must lend him some things."

"I will not. Besides, the fellow is too large. He would split my tailored coats."

"Then we will find something. So, it is decided," his aunt continued. "Send the fellow to Strathniven. We will tutor him and introduce him as Lord Darrach."

"That is not decided either," Sir Hector cautioned.

"I have grave doubts," Corbie insisted. "A crofter and a thief in plaid rags who speaks no English, has not seen the sharp side of a razor, and does not know a soup spoon from a sugar spoon. Civilizing him will need more than a frock coat and some English words. Remember, if this fails, all our reputations will be at risk."

"You can be so dreary sometimes, Adam," his aunt said.

"MacGregor was probably educated in a glen school," Ellison said. "And if he creates a whisky so extraordinary the very king loves it, he is smart and discerning."

"Exactly," the viscountess said. "We shall sew up the rest into a fine gentleman."

"Sow's ear into a silk purse," Corbie muttered.

"Yes!" His aunt smiled. "Hector?"

"Papa?" Ellison asked, turning expectantly.

Sir Hector threw his napkin on the table. "I see no other solution. I will arrange something. A temporary warrant of release may do for a fortnight."

"Thank you, Papa."

"Just tutor this fellow in the basics and be done with it. But I must insist, Ellison, that you are never alone with him. Understood?"

"If I must provide lessons—"

"I agree." Corbie spoke over her. "Sir, I should go to Strathniven as well."

"You are needed in Edinburgh," Sir Hector barked.

"I will chaperone," Lady Strathniven said. "We will teach him proper manners. Perhaps some dancing lessons too."

"Dancing! Outrageous," Corbie grumbled.

"He will be quite the success. So handsome and appealing!" Lady Strathniven smiled.

"Heaven forfend," Sir Hector muttered.

SEATED IN HER father's library reading, Ellison looked out a tall window, watching for Lady Strathniven's coach. Her baggage was packed and she was excited to start the adventure she secretly craved.

Again her thoughts went to Mr. Ronan MacGregor. Papa had promised a safe warrant to grant the man a temporary release. But MacGregor seemed proud and strong-willed; he could refuse to comply with the proposal.

She frowned, wondering if her father and Corbie would inform him of the plan. Sighing, she knew Corbie was adamant against her involvement. He was oddly possessive of her, though he claimed fondness. He might seem an excellent match for her. His persistence and remarkable head for detail could bring him more responsibility in the government; he had a good income, and he was Lady Strathniven's sole heir. His prospects were excellent. He was nice-looking, short but strong, with pleasant if plain features, sandy-colored hair, brown eyes, and a solicitous manner.

Having known him for years, she knew his tendency to criticize, knew the lack of sympathy he could show for those in lesser circumstances. His arrogance could be too much in evidence. But she found it less easy to define her feeling of discomfort around him; she never fully relaxed in his company. Corbie was interested in Corbie, a quality she found difficult to comprehend.

Yet Sir Hector relied on him and Lady Strathniven cared about him. Both would favor a marriage between Ellison and Adam someday. She wondered if Corbie had mentioned his interest to her father yet. She had a feeling that would come soon.

And lately he seemed jealous of MacGregor. However unfounded, it explained his obstinance regarding any plan that elevated MacGregor and brought her near the man.

All that mattered to her was her father's well-being. She had a unique chance to regain his respect and bridge the gap in their troubled relationship. As for Adam Corbie, she would continue to keep a cool distance and hope for the best.

Turning the page to read on, she could not concentrate, eager for the carriage to arrive for her escape north. She had looked forward to time alone to write and think about her life. Now she had work to do.

Exciting work! Smiling, she turned another page without reading.

Adam Corbie was a doomsayer and her father was skeptical, but she felt deliciously eager for this challenge. She was glad MacGregor would have a little freedom in the north too, and she was sure he would make a convincing gentleman.

She refused to think about what might happen to him after the royal visit.

In the hallway, she heard her father and Corbie talking. Setting the book aside, she glanced around the library with its high bookshelves, polished table, handsome chairs. She loved the comfortable refuge of a beautiful, peaceful library. Strathniven House had two handsome libraries where she could—

Papa and Corbie entered, dispelling peace with some petty argument.

"I do not want a military translator," Sir Hector said. "Ellison will do that. This must be kept among the few of us."

"I arranged for a regiment soldier to translate on the journey, since MacGregor will be taken north under military guard. It is part of the agreement for temporary custody, sir."

"I am looking into a conditional pardon, which relieves me of direct custody."

"The escort ensures that the ladies need not travel with him."

"Fine. Otherwise, Ellison must be the only translator and

tutor for this infernal nonsense. You have arranged all the details?"

"Yes. He will be taken north in a few days and cautioned not to set a foot wrong. Ah, Miss Ellison! We did not see you hiding there."

She peered around the chair. "Good morning. I was not hiding, Mr. Corbie."

"Silent as a mouse. I have prepared a list of the tasks that require your attention." Corbie took folded pages from a pocket. "Sir, if your daughter follows my directions, all will go smoothly."

"Fine," grunted Sir Hector, taking the paper Corbie handed him.

Approaching them, Ellison took her copy and read the list written in Corbie's spiky handwriting.

Barber and a bath, it said. *Burn the plaid and Highland kit etc. Acquire one set of proper clothing and shoes from a man of matching size. Avoid unnecessary expense.*

Blushing at the quick image of MacGregor in a bath, muscled and gleaming—*stop that*, she told herself—she tried to envision him neatly groomed in a dark coat, snowy cravat. But she could only imagine him in Highland plaid looking grand.

She cleared her throat. "Mr. Corbie, we cannot burn a Highlander's plaidie. It is an insult."

"Fleas," Corbie said curtly.

Ellison went on reading. *Teach simple English phrases suited to the occasion. Give school examination for reading skills.*

"An examination intended for children? I will not do it."

"Meals are to be taken alone in his room," Sir Hector said, reading his copy. "He may join an evening meal only to practice manners. Very thorough. This will do."

"It will not do," Ellison protested. "You must allow the man some dignity if you expect him to act the gentleman. And I should decide on the lessons."

"The list is just to ensure the process goes quickly," Corbie said.

"Papa, you know this will need time."

"I do not know how much time we can spare, my dear."

"Two or three days ought to do it," Corbie said.

"Tutoring and even finding appropriate dress will take more time than that. Unless you want to present him to the king as he is."

"A filthy smuggler in rags?" Adam Corbie scoffed.

"A Highlander. There will be many Highland gentlemen at the royal assemblies. Most will be in full Highland regalia. Sir Walter is encouraging it," she said.

"The man should not look like a Scottish chief. He will attract too much notice."

"Sir Walter is keen to show what is unique and special about Scottish culture at the royal assemblies," she countered. "That includes tartan dress for Highlanders."

"A parade of peacocks in plaid," Corbie said.

"Adam," Sir Hector warned. "Yes, Scott is keen to create a sense of the Celtic heyday of Scotland. But we risk overblown pageantry. Many gentlemen will wear formal attire that is elegant and appropriate to the occasion. Ellison, your Highlander must not be allowed to adopt excessive attire."

"He is not my Highlander. A Highland gentleman dressed authentically is a magnificent sight. The king will appreciate Scottish culture even more."

"My dear, do not idealize Highlanders. Especially this one."

"But they are, at heart, a noble race brought down by oppression—"

"Enough! Romanticizing only brought you trouble in the past."

"Years ago, Papa, and I have paid dearly for it."

"You have a sensitive nature, Miss Ellison." Corbie smiled, brown eyes doting, reminding her of treacle. "Teach the man his please-and-thank-you's and be done with it. Sir, I fear your daughter is a little infatuated."

"My dear, just see that the man is presentable. Do not let

your imagination take hold of your senses."

"Papa." She fisted a hand, simmering, then forced a smile. She would prove them wrong and make her father proud of her again.

"I repeat, sir, I must be at Strathniven to ensure the man's behavior."

"And I repeat that you are needed here. Your aunt will chaperone."

"With due respect, my aunt cannot protect Miss Ellison physically."

"I do not believe Mr. MacGregor is a threat," Ellison said.

"I doubt you are the best judge of that, Miss Ellison," Corbie retorted.

"We cannot assign a guard at Strathniven," her father said. "This must be private. Besides, every military man will be needed to manage the crowds coming into the city. Soon the streets will be full day and night. They say every bed and broom closet will be rented out as people arrive from all over Scotland."

"I am taking Balor with me," Ellison said. "He is fiercely protective."

Corbie laughed. "That little mop! He snaps at boots and chews carpet."

"That pup is more bother than he is worth," Sir Hector said.

"He chewed a little carpet, but he grew out of the habit. Lady Strathniven adores him. You know she keeps a full staff in summer. The house will be busy."

"Then someone at Strathniven can be enlisted to help. Who is that strapping young lad who helps there? Donald. Douglas," Sir Hector said.

"Donal Brodie," Ellison said. "A good lad, very smart. He works with Mr. MacNie in the stables sometimes. Mr. MacGregor will need a valet, and Donal would do."

"Valet!" Corbie said. "Someone needs to watch his every move, not tie his cravat."

"Donal will do. Mention it to Lady Strathniven," Sir Hector

told Ellison.

"I will." A question burned in her mind. "Did Mr. MacGregor agree to the plan?"

"He will comply, trust me," Corbie said.

That made her wary. "What do you mean?"

"Once he leaves Edinburgh, his conspirators will be transferred to Calton Jail. MacGregor will soon learn that their wellbeing depends on his cooperation."

"I do not recall ordering that," Sir Hector said.

"Sir, you mentioned some details that I appended to the petition for safe warrant. You signed the papers. Busy as you are, you may have forgotten."

Sir Hector frowned. "I would not forget a detail such as that."

"The other two could hardly remain in the Castle dungeon once MacGregor was removed. Questions would be asked. Moving all three at once attracts less notice. You said MacGregor must understand that his cooperation is essential."

"Ah. Well, if I ordered it." Sir Hector looked perplexed.

None of this felt right, Ellison thought. "What consequences?"

"Just what has been done for centuries," Corbie explained. "MacGregor will cooperate in exchange for the treatment of his accomplices."

"Hostage for blackmail? It is medieval and despicable! Papa, you cannot do this!"

"Transferring the other two is sufficient, Mr. Corbie."

"Sir, we have no guarantee—"

"You cannot betray the man when you need his help!" Ellison said.

"He benefits from this arrangement. And we must exercise caution."

"You need me, but I will not be party to betrayal."

"You are already part of this scheme," Corbie said. "You must ensure its success."

Without answer, she went to the door, taking the handle in

trembling fingers.

"Ellie, stop." Her father's quiet use of her childhood name made her pause.

"Papa, I will not be art and part to betrayal."

"All you need do is turn a frog into a prince," Corbie said.

"Pity. I quite like frogs." She shut the door firmly behind her.

Chapter Six

*F*REEDOM. HE HAD nearly forgotten the feeling.

Through the window of the rolling carriage, Ronan watched the morning fog lift away from buildings crowding the High Street. Two Regiment of Foot guards had escorted him from his cell to the castle forecourt and a waiting vehicle. Now the coach lurched along so quickly that he tilted on the cracked leather seat, hands and ankles bound with rope.

Where the devil were they taking him?

He gulped in cool summer air, enjoying the earthy scent of the cobbled streets, the tantalizing smells of bacon and new bread wafting from booths in the Lawnmarket where merchants were setting up for the day. Everywhere he saw farmers, merchants, women with baskets, children running, and a few soldiers of the Regiment of Foot in red coats, tartan trews, black hats. Overhead, the bells of Saint Giles rang out.

For them, an ordinary morning; for him, extraordinary.

The shabby vehicle was a hired hackney. Curious, he thought. A cart might mean he was headed for trial and hanging. A carriage meant a longer trip.

Earlier, MacInnes and Linhope had watched in alarm as the sentries removed him without explanation. He could not guess their fate now, or his. Whatever the day would bring, he must face it with fortitude.

Ahead he saw the rooftops of Holyroodhouse; to the left, the rugged incline of Calton Hill. Instead of heading there, the coach turned into a shadowed close and halted. Frowning, he recognized the building as the offices of the Constabulary. Dread punched through him.

Leaning to the window, he saw two guards walking with a portly gentleman in a black coat, his expansive chest draped with a blue ribbon, gold badge, silver whistle on a chain. An Edinburgh constable.

A guard opened the door and entered the coach; Ronan recognized Bain, the young sergeant who had interpreted Gaelic for the prisoners in the Castle. The constable thrust his beefy head inside and waved the papers clenched in his hand.

"Ronan MacGregor of Glenbrae in Perthshire, accused of offenses against the Crown, including trafficking of illegal goods," he intoned.

Bain repeated in Gaelic. Ronan nodded; they believed he spoke no English.

"Mr. MacGregor, there are new orders for you," Bain said in Gaelic.

"Am I bound for the gallows?"

"I only know that you are to be taken out of the city."

"Did some rural court lay claim?"

The soldier leaned forward to speak low. "Listen now, for you are a Gael and a MacGregor, and my mother is a MacGregor, and so I will be honest with you."

"*Tapadh leat,*" Ronan said. Thank you.

"What are you saying in there?" the constable demanded.

"The arrangements," Bain answered. "Listen now, Glenbrae. Agree to whatever they ask on pain of consequences. Comply with any conditions proposed for you."

"Why?"

"MacGregor!" The constable rustled the papers in his hand. "This writ is signed by the Right Honorable Sir Hector Graham, Deputy Lord Provost. You are to be released." Bain's Gaelic interpretation was unnecessary, but Ronan waited.

"On what condition? Who paid the surety for the release?" Ronan asked. Bain spoke to the constable.

"Criminals think they know the law better than lawyers," the man groused. "Tell him he is discharged by petition to the Magistrate's office. But he can be confined again for any offense not subject to the terms of this release. On one condition."

"If I am free on discharge there should be no condition," Ronan murmured in Gaelic.

"He is in the judicial custody of Sir Hector Graham," the constable said.

"What interest does Graham have in me?" he asked.

"I do not know," Bain answered. He relayed the question but got no reply.

Scowling, Ronan recalled that Miss Graham had mentioned that someone important was interested in Glenbrae whisky. Was this conditional release part of that odd request?

"Wait here." The constable walked away. Ronan and Bain sat silent.

Shoulders tight, tension growing, Ronan puzzled over pieces that did not fit. Even if someone in authority wanted to see him, it was unusual to free a prisoner and even odder for the chief of the constabulary to guarantee it. Outside came more footsteps, and the coach door opened again.

Recognizing the man who had accompanied Miss Graham to the dungeon, Ronan felt a warning chill spiral through him.

"This is Mr. Adam Corbie," Bain said in Gaelic. "Secretary to the Deputy Lord Provost of Edinburgh. He has some information for you."

"And I have questions. Ask if I am a judicial ward of the provost's office or free on my own accord." Bain did so.

"Temporary. Conditional," Corbie said. "Ask MacGregor if he is responsible for Glenbrae whisky. Ask if he smuggles it."

"Miss Graham asked that and I answered. Mr. Corbie cannot trick me into admitting a crime. I need not answer his inquiry, as he is not an officer of the court."

The translation earned him a flat stare from Corbie. "Remind MacGregor he is liberated temporarily on a minor detail. Sixty-five days have passed since his arrest without trial. That entitles him to release. Such privilege is rarely granted. He is under Sir Hector's protection and would be wise to accept it."

"Then my friends should be released as well," Ronan said, as Bain translated.

"They would require separate petitions. There is no time for that," came the reply.

"Ask what the devil he wants," Ronan snapped.

"The king is fond of Highland whisky." Corbie sneered as he spoke. "We require a supply of your product as a gift for the king."

"Tell him to send word to Glenbrae distillery to purchase what is needed."

Bain translated and Corbie flicked his fingers dismissively. "It is complicated. MacGregor will learn more later."

Was King George the important person? It seemed preposterous.

"Does the Provost's office want to avoid embarrassment because the Glenbrae distiller is accused of smuggling?" Ronan asked. Bain repeated it in English. "Am I released to be located elsewhere until the king leaves Scotland?"

"MacGregor is heading north. That is all he needs to know," Corbie said stiffly.

"What of my friends?" Again Bain translated.

"Tell him to be grateful for his situation. His friends' welfare depends on his cooperation."

"What the devil!" Ronan growled in English, glaring at Corbie.

"Ah, you do speak English," Corbie drawled.

"Some," he bit out.

"Tell him he is under the protection of Sir Hector Graham until otherwise decided. Comply, or his accomplices will pay the price. And he will be sent to Calton."

"I will not comply with blackmail," Ronan snarled in Gaelic. Bain interpreted.

Corbie lifted a hand. "Take him north, Sergeant. Ride with him until you meet the second coach. Then return to the city in this one." Corbie opened the door, then turned.

"Tell MacGregor," he added low, "when he sees Mrs. Graham-Leslie, he will keep his distance and speak only when chaperoned. Or else," he growled, looking at Ronan, "I will see him arrested and hanged. Or kill him myself." He walked away.

Bain did not translate.

Silent, Ronan fisted his hands, wrists still bound. Moments later, the driver stirred the horses and the vehicle climbed the slope to the High Street.

"Since they declared you free, there is no need for these." Bain leaned forward, produced a small, sharp knife, and sliced through the ropes binding wrists and feet.

"Thank you." Ronan rubbed his wrists. "Where are we headed?"

"North to Kinross to meet another coach. That is all I know."

Heading north, Ronan watched the landscape flow past and nursed simmering anger over his baffling encounter. Freed by unexpected writ, he wanted to enjoy the luck, but could not. Threats, mystery, betrayal laced through the situation.

Hours passed as they took a barge over to Fife and headed northwest for Perthshire and Kinross. He knew the route well. Bain dozed. Ronan rested some, but turned the conundrum over in his mind.

Somehow the delectable Miss Graham was involved in this. *When he sees her*, Corbie had said. Not *if*.

Watching rainclouds over distant hills, he wondered if Graham and Corbie knew they had sent him home, where he had opportunity and hope.

"Aye, Mr. Balor, we will go out soon for a good run before supper," Ellison said as the little terrier jumped about by the door that led to Strathniven's kitchen garden. She bent to pat the terrier's head, and Balor, his long dark coat nearly brushing the slate floor, stood as patiently as possible, his little body quivering with excitement.

Tying the black ribbons of her straw bonnet and adjusting the wide brim with its crescent of silk flowers, she smoothed the flounced skirts of her lavender day dress and plucked a tartan shawl from a hook to drape it over her shoulders in case of rain. Remembering the boots she kept at Strathniven for traversing the hills, she slid out of her black slippers, found the boots, tugged them on and tied the laces.

"Sensible shoes!" Lady Strathniven said as she stepped into the dim corridor. "These hills can be muddy. There was quite a bit of rain lately."

Ellison straightened. "I fell once in slippers on a hill, which taught me a lesson."

"Yes, you broke an ankle! I am glad you came up here for a little respite, dear."

"We will not have much of that once our guest arrives." She took the dog's leash.

"You are the perfect tutor for the task. That sky looks ominous." Lady Strathniven peered through the window. "Let one of the maids take the pup out."

"Your staff are busy, and I enjoy walking him. Donal Brodie offered earlier today, but I have not seen him since."

"He went to Kinross with Mr. MacNic to pick up the wee man. Sir Ronald."

"Ronan," Ellison said. "I did not know Mr. MacGregor was expected today."

"Did I not mention it? What should we call him? Lord Darrach or Sir Ron—Ronan."

"Glenbrae or Mr. MacGregor should do. We may need to call him Lord Darrach in company later, though I doubt he will like it much."

"We shall see. MacNie will pick up some things while he is in town, including the post. They leave it at the inn now rather than bring it around as before. Efficiency for them is not very efficient for us. Hey, Balor!" The lady bent to pat his head. "Sweet pup!"

"He adores you. Papa thought I should leave him in Edinburgh to save your Turkey carpets."

"I would rather he chewed all my carpets than stayed with that old numpty. Hey, my laddie," she said to the dog in a silly voice.

Ellison laughed. "He loves the freedom here. So do I."

"We do as we please here, my dear. It is part of why I love the Highlands." She sighed. "I wish my nephew appreciated it as much as you do. I should leave the estate to him as my heir, but he has become such a sour fellow. I told him he must marry a practical and kind wife if he wants Strathniven. You know he is quite fond of you."

Was that a hint? Tugging at her gloves, Ellison frowned. "I had that impression."

"I am sure your father would approve."

Ellison busied herself with the dog's leash. She did not want to talk about the possibility of marrying Corbie.

"Adam did not inherit much from his father, alas, but he has a respectable income and an ambition to succeed."

"I have noticed. Oh, look how anxious Balor is to be off. We will be back soon."

"I know Adam does not think MacGregor should be treated as a guest here," the lady went on. "And you two disagree at times. True, Ronald MacGregor must feel like a gentleman if he is to act like one."

"Ronan," Ellison said absently. "My lady, does this ruse trouble you?"

"It is necessary. With all the kerfuffle around King George, no one will think much about another Highland lord. Go, now." The lady opened the door. "Hurry back."

Balor half-dragged Ellison down the kitchen path toward the lawn and flower gardens. She guided him firmly beyond the low garden wall, crossing a meadow toward a hill behind the house.

On the incline, skirt hems brushing wet heather, she glanced back at Strathniven House. Golden sandstone walls soared on green lawns under gray clouds. An elegant windowed façade and jumble of slate roofs defined the main house, and an old stone tower, all that remained of the original castle, capped a far corner. Tucked against the foothills, it looked like a fairytale castle.

She loved every stone, every acre. Someday Adam Corbie would be its master, but for now, she was grateful to be here. She wondered if Corbie could truly care about the estate, cultivate it, protect it, be a fair landlord to the tenants on its vast acres. Lady Strathniven was right. Her nephew would need a capable wife and helpmate once he inherited the estate.

Much as she cared about Strathniven House, she could not be that helpmate.

THE HILLS GREW higher, steeper, and pines rose green and strong against rugged slopes misted in purple heather and yellow gorse. Here and there, wild roses clustered. Ronan savored the comfort of familiar beauty, grateful for the luck that had him rumbling toward home.

But he did not know his fate here, and dare not think longingly of Invermorie Castle, his property in these heathery hills, or of Darrach Castle, the stone tower that may or may not be his right someday. The tug in his heart felt almost physical.

Instead, he puzzled over the curious arrangement that had brought him this wee bout of freedom. It was cause for concern. What did the lovely Miss Ellison Graham have to do with this? He doubted King George cared a whit who distilled the whisky in his glass so long as it was abundantly supplied.

But he smiled, certain that Glenbrae whisky was just that good, especially the casks released earlier this year. Aged five years, it was exceptionally smooth and rich. A cache of Glenbrae whisky had made it to the king's table two years ago, courtesy of a kinsman. That the king preferred it was fine news indeed.

The landscape streaming past grew even more familiar. In these glens, he knew every hill, path, and cave; every castle, croft, and bothy. There he would find home, kin, friends; enemies too.

Soon he saw the church steeple and market cross of the small town of Kinross. The coach drew to a stop in the forecourt of an inn he knew as well. And he was wary of being recognized by its patrons.

Bain stepped out of the hackney, stretching. "A coach waits for you over there," he said, pointing. "The driver will take you onward. I wish you *slàn leat, deagh fhortan.*"

Ronan stepped down into a drizzling rain. "Luck to you as well," he replied in Gaelic. "If you and the hackney man want a pint and a meal before you return to the city, the fare is good here." Across the yard sat a black brougham, old but well-kept, with two stocky horses, black and chestnut. The driver, an older fellow, sat beside a youth. Both pulled plaids and caps against the rain. Waving, the driver climbed down to approach.

Feeling a jolt to see a man he knew, Ronan pulled a swath of his own plaid over his head against rain and recognition.

"Ben MacNie here for the guest, sir," the older man told Bain, and gave Ronan a keen glance. Head lowered, Ronan nodded in silence, glancing at the familiar face of a friend. MacNie had rough-carved, amiable features, a gray beard, and sharp blue eyes that studied him. Glancing past him, Ronan felt another tug when he saw the face of the young man seated on the driver's bench.

He caught his breath. His ruse was all but done, and depended on these two.

"This is Mr. MacGregor. He speaks little English," Bain told MacNie.

"Does he now," MacNie drawled. "Come from Edinburgh

with a military guard? I thought we were to fetch a gentleman guest."

"He is a guest of Lady Strathniven."

Keeping his head down, Ronan nodded curtly at the introduction, and wondered why the devil they would send him to Strathniven. What did they want of him?

"Aye well." MacNie watched Ronan. "Sir, I am steward and factor at Strathniven House and estate, and keep the stables too. I will say the MacGregors are a good lot. My stable lad is of that ilk. *Fàilte*," he added in welcome.

"*Tapadh leat,*" Ronan murmured, head down.

"Lady Strathniven looks forward to your visit. We should go."

"She is a kind lady," Ronan replied carefully.

"Aye. This way, sir. Good day, Sergeant."

Ronan thanked Bain and followed MacNie across the yard. The driver had guessed by now, no doubt, and soon enough the lad would too. He had to count on their silence. And he was determined to discover why he had been sent here.

Chapter Seven

"BALOR!" ELLISON CALLED as the terrier scampered ahead, pausing to glance at her as if considering his choices, though the leash limited those. Tail wagging, he came to her when she called again, and took the bit of oatcake she offered from a pocket.

Keeping pace with the dog as he explored the damp hillside, Ellison raised her face to the drizzling rain, enjoying its soft, clean wetness and the freedom she felt. At Strathniven, she felt untethered and could reclaim herself for a little while.

Balor enjoyed the same, and because he was good about returning when she called, she let him off the leash. Then she called him back for a pat and praise, and followed where he went.

She was glad of a little time to think about what was expected of her with these lessons, how she should proceed with tutoring, and how she felt about this scheme. A gentleman was essential for this royal request. She knew that. But she disliked Corbie's barely veiled threats and her father's desire to have little to do with it.

Thinking of Corbie, she shivered. His disrespect toward MacGregor revealed a colder heart than Ellison had realized. For all his haughtiness, she had not thought him capable of cruelty before, but now, she was not so sure. If her father expected her to accept a match, he and Corbie would be sorely disappointed.

Looking around, she saw Balor happily nosing nearby. A

burst of wind stirred her skirts, and fat raindrops splattered the turf, the rocks, her bonnet. "Come here, Balor!"

Digging and busy, the dog ignored her. Walking closer, Ellison glanced down to see the road that swept north from Kinross to curve around the foothills. Mr. MacNie would bring the coach carrying MacGregor along that road, and soon the lessons would begin. She breathed in, feeling a thrill at the thought of this adventure.

Hearing a bark, she saw Balor running along the slope, tail wagging madly. She followed a rough path between heather, gorse, and rocks, determined to fetch him. Rain was falling in earnest now, and it was to head back to the house.

"Balor!" The dog forged ahead through brush and bramble, nose down, tail straight, silently intent on a quest. Sighing, Ellison followed. "Come here!"

Distant thunder rumbled, and the dog bolted like an arrow. Ellison knew he hated thunder and lightning, usually hiding under furniture. Now he ran in a panic.

"Balor!" She turned, searching the slopes. He had vanished, having found some niche behind a rock or a bush. Spotting his little dark rump beside some gorse, fearing his coat would be full of the painful spines, she ran toward him.

More thunder, then a bright crack of lightning overhead. The rain turned to a downpour. Running, heels sliding, she nearly fell, catching herself with a hand splayed on the turf, a knee to the mud. Scrambling to her feet, she hurried, calling out. The delay of her fall, then a new round of thunder, caused Balor to flee again.

Pausing to catch her breath, spinning, Ellison did not see the dog, but noticed how far she had come from the house. The wind and slanting rain grew more forceful, and she drew the plaid close, lifting the drooping brim of her straw hat to look around.

"Balor!"

Desperate, she spun again and saw movement on the road. The black Strathniven carriage came around a curve, its red-painted wheels a blur. In a panic, Ellison hurried down the hill, waving her arms.

"MacNie! Mr. MacNie! Stop!" She ran, heels sliding on the slope, damp skirts clinging as she stepped onto the road. The carriage pulled to a sudden halt.

"Miss Ellison!" MacNie called. "Ye look a right banshee! What is it, lass?"

"Mr. MacNie! Donal!" She hurried toward the carriage as Donal Brodie climbed down to meet her. "Balor ran off in the storm. I cannot find him—I am so glad to see you! Can you help?" She spoke breathlessly, knowing she must look like a drowned harpy. Donal came near, and beyond, she saw a face at the coach window.

Dark hair, rough-bearded jaw, shoulder pressed to the glass. She felt a leap in her heart to see MacGregor there. But Balor was all that mattered.

"Miss Ellison, where did you see the dog last?" Donal asked.

She pointed. "Up there. He found a hiding spot somewhere. He is frightened of thunder." Another roar punched through the clouds. She jumped.

MacNie climbed down, red plaid wrapped over coat and trews and draped high over his head and shoulders. "Which way, lass? The wee rascal! Donal, wi' me." He turned for the hill. "Wait in the coach, Miss."

"I can help you find Balor!"

"Ye're soaked through. Her ladyship will have my hide should ye take ill. Inside, now. Dinna mind the young man there. He's all right," he added, waving her away.

Just then MacGregor stepped out of the vehicle, pulling his dark plaid over his head too against the downpour. "Miss Graham! What is the trouble?"

"My dog is lost on the hill," she said, distracted, pointing that way.

"We're off to fetch him," MacNie called. "Lass, to the coach!"

"Let me help," MacGregor said. With a fleeting touch to her elbow—she felt the tender shock of it through to her knees—he hurried away, taking the slope in long strides. Watching the men, she then went to the coach and climbed inside.

Something tapped at her awareness, but she had no time to study it, anxious for the dog's safety. She shook her skirts, stamped her muddy boots, sat on the edge of the leather bench, and watched the hill. Rain pounded on the roof, thunder rumbled, lightning cracked. Tugging off her wet gloves, she leaned to look up the slope.

On the hill's crest, the men moved through a haze of rain, shouting, waving arms as if to herd the dog. Had they found him? Opening the door slightly, she listened to their shouts through the sound of the rain.

"Here—no, there! Over there! Hey! To me, wee rascal! Och, beastie, here to me!"

She could make out MacNie in his trousers and flat cap, Donal, lanky and fast, and MacGregor, tall and strong, arms extended, plaid flapping. When a small dark shape darted across the ridge, MacGregor spun after it and dove down.

Moments later came victorious shouts as the men headed down the hill. Seeing MacGregor clutching a squirming bundle inside his plaid, Ellison jumped from the coach and ran toward them.

He patted the bump in his plaid and glanced up at Ellison. He grinned. MacNie spoke and MacGregor replied, laughing, the sound warm through the rain. Here was a man at ease, confident, untroubled—no wary prisoner, but a Highlander in his element.

And he had rescued her pup. Grateful, relieved, she ran forward, tugging at her drenched shawl. The men were soaked, too. They would arrive at Strathniven in a sorry state. She hardly cared.

Donal spoke then, and MacGregor and MacNie laughed. Ellison smiled too, eager to join them. Then that sense of something missed, forgotten, suddenly came clear.

They all spoke English. So did MacGregor, with great ease.

Then Balor's little snout poked out of the Highlander's plaid.

Crying out in relief, Ellison hurried forward.

"Is this the small one you are wanting?" MacGregor asked in Gaelic.

"*Tapadh leat*," she said, hands open to lift the dog away. MacGregor cupped his large hand gently over the dog's head.

"He is excited and may bolt again." This in Gaelic too. "Come into the coach. You are wet and will catch your death." He touched her elbow to guide her there.

Another incidental touch, another rush of safety and strength. She stepped away.

"I will walk, Mr. MacGregor," she said in precise English. "Give me my dog."

THUNDER BOOMED, LIGHTNING snapped, the dog in his arms yelped. Ronan took the girl's elbow firmly. "*A-steach don charbad, mo nighean.*" Into the carriage, my girl.

She glared at him, eyes gone stormy gray. He frowned, wondering what had sparked her temper. And then he knew.

What a fool to forget his ruse. He had naturally used English while the men chased the dog, reverting to Gaelic when he spoke to Miss Graham. She, a clever girl, had noticed.

Thunder again. The dog jerked. Ronan guided the girl toward the carriage. She relented, letting him assist her inside. Her fingers were slender and cool, attitude cooler.

She sat, smoothing her damp skirts. He sat opposite, cradling the pup in one arm. He knew she was angry and knew he deserved it.

"You can take the pup and I will do the walking," he offered in Gaelic.

"Then you will be the one catching your death," she responded in that tongue.

"If I do not catch it from you first."

She opened her mouth to speak just as the carriage lurched forward. Ronan swayed, holding the dog. The girl nearly tumbled from her seat, righting herself and turning indignantly away from him. He noticed her gown had fared poorly in the rain, soggy flounces at the hem, wet lace at the bodice. When dry, the thing would be fetching; the lavender hue would complement the flash of those irate eyes.

His mouth twitched. He stroked the quivering dog's head, waiting. Miss Graham lifted her chin, fussed at the damp shawl, pushed at her drooping bonnet with its bedraggled silk flowers, her wet golden curls straggling free. She glanced at him, cheeks high pink, rain-colored eyes snapping.

"Do you want the pup?" He used Gaelic stubbornly to push against the strong attraction he felt. Tension hung between them. She did not reply.

Wriggling and warm, the dog stretched its snout to lick Ronan's bearded chin. He laughed—he could not help it. The girl melted a little and reached out.

"Wee laddie, come here," she cooed, and took the creature, cuddling it, heedless of mud and damp. The love between the two warmed the dreary carriage interior like sunlight.

It warmed Ronan's heart, too, though he folded his arms over his chest, suddenly aware just how easily he could fall for this sopping, messy, indignant, beautiful girl and her mucky wee pup.

He needed to stay aloof, needed to mistrust her, her father, and Corbie. With his freedom in question, his friends threatened, and this journey benefiting others somehow, he had to remain vigilant.

Thunder rolled above, loud and startling. The dog barked, and the girl squeaked as the carriage hurtled onward. "MacNie and Donal are seated outside in this awful storm. It is dangerous for them to be up there." She spoke in English.

So did he. "Your man drives like the very devil."

"He drives fast no matter the weather." She held the whimpering dog close. The coach rocked, pitching her sideways. Ronan straightened his leg, bracing his boot against the opposite seat to keep her from falling.

"Beg pardon," he muttered, dropping his foot to the floor.

She watched him over the dog's head. "So you have English."

"I have." He felt a little of the burden lift.

"A good bit, I think." She lifted her chin defiantly, a habit he had noticed in her.

"Aye so." He inclined his head.

"Did you need the Gaelic for protection?"

"It proved convenient." Her observation was kind as well as perceptive. But he could not allow kindness, or this drenched, charming, delicate vision, to sway him.

"May we use English between us, then?" An offer of peace rather than an accusation, it revealed her character. He liked that. He nodded.

"The ruse has been helpful," he said.

"Ruse?" Her hands clenched. "I will not keep your secret. But tell me—are you a true Highland man? There is more to you than one might guess."

"One might say the same for you, Miss Graham." She was learning about him as fast as he was discerning her. "I am Highland born and bred and have spoken the Gaelic since my first words. English too. Lately the native tongue suited best."

"It would have been risky to reveal too much about yourself."

"I can hide little from you, Miss Graham. I am warned."

"I am not your enemy." She watched him for a moment, then looked out the window. *"Cha mhòr an sin."* Almost there.

Gaelic again. Bless the girl. "Strathniven House?" Looking through a haze of rain, he glimpsed the massive sandstone façade in the distance.

"It is." Tugging at her bonnet, she swept her fingers through the wet, honey-colored curls spilling along one shoulder. "I look a fright."

"Not at all." She looked a wee goddess. Not just lovely, but intelligent, forthright, unpretentious. Such virtues in a woman were his downfall. He yearned for a woman with inner strength, a sharp mind, kindness, even a touch of whimsy. One such woman had slipped through his grasp years ago, and his uncertain future might not allow him to find another. Yet this girl fair glowed with allure, wit, compassion, and more. He felt himself falling.

Careful, lad. This fleeting moment was no place to rest his hopes and dreams.

"Miss Graham, only your wee hat looks a fright."

She laughed, touched the woebegone flowers. "Your things are soaked too. Thank you for fetching my dog. I appreciate it more than I can say."

"It is I who must thank you. I enjoyed chasing about in the rain. It has been too long."

"Thank Balor for running away." She ruffled the dog's head.

"Balor, is it? Chief of the Fomorians in Irish myth—the 'deadly one'—a formidable name for a wee Skye terrier." He reached across the gap to scratch the little head and received a licking of the fingers in return. "Fierce laddie."

She laughed again. "Do you have a dog?"

"Two deerhounds, staying with kin while I have been away." He went silent, having eased up caution too soon. The girl broke his focus.

She giggled as the dog licked her chin. Ronan enjoyed the silvery sound and her impish, fairylike smile. Affection and contentment warmed him out of nowhere.

"Regardless of the reason," he ventured, "it is good to be out in the world again."

"I am glad. So you agreed to what was asked of you?"

"I was told the king has a fondness for my whisky. I saw your Mr. Corbie."

"And he explained the rest?"

"The king would like a supply of Glenbrae whisky, and it seems I am expected to provide it. That may take some doing."

"You have a few weeks to arrange it."

"Mr. Corbie hinted at some difficulty for my friends if I do not comply. With what," he murmured, "should I comply?"

"Oh." She worried her teeth against her lower lip. "I thought you knew."

"I am to obtain whisky. And it seems I am being removed from Edinburgh to avoid embarrassment for Scotland."

"That is part of it." She paused. "Do you not know?"

"Know what?" He waited.

"Mr. MacGregor, I must warn you."

He leaned back. "If you feel this space is too close, I apologize. But you are safe from me. Your Corbie warned me to keep my distance from you."

"He is not my Corbie. And he should not have told you that. He misspoke."

"If I am missing something here, best say it out."

"I must warn you that Mr. Corbie thinks you should be a—a hostage."

"Does he," he drawled. "Are you my custodian, then?"

"Not me. But there are expectations of you. Truly, he did not explain?"

"All I know is that I have been liberated. What expectations?"

"Liberated?" She tipped her head in surprise.

"A nicety of the law fell in my favor. I hope to extend it permanently." He waved a hand. "What is expected of me, Miss Graham?"

A worry, something unsettled, flickered in her eyes. "I believe Mr. Corbie meant hostage in the old sense—a hostage for good behavior, as in earlier days."

"I know what it means. Held in abeyance. My good behavior in exchange for the safety of my friends. What is expected in return?"

"Please understand that I am not part of any threat to you."

"I would quake in my boots if you were. Out with it, Miss."

"There is an arrangement. It should have been explained."

"I am to keep my distance from you. Must I also display excellent manners at your country house? Pretend to be a better man than I am? I can manage it briefly. It will try me so," he snapped.

She winced, cheeks going pink. "M-manners?"

"I assume I must be isolated here while the king is in the city."

"I know you are upset, but you must agree to what is asked." Above the sound of rain and wheels, her voice turned urgent. "And you must not try to escape."

"Or your spiteful wee clerk will be after me?" He huffed a laugh.

"He is my father's secretary."

"And in love with you, if I am not mistaken."

"I do not know what he thinks of me." She looked away.

He did not believe that, but he was after a different truth. "Miss Graham, I sense something afoot here. It seems your Mr. Corbie has gallantly left it to the lady to explain. And he calls himself a gentleman," he muttered.

"Gentleman! Oh." She held the dog tightly against her.

"You will smother that pup. Tell me."

"You are to be introduced to the king," she blurted. "At one of the assemblies. As a gentleman. Perhaps—under another name. Because of your—predicament."

Of all the possibilities, he had not expected that. "How absurd."

"The king expects to meet the distiller of Glenbrae whisky. He likes your whisky very much."

"Ah." The pieces came together swiftly. "Alas, the distiller is a smuggler, even worse, a prisoner, but the Provost's office cannot refuse the king. What to do? Aha!" He spoke swiftly, with an edge. "Hide the scoundrel away until the king departs—or shall we clean him up and trot him past the king? Is that it?"

"Uh—oh, look!" She pointed out the window. "Strathniven House."

Now he noticed they were rolling between two stone gates to enter an earthen courtyard edged by pine trees. Sandstone walls were articulated by rows of gleaming windows overlooking lawns and gardens. To one side were stables and sheds; to the other, soaring blue and heathered hills.

This was the fine house and estate his great-grandfather had lost long ago.

Strathniven is no longer ours, lad, his father had told him once. *But Glenbrae and Invermorie will be yours after I am gone, and your cousin will have Darrach. The two of you must guard the land and tenants.*

A task that had proven all but impossible.

"May we speak of this matter later?" she asked. "Mr. Mac-Gregor?"

"What? Aye." The carriage slowed. "Have MacNie leave me at the servants' door."

"You are a guest here," she said as the coach stopped. "Welcome to Strathniven, Mr. MacGregor. Shall I call you Glenbrae?"

"If you like," he said, distracted, thoughts racing.

The carriage door opened, and Donal peered inside, tall and thin, black-haired, with the rounded beauty of a young man who would one day grow into handsomeness.

"Miss Ellison," the lad said, handing her out.

"Donal, this is MacGregor of Glenbrae. He is our guest. Sir, this is Donal Brodie, one of our grooms."

"Sir." The lad touched his cap. Ronan nodded in silence, stepping down. Lanky young Donal took the dog from Miss Graham and set the pup on the ground. "I will take Balor to the kitchen and dry him off, Miss."

"Thank you. Oh, Donal," she said, turning, "Glenbrae does not have much English. Your Gaelic is good enough for conversation, I think?"

"Gaelic?" The lad's brows lifted under the dark gloss of his hair, and his whisky-brown eyes widened in surprise. "I know a bit."

"Good. That will be a help." She turned for the house.

Ronan waited until she was out of earshot. "Donal Brodie,"

he murmured, "you have sprouted since I saw you last."

"That I have. Welcome back to Perthshire, Uncle." Donal grinned.

Ronan's throat tightened. For a moment he could not speak. Then he clapped his brother's stepson on the shoulder and walked with him toward the entrance.

Chapter Eight

"WELCOME, GLENBRAE! WE are so pleased you are here!" Lady Strathniven enunciated loudly, her voice echoing in the foyer. Ellison was pleased that Lady Strathniven acted as if she had never seen the man before. But he was not deaf.

MacGregor bowed his head. "My lady, thank you," he replied in English.

"He speaks English?" Lady Strathniven said, turning to Ellison in surprise.

"A little," Ellison said as she untied her soggy bonnet.

"Thank you for saving the pup today! Mr. MacNie told me all about your rescue!" As the lady continued to shout, the Highlander smiled amiably.

Ellison translated in Gaelic, though she knew it was unnecessary. Seeing sparks of humor in his blue eyes, she wondered how she had not discerned the truth sooner.

"He seems a nice young man to me." Lady Strathniven turned to Ellison. "I do not understand the kerfuffle over bringing him here."

"Please, my lady, may we talk about this later?" Ellison asked.

"Mr. MacNie says the dog likes him very well. Balor's good opinion is golden."

"It is. Dear me, I am drenched. I hope we did not track mud over the floor."

"It can be cleaned. Did you have a nice chat with Glenbrae in the carriage?"

"A bit." Ellison was keenly aware of the man standing so tall, so close, so attentive.

"You must continue to practice polite conversation with him. It is why we are here." As the viscountess spoke, Ellison glanced at the Highlander. He cocked a brow.

"We are here for polite conversation?" he asked in Gaelic, with a tight smile.

"And other matters. Later, sir," she said in Gaelic, unwilling to expose his ease with English. "My lady, our guest will want to rest after his long journey."

"Mrs. Barrow prepared a room in the tower for him. My nephew wanted me to put him in the servant quarters. But I do not take instruction well."

Ellison laughed. "You do not, to be sure." She translated for MacGregor—*your room is in the old tower. It is very private. You will be comfortable there*—while avoiding his steady gaze. Looking down, she noticed his mud-plastered boots were worn and scuffed, the soles gaping in spots. His feet were long and large. His plaid and other garments were soaked and grimy. And the man had an earthy aroma that was not very gentlemanly.

She remembered Corbie's list—bath, shave, clothing. She had to agree.

Now she wondered if the clothing she had asked Donal Brodie to find for their guest would suit him. Informing Donal that they expected a gentleman who was tall and fit and in need of clothing, she had told him to look at some things she'd stored in a chest in one of Strathniven's attics. Because she and Colin had spent so much time at Strathniven, they both had clothing left here.

But she had misjudged. MacGregor was taller, heavier, more muscular than her late husband. Colin Leslie, tall and lean with a poet's soul and an artist's elegance, had preferred closely tailored suits and fashionable boots. Brawny MacGregor, quiet and powerful, could fill a space with his very presence; his build was only part of that.

"Will Glenbrae join us for supper? I asked Cook to prepare a simple meal."

Turning, Ellison asked in Gaelic if he would care to have supper with them.

"An honor, but I must decline," he replied in that language. His voice, even softly modulated, had a resonance that sank through her like whisky. "Please tell the lady that I am fatigued and would not be good company."

"Just as well. You must be tired too, my dear," Lady Strathniven said. "Let Mrs. Barrow see Glenbrae to his room. Your dress is quite ruined. A pity you did not bring a maid to see to your needs. My Jeanie is here, but keeps busy seeing to me. Young Mary can be assigned to help you."

"Thank you. If she can clean my dress, I can make any repairs." Glancing around for the housekeeper, Ellison was reluctant to leave the Highlander with the viscountess in her current talkative mood. He would hear too much before she could explain the plan. She needed an opportunity to talk to him in private.

"I vow, Adam thinks this fine Highland rascal cannot learn to act properly no matter what we do, but I disagree—"

"Mrs. Barrow!" Ellison called in relief, hearing the woman's footsteps.

AFTER LEADING RONAN through the house to a short corridor and the entrance to the old structure, Mrs. Barrow preceded him up spiral stone steps and flung open a door. "This is your room, Mr. MacGregor," she said as loudly as the viscountess had done.

"Thank you." Ducking slightly under the old lintel, he followed her inside. "A fine room." He kept the English simple. She smiled.

The chamber was small but well-appointed, cozy, and somewhat antique, with whitewashed walls, a beamed ceiling, and worn patterned carpets on the planked floor. A large canopy bed with a red brocade coverlet filled much of the space; a small table and wooden chair sat beneath a mullioned window framing a misty view of hills. The room had an air of solitude, high in the old tower. He liked that.

Long ago, a MacGregor ancestor had designed and constructed this very tower. Bemused, he nodded. "Thank you, Mrs. Barrow. Very nice."

"You-speak-English?" she enunciated.

"Some. Thank you."

"Lady Strathniven thought you would be comfortable here." The housekeeper pursed her mouth.

"Aye."

"Huh, and Mr. MacNie out in the rain at his age, catching his death to fetch you," she muttered half to herself, "and you bringing mud inside and much in need of a barber and a bath. What are we to do with you. Why are you here at all, at all. Curious, I say."

"Thank you, Mrs. Barrow." He set a hand on the door.

"Glenbrae is a local name. Are you kin to the MacGregors of Glenbrae and Invermorie? And the late Darrach, God rest him?"

"Kin? Some."

"I didna know the young viscount, but I knew his father. And you have the look of the Glenbrae MacGregors." She squinted. "A handsome folk."

He smiled. "Thank you, Mrs. Barrow. The room is good."

"*Och,* not a word did he get," she muttered. "MacGregor, if you wish a bath, we have a bathing apparatus here. Lord Strathniven had it brought up from London. You-may-use-the-bathing-apparatus," she said loudly.

Ronan huffed in amusement. "Bathing apparatus. Thank you."

"Down-the-stairs!" She pointed out and down.

"Aye." He wanted a bath desperately. A basin and cloth would do, but he would try the shower machine, though he hated the things, having encountered them before.

"Clothes." She pointed to the chair and the bed, where items were folded and stacked. "Towels. Soap. Bath!" she repeated with a sniff.

"Very kind."

On the bed, he saw folded white linen towels, a fat ball of soap, and grooming items. The canopied frame was a dark, hefty monstrosity draped in red damask; the thick mattress was piled with pillows, and looked tempting after months on straw mats in a dungeon. A stiff chair held clothing items; polished boots sat on the floor.

He smiled, gritting his teeth, eager to be alone to bathe, change, rest, and think.

"Why does a guest arrive without his things, I wonder? But your manservant found some items for you to use."

He raised his brows in surprise. "Manservant?"

"See, you know some words! Young Donal. Your manservant here."

"Ah." His nephew might be expected to guard him as well. A fortunate choice.

"Do-you-need-anything-more," she boomed.

He shook his head. "Thank you, Mrs. Barrow. Kind."

"Supper? Hungry? I will send up a tray. Tomorrow, breakfast is in the main house. That way!" She pointed out again. "Dining Room. Understand?"

"Aye. Breakfast. You are kind."

"Hmph," she muttered. "You have more English than anyone knows, I suspect."

When he twinkled his eyes at her, she brightened. "So, Glen-brae! They think you a simple Highland man, but I think differently. I know a few MacGregors hereabouts."

"Aye?" He went wary.

"Most are good folk, but there are smugglers in these hills.

Are you with them?"

"I bring no trouble here." Her question deserved an immediate answer.

"Huh. We shall see. Good evening." She left the room, closing the door.

He sighed, ran a hand through his disheveled hair, rubbed his scruffy beard, and reminded himself again to be extremely cautious at Strathniven.

Exploring the room, he sorted through the clothing—linen shirt, neckcloth, waistcoat of brown damask, and a coat and trousers of black superfine. He wondered whose they were; the cut was suited to a tall, trim man.

First, he needed to feel clean again. Gathering the towel, soap, and a leather case of grooming items, he went in search of the bathing machine.

Going down the stone steps, he opened one door after another, finding rooms with furniture draped in dusty sheets and a compact room that held bookshelves, a table, a couple of chairs. A library. He would like to use that if he had time.

On the lower level, he found a small room with a high raftered ceiling and walls covered in blue Delft tiles. The tall apparatus filled the center of the narrow room.

He eyed the contraption skeptically. A wooden tub fitted with tall iron struts formed a cage-like enclosure; above it, a metal tank bolted in the rafters connected through pipes to the showering cage. Water was drawn downward by operating a long cord inside the cage; pulling it would produce a rainlike shower.

That was the theory behind such things, but in Ronan's experience, they spit and shuddered and trickled and were more trouble than convenience. Pipes could leak and refilling the tank required at least two men to do the job.

This beast acted as expected. Ronan tugged a lever and then the cord, and water spit slowly downward. Stripping out of his things, he stepped inside, catching just enough tepid trickle for a decent wash. Wary of the rickety frame and creaking valves, he hurried to lather his hair and body with the pine-scented soap ball.

Earlier, the downpour on the hillside had given him a natural shower, so the machine completed the task. Rinsing the soap, he pulled the cord and stepped out. Clean was clean, and he felt good and grateful.

Toweling off, he trimmed his beard with the grooming tools, then combed his too-long hair. His plaidie and other garments were filthy; he would ask Donal if someone could clean and repair them. Dressing in the things provided, he found they fit, just, the shirt and waistcoat snug, the trousers too short. The boots, hardly worn, were tight.

Climbing the stairs to the guest chamber, he winced with each step. Such footwear would discourage a man from escaping, he thought; his old brogues, hard-worn but comfortable, would need repair soon. Even so, his worn brogues were unsuited to a royal audience. He huffed at that thought.

At any rate, whether at court or at home, he would prefer to wear good Highland gear, with its handsome distinction and comfort. Another request for Donal, then; the lad would know just where to find Ronan's things.

Supper waited on a covered tray in his room, left in his absence by a servant. Sitting by the window, Ronan tucked into barley soup and crowdie cheese on an oatcake, washed down with ale from a jug. There was a squat pottery jug of whisky, too. Perhaps Donal had been here to leave it. Pulling the wax plug free, he sniffed and sampled.

Pitlinnie. He knew the taste. Intrigued to find Pitlinnie whisky at Strathniven, he wondered if Mrs. Barrow had purchased it for the household from Sir Neill Pitlinnie. Perhaps the fellow gifted a supply to the household to buy silence and loyalty where goods were often smuggled. Ronan suspected the latter.

A folded paper was tucked under the china plate; the creamy stock was creased repeatedly in the manner of a secret note. Opening the tiny quartos fold by fold, he saw a missive written in a feminine hand.

Mr. MacGregor,

Lady Strathniven requests your company at breakfast tomorrow morning at nine o'clock in the dining room of the main house.

This evening, please visit the tower library at half eight. A message awaits you there.

E. S. G.

Ellison Graham's writing hand was lovely, but a blot or two spoke of haste.

Hoping the message would add clarity to this odd situation, he sat back, sipping the Pitlinnie. The mantel clock chimed softly; he had a little time to spare. Grateful to be free, he thought of Linhope and MacInnes on Calton Hill by now. Their fate depended on what he did here.

He gazed at the evening sky, its clouds lessening, and felt weariness pull at him. He closed his eyes, dozed—and startled awake to see the time was nearly half eight.

Shrugging into the black coat—tight across the shoulders, sleeves too short, but it must do—he left the room, wincing as the boots pinched.

THE DOOR TO the small library was ajar, showing lamplight and bookshelves. Miss Graham stood by the mullioned window, haloed in the glow of the twilight sky.

No message, then, but a conversation. Knocking softly, he entered, taking in the room—old ceiling beams, planked floors, hefty furniture—and bookshelves crammed with volumes, vases, globes, and more. Sturdy wooden chairs flanked the table and an oil lamp shed golden light on books and papers.

Ellison Graham turned. In the small room, she stood but a dozen paces away. "Mr. MacGregor—Glenbrae. Please come in." She spoke in English.

"Miss Graham, good evening." He too set the Gaelic aside.

"Please sit." She indicated two armchairs by the window, upholstered in red brocade. He could look only at her for a moment—rosy light shone over the soft golden curls framing her face. She wore a dark blue gown, a prim thing with a high collar and long full sleeves that made her seem small and fragile. Nervous too, she twisted her fingers in a graceful yet anxious way.

Ronan eyed a red chair warily, which looked too slight to support a large male. Instead, he drew one of the wooden chairs close, angling it toward her.

"I thought to meet privately here," she said. "Though it is not the most proper."

"So long as you are comfortable, Miss Graham."

"Aye. The sky is lovely now. The rain is lifting." She flexed her clasped fingers. The light made her eyes translucent silver.

"Beautiful, aye." The sky, his freedom. The girl.

"You and your friends have been quite popular in the city. The Whisky Rogues have won the public's imagination."

"We have Sir Walter Scott to thank for the name."

"His opinion holds weight. My father said he called you the Whisky Rogues at a dinner party and mentioned that Highlanders move whisky efficiently and illegally, using the profits to help crofters in dire conditions. He compared you to Robin Hood and his merry men. A journalist overheard and it reached the newspaper."

"It is a romantic notion and not quite truthful."

"Sometimes Highlanders smuggle whisky simply to protect their families. Good intentions can cause good men to break laws. I find nobility in that."

"An interesting thought from the daughter of a government official."

"I respect Highlanders. I have seen the difficulties they face."

"Ah." Best to not pursue the subject of what Highlanders lacked under English governing; he might say too much. He glanced around. "What a fine library. The tower is very old, but well cared for."

"I like the medieval part of this house. If you prefer something more modern, I will let Mrs. Barrow know."

"Probably best to separate the rogue from the household," he drawled. "Thank you for the hospitality and the excellent clothing." He brushed at the coat sleeves.

"We have clothing in storage here, so I asked Donal to find something for a tall man." She tipped her head. "If I may, sir, I wonder if the fit is comfortable."

"These may have been tailored for a slighter gentleman," he admitted.

"He was tall, but not as—robust. We can have your things cleaned."

Curious, he did not ask whose suit this had been. "A Highland plaid may not be proper here." He shifted, praying the coat seams would hold.

"Tartan is considered proper in Scotland again. And Lady Strathniven loves the Highlands, I assure you. As do I."

He nodded. "So, Miss Graham. There is a message for me?"

"You are owed an explanation."

"I am listening." He watched her. Graceful, lightsome, yet something troubled her. Beneath her calm, fine-tuned beauty he sensed tensile energy and a strong spirit. Her fingers folded, then opened like a lotus.

"We—need your help, Mr. MacGregor."

"I will provide the whisky. Just give me time. You mentioned the king earlier, but I see no need to meet him."

"His Majesty requested to meet the distiller. Papa's office is obliged to honor it."

Questions crowded his mind, but he would be cautious. "What a fuss this visit will be for Scotland. The last English king to visit here, other than those who came here to make war, was Charles the Second, I think."

"Your education was good in the glen school. My father will be pleased to know it."

Good Lord, Ronan thought; this Highland savage act had gone too far. "I can read, write, and count on my fingers. I attended the glen school and a public academy in Perth." He was sore tempted to add that he had studied law in Edinburgh, apprenticed in a law office in Perth, and practiced there still. "Tell Sir Hector the Highlander can quote the Greeks and Romans, spool on about history, philosophy, and maths, and even discuss points of law."

Indignation flamed in him. He wanted an end to the ruse, but his friends needed protection. He waited, nostrils flared.

"I see." Color rose in her cheeks. "But the king wants to meet you. He likes your whisky very much."

"Then I assume this will be a fast introduction. I would bow, say something proper, and then be whisked away to meet my punitive fate."

"Not so dire as that, I hope."

He huffed. "And your role in this?"

"Tutoring you in protocol and manners."

"I am not a savage, madam." He took quick offense—tired, perplexed, insulted. He breathed out, willing his temper to subside.

She lifted her chin. "I know that. It is a complicated situation."

"I dread to ask."

"The king believes the distiller is a gentleman of rank. A peer."

"Ah." Pieces clicked into place, beads on an abacus. "Presenting a filthy prisoner is unthinkable, so he must be cleaned up and properly trained. A frog-and-princess tale, is it?" He tipped a brow.

Her cheeks burned deep pink. "I am to tutor you and translate, but clearly you do not need much."

How ironic, he thought, to trade one ruse for another. "I can behave cordially enough—if I decide to do this."

"Mr. MacGregor." She sat forward. "You have little choice."

"'What a tangled web we weave,'" he quoted, "'when first we practice to deceive.'"

She blinked. "Scott."

"Appropriate, I thought."

"The other reason for this plan involves the licensing of your whisky."

"Ah. The landowner is legally the distiller no matter who makes it. So, Viscount Darrach. But he is dead."

"Did you know him?"

He shrugged. "Somewhat. Surely you do not expect me to pose as Darrach."

She sighed. "You see our dilemma. It is—complicated."

"Simplify it," he clipped.

"The king expects to meet a viscount, not a prisoner. The Darrach inheritance is undecided." She glanced down, as if her conscience troubled her. "Papa thinks the inheritance will not be decided for some time yet."

"Possibly." He knew the issue would go to court soon and he had a solid claim. "If an heir is found, Sir Hector's scheme will collapse."

She blushed, nodded. Her thoughts and feelings were transparent, a charming but vulnerable quality. He folded his arms against a protective urge.

"The royal assemblies will be huge, hundreds or thousands in attendance," she said. "An unfamiliar viscount of a small estate would hardly be noticed. It would all go very quickly."

"Whether a minute or a lifetime, impersonating a peer is punishable by prison or exile. Or worse. If this insult to the Crown is discovered, we could all be charged and sentenced with conspiracy. Even you."

"You know something of the law."

"A bit."

"I know there are risks." Her brow furrowed, her hands fluttered. She was frightened, he realized.

"So, you must train a peasant to act a peer, run him past the king, hope no one notices, and then escape the whole mess as fast as you can."

"Do you need a tutor at all?" she snapped.

"Aye," he bit out. "If I set a foot wrong and ruin your lunatic scheme, my friends could suffer. I can manage to be polite—briefly." He spoke bitterly, but knew she did not deserve his anger; her father and his secretary did.

She wove her fingers in and out fretfully. He wanted to reach out and calm her hands. Calm her. She looked as delicate as porcelain, yet beneath her nervousness, he sensed strength, regret, and sadness. He had secrets and sadness too. His sympathy toward her grew, and something inside him succumbed.

"I apologize, Miss Graham. This appears to be none of your doing."

"Will you agree to see this through?"

He ought to refuse, but his friends in Calton depended on him. The Highland rogue was more a gentleman than the schemers knew. But he must hide it.

He nodded. "I will."

"Thank you." She breathed out as if in relief.

"So, what will you teach me?"

"We will cover polite conversation, how to properly address nobility and royalty, some aspects of gentlemanly behavior, costume and comportment, and so on. And perhaps a dancing lesson." Her fingers were like gentle, fluttering butterflies. He felt keenly that she had been forced into this, just as he was.

"Using the wrong fork is a serious matter, is it? Tie a cravat properly or someone will die?" He raised a brow. "A dangerous wee game, this. Then what?"

She ducked her head, went rosy. "I am not sure what happens afterward."

"*Bidh a h-uile càil gu math,*" he said softly. All will be well. "I suppose polite chatter and a little dancing are preferable to hanging."

Her earnest nod was endearing. That was dangerous too. He

stood. "We have been alone too long. We must practice propriety."

She stood, just at the height of his shoulder. He felt very tall and protective. Going to the door, he reached for the handle and paused.

"Miss Graham," he murmured. "Whatever happens to me is my concern. Do not fret over it. You did a brave thing tonight."

"Brave?" Her eyes were dark, sincere gray now. His breath stirred a soft curl at her brow. Aware he stood too close, he did not move, nor did she.

"You delivered a message that two men were too cowardly to give. Just who needs to learn some manners?"

She smiled. "Tutoring you should prove easy enough, sir."

"See how quickly I learned English tonight. What shall we do tomorrow?"

"Whatever you think is best."

"I always do that," he murmured, and reached over her head to open the door.

Chapter Nine

"I SO ENJOY a cup of tea in the morning rather than coffee." Lady Strathniven took a sip from a china cup. "Ellison, you have had two cups already. Are you fatigued?"

"I am fine. Strong tea is so bracing early in the day." Ellison glanced at the man standing by the sideboard and recalled their meeting last night. Dressed in the black suit that closely fitted his tall, muscular figure, with his dark hair swept back and his beard all but gone—just a shadow this morning—he was not just handsome. He was perfectly distracting.

Her gaze kept sliding toward him, her awareness keen. Standing in the sunlight filtering through ivory silk draperies, MacGregor was a powerful masculine contrast in the pink and cream dining room. He opened the spout of a silver samovar to pour himself more coffee, and then glanced up to meet her gaze. She looked away quickly.

"Glenbrae, is the coffee to your liking this morning?" Lady Strathniven asked.

"Very much, my lady." He stirred cream into the cup. "Thank you for your hospitality." He resumed his seat on the other side of the table.

"Of course. Mrs. MacNie was very glad to prepare breakfast this morning for a gentleman with a healthy appetite. All we usually take is tea and toast or porridge."

"It is a delicious breakfast." He took up knife and fork to slice into a fat sausage.

"Better than prison fare, I trust!" Lady Strathniven leaned forward. "What did you eat there? Moldy bread and old beer?"

MacGregor stifled a laugh. "You have a vivid imagination, my lady. Bread, cheese, thin ale or weak tea. Porridge. Soup. Occasionally meat."

"Oh dear. We shall feed you well, I promise." Lady Strathniven tipped her head. "I must say, your English has improved overnight."

Ellison began to translate into Gaelic, but he caught her eye and shook his head.

"Lady Strathniven, I have a confession," he said.

"That you speak excellent English after all, and do not require an interpreter?"

"I speak both English and Gaelic fluently."

"Glenbrae found Gaelic more useful in his previous situation," Ellison explained. "Papa and Mr. Corbie assumed he needed a translator. It is not necessary."

Lady Strathniven clasped her hands. "Well, this will make our conversations easier! Oh! Is he aware of the arrangements? Did I speak out of turn?"

"I am aware, my lady." MacGregor inclined his head.

"Since you speak like a gentleman, may we assume you require little tutoring?"

"My mother taught her children excellent manners, and our parents ensured that my siblings and I were well-educated, regardless of diminished fortune. Like many after Culloden, my great-grandfather lost his lands and title," he added.

"How unfortunate. I am sorry," Lady Strathniven said.

"Nonetheless, I would benefit from instruction. I have not met royalty before."

"Most Scots will require lessons in royal protocol, I think," Lady Strathniven said. "Sir Walter has written a book of advice. For example, ladies are told to wear gowns with trains several feet long, with nine ostrich feathers in their headdresses. Elly," she added, "we will need to study his etiquette guide carefully."

"We will," Ellison agreed. "Papa gave us copies of Sir Walter's pamphlet," she told MacGregor. "It is written by an 'anonymous citizen,' but we all know it is Scott."

"He does enjoy anonymity," MacGregor agreed. "He still denies being the author of the Waverley novels and prefers to be called a poet."

"Some think novel writing is not as respectable an occupation as writing poetry," the lady said. "Ellison writes lovely poems. Though I do love a good novel."

"Poetry?" MacGregor quirked a brow, looking at Ellison.

"Some." And a novel she was secretly writing. She felt a fierce blush growing.

"I too prefer a good novel." He sipped his coffee.

He was more educated than he let on, Ellison thought. He was no ordinary Highland smuggler, to be sure, and had secrets. She could only hope nothing would complicate this lunatic scheme, as he had called it.

"Let the pageant master help us prepare for the king's visit," the viscountess said.

"Pageant master?" MacGregor asked.

"Sir Walter. It is not meant in a flattering way, my lady," Ellison clarified.

"Well, his wee book will be useful. Glenbrae, you can borrow my copy to read the details. Then you can tell me what I must know. I will leave my copy in the library for you."

"The library in the tower?" he asked. Ellison avoided his glance.

"My late husband's library, just along the corridor. Not the musty old tower library that Ellison prefers."

"I saw the tower library last night, madam. A fine collection of old volumes."

"Feel free to explore both collections, sir. My husband took great pride in his books and was pleased to share them. You enjoy reading and scholarship, I think?"

"I do," he murmured.

"Ellison, your task will be an easy one, I think. Sir Hector and Adam will see quick progress when they arrive to judge for themselves."

Sipping her tea, Ellison sputtered a little. "They are too busy to come north."

"Your father said he may send Adam up to be sure everyone is prepared."

Her stomach sank. She did not want that scrutiny. "We will be ready."

"Glenbrae." Lady Strathniven looked at MacGregor. "I have the utmost confidence in you and your excellent tutor. But let us be honest here."

"Madam?"

"This venture is chancy, but may be the best solution."

"I wonder for whom it is best, my lady," he murmured. "If we are being frank."

"True. I see no reason for them to know that you speak English as well as anyone and already comport yourself as if born to the peerage. I, for one, will not mention it. Let them be pleased with Ellison's work, and with you."

"If we are fortunate, my lady." Catching Ellison's glance, he tilted his head, eyes sparkling with amusement. He was enjoying this too much, she thought. "Please excuse me, ladies. I thought to find Donal Brodie this morning to see if we can ride out. I would very much like some air and exercise."

"Donal is at your disposal, and so is Mr. MacNie. We have horses, a carriage, a gig, and an estate you can explore. I hope you will be back in time for luncheon."

"I will do my best. My lady. Miss Graham." He stood. "Will lessons begin today?"

"After luncheon," Ellison replied. Nodding, he left the room.

"My dear," Lady Strathniven said, "I believe your work is done before it has begun."

"He does have the makings of a gentleman," she agreed faintly.

"Now that we know MacGregor's secret about speaking English," the lady whispered, "we must keep it safe."

Nodding, Ellison felt sure the Highlander had far greater secrets.

"HOW ARE YOUR mother and Sir Ludovic?" Ronan asked as he and Donal walked toward the stables. Pausing in the shade of a few birch trees, he turned.

"Mother is well. She is busy with herbal concoctions and helping those who come to her. She is much needed in the glens, at Strathniven too at times, and she sells her potions on market days. Grandda Ludo helps keep her healing garden."

"Is Sir Ludo still writing his history of the clans?"

"Aye. It is enormous now. He hopes to publish the manuscript someday, though Mother thinks he will never finish. He constantly adds more, but it keeps him content."

"I am glad they are well." He clapped a hand on Donal's shoulder. At sixteen, the lad was tall, black-haired, and handsome, with his mother's brown eyes. Ronan had known him since his birth; he was Mairi's only child with her first husband, who had succumbed to a fever when Donal was small. In the years Ronan had been at university and thinking himself in love with Mairi, his brother William, a year younger, had married her. He had managed to accept the shock of it. Will had been a good father, the only one Donal knew. Since Will's death, Ronan had done his best to take care of the family.

Although he held Invermorie Castle as Glenbrae's laird, he had invited Mairi to live there with her son and her father, Sir Ludovic Brodie, an impoverished knight; Ronan had moved to a cottage on the distillery grounds. Invermorie Castle needed a family, not a bachelor. And he wanted distance from Mairi Brodie, far enough for his heart to recover, close enough to keep an eye on William's family.

He had thought to marry someday, but now, thirty years old and recently a prisoner, he had suspended thoughts of the future. Time would tell.

"I help at Invermorie and here at Strathniven, and the distillery too," Donal was saying. "I bring in some coin since Da died—and then your arrest."

"Lad, whatever happens, I will always take care of you, your mother, and your grandfather. Now, tell me what you have heard."

"We knew last May that the Whisky Rogues were taken, though only we knew exactly who you were. The reports said excise men grabbed you unfairly in Culross."

"More or less."

"Then how are you here at Strathniven, Uncle?"

"Liberated on a detail of the law, but temporarily, if Sir Hector Graham and his secretary have their way."

"I know them. Sir Hector is decent enough. His clerk is another sort."

Ronan huffed in agreement. "Your work here is appreciated, I am sure."

"Mr. MacNie sent a message last week asking me to work at the house for a while to act as valet to a guest. I agreed. Luckily it was you!"

"Lucky for both of us, even if you do not know how to tie a cravat."

"Grandda and Mother gave me advice. Will you visit Invermorie soon?"

"If there is time. I suspect you were hired as my guard more than my valet."

"But you are a free man now."

"It is complicated. Best keep watch over your rascal of an uncle," he teased. "How goes it at the distillery?"

"The Muir lads are well. We set up a new batch—made three hundred pounds of barley into mash, and got a fine barley brew sealed in oak casks and kegs to wait at least three years, as you prefer."

"Or longer if we can. Excellent. You could be a distiller one day too, though you wanted to be in school soon. You heard from Saint Andrews?"

"Aye, I am to start next year. But I am needed at home."

"My brother set the fee for your schooling aside."

"But I am undecided. I might like to study medicine like Lord Linhope. I spoke to him about it before you went off to Edinburgh. How is he, and MacInnes? Free as well?"

"Still held, but it will be resolved soon." He smiled flatly.

"Mother will be pleased. She and Linhope were corresponding about treatments, but his letters stopped. She was worried."

"He will write again." He knew he must talk to Mairi soon, though he had not seen his gifted, stubborn, beautiful sister-in-law for months. His habit of avoiding her still stuck. After Will's death, time and need began to heal the gap, yet he still felt hesitant to see her.

He felt he had failed as a brother-in-law, uncle, friend, protector. Though he was a lawyer with a strong sense of justice, he had ventured into smuggling. Frowning at his thoughts, he caught Donal watching him.

"Uncle Ronan, do come up to Invermorie soon."

"I will. Lad, call me Glenbrae here at Strathniven. If you are told to call me Darrach, do so."

"Darrach? Why? Is there good news of the title and estate?"

"Not yet. It may never fall to me. But they know very little about all that, so I need to be careful."

"Is there some trouble, Unc—Glenbrae?"

Ronan leaned a shoulder against a birch tree, considering what to reveal. "You know the king is coming to Scotland?"

"Everyone in Scotland knows that!"

"He likes Glenbrae whisky quite a bit and wants to meet the distiller. The Scottish government is eager to please him, so I am to be presented."

"To the king!" Donal widened his brown eyes.

"So I must behave myself, and need your help." As Donal nodded eagerly, he continued. "For now, keep the truth close. There is something else." He shifted from foot to foot. "Fetch me my good boots, lad."

Donal looked down. "Miss Ellison wanted you to have those fine boots. Too tight? The other things too? They were her husband's. He was tall, but not as big as you, sir."

"I believe that. In the cottage at the distillery, there is a chest of my things. Bring my good boots, and my plaids and Highland kit stored there, if you will."

"I will. Better to wear your own gear than a dead man's, hey."

"Huh," Ronan agreed. "Did you know him? Her husband?"

"Colin Leslie? I saw him a few times. A polite man. Young and shy. He would always thank me for doing something. Not everyone thanks a servant," he added.

"True. What happened to him?"

"An accident. Fell from a horse when out with friends, they said. Nearly two years now, and Miss Ellison has still not come full out of her mourning."

"A tragedy." Ronan frowned, realizing what the girl must have endured. He also had the sense she was under her father's thumb, which seemed counter to her delightful nature. He felt a wrench of sympathy, understanding why she sometimes seemed lost or uncertain. Yet he also saw glimmers of strength and spirit in her, as if her true self was on the verge of bursting forth, if only she would allow it.

"Son of a Lowland viscount, I heard," Donal went on. "A poet or some such. Mrs. Barrow said they eloped and Sir Hector was angry. Miss Ellison is not the same lass as before, Barrow says. All quiet and meek now." He shrugged. "How long will you stay?"

"A fortnight or so."

"I will fetch your things today. Is there anything else?"

"Can you get word to the Muirs? I need to talk with them."

"I can do better. You wanted to ride out today. Aleck Muir often goes up and down the Lealtie Burn that flows through the distillery, making sure the water is clear of debris. We may see him if we ride that way."

"Aye, then." Ronan headed with Donal toward the stables.

WITHIN THE HALF-HOUR, Ronan saw a young man strolling along the edge of a fast-flowing stream: he knew Geordie Muir, younger of two brothers, by the rangy build and red hair. Spurring his horse forward, he cantered across the meadow, Donal following.

Geordie looked around as Ronan called, and then waved to another young man further down the stream. With a shout of elation, Aleck Muir came running.

Dismounting, allowing the horses to graze on sweet grasses, Ronan slid from the saddle as he and Donal met the Muir brothers under some nearby trees.

"Ronan, God above! I hardly knew you at first!" Geordie said. "Dressed like a city gentleman. We heard you were taken in Culross. You are released?"

"Aye." Ronan shook hands, patted shoulders. "You both look well. Donal says you are looking after the distillery in my absence. How is Auld Rabbie?"

"Grandda is well, or nearly so. Getting older," Aleck said.

"You were checking the burn?" Ronan looked past them. "Wild garlic and such?"

"And making sure the flow isna blocked where it turns toward the property," Geordie said. "Some say the water doesna make a difference to the whisky, but it all goes toward the taste, as Grandda and you have taught us. For the latest batch, we kept the peat fires hot to dry the mash longer than usual, as you prefer, for a good smoky flavor."

"I have left the place in good hands." Ronan smiled.

"We do our best. But sir—while you were gone, you should

know Pitlinnie is taking an interest, coming around with questions, wanting to buy up our kegs. I do not like it," Aleck said.

"How much has he purchased?"

"More than he needs. We canna trust the man," Aleck said.

"How much is stored? If I want to send kegs down to Edinburgh, what's there?"

"Enough. Tell us how many and we will see to it," Geordie said. "There are various casks at the distillery, many still aging. Our best store is set aside and not at Glenbrae. You know."

"Aye. Still safe where it is?"

"Auld Rabbie checked it recently. Pitlinnie also asked what we have in store, how many casks in the barn aging, how many elsewhere, how old, and such."

"The longer those casks are undisturbed the better. He knows it will be years before they are ready. Make sure he stays unaware of the other lot. What does he want?"

The brothers exchanged a grim look. "He offered to buy all of it."

"The kegs?"

"All of it. The distillery, the property, casks, kegs, the lot," Aleck explained. "We think Pitlinnie wants to merge Glenbrae with his distillery."

"Lord save us. Tell me you agreed to nothing."

"Aye. Something else he wants." Geordie glanced at Donal. "Mairi Brodie."

"Indeed." Startled, Ronan did not show it. "Donal, did you know?"

"He comes around and acts the charmer. I did not think much of it."

"The man is smitten," Geordie drawled. "Mairi Brodie may mention it."

"Perhaps." Ronan glanced upward to see rain threatening in high gray clouds. He had promised to return to Strathniven for luncheon. The horses whickered. A light drizzle began. Time was passing. "I must go."

"Where can we find you?" Aleck asked.

"At Strathniven for now. I will find you," he added. "Better yet, I will come to the distillery. We need to count how many kegs can be sent out."

"To be taken over the hills by night, with a fine profit for all?" Geordie smiled.

"None of that now, lads." He lifted a hand in farewell.

Chapter Ten

O F ALL THE rooms in Strathniven House, Ellison loved its large library almost as much as the one in the old tower. Standing in its expansive formal space, waiting for Ronan MacGregor, she inhaled the scents of wood and leather, old paper, the earthy scent of linseed oil polish used on the wood furnishings. The table's walnut surface was a smooth, dark gloss under her fingertips.

She loved the soaring bookshelves crammed with volumes; loved the reading nooks set with comfortable chairs, and the balcony level accessed by a wrought iron spiral stair. She strolled through the library choosing books suited to etiquette lessons and set them on a small table between two sage green upholstered chairs beneath a tall window draped in gold damask. She felt ready to begin.

She glanced at the portrait of Viscount Strathniven over the fireplace; he looked stern but kind, overlooking his beloved library. She suspected Lady Strathniven spent little time in the room simply because she felt sad to see his likeness.

Had there been a portrait of Colin Leslie, Ellison thought, she might have avoided it too. The wound, the regret, the conflict still hurt. She had been young, foolish, believing she was in love. Yet she had brought only grief to her family in the end.

Hearing a knock, she turned as Ronan MacGregor entered the room. He looked fine in the black suit that had once belonged to Colin, though he filled out every stitch of it with muscle and brawn. Amused, she saw he wore his old boots again, buffed but frayed.

"Sir," she said, and set a hand to her midsection, feeling a flutter that no other man had caused in her. Not even Colin, despite her love for his intellect, his art, his elegance. Yet this man, a stranger, stirred excitement with an undercurrent of safety. Near him, she felt steady. Invigorated.

"The rain has stopped." He approached.

"Aye. Did you and Donal have a pleasant ride?"

"We did. Highland air is refreshing in any weather."

"It is. I thought to walk out later with Balor. As long as there is no thunder!"

He smiled. "Where is the wee rascal?" He looked around.

"Napping elsewhere. He is banished from the library. He has a taste for carpet fringe. Shall we begin? I thought we might look through some books on etiquette." She indicated the table and chairs, the stack of books.

He made a wry face. "My assigned reading? What a fine library." He turned to survey the expansive room. "Two libraries in one household? It is a scholar's paradise." He glanced at her. "Is Lady Strathniven so fond of books?"

"She appreciates the collection but is not overly fond of studying. This was Lord Strathniven's project."

He nodded, moving to examine a tall section of shelves. "Poetry, mythology, botanical studies, sciences, medicine. And novels," he murmured. He paused here and there to pluck a book, sift through its pages, slide it back into place.

Ellison moved beside him, her gray skirt shushing along the wooden floor. In the rainy light, his eyes were intent as he looked through books, caressed gilded leather, flipped pages, his touch tender and sensual. Suddenly she felt a sweet chill, as if he had touched her with the same affection. A love of books radiated from him like a current, a yearning. She caught her breath, recognizing the feeling.

"You truly appreciate books." Her heart swelled with an impulse to share her favorites, see his pleasure. For a moment she glimpsed the true man, peered into his secrets. He wanted others to think him a simple man, laird, crofter, smuggler. He might be those, but he was far more. Educated. Complex. Thoughtful.

He touched another book. "Percy's *Reliques of Ancient Poetry.* My mother had a copy. I read it as a boy."

"I loved it as a child too. I still go back to it."

He moved on, looking at matching sets of black and red spines. "Law books," he murmured. "Erskine's *Institute of the Laws of Scotland.* All four volumes. Burnett's *Criminal Law* . . . excellent."

"You are familiar with those?"

"A rogue must understand the risks," he drawled. "How many books are here?"

"A count was done for the estate when Lord Strathniven died. Four thousand, two hundred ninety-eight volumes. I remember because Lady Strathniven bought two books to make it an even number." Ellison smiled. "I have added others since."

"You and I have something in common."

Her heart quickened. "I love to read, love to write, too—" She stifled an effusive urge to say more. "Well. Browse and read as you like in both libraries."

"Thank you. Perhaps someday you will tell me what you like to read—and write," he added. "The viscountess mentioned you write poetry?"

"Some." Feeling silly and hopeful, she only shrugged. "But we are here for tutoring. Shall we begin?"

"Aye, or greatly disappoint your Mr. Corbie."

"He is not my Mr. Corbie," she said stiffly, and led him toward the chairs by the window. She sat, as he did, and reached toward the stack of books.

"We need only review these. Most books on manners address what is proper for girls and women. I found just one or two that address gentlemen's manners."

"Both genders need sensible advice." He took up another book.

She opened the volume in her hands. "This one discusses how a worthy gentleman must act . . . Ah, here. Social encounters."

He shifted to lean an arm on the chair, which was snug for a man of his height. The chair she had was too large, her toes barely touching the floor. Suddenly she felt conscious of the room's fussy formal setting; neither she nor MacGregor could relax.

She began to read. "For most social occasions, standing is acceptable and common for a gentleman, except at meals. While standing, it is frowned upon for a gentleman to thrust his hands into his pockets or warm his back at the fire."

He stood then, towering over her, a smile teasing his lips. He lifted a side flap in the black coat. "This has an actual pocket. Excellent. What is proper to keep there? A wee page with what I should say to the king?"

She stood too, laughing. "Do take this seriously."

"Trust me, I do, for your sake and mine."

"No hands in the pockets, then. When you take a seat, re-member that a gentleman never drops down loosely. Especially a tall man. It is most unbecoming."

"I shall try to remember." His eyes sparkled. "Next? Shall we practice going into dinner?" He extended his elbow. "Miss Graham?"

She wrapped her hand lightly around his offered arm, sensing hard muscle beneath smooth wool. He walked her forward, turned, came back. "Neatly done, sir. A gentleman never jabs out his elbow in case he should hit the unsuspecting lady."

"I would never hurt a lady." His eyes caught hers. She felt herself blush.

"Common sense. Most good manners are." She looked away, cheeks hot, too aware of his closeness, his strength—and glad of his charming willingness and droll humor. His upbringing had been proper indeed, which only raised her curiosity.

"We only need to review the protocols relevant to meeting royalty," she said. "Though more might be expected of you." But if Papa and Mr. Corbie knew how easy this was, she thought, they might take MacGregor back to Edinburgh sooner, even back to prison if they could. She would not be the cause of that. "We will take our time."

Seated again, she chose another book. "Lord Chesterfield's letters to his son."

"The infamous Chesterfield. My father gave me a copy as a boy, advising me to take some to heart and reject the rest. The author's sour attitude actually shows us how *not* to behave."

"Oh dear. I have not read it, I confess."

"Nor would you. But if you have a son someday, be warned." He took the book from her. "Chesterfield emphasizes hard work, persistence, truth, and honor. What is worth doing is worth doing well, and so on."

"That sounds reasonable."

He skimmed his fingers along a page. "A man should keep his eyes open and mouth shut and avoid gossip. Also sensible. But he advises gentlemen to impress others of superior rank by copying their dress and mannerisms, even if those are foolish fashions."

"That will not do!"

"His thoughts on women are interesting as well," he added, turning pages.

"I can hardly wait."

He chuckled. She loved the sound of it. "'Women are only children of a larger growth; they have an entertaining tattle and sometimes wit; but for solid, reasoning good sense, I never in my life knew one that had it.'"

"What! You invented that." She reached for the book, but he held up a hand.

"On my honor, madam. Listen. 'A man of sense only trifles with women, humors and flatters them . . . but neither consults them nor trusts them with serious matters.'"

"Let me see!" As she reached for the book, her fingers grazed his. A gentle thrill ran through her.

"There is more. He says women love to dabble in business, which they always spoil, and believe they are beautiful even when they are ugly." He glanced up.

"What a hateful man!"

"None of this, by the way, applies to you."

"Or anyone!" But her heart gave a little fillip with the sweet, casual compliment.

"Trust me, I disagree with Chesterfield in most things."

"I should hope so. Give it here, sir." She extended an open palm.

"One last piece of advice. 'One must be careful never to laugh in company. It is rude and unfashionable.'" He looked up. "Do not dare laugh, Miss Graham—"

Too late, laughter bubbled up in her even as he waggled his finger like a schoolmaster. His lips pinched to suppress his laughter. "Such a rude wee lass!"

"Give me the book!" She took it with two fingers as if it were vermin and set it aside.

"It does not describe you," he said, sitting back. "You are exceeding proper and very capable, it seems to me."

"Not quite, though my father wishes so," she said quickly. "Most of these other books advise that a woman's chief purpose in life is to make a perfect and comfortable home for fathers, husbands, and children. I am not very good at that, I think."

"You would be. But women are capable of far more."

"We are as capable and intelligent as men, but do not always have the education or the chance to prove it." She set her chin defiantly.

"I learned early from the example of my mother and sisters that the female is often superior to the male in common sense and consideration. If I have proper manners, it is due to the women in my life." His eyes crinkled in a smile.

"Wise man." She smiled, and felt as if the keen blue lights in his eyes saw straight through her somehow. If he knew about her hasty marriage, her dream of writing novels, and the low opinion her father held of her, he would not think her so worthy.

"What is this?" He plucked up a slim volume with marbled covers.

"Mr. Scott's pamphlet of protocols for the royal visit. Lady Strathniven left her copy for you to borrow. We can discuss that book later."

"And so we have survived our first lesson in etiquette."

"We have. Oh, one matter before you go, Mr. MacGregor. I had a note from my father this morning when MacNie fetched the mail in Kinross. Papa says Lord Darrach will be invited to attend the royal levee. It is planned as a small gathering for gentlemen who are to be introduced to the king."

He frowned. "Lord Darrach?"

"My father submitted that name. I suppose we should address you as such now."

His curt nod told her he was displeased. "I doubt any of the events will be small."

"This one will be hundreds of guests, I believe. Other gatherings are expected to number in the thousands. The invitations will be delivered a day or two ahead of the levee. The king's secretary requests an address. Do you know where you will be?"

"Hopefully not in the subterranean accommodations of Edinburgh Castle."

"Never that! You have a warrant of release."

"Conditional, according to Mr. Corbie."

"Accommodations are filling up quickly, Papa says. Rooms and houses are being rented for exorbitant fees. A tiny room for a week could cost the same as a year's rent. Outrageous! Lady Strathniven mentioned that she would be pleased to have you stay at her home on Charlotte Square."

"Very generous. I will let you know my arrangements soon. We must be certain of this scheme before too many plans are made."

"It will succeed. It must," she added, glancing down.

He stood. "Your father and your suitor may be disappointed to learn that I have not yet mastered forks and dancing."

"He is not my suitor! And he did not want me to teach you to dance. Mr. MacGregor," she said, standing too, tilting her head to look up at him. "I know you are not happy with this situation. And I see there is little I can truly teach you."

"On the contrary, there is much I can learn from you. And perhaps you can learn a little from me," he murmured, gazing down at her. His way of focusing intently, of listening closely, was compelling. She felt noticed, important to him, even if it was only a passing illusion.

A swirl in her midsection drew her toward him like a lure. She raised her chin. "What," she said softly, "would you have me learn?"

He touched her shoulder, lifted away. "Just this—to straighten your spine as you do now. To know you are strong and intelligent. And to tell your Papa and his clerk that you are not at their beck and call."

"Oh," she breathed. Shivers chased down her spine. "Oh."

"Until later, Miss Graham." He strode for the door.

IN THE HALF-LIGHT of dawn, Ellison tiptoed through the silent, sleepy house. Seeing a maid stoke the fire in the parlor—even in summer the house could be cool in the mornings—she passed the library, where tall windows showed gauzy shawls of mist draping the hills. She half-expected to see Ronan MacGregor in the library, rising early as she had, but the room was empty.

In the kitchen, bacon crackled on the griddle as Mrs. MacNie chopped fruit into a bowl. Ellison murmured a greeting and plucked a fat strawberry, eating it as she went to the door. Balor jumped up from beside the hearth to trot after her.

Grabbing a straw bonnet and a red and black tartan from hooks by the door, she tossed the plaid over her lavender muslin gown, now cleaned and pressed. She could leave mourning behind and thought of it often, but somber colors still suited her. She was not ready yet. Fastening the dog's leash, she opened the door.

Mist obscured the gardens and the surrounding hills, but the pleasant air promised sun and warmth soon. She walked past the gardens, letting the dog tug her along. Something inside her craved freedom this morning.

Perhaps the feeling stemmed from Ronan MacGregor's words yesterday. *Know you are strong*, he had said. How unsettling and yet liberating to be seen like that.

Balor pulled ahead and she let him take the lead as he headed past the gardens and away from the hills toward a grove of birches and a path to a lochan on the property. Through the trees, the water shone like glass and she could hear ducks gently calling and splashing. Ripples arrowed through the water as ducks swam past reedy patches. Stepping into the clearing, she felt as if she entered an enchanted world.

Balor pulled her ahead, earnestly following whatever trail he had picked up, while she kept a tight hold on the leash, unwilling to let him off the lead again. Ronan MacGregor was not here to rescue the pup today.

The man was never far from her thoughts. Truly he was a mystery: an educated man, a gentleman, a man of integrity and secrets contradicted what she had expected.

Then Balor lurched forward, barking, dragging her toward the water's edge. He was deceptively strong for his size; beneath his long peppery coat, he was all muscle and determination. And he was on a mission.

His noisy barks caused a commotion of flapping wings as ducks rose from the water, quacks echoing in the quiet. Balor jumped, furiously yelping as if he wanted to snatch the birds out of the air.

Tugging on the leash, his head smaller than the breadth of his neck, he slipped free and ran along the shoreline. Calling out, Ellison stayed close on his heels. The dog slowed to explore the slow sweep of the water where stones gleamed and reeds thrust upward. He drank a little, trotted along, dancing in and out of the shallows. More ducks flapped up and away, quacking loudly.

"Give up, you cannot catch them," she said, approaching with the collar and leash. Then Balor barked wildly and leaped into the water, surging ahead to paddle after something that caught his attention.

Kicking off her slippers, Ellison lifted her skirts to step ankle-deep into the water, gasping at the chill as stockinged feet found purchase on stones and muck.

"Madam," came a deep voice. "Please stay where you are."

Startled, she looked around. No one stood on the grassy shore or in the lacy screen of nearby birches. Whirling, she gasped as a man rose out of the sun-sparkled water like a selkie from the sea. Water sluiced off his dark hair and wide, bare shoulders.

Ronan MacGregor stood chest-high and shirtless in the water.

"Madam!" He held up a deterring hand. "Come no further, if you please."

"Mr. MacGregor!" She stood calf-deep in water, skirt bunched in her hands.

"Go back. I will get your wee dog." He dipped lower in the water and pushed toward the little black dog paddling earnestly toward him. Reaching out, he grabbed Balor close. "Here, lad. Aye, there we go." With one arm treading water, he waved toward Ellison. "I'll send the dog toward you. Wait there."

She was already surging forward. "I will come to you."

"The water is deeper here than you are tall. And I am not in a state for company."

"I will not look." She came forward. The water rose higher around her, though for him it was at mid-chest. Watery reflections danced over his muscled shoulders and chest, lapped at his hair and broad neck.

"Do not come closer!" he called, while Balor busily licked his chin.

"A man in bathing attire does not frighten me. I was married, sir."

"It alarms me, if not you. And you will ruin another gown."

"Too late!" The water reached her waist, then her chest. But he was correct, for the mucky floor suddenly dipped away under one foot. She stopped.

"Wait there." He approached, keeping low in the water, holding the dog.

She threw out an arm for balance and reached forward with the other. The water licked around her bodice, splashed her chin, dampened her hair.

"Here, reach for your wee kelpie." He pushed the dog toward her. Obedient for once, Balor paddled toward her and she caught his wriggling little body.

"Thank you, Mr. MacGregor, for rescuing him once again."

"Nothing to it. So it is Mr. MacGregor? Not Lord Darrach?" he teased.

She looked away, for her gaze kept dipping from his bearded, handsome face to his wide shoulders, strong collarbones, and chest with its dark, wet mat. Even in cool water, she knew her cheeks burned.

"I can hardly call you Lord Darrach here. It would be even more embarrassing."

He chuckled, arms treading, circling. "Ronan, then. Certainly after Balor's latest escapade, we can consider each other a friend."

"Friends with a secret," she laughed.

"Many secrets," he said, as his eyes cast quickly down, then up.

Glancing down, she saw her bodice and chemise ballooning with water, exposing far too much. Tugging at the cloth, she pressed the dog closer. But the tall man standing just an arm's length away had an easy view.

He looked away politely, dipping down so that water covered all but his head, while his hair floated out like a dark fan. He leaned backward, hands circling, distorted by the rippling water. "Take that wee rascal to the house and get dry. And be sure to tighten his leash. He is bent on mischief, that one."

"He is spirited," she agreed, easing backward in the water, dog clasped close.

"Farewell." He waved her toward the shore. "I will wait until you are well away."

"I apologize. I had no idea—do you often bathe in a loch? Is it a Highland habit?"

"Aye, common in the hills. I came here hoping for a quick private swim. I am not fond of that beast in the tower."

"Beast? Oh, the shower machine! It can be difficult." She waded backward. "Thank you again, Mr. MacGregor."

"Ronan. Surely we are friends now." He spread his hands, bare shoulders out of the water, to indicate his state.

"Ellison," she offered, moving back, water sluicing from her gown.

"Ellison Graham." He smiled. "E. S. G., as in your note. What is the 'S' for?"

"Sophia. My mother's name."

"Ellison Sophia, I enjoy your company, I do. But you cannot be seen here with me. Go on, and take the wee one with you." He waved.

As she turned, Balor struggled to get free, yelping as if insisting he stay with the man in the water. She pressed him tightly to her as she walked over slippery stones, water surging around her. But her foot found an uneven dip and she stumbled, going nearly under for a moment. Holding the dog high, she gasped and tried to regain her balance.

Strong hands grabbed her around the waist. Sputtering, she swirled to face Ronan as he held her securely so she would not slip again. Pushing her hair out of her eyes, she held the dog, coughed, sniffled. "Thank you," she said breathlessly.

He let go but kept one hand firmly on her shoulder. "Steady, now. Good?"

"Aye." Sniffling, she stepped back, though Balor struggled to reach the man he clearly adored. "Best no one knows about this."

"Agreed." He surged backward. "Go on. I will follow in a bit."

"You should come out of the water. You will catch a chill."

He laughed. "I am a hearty sort. And we have had enough compromise for one day, Ellison Graham." His eyes were even bluer than the water in the morning sunlight.

She nodded, then emerged from the water, aware that her gown clung to her body. She felt him watching as she pulled at the fabric and stooped to attach the dog's collar and leash. Finding her shoes and bonnet, she picked up the plaid and glanced back.

He lifted a hand in farewell, then leaned back to float, chest exposed, arms relaxed, hands nimble as he boated himself along.

She left the plaid on the grass for his use, then tugged the dog along, though he wanted to turn back. So did she—how lovely to run back to the water for loch's cool caress, for the freedom of a little rebellion and laughter on a summer morning, and for the delight of being with Ronan MacGregor.

Enough, she told herself sternly, and hastened toward the house.

"MY DEAR, I have news," Lady Strathniven said when Ellison joined her later for tea in the parlor. "I promised your father that I could act as chaperone here, but I need to leave for a short while. I am sorry."

"Is something wrong?" Ellison asked, glancing up as Ronan MacGregor entered the room. He wore a Highland outfit now rather than the snug black suit of the last few days: a belted plaid of forest green and wine red, a brown jacket and waistcoat, a creamy shirt and neckcloth, along with tartan stockings and leather brogues. Ellison caught her breath at the stunning sight of the man. And she sensed her cheeks burning in renewed embarrassment as she recalled their encounter earlier.

Beside her, Lady Strathniven gasped a little, seeing him, and Ellison smothered a smile that dispelled the distracting image of MacGregor in the water. She had not seen him until now; he had been gone most of the day with Donal and MacNie. Perhaps he avoided her as she had avoided him. Surely he thought her a silly girl with a silly wee dog, though he had been kind about the incident.

"I hope I am not late, my lady. Miss Graham," he murmured, taking a seat.

"Not at all. What an excellent costume, if I may say, sir," the lady said.

"Thank you. Donal kindly fetched some of my things from my home."

"And where is home? Of course you would want your own things."

"The hills of Glenbrae, and aye, it is good to have my own gear, my lady."

"We are to call you Lord Darrach now, I understand?" she continued.

"So it seems. But I will answer to whatever you choose." His smile seemed tight.

"We shall practice using Lord Darrach, shall we, Ellison? It suits him. Now, sir, I was just telling Ellison as you came in," she continued, "that I had a note from my sister, Mrs. Harold Beaton. She just arrived at Duncraig, her Highland home, for the summer to rest after the stress of organizing her daughter's wedding last month. Her youngest came up with her—Miss Sorcha Beaton, whom you will remember, Ellison."

"Aye, a lovely girl. She will debut later this year in Edinburgh, I think."

"She will, yes. My sister's son, Archibald, may come up later. But he is a busy man. He is a judge, you see, Darrach."

"How nice to have family nearby," he said politely. Ellison noticed a muscle bouncing in his cheek. She frowned, wondering if the mention of a judge troubled him.

"Beth's wedding in Edinburgh was wonderful. I was good friends with her in school, sir," Ellison said. "I feel like an older sister to Sorcha, who is sixteen now."

"Nearly that, and her Mama is planning the girl's debut—another stress. You see, Darrach, I have two nieces and two nephews, the children of my sisters," the lady explained. "My youngest sister was Adam Corbie's mother. Foolish girl eloped with a reprobate. Both she and her husband are gone now, and I shall not speak ill of the dead." She sniffed. "I have kept a watchful eye over Adam, though he spent some of that time away at school. One never knows what influences boys encounter in those places. Which school did you attend, Darrach?"

"A glen school, and Perth Academy. I lived with my uncle in those years."

"My lady," Ellison said, hoping to bring the lady's attention away from probing. "How long will Mrs. Beaton and Miss Sorcha be at Duncraig?"

"My sister is undecided, although she asked if Sorcha could return to Edinburgh with me for the festivities. There will be an exodus from the Highlands to the city in a few weeks. Well, to my point," she went on. "I am invited to visit Duncraig. My sister has a nervous constitution and I am a calming influence on her. But I gave my word to be here with you, Ellison. So I am torn."

"You must visit Duncraig, my lady. Mrs. Barrow and the MacNies are here, the servants too. And Mr. Mac—Darrach and I will be busy with the work to be done."

Lady Strathniven tipped her head to consider MacGregor. "Sir, my instinct says you are a true gentleman. But propriety, and Sir Hector, insist on a chaperoning presence. I have a thought!" She turned to Ellison. "I will ask Sorcha to come here as your companion. She could be such a help to you."

"I would love to see her." A little qualm went through her. She cared about Sorcha, but was intrigued by the thought of more freedom in MacGregor's company.

"MacNie will take my note directly to Duncraig today. The

post takes so long now to go back and forth," she complained.

"Sorcha is welcome, though I do not need a chaperone these days." She felt another blush rise, the tell-tale curse of her delicate skin.

"Because you are a widow? Sadly, we trade loss for a little freedom, my dear. But your father insists on propriety while you are here this time."

"I know." Ellison was keenly aware of MacGregor's silence.

"Adam seemed eager to come up. I could write to him," the lady offered brightly.

"That is not necessary," Ellison said quickly. "You will only be gone a few days."

"Perhaps longer. My sister feels very drained. But when I return, Darrach will be a fine gentleman indeed, and we will be off to the city. Do you not agree, sir?"

"I will do my best to fulfill expectations, my lady."

"You are doing that already. Ellison was told to turn a frog into a—"

"Here is tea!" Ellison said in relief as Mrs. Barrow entered the room with a tray.

RONAN HOPED HIS stomach was not growling audibly. He had eaten little that day, and months of a prison menu had honed his appreciation of good food. Ellison Graham served tea, hot and dark, steam floating from dainty cups, and filled small china plates with pretty cakes and a heartier fare of sausages, cold salmon, and rolls.

"This is excellent," Lady Strathniven said. "Is that Mrs. Barrow's lemon cake? And fresh strawberries? Marvelous! But I should have a little salmon first."

Watching Ellison prepare another plate, Ronan noticed how petite and wan she looked in gray-blue trimmed in somber marching rows of black lace. Her morning dress had been soaked, he remembered vividly, showing how thin she was, though lush in places too. He was glad to see her appetite in selecting sausages and a roll for herself, while Lady Strathniven's plate rivaled a farmer's.

He smiled, accepting a teacup. She then provided him a plate of savory sausages, salmon, and a buttered roll. She had remembered that he took only a dollop of milk and no sugar in his tea. But even if she had loaded it with sugar, he would have sipped it just to see her smile.

"Despite what your father believes, my dear," Lady Strathniven was saying, "Sir Hector will always think of you as his little girl no matter what. But you have earned your independence, and it is time he realized it."

Ellison nodded, glancing quickly at Ronan. "Aye, my lady."

"Doing what you please is a hard-earned privilege of widowhood. Sir Hector cannot protest if you follow my example. I do as I want."

"It is good advice."

"I do wish your husband had left you an unencumbered property. Have the lawyers sorted out your Edinburgh house?"

"Not yet." Ellison sipped her tea.

"It should be yours without question. The house is suitable for now, but if you marry again, which I am sure you will do, it may be too small."

The girl blushed furiously. Silent, listening, Ronan sipped tea.

"Mr. Smithson believes it will be mine as soon as the dispute is solved."

"A good house in a desirable area is a treasure. I do wish the poor fellow had left you more secure, my dear. Do prod the lawyer again. Some of them are not worth their salt and we must continually press them, isn't it so, Lord Darrach?"

Ronan swallowed quickly. "At times, aye."

The lady picked up a scone and spread it liberally with butter. "Hearts heal, but property could be lost forever. Colin's cousins need to leave that house now."

"It is a bit of a problem," Ellison agreed quietly.

"Squatters," Lady Strathniven declared. "You see, Darrach— her late husband's relatives insist the house is theirs. They moved in last year and refuse to leave."

"That must be very distressing," he commented carefully.

"My husband's will was not specific about the property," Ellison explained, "so his cousins claimed the house because the will stated they could choose whatever family items they wanted. After his death, I moved back to my father's house, and they took up residence without asking. They had a key from years before."

"An unfortunate situation," he said, but inside, he simmered over the injustice.

"Squatters!" Lady Strathniven repeated. "Uncouth and un-mannered."

"I am sure the lawyers can straighten it out," Ellison said. "Mr. Smithson is here in Edinburgh, and his partner Mr. Cameron is sometimes here and sometimes in Kinross. Perhaps you know them."

"I have heard their names." He was more than familiar with both.

"Do you know much about the law, Lord Darrach?" Lady Strathniven asked.

"Some, madam." He noticed Ellison glance sharply at him. She was too alert to his truths and half-truths, he realized. He needed more caution—or more confession.

"Those involved in the whisky business should know the laws," Ellison said.

"Exactly, Miss Graham," he agreed.

"Crofters deserve to earn a livelihood from their barley and their whisky," Lady Strathniven said. "A local distiller, Pitlinnie, brings us a regular supply for free."

"It is a good whisky. I would be happy to supply Glenbrae's brew to you also."

"I would like that! I do enjoy a dram now and then. Do you

think they will change the whisky laws, Darrach?"

"They say the laws may change substantially next year."

"Best you are done with such nonsense, then, and distill it legally."

He chuckled. The lady's honesty could be brutal at times.

"Ellison," the viscountess went on, "perhaps Darrach has some thoughts regarding your town house. What would you do, Darrach, if it was your house?"

He cleared his throat, seeing Ellison's obvious discomfiture. Increasingly aware of her subtle responses that told her thoughts, he warned himself to be careful. But he was not sure he could remain neutral much longer.

"How can I help?" he asked.

"We should not bother Darrach with it. Here, let me serve the cake." Ellison stood, her lovely butterfly hands flexing, folding, and went to the sideboard where Mrs. Barrow had left the larger dishes. She took up a knife and thrust it into the cake. Ronan sensed temper and frustration all through her.

"Darrach, if you know Smithson, perhaps you could visit him," the lady said.

"If it would help. But Miss Graham may not want assistance."

"She may not." Ellison sliced cake, slid it to a plate, scooped up strawberries from a bowl and slapped them on top. "She might want to sort it out on her own."

Lady Strathniven frowned. "I suppose it is your concern, my dear, but—"

"Cake, my lady?" Ellison thrust the plate toward her, cake and fruit sliding dangerously. Ronan quickly took it and handed it to the viscountess.

"Thank you, sir. What is your advice for Ellison?"

The girl slapped another helping of cake and strawberries onto a second plate and thrust it at Ronan. She also gave him a snapping glare. Taking the dessert, he smiled.

"The last version of the will would help decide. But the lawyers know that. I am not qualified to comment," he added.

Though he deuced was.

"You must have some sense. Men know these things."

"Ladies may know these things too," Ellison said, stabbing a strawberry.

He needed to extricate himself, but he wanted to make something clear. "If the will was signed and witnessed and is authentically by your husband's hand, it is valid. If the wording is vague, it might be the solicitor's fault, though they can interpret it to some extent. But if the intention cannot be agreed upon, a judge may need to decide it."

"There, you see," Lady Strathniven said. "He knows a good deal, does Darrach."

Ellison speared another strawberry. "Perhaps."

"If I can help, I will," he said, and let the offer stand.

She poked her spoon at a bit of cake, mashed it about, then sighed. "I want to avoid a confrontation over the house. It is just a house. I want no harm to anyone."

"Your rights are important too." He should avoid involvement, he thought. Too soon he would see her for the last time, and then face legal problems of his own. He should not entangle himself in this.

Oh, but this lass, he thought; this strong, fragile, outspoken, yet soft-spoken lass. She was scrambling all his intentions.

Ellison set down her spoon. "Fine, sir. Do you have another suggestion?"

"Ask your lawyer to evict them from the property. Until the will is sorted out, they have no legal right to be there. The police can assist."

"I cannot do that. They were his only kin."

"She has a soft heart, you see," the viscountess said.

"Then let the lawyer show a harder heart. Then you need not compromise your kind nature, Miss Graham." He watched her eyes widen, then seek his.

"Could you—perhaps talk to someone?" she asked.

"The lawyer or the squatters?" Lady Strathniven interrupted.

"Either or both," he agreed.

"Never mind. I will not trouble you." Ellison paused. "But if eviction comes next, perhaps you would know what to say."

"I can deliver a message to the lawyer."

She nodded. "I just want no one harmed."

"Of course. Your lawyer would handle it directly and then report to you."

"Good, it is settled. This cake is delicious," the viscountess said.

"Thank you." Tilting her head in a sunbeam, Ellison's gray eyes went silvery. She shone, he thought—beautiful, vulnerable, relieved. She looked suddenly hopeful too, as if she saw a light in the darkness. He gave her a silent reassuring nod.

And felt suddenly as if he were the one lost, reaching for a silvery light that could lead him to all he had ever desired. He looked away then, dipped into cake and fruit, sweet and tart, and hardly tasted it.

Chapter Eleven

"T HANK YOU FOR inviting me to come along with you this morning," Ellison said.

"A privilege on a beautiful day." Ronan slowed his mount to allow her to pull even with him as she rode a stocky Highland pony, the best mount for negotiating steep, rough slopes as they progressed into the hills.

She smiled, savoring the sun's warmth and the fresh breeze that ruffled the skirt of her black riding costume. She looked out at the expanse of rugged hills surrounding the bowl of a green glen ahead. "Where would you like to go today, Mr. Macgregor—er, Darrach? Likely you know the area well."

"I do. Darrach is not necessary between us," he said quietly. "I thought we might visit the Glenbrae distillery, just across this glen."

"I would love to see your property."

"Mine in a sense. The glen and distillery are part of the Darrach estate, but for a long while have been leased to my family, going back to my great-grandfather. I am a tenant."

"And the laird. If there is no viscount, whose tenant are you now?"

"The estate's tenant until the inheritance is decided. This way. See that branch of the military road?" He pointed ahead, where the cobble-and-dirt road forked, one north, one northeast toward forested slopes.

"I have ridden in this glen before, but have not seen a distillery. Is it far?"

"Not far," Donal said, joining them to ride three abreast on the solid, shaggy Highland ponies. MacNie kept a few of the animals at Strathniven for riding on steep terrain. Ellison's smaller mount suited her, but the taller men outsized the horses. Yet they looked natural, she thought, part of the raw strength and beauty of a Highland glen.

For a moment, she wished she had brought her sketchbook and pencil to capture some images that might inspire her story. The manuscript, growing slowly, was locked in her writing box at Strathniven. Each day she learned more that could benefit her novel, and learned more about Ronan MacGregor too. She hungered to ask him about his life. Hungered, she thought, to be near him. He fascinated her more than anyone she had known. That in itself was a revelation.

"This way to the distillery," Donal was saying. "The other road leads to Invermorie, where my mother and grandfather live."

"How nice! Can we stop there? I would like to meet them."

"Another time," MacGregor said curtly. "The distillery will take time, as I must determine what is available and make arrangements to send whisky to Edinburgh."

He rode ahead, Ellison and Donal following the road that cut a straight, unforgiving line through the hills, as if the engineer had neither patience nor sensibility for the beauty of the glen's slopes and curves. As they left the hard road to follow a drover's track of earth and turf, Ellison fell behind, gazing with awe at Glen Brae.

"Here we are," Ronan said, looking back. "The glen is named for that high, steep hill that juts above the slopes, the braes or *bràighean* in Gaelic, that form the glen."

Looking about, she saw a small stone castle in the lee of a high hill. The structure looked very old, its gray stone and blunt shape stark against heathery hills.

"What castle is that?" She saw rambling fieldstone walls and outbuildings surrounding the structure, while goats and sheep grazed on a nearby hill.

"That is Invermorie," Ronan said.

"Your home, as laird of Glenbrae?" But Donal's mother lived there, she thought.

"I lived there as a boy. My home is elsewhere now. Tenants live in the castle."

"Donal's mother?"

"And grandfather." He lifted a hand to shade his brow.

Then Ellison noticed a dark-haired woman crossing the yard to step into a side building. Ronan took up the reins and turned his horse. "This way, Miss Graham."

Enchanted by the little square castle, she gave it a last look, then followed.

As soon as he heard the burble of water near the distillery, Ronan felt himself relax. The soothing chuckle of the Lealtie Water had always seemed to wash troubles away in its flow. His troubles would not so easily rinse away now, but he felt them ease.

He guided his pony over the stone bridge spanning the fast-flowing burn, with Ellison and Donal following. His gaze, his very heart, was transfixed by his distillery, with its whitewashed walls and slate roofs of its three buildings, by the trees and rumpled hillocks that held his little enterprise like a safe and cushioning hand.

His next breath was infused with pride and love. Beyond the main building sat his stone cottage, thatched roof golden in the sun, quietly waiting for him. Home.

"Beautiful," Ellison said when they crossed the bridge and halted the ponies in the yard. "So peaceful."

"It is," he agreed. "And hardworking as well."

"I will see who is here." Donal dismounted and walked toward the main building, opened its red door, vanished within.

"Just one or two men are needed here most days, depending on the work. Come inside." Ronan dismounted to tie the reins of his horse and Donal's to a post, then turned to help Ellison down. Her body slid against his unexpectedly, so that he felt a leap and heat within. He set her down and stepped back, while she turned away quickly.

Donal called from the doorway. "Auld Rabbie is at the spirit safe!"

"Ah," Ronan said, and led Ellison toward the door.

"Spirit safe?" Ellison asked.

"You will see." He noticed that her cheeks were still pink after their bodies had touched. She was a delectable sight, he thought, and did not seem out of place here. Her quiet simplicity matched the surroundings. He wished she could be here with him always. He pushed the thought away.

"This way," he said gruffly, holding the door open.

As they stepped into the cool, dim interior, Ronan led her into a wide, plain room that held three huge copper stills. Sunbeams poured through a narrow window, gleaming over bright metal. Ellison turned in wonder.

"What are those? And that smell—ale? And smoke?"

"Those are the stills," he said. "We brought them here from Perth. That beery smell is given off by malting barley, and the smoke is the peaty sweetness of the low fires in the drying room next door. The malt house, the drying rooms, the still house are all connected by covered passages. Over years, the odors have permeated the whole place."

"It is a comforting sort of smell."

"Some dislike it." He was glad she appreciated it. He rested a hand on the warm copper shoulder of one of the stills proudly, cognizant of the challenges of bringing the huge stills here and building the place up from a cluster of old cottages. For several years, he and his brother Will and their cousin, Darrach, with the help of a few others, had worked tirelessly to create what he had finally licensed as a legal distillery.

Soon after, his brother and cousin were killed. Then the secrets they had kept from him had emerged as the crisis that altered his life and that of his friends.

He had done all he could to right things, but at a cost. Now he must reclaim his life and rebuild Glenbrae into what it could be. But he was beginning to realize that he needed something else, too. He glanced at Ellison.

"Ronan MacGregor?" She watched him.

He liked the way she said his name, a Highland way. He moved away from the copper still to usher her through a doorway into a connecting room.

Donal was standing beside a man who was elderly and ropey thin, swathed in a shabby plaid and bonnet. Beside them was a metal tank fitted with brass pipes, and a large glass box banded in brass and set on a pedestal. A stream of liquid was channeling through the pipes into the transparent box.

Donal waved. "Good as gold, sir. Auld Rabbie Muir has been watching it."

"Ronan! *Fàilte air ais gu Gleann Bràigh!*" The old man grinned.

"Rabbie, *tapadh leat!* It is good to see you," Ronan continued in English.

"And you! We heard you was taken, lad!"

"But I am here now, come to see for myself the excellent work you have done while I was away. This is Miss Graham," he said. "This is Robert Muir, who has been making whisky in Glenbrae since my father was a lad. Or was it my grandfather," he added with a chuckle.

Rabbie tipped his cap. "Miss, welcome. I was a lad with this one's Grandda, to be sure." He winked. "And I taught his Da and himself, here, to make the *uigse beatha,* our water of life, our whisky. Ronan took to the art of it young, and had a gift for the brewing. He has made our whisky into a very fine thing that makes our glen proud."

"How lovely to meet you, Mr. Muir." She held out her gloved

hand, which he took in both of his. "It is a very nice place and a very bonnie glen."

"Och aye. But not near as bonny as the lass Glenbrae brings with him today." He gave her an impish grin. She laughed.

"Enough charm, sir." Ronan tapped the glass lid. "How goes it?"

"We expect a fine brew from this. It goes in the casks soon. See, Miss Graham," Rabbie explained, "this is our spirit safe. It collects vapors from the barley mash that is fermented in another room. It is heated and stirred again and again, and the vapors are the gift of the spirit, see. What escapes into the air during the distilling and the aging of the whisky, well, that we call the angel's share."

"Angel's share," she repeated. "How lovely."

"It makes for good luck, you see. We store the liquid in casks where it ages to become the best whisky. It takes time to make the best water of life," he went on. "It takes good barley and Highland water, peaty smoke from the fires, and the flavor of the water too, influenced by rocks and flowers along the burn that runs through here. Needs it all."

"It takes a love of the craft, too," she said.

"Och, aye, love and care, time and patience, to make the best whisky we can. And skilled hands too. My grandsons work with me. They are out and about," he told Ronan.

"I saw them recently," he murmured. Rabbie nodded.

"From here it goes in the casks? Where are those kept?" Ellison looked around.

"The liquid essence captured here," Ronan said, "is transferred and stored in oak casks, the older the better to add richness. The best casks have held either whisky or Spanish sherry. They rest and mature for years in another building."

"Years, aye," Rabbie said. "The longer it rests, the better it is. Ronan MacGregor has the patience for it, and the love, as you say, Miss. It makes all the difference."

"You're an auld poet," Ronan drawled.

"We Gaels are an ancient race of poets, are we not, and our whisky carries the heart and spirit of Scotland in it. Do ye take a sip now and then, Miss? Some ladies will and some will not."

"I have on occasion. It is invigorating."

He laughed, then turned to Ronan. "I do not know where the girl was born," he said in rapid Gaelic, "but this one is a Highland lass in her soul."

"And she speaks the Gaelic, too." Ronan cocked a brow.

"Aha! *Ciamar a tha thu an-duigh?*" Rabbie asked her in a renewed greeting.

"*Tha mi gu math, tapadh leat,*" she responded, and Ronan suddenly felt as proud as if he were her tutor—or something closer, more intimate.

"She will do, Glenbrae," Rabbie approved.

"Aye so. Donal, please take Miss Graham around to show her the place, while Rabbie catches me up on the business."

"Miss Ellison, this way." As she murmured thanks, Donal led her to the door.

"God above, we heard you were all taken," Rabbie told Ronan.

"But with a bit of luck, I was released. How goes it here?"

"Well enough. Though that scoundrel Pitlinnie comes around with questions, buying kegs and casks. I do not like it."

"How much has he purchased?"

"More than I want him to have. I do not trust the man."

"How many casks and kegs are in storage? Do we have enough to send a supply south quickly?"

Rabbie rubbed his chin. "Most of what is here is too young to go. We have a good store set aside, but not here. You know where it is."

"Aye. Is it safe there?"

"Far as I know. I have not looked for a while. I will send my grandsons to see. Ronan, I tell you, Pitlinnie is too curious. He asks how old our kegs are, how many are here and elsewhere, as if we were friends and allies."

"It is not his business where it is kept. Does he know about the hidden stock?"

"I do not think so. But he wants to buy all we have. Casks, kegs, bottles, all of it. Distillery too, property, stills, buildings, the lot. When word of your arrest got out, he came around. He wants to join it with Pitlinnie. He does not say so, but I ken it."

"And you refused him," Ronan prompted in a growl.

"It is not for sale, said I. Whatever becomes of the laird, we will never sell, I told him. But if aught happened to you, Ronan, what then?"

"Donal," he answered. "As my brother's stepson, he is my closest kin."

"You know Pitlinnie thinks to court Mairi Brodie."

"I know. I will visit soon." He stepped back. "I am indebted to you and your lads, Rabbie Muir."

"*Tcha.* Let us look at the resting casks, now, where we will find your bonny lass."

"Not my lass." But the words did not ring true.

Rabbie gave a little huff and preceded him through the connecting door.

Damn Neill Pitlinnie, Ronan thought as he walked. The man might vie for advantage in the laird's absence, but that was about to change.

"HOW GOOD TO see you, Sorcha!" Ellison took her friend's arm as they walked back to Strathniven's main hall after she'd shown the girl around the house and gardens. Just a reminder, for Sorcha had visited her aunt's home before and admired some changes, including the handsome new Oriental carpet in the library, Balor having chewed the edges of the previous one. As they walked, Ellison glanced around for Ronan MacGregor, but did not see him; Mrs. Barrow then mentioned that Lord Darrach—said with a sniff—had gone to the stables.

Ellison was glad that Sorcha meant to stay, for the girl was gracious and kind, with a sweet and cheerful enthusiasm. Perhaps Sorcha could charm MacGregor, who could be dour at times, Ellison thought, considering his situation. A true gentleman, he hid it well, though she saw through him more often now—somber and reflective, yet amusing and kind too. All of it stirred and intrigued her.

Infatuated, Adam Corbie had once called her. Perhaps he was right.

"Lovely to have luncheon with you and my lady aunt today," Sorcha said then. "She seems eager to leave for Duncraig, and Mama will be happy to see her."

"And we are happy to have you here," Ellison said, recalling that MacGregor had missed luncheon, for he and Donal Brodie had gone out to exercise the horses and visit a few Strathniven tenants. Glad he was finding things to do, she wished they had more time for the lessons. But the longer his supposed transformation took, the better. She dreaded his return to Edinburgh.

"Lady Strathniven is nearly packed and ready to go," she told Sorcha. "And your Duncraig man had lunch in the kitchen after the long drive. He needed a chance to rest before driving back today. Ah, my lady!" She turned as the viscountess approached.

"There you are! Did you see the house, dear?" Lady Strathniven asked Sorcha. "You have not been here for a while. We are so pleased you could stay."

"Thank you again for inviting me," Sorcha said as her aunt enveloped her in an embrace.

"You are always welcome here," the lady responded, eyes twinkling.

"My lady, Mrs. Barrow said all is ready for your journey to Duncraig," Ellison said. "It should take three hours, depending on the roads after the rains."

"I am just waiting for Jeanie to bring down the last of my things. My goodness, Sorcha, you look so grown-up now! Such a pretty girl, the image of your Mama."

"Truly you do," Ellison said, admiring Sorcha's bright, happy countenance, with large hazel eyes, a scattering of freckles on her upturned nose, and honey-colored hair in soft curls. The sunny little girl she remembered was now a graceful young lady, and as straightforward as ever. Sorcha was a smart and uncomplicated girl with a clear-sighted outlook and a practical nature. She would be delightful company.

"I will be gone a week or two, depending on your Mama," Lady Strathniven said.

"I wish I had the patience for Mama that you do, but when I offer solutions, she only wants sympathy. You lift her spirits and make her laugh. She needs that. She misses Beth now that she has married."

"My sister has always had a nervous constitution. But she did mention in her letter that she might hold a dinner party if she feels strong enough."

"She is considering it. Perhaps you can inspire her in that. It would do her good."

"We would all enjoy it. Ellison, my dear, has Sorcha met Lord Darrach yet?"

"Not as yet. He will be here soon, I expect."

"I wonder if he could accompany you over to Kinross this week," Lady Strathniven said. "The seamstress there is finishing two dresses, one for me and one for you, Ellison. I took the liberty of asking her to make something new for you to wear in Edinburgh to attend one of the dances."

"Thank you, my lady," Ellison said, surprised and pleased.

"With all you are doing, you deserve something special. Ellison is such a help here at Strathniven," the viscountess told Sorcha. "We could not get along without her."

"Thank you," Ellison repeated. "It would be nice to go down to Kinross."

"Excellent. Sorcha, dear, you must have something new for Edinburgh too. Tell the seamstress to bill me for it. Though she may have to work quickly."

"Oh, my lady aunt, I could not—"

"You certainly can. Something to match your green eyes, perhaps. But be sure to go with Lord Darrach, Ellison. A gentleman should bring you two into town."

"I am sure we could manage without an escort," Ellison said.

"One could encounter rogues in these hills. Better he was with you."

"Aye." The man was as much a rogue as any, Ellison thought with a wry smile.

"Lord Darrach? I know the name," Sorcha mused. "My mother mentioned him. Viscount Darrach was a neighbor in another glen who died mysteriously two years ago. My brother told her about it, knowing local gossip cheers Mama out of her doldrums."

"Our guest is another Lord Darrach," Ellison said quickly. "A friend of Lady Strathniven."

"Yes, another Darrach. That estate is very grand," the lady continued. "It touches Strathniven on our western boundary, with Glen Brae between. Castle Darrach is a few hours ride from here. Our Darrach," she added, "is the heir."

"But he is staying here rather than at his own castle?" Sorcha asked.

"Matters are still being settled," Ellison said hastily. They had not considered all the ramifications of preparing a smuggler to meet the king. At first, she had only thought to please her father in this. But MacGregor was becoming even more important to her than her quest for Papa's approval.

Oh, what a tangled web we weave when first we practice to deceive, MacGregor had quoted Scott. A tangle indeed.

"Darrach is with us until we all go to Edinburgh for the king's arrival," the viscountess said. "He is quite an eligible bachelor— title and lands, and very handsome. I imagine many young ladies will want to be introduced to him."

The tangled web just became more snarled. "My lady," Ellison said quickly, "your carriage is ready."

"When Jeanie comes down, we will leave. I had hoped to introduce Darrach."

"I can do that," Ellison said.

"Perhaps Mama will invite Lord Darrach to supper at Duncraig," Sorcha said.

"A splendid idea! I will mention it to her. Ellison, what an excellent thought!"

"Excellent," she replied. Tutoring the man to prepare him for a royal interview was one thing, but introducing him as Lord Darrach at a local party was quite another, and risky. If he was exposed, the consequences could bring down her father as well.

"Mama needs a distraction. A new bachelor in the area is a good reason to host a country dance," Sorcha said. "We could have fiddlers and dancing and supper. Our friends here are eager for news and a little society before people travel to Edinburgh in time for the king's arrival. It would be perfect!"

"Perhaps that is better done in the city," Ellison suggested.

"Lord Darrach might enjoy a chance to practice his . . . dancing," Lady Strathniven said, looking hard at her.

"Think of everyone eager to meet him and dance with him." Sorcha giggled.

"Perhaps," Ellison said. Dread ran through her like ice.

"Here is MacNie—oh, and Darrach too!" Lady Strathniven turned as the front door opened and the men stepped into the foyer. Sunlight flooded in with them.

"My lady." Ronan MacGregor raised a brow, seeing the women gathered. His gaze touched Ellison. "Miss Graham. And—?" He inclined his head with a polite smile.

"Lord Darrach, this is my niece, Miss Sorcha Beaton, just arrived from Duncraig."

"Ah, Miss Beaton. A pleasure to meet you." He held out his gloved hand.

Sorcha bowed her head a little and took his large hand, beaming. "Thank you, my lord. I have heard so much about you."

"Have you?" he asked pleasantly.

"Not much, sir," Ellison said. "Just that you are a guest here."

"Ah, and grateful for the hospitality of friends," he said.

"We were just saying, my lord, that you might enjoy visiting Duncraig," Sorcha said. "My mother is there, and my brother, Lord Justice Beaton, will come up from Edinburgh for this. He is fond of Glenbrae whisky, which I understand is yours?"

"It is," he murmured. "So Justice Beaton is your brother?"

"Yes, do you know him? He was a lawyer and is now a lord justice of some kind. There are many justice ranks. I have never sorted them out," she added with a laugh.

"I know the name. He is in the Court of Justiciary, I believe."

Ellison felt a flutter of fear on his behalf; his reply was smooth but she heard a tense underlying note.

"Jeanie, at last," Lady Strathniven said a tall maid in black came down the stairs carrying what seemed to be a heavy valise. "Where is MacNie? He was just here. Give that bag to the Duncraig driver. Where is he? We should be off soon."

"Aye, madam."

"Miss Jeanie, let me take that for you. Nonsense," MacGregor said, reaching for the leather bag as she protested. "I do not mind at all. I am just headed outside myself."

Ellison frowned. A lord offering to help a servant was a bit of a *faux pas,* although a kind gesture could rise above manners and earn praise and loyalty from household staff. She saw it as MacGregor's nature—and perhaps he wanted an excuse to depart.

"Ellison, I nearly forgot," Lady Strathniven said. "I had a letter from your father this morning when MacNie brought the mail."

"Papa? What did he say?" Ellison did not dare glance at MacGregor, who paused at the door, valise in hand.

"He has decided to send Adam here after all."

"Cousin Adam! How delightful," Sorcha said.

"When?" Ellison asked in a flat tone.

"In a week or so. They will send word. I may be back by then."

"Ah." Heart hammering, wanting desperately to look at Ronan, she kept her gaze trained away. She felt his silence keenly.

"Adam is looking forward to seeing Lord Darrach," Lady Strathniven went on.

"Is he," MacGregor clipped. "Good day, ladies. I have an errand. My lady, I wish you a wonderful visit." He inclined his head. "Miss Beaton, good to meet you. Miss Graham, good day."

Ellison met his frowning gaze. "Darrach."

"Well, I am off, my dears!" The viscountess leaned in to kiss Ellison and then Sorcha on the cheek. "Do not get into mischief while I am gone," she teased.

"Of course not," Ellison answered stiffly.

"All will be well, my lady," MacGregor said, and held the door open.

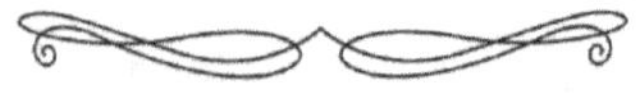

Chapter Twelve

Ruari MacAlpin had adored redheaded Isabella since they had been small. Tender years had led to innocent kisses, then shared whispers of love and devotion, and finally marriage. The guarantee lay in the friendship of their fathers, who had guarded each other's backs on the battlefield. But when Grant's death revealed his debts, his grieving widow wed a high judge who could pay that for her. He then arranged to betroth Grant's daughter to Strathearn, a powerful royal advisor, who would give her a life of privilege in London. But the wedding would take place soon.

"Tell the lass your feelings before she flies south forever," a friend urged Ruari. "Losing her will be your undoing."

"That beauty—and this beast?" Ruari, tall and strong as an oak, bearded and plaided, his hands used to heavy work, laughed bitterly. "I canna give her what she deserves. The beautiful bird will fly and the beast will go to ground."

So he saw her go in silence, just a hand lifted in farewell in the kirkyard. He turned away without seeing the tears in the bride's eyes.

Five years, five seasons of barley and oats, of midnight cattle forays and drives to market along ancient tracks; five years of having no lass to warm his heart or his hearth. None could compare to the one he had let go.

Five years, and then the winsome Lady Strathearn returned to the Highlands, a young widow draped in black. She brought a small son and a fortune to protect for him. The glen folk said the lady had fled to protect her child's life. Strathearn's foes in the south were bent on destroying his family and his legacy. The lady, said they, sought to hire a sword-arm, a man keen for mischief and danger, a seneschal who would hold Strathearn Castle strong.

That night Ruarie of Garslie sharpened blade and dirk on the whetstone, cleaned and oiled sheath and targe, unlocked the chest that held his father's armor, and made himself ready.

Ellison paused, reading softly aloud, jotting changes here and there. The hour was late, and the little tower library was silent and cozy. Candles flickered, rain shushed against the window glass as she wrote. Earlier she had crafted a title page on a creamy sheet of paper to cover her growing manuscript: *The Highlander's Lament by E. S. Leslie,* she had written, and made a little ink sketch of a castle on a hill.

She was thrilled with her story. The hero, Ruari MacAlpin, a proud descendant of Scotland's ancient kings, lived under English rule in the time of the Covenanter's dispute, when no Scotsman dared claim royal blood or a Papist education. A man of tremendous heart and loyalty, he nurtured an unrequited love for Isabella, who did not know how deeply he loved her. Though he never spoke of it, he would have given up his life for her. Nor did Ruari know that Isabella hid her love for him.

Ellison sighed, for the story made her hopeful as well as sad. She had to think of a way to bring noble Ruari and foolish Isabella together, and make each one better for it. She scribbled some thoughts in the margin, chewed on the end of the pen, and wrote on.

Tapping her fingers on the tabletop, she wondered how to place the hero in yet another pickle. He must face a foe with swords drawn and defend the lady, her son, and her castle from attack.

A little clock on the mantel chimed softly. The hour was late and the household asleep. Coming to the old library mouse-quiet, she'd thought MacGregor to be still in the main library, where she had glimpsed him earlier. Once Sorcha had retired to bed,

Ellison had gone to the larger library hoping to write, only to see MacGregor seated with books, intent on his reading. She had retreated and headed to the tower library, not wanting to distract him.

Yet the Highlander was a distraction under any circumstances. Just a glance or a quiet remark could set her deliciously off-kilter. But tonight the writing itch was upon her, and so she managed nearly two hours of writing in the silence and privacy of the medieval tower.

Standing, stretching, she glanced out the window at the dark, drizzly, summer night. Then she opened a glass decanter to pour a little bit of ratafia into a small glass. Mrs. Barrow's recipe of sherry mixed with berries, oranges, cinnamon, and water was refreshing, and the housekeeper made sure to keep some of the drink, a favorite of Lady Strathniven's, in the old library for Ellison, who used the room most often.

Sipping the homemade cordial, hoping it might help her sleep later, she had another idea, and covered a page with writing, pen scratching in the quiet.

She froze when she heard the scrape of boots on the stone steps. MacGregor must be going up to his room for the night, for the footsteps passed the library. Above, a door latched shut.

Breathing out, she dipped the quill and wrote on, but could not focus on her story. In the noiseless room, her thoughts kept sliding to Ronan MacGregor. The mere scrape of his foot on the step had made her heart beat faster.

Just infatuation, she told herself, and she must ignore it. He did not seem to return her interest, and a romance was unthinkable for the daughter of the deputy provost and a man who could return to prison. MacGregor was gentlemanly, polite, and kind toward her and she could expect nothing more.

Part of her wished he would abandon propriety and show reciprocal feeling for her—a long while had passed since a man had cared about her. Her widow's existence sealed her off from affection and love, and so she might feel isolated the rest of her life.

Outside, the sky was the purple of a late summer night. She ought to go to bed. Tomorrow would bring them closer to the day Ronan MacGregor must carry out this risky scheme in Edinburgh. Then he would depart, never knowing how she felt. She could not tell him—it would not do.

But she could write about it. A sense of unrequited love infused her story. Taking up the pen, she began to write, soon surprising herself as an impassioned scene emerged with each scratch of the quill. Isabella secretly loved Ruari, but had married a man who would help her family. Now she was widowed and had to seek help from the Highlander she had once rejected. The scene poured through the pen.

Pausing to think, she slid her fingers through her loosened braid. As she wrote of the love between her characters, tears welled and spilled, blotting the ink.

She looked up to see her face reflected in the window glass. Then she saw a face just above hers, as if her Highland hero stood there, tall, handsome, mysterious. She gasped, for she realized Ronan was in the doorway, reflected in the window too.

"Miss Graham," Ronan said, sensing her surprise. "I did not mean to startle you. It is late, and I apologize." As she beckoned, he entered the room. "I could not sleep and came downstairs, for I had seen a light earlier. I wanted to be sure no candles or lamps were burning. I did not realize you were here."

"Sometimes I come in here to write or read. It is so private."

"Or was, until I arrived. Letters?" He glanced at the pages on the table, noticing watery blots of ink. She covered the topmost page with her hand.

"A story. A book someday," she blurted.

"Ah." Sensing fragility, Ronan paused. Strong though the girl might be, life had made her hesitant and fearful; perhaps her dreams seemed risky. The thought of anyone diminishing the shining spirit within her made him feel indignant and protective. He frowned, wishing she would trust him, but she watched him warily.

"A book? Excellent."

"You might think it a frivolous waste of time." She tucked the pages together and folded her hands over them as if to shield them. "But I enjoy it."

"If reading a book is a worthy occupation for men and women, how could writing a book be unworthy?"

"Writing poetry is considered more suitable for a lady than a novel."

"I enjoy novels more than poetry. But then some think me a ne'er-do-well."

"I do not think so."

"Thank you. There is much to admire in those who take on the task of writing and accomplish it." He smiled. "I will not interrupt your work." He stepped back.

"I am done for now. Sit if you like."

He took a chair by the table. "So you work on something in solitude. I will keep that secret for you, I promise."

"I appreciate it." She spread her fingers to cover the pages.

"I only came in here to check the candles, and to look for a book that might help my own secret work."

"I saw you reading in the library earlier. Law books, I think?"

"Aye. I am hoping to find a solution to a certain dilemma. I confess I also came in hopes of finding a decanter of whisky. A wee sip is good for a sleepless night." He rose and went to a shelf where two glass decanters and drinking glasses sat neatly arranged. One decanter was full of amber liquid. A smaller decanter held a darker liquid. "Sherry?"

"A ratafia with berries and spices. Mrs. Barrow makes it. Help yourself, sir."

"Ratafia is more of a ladies' drink. I shall try a dram of this one." He poured a little amber whisky into a small glass. "Would you care for some?"

"I had the liqueur earlier. Though—aye, a little taste of whisky will do. I feel a bit restless tonight too."

"Highland ladies enjoy a dram whenever they like." He

poured a wee bit into a second glass. "It seems that Lady Strathniven agrees."

Ellison laughed. "She does. Thank you." She took the glass, sipped, grimaced.

He lifted his glass, watched candlelight flicker through the honey-gold liquid, and sipped. "A handsome whisky. Made by Pitlinnie, if I am not mistaken."

"I believe so. He is a local baronet, I think, and makes his own whisky."

"Aye, he has a small Highland estate and a recent title, which I hear he earned in return for a monetary gift to the English government."

"Oh! That seems—rather crass."

"A bit. His grandfather was appointed a knight for a similar reason, but they never let their neighbors forget their raised status. To Sir Neill Pitlinnie," he drawled, raising his glass. "May he prosper and enjoy his titles and such."

"You do not seem fond of him."

"Not especially." He drank.

"What were you looking for in this library? Can I help find it?"

He liked to keep his secrets safe, as she apparently did too, but he felt at ease with her. "I am searching for a small archaic point of law. I thought the older volumes in here might have something."

She waved toward the bookcases lining the walls. "There are some older books on Scots law in one corner. Lord Strathniven shelved them here, finding them outdated. But that might be what you need."

"Thank you. But I do not want to disturb your writing session."

"The inspiration has passed." She smiled, lifted a shoulder.

"Inspiration—and tears?" He glanced at the pages beneath her hand. "Sorry, I should not ask. But it must be a good story to touch you so."

"I like it, but Papa thinks—" She stopped, shook her head.

"Thinks it unsuitable?"

"Worse. Folly." She shrugged, took a sip. "Oh, my. That does warm the throat."

He saw a blush rise into her cheeks. "What is your story about, if I may ask?"

"It will seem silly to you." But her eyes sparkled, and he had the feeling she wanted to talk about it.

"Not at all. Can I help?"

She looked down, the movement spiraling a golden curl out of her braided hair. "Kind of you. Perhaps someday."

"I wonder," he murmured, "if we will have a someday, you and I."

"I know," she said softly.

Something tugged in his chest. Leaning back, he folded his arms as the relaxing warmth of the whisky ran through him, loosening candor. "Tell me about your story."

She sipped the whisky, coughed, and began to talk. At first quietly, then with spirit and enthusiasm as she described the story. He smiled, seeing her excitement.

"So Ruari must protect his heart against more hurt. And Isabella is caught in what her family needs and does not—oh, I am sorry," she said.

He opened his eyes. "Sorry about what?"

"I thought you were bored. Getting sleepy."

"I am listening intently to a charming narrator." He smiled. "Go on. This Highlander is a strong fellow of high morals and proud birth, though he indulges in a bit of cattle thievery now and then. He cannot reveal his love for the daughter of a rival clan chief because of an ancient feud. And her family betrothed her to another."

"He wanted what was best for her, and tries to accept it. Do you think it is silly?"

"I think it is a classic and perhaps tragic love story. And I like your hero."

"I gave him some of your traits," she said. "Oh, I should not have said so."

"As long as they are my better traits, I am flattered." He smiled, feeling relaxed. "Your Highland laddie is in some hot water, about to lose his lands and all he treasures in life. What will he do?"

"He must choose exile or risk death. But first he must defend Isabella when she returns to the glen."

"Ah. So he dons armor and weapons and offers to be her guard. But that is a great risk for him. Death and hanging if he is caught, aye?"

"Aye. If English officers come to her castle, they might find him there."

"Then we must save him from the gallows and reunite him with his dearest love, so he can profess undying love and she can—"

"Please do not mock my story." She rustled the papers together.

"Miss Ellison." He leaned across the table and laid a hand upon her wrist as she gathered the papers. "I would never mock it. I like it very much. But—"

"But what?"

"Sometimes it is easier to make light of feelings than to be honest about them."

His heart began to thump with that statement.

"About his love for the heroine?"

"Aye. Some men find that sort of thing difficult." Well, he certainly did. Her expression just then—soft, compassionate— nearly undid him. "I feel for your Ruari. I know what it is to love and—feel betrayed."

"Do you?" She tipped her head.

"It was a long time ago. Go on," he said. "The lad loves the lass, the lass loves the lad, and neither is able to say so."

"They can never marry, you see."

"Why not?" he asked abruptly.

"He thinks her unreachable and believes she does not love him."

He watched her for a moment. "Is she? Unreachable?"

She shook her head. "She loves him. She would do anything—to be with him."

"Then they need to declare their feelings."

She laughed. "But then, the story would be over in a chapter or two. There must be complications. Challenges to overcome."

"Magic," he said suddenly. "Do you admire Mr. Scott's work? He might bring magic or something otherworldly in to such a tale."

"Aye, magic! But how?"

"The Highlands are full of such stories." The far-fetched idea had some appeal, he thought. "Not far from here, there is a loch that is said to be cursed by the fairies. Now and again the fairies take its island back to their realm, so it is said."

"How could they take an entire island?"

"It disappears."

"Truly?"

Ronan smiled. "I will take you there. It may not disappear, but you can see it."

"You just want another excuse to ride out." She smiled.

"True. I should ride out with my band of smugglers to make a whisky run before I meet the king and return to prison where I undoubtedly belong."

"Stop it, Mr. MacGregor," she said, half-laughing.

"I will take you fishing, how is that? We will look for this loch. Miss Beaton and Donal Brodie could go too. The lad will ensure my good behavior."

"We could make a picnic of it."

"You must teach me picnic etiquette in case the king wants to picnic with me."

She laughed again. "We could do that. What other fairy legends do you know?"

"I have a cousin who makes *uisge-beatha sìthiche*."

"Fairy whisky?" She tilted her head, a curl sliding down. "I have not heard of it."

"You may have the Gaelic, but you were not raised in the Highlands."

"Is this it?" She lifted the whisky glass.

"This is good stuff, but hardly magical. Fairy whisky is made to an ancient recipe known only to a few. It is a carefully-guarded secret in my cousin's family. He has the knack of making it."

"Does everyone in your family make excellent and very illicit whisky?"

"Not all of us. My cousin's branch has kept the recipe secret for generations. Not many have tasted it, for it is neither sold nor traded, just given away to a select few."

"Have you tasted it?"

"I have. And Glenbrae brew does not hold a candle to it."

"Best not let the king know about it, then."

He laughed, delighted. "True! Even the king could not obtain this stuff. Only those who are born with the Sight can tell what it is. To others, it is just an excellent Highland whisky. There is some magical secret in the process. My cousin's ancestor once saved the life of a fairy, so the legend goes, and the recipe was his reward. When I was a lad, I thought my family rather dull by comparison to my cousin's."

She smiled. "Were your kin free traders too?"

"Oh, we were a very respectable bunch." He would not tell her more, for they now sat in a tower that had once belonged to his ancestors. "No fairy legends, alas."

Her smile was pure whimsy. "Fairy whisky sounds very romantic."

"Include it in your story. But I do not know the recipe."

"That would be wonderful." She lifted her glass, drained the trace there. He watched the line of her throat as she swallowed, felt a pull inside, leaned back as if to distance himself. *Be careful*, he thought, as the yearning began.

"Perhaps one day I can get some for you." But that day would not come if her father had his way. Yet Ronan's desire to be near her was strong and astonishing.

"I could add a legend, and complicate my story."

"Aye, do weave legends and magic into the story."

"You should write this, Mr. MacGregor." Her wider smile showed a dimple. She glanced out the window, then stood, skirts whispering. "It is very late."

He stood quickly. "I enjoyed our chat."

"So did I. Though I had a bit too much of the magical whisky, I fear."

"You will sleep well." As she proceeded him to the door, he blew out the candles. Then he reached past her to draw the door wide. Light from a narrow window in the stairwell flowed gray-purple into the darkness.

She moved past him, shoulder brushing his chest. Ronan set a hand briefly to her elbow. Pausing, she looked up.

"I do not know what will happen after the king's visit," she murmured. "But if you need anything then, please let me know."

His heart pounded hard. "Thank you. I appreciate your friendship."

"Are we friends, then?" She tipped her head, watching him.

"More than friends, if you like," he murmured, pressing her elbow, drawing her closer. Lowering his head, taking the chance, he touched his nose lightly to hers, angled his head. Waited, invited.

She tilted her face, nudged his nose, allowing. He drew in a breath and touched his lips to hers gently. Her lips met his in tender answer. Resting a hand on his chest, she leaned against him, and the kiss deepened of its own accord.

With one arm, he pulled her snug against him, and as she melded willingly into him, he sought her lips in a deep, exploring kiss. Sinking his fingers into the silky mass of her hair, he felt her sigh, press into him, open her lips to taste more. The feeling that plunged through him pulsed, strengthened. Then he pulled back.

"Friendship," he breathed, "may have to be enough."

"And secrets," she whispered.

"Yours are safe with me."

"And yours with me." She did not pull away, but he let go, creating space between his body and hers.

"Forgive me," he said. "Talk of fairies and romance skewed my thinking."

"Hush. Do not apologize." Reaching up, she touched a finger to his lips. "You do not seem the romantical sort. Perhaps it was the whisky."

"Perhaps. But I do apologize. Neither of us needs a complication."

"I am no innocent girl, but a widow."

"I know," he whispered.

"Ronan MacGregor," she said, face close, bodies apart, tension rising like lightning between them. He felt it and would not allow himself to pursue it. "I trust you. And I—would be yours, if you wanted. If we agreed. I think we might."

He sucked in a breath. "Go gently, lass. Do not trust me, or this moment."

"I do. You are not the rogue people think."

"Am I not?" He stepped past the threshold to the stone platform, where the steps led up to his room, or down and away. A precarious place. A precarious decision. He took her elbow. "I will take you to the tower door. The steps are treacherous in the dark."

"Wait. I should apologize." She took his arm. "It is unlike me to speak so—boldly. It might be the whisky."

"It has a way of loosening tongues. Come ahead." He guided her down a step.

"I have made a fool of myself," she fretted quietly.

"Hush. What you are doing for me, lass, and what you said made me feel like—"

"A viscount?" She half-laughed.

He tipped her chin upward. "Like a Highland hero, kissed by a fairy queen."

"Oh," she whispered.

In the half-light, her soul seemed to shine in her eyes for a moment. It was all he needed, all he could ever want, but could not have. He was very like the sorry Highlander in her story, filled with love he could not express.

Enough, he told himself. "Best go, lass, before I lose myself utterly and you lose your trust in me."

"I do not think that can happen now."

"Miss Graham, you are a delicious and idealistic creature." He led her down another step.

"Papa says I am full of dreams and had best wake myself up to the real world."

He frowned. "Hold onto your dreams. Keep them safe."

"I will try." She hesitated as he stepped down again. He turned, finding her height closer to his. "Ronan, would you—kiss me again? Before we go?"

He did, and then did again, pressing her close so that she would know his desire for her, while he felt hers blooming in the curve and warmth of her body. Moments and kisses passed, until at last he drew back, letting go of the dream that could never be.

"Miss Graham. Come this way."

"Ellison," she said.

"Elly, my lass. This way." Gently he guided her down to the door that connected to the main house, to reality, and tomorrow.

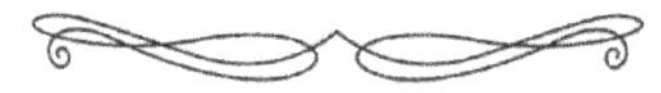

Chapter Thirteen

"SUCH A WARM day," Sorcha said, fanning herself with a painted silk fan as she sat beside Ellison in the carriage. "Perhaps it will feel cooler in Kinross."

"The closeness in here makes it warmer," Ellison said.

"Kinross feels good breezes off Loch Leven," Ronan said. "You will enjoy the outing either way." He looked toward Ellison and she turned her head, remembering shared kisses in the tower stair. She had brazenly asked him to kiss her again. Embarrassment whirled through her.

At supper last night and breakfast today, he had been polite but distant, and Ellison was sure his opinion of her was unflattering. Never again would she follow a ratafia nightcap with strong whisky. But that had led to those unforgettable kisses.

"How nice you could come with us today, Lord Darrach," Sorcha said.

"Aye," he said, though Ellison noticed a subtle wince at hearing the title.

"We need not stay long," Ellison said. "We only need to visit the seamstress and do a few errands."

"It's so exciting," Sorcha went on. "My aunt is kind to include me in her party in Edinburgh so I can attend the king's reception for the ladies, too. Mama does not care to go, since the crowds are expected to be so large. She has a delicate constitution."

"More than enough reason to avoid the city this summer."

MacGregor flashed a blue glance toward Ellison, then away.

"Sir, do you have some business in town as well?" Sorcha asked.

"I can visit one of my solicitors, who has an office in Kinross."

Interesting that he wanted to see his lawyer, Ellison thought, frowning. She hoped it would not involve talk of smugglers, prisons, or some means of escaping the king's introduction and any connection with the Grahams.

Trust him, she reminded herself. She had agreed to do that. If she had made a blunder last night, it was not only the drink, but because she felt at ease with him. Would he feel the same now, or think her a silly young woman—worse, a desperately lonely widow?

Reaching the main street through Kinross, MacNie drove the carriage at a leisurely pace, passing Muir's Inn on the left, then headed toward Green's Hotel, closer to the shops. Ellison had requested they stop there, thinking it would be a good meeting place once they finished their errands. Green's served an excellent tea, and she hoped there might be time for that.

As a groom ran through the yard to help with the horses, MacGregor stepped out first, turning to hand Sorcha, then Ellison down. Setting her hand in his, she thought he pressed it slightly in some silent message. Apology? Promise? Affection? She dared not hope as she stepped down.

He pulled his hat low over his brow, tugged at his coat collar, and glanced about, as if wary of being recognized. Ellison felt sympathy more than suspicion, seeing that.

"Where would you like to go first, ladies?" he asked.

"The seamstress's shop is there along the High Street." She pointed nearby. "We can easily walk. Where is your solicitor's office?"

"Near the town hall." He gestured the other way. "I will go there, and meet you here at the hotel later. Would that suit?"

"You need not hurry," Ellison said. "We will visit other shops as well. Lady Strathniven gave me a list of errands. But I hope we have time for tea here at Green's."

"I would enjoy that," Sorcha said. "Lord Darrach, I hope you can join us."

"An honor, Miss Beaton. Will an hour do?"

"Perfect," Ellison said, turning to see their driver returning. "Mr. MacNie, we will come back here in an hour. I think you have errands of your own, am I right?"

"I do, Miss. Mail and such, and I will see the blacksmith about getting some new harnesses."

"Very good. We will see you soon." She took Sorcha's arm and turned away.

Pulling down her bonnet brim against the sunlight, she walked with Sorcha along the High Street. After a moment, she looked back to see MacGregor walking in the opposite direction. He had not worn his Highland gear—perhaps because some might know him, she realized. In dark trousers, coat, and tall hat, he looked like an ordinary gentleman on an ordinary day, though so tall and striking a figure would catch attention wherever he went. The sureness in his stride said he belonged here, knew where he was going, and knew what he meant to do.

He had more secrets than he would ever reveal, she thought.

"RONAN! I AM surprised to see you in Kinross—and pleased." Hugh Cameron took Ronan's hand, his clasp warm and strong. "I thought you were still in Edinburgh. I recently had an interesting letter from the Provost's office concerning you. A pardon, of all things. Very unexpected."

"It was. I will explain. Do you have time to talk?"

"Time for the lad who memorized every law book in the university's library with me, matching pint for pint and book for book? Always! It is good to see you after these troublesome months for you. Take a seat." Hugh sat in the leather chair behind his desk while Ronan took the chair opposite. "So, out and free. How the devil did you do it?"

"Free for now. I am skeptical, but I had some luck via the king, if you believe it."

"I must hear this. Are you back in Perthshire to stay? The letter was unclear."

"Soon I must return to the city for the royal visit. First, have you had any word about Linhope and MacInnes? I understand they were transferred to Calton Jail."

"Aye, notice of that came to our Edinburgh office—Alan Smithson is looking into their situation." Cameron shook his head. "Calton is not a good place."

"True. Alan will make sure of their treatment."

"He will. He wrote that Linhope told the warden about his medical skills, which are needed there, so he has some privileges, and MacInnes is allowed to assist him."

"Good. Did they need to reveal who they are?"

"No questions, I think. Any medical experience is useful there."

"That is the best we can hope for until I find a way to get them released."

Hugh shook his head. "Not easy. What do you have in mind?"

"I found a detail that might help lift the charges. Innocence is not enough."

"Innocence has gradients. You were lucky to obtain a pardon. But once a trial date is set for the others—well, we will try to avoid that. Let me know what you need."

"Aye. Otherwise, is there news about the estate?"

"Nothing much. I was preparing a letter for you and was going to send it to Smithson so he could find you. But here you are."

"Here I am. What more do you know? Sorting out the estate is a slow process."

"Given the commotion of the king's visit in the city, even

slower." Cameron picked up a sheaf of papers and rifled through them, choosing a page. "I wonder if you had much news in the dungeons. Are you aware that old Sir John Murray-MacGregor died this summer?"

"I heard. Sad, that. And Sir Evan is now clan chief."

"Then you will have guessed that your cousin will take time to review clan issues before any decisions can be made. The Darrach matter will come to him."

"Aye, the clan chief has the right to absorb forfeited or abandoned lands and titles into his own holdings. He may decide to do that and have done with it. My cousin Darrach left a bit of a tangle."

"He did. The matter went to the Court of Sessions and the Lyon Court to help sort out the heritable claim, but it is difficult, since Darrach left no will."

"He talked about it but never completed one, as I recall. He never thought it was pressing. He was young, and had other things on his mind."

"The business with your brother William."

"Aye. We do not know what Darrach preferred. He was not married, and might have left some to William, but both are gone and we may never know."

"No one has come forward in all this time, so there are no claimants so far. The court might have sent it to Sir John MacGregor as a clan matter, but his death delayed that. So it will go to your cousin Sir Evan, as clan chief, to decide."

"The courts will be glad to be quit of it."

"The land and title could still come to you."

"Evan may be disinclined to choose a man accused of criminal activity." He knew Evan MacGregor well, though they had kept their distance over the last few years.

"But now that you are free and clear, according to the documents I saw, you could write to Sir Evan to inquire. I hear he will be in Edinburgh soon for the festivities. You could meet with him there to discuss it."

"I doubt he would welcome seeing me."

"Surely time has softened that old matter?"

Ronan shrugged in silence, feeling the old hurt surface. The rift was strong between him and his cousin following the events after the battle that had wounded both of them.

Hugh sighed. "Aye, well. You should know he has agreed to lead the Highland contingent in Edinburgh during the royal visit. Sir Walter Scott and the Lord Provost wanted to honor him as a war hero admired by many."

"They could not find a better representative of Highland dignity than Evan Murray-MacGregor. He will assemble an impressive tail of chieftains in full regalia."

"He will, as will the other clan chiefs in attendance. They will muster men, horses, weapons, plaids and all to roll out a great showing of Highland clans. They say all of this may even cause a shortage of tartan cloth, with thousands eager to show Scotland at its finest. We may never see its like again. A great celebration of Scottishness."

Ronan nodded. Reluctant to be part of a ruse in meeting the king, he yet felt a strong pride within about being Highland and Scottish. He wanted to witness the spectacle, feel the swell of Scottish strength borne on this wave of royal excitement. But he would rather avoid any debacle.

"I will write to Sir Evan to let him know you are free, since he is aware of the arrest as chief of your clan. As for the charges, which I am certain were unfairly assigned to all three of you, Smithson and I can make some headway."

"The charges were unclear and remain so. It is to our advantage."

"True. Ronan," said Hugh, giving him a severe glance, "would you be willing to speak frankly about your situation if this comes to trial?"

"About William and Darrach? I will not expose them. Let them rest in peace."

"Your stubbornness is only to your detriment."

"We agreed to hold back the full truth, short of hanging. I will not dishonor my brother and my cousin."

"To your peril, you are an honorable man."

"Huh. If you have word on the other matters, you can send a message to Strathniven House for now. But in Edinburgh," he said, "send word either to Lady Strathniven in town or Miss Ellison Graham at her father's home. Only those two. There are few I can trust."

"The deputy lord provost's daughter? I did not realize you knew the Grahams, or Lady Strathniven either."

"We met only recently. Both have shown me kindness and discretion."

"Do they know your history?"

"Not entirely."

"I see. What is this business to do with the king? You mentioned something."

Ronan huffed. "King George is so fond of Glenbrae whisky that he wants to meet the distiller."

Hugh chuckled. "No wonder Sir Hector found a way to release you. Save face, clean up the prisoner, is that it?"

"Exactly. Once I am presentable, I will be introduced at the royal levee."

His friend laughed again. "They must be scrambling to hide the truth about you."

"My incarceration did pose a dilemma."

"Do they know about your connection to Darrach?"

"Not entirely. They decided to elevate me to the viscountcy on the chance. An odd coincidence, that."

"You must be joking." Hugh's grin faded. "Very well. I do not want to know the details. Not good for either of us. But I will write to Sir Evan on your behalf."

"I doubt it will do much good. He has been angry with me for years."

"It would be helpful to have his answer and be done with it." Hugh tapped a finger on the desk, his brow furrowed. "Well.

Aught else I can do, Ronan?"

"This." Ronan reached into a pocket to bring out a note he had written late one night after poring over volumes of law in the Strathniven collection. "I suspect they were so eager to grab the Whisky Rogues that they may have overlooked some details."

Hugh studied the page. "This is accurate? The first of May? Interesting." He returned it to its envelope.

"Another matter, if you will. Do you know much about the will left by Colin Leslie? I believe it was made in your Edinburgh office. He died less than two years ago in Edinburgh. A poet, I think."

"Sir Arnold Leslie's lad? Aye. Not my client, but I know something of it. Tragic, that. Drunken fall from a horse. Young lad, I believe."

"Aye."

"He left a young widow."

"The deputy lord provost's daughter, aye. She inherited Leslie's house on North Castle Street, but she cannot gain access to it. Some of Leslie's relatives are protesting the will and have taken up residence there."

"That cannot be allowed if the dispute is unresolved. I will send word to Smithson to look into it. He might be aware of the situation. If they refuse to vacate, I will go there myself and toss them out."

"Leave it to me. You do not need to be arrested for disturbing the peace."

"Just get them evicted. If the place needs cleaning and repair, I will pay for the work. You have access to my account per our agreement before I, er, became a tenant of Edinburgh Castle." Hugh quirked a brow and Ronan nodded. "It is a favor for a friend."

"Quite a favor. Quite a friend, is she?"

"I owe the young lady a debt of kindness."

"Write out a draught, then, if you will." Cameron opened another drawer and drew out a leather wallet of bank drafts, which he slid across the desk surface.

Writing out a generous amount, Ronan handed it back. Hugh nodded. "It will be done. When you return to Edinburgh, where will you stay?"

"The hotel on Princes Street. My usual place."

"You had best inquire. Every available hole is filling fast with the crowds expected. I will stay with my mother in the Canongate during the royal visit. You are welcome there. She has always been fond of you."

"Thank you. How is your mother?"

"Very well, but the royal visit has her at sixes and sevens. She is no fan of the Crown, being raised by staunch Jacobites, but she is insatiably curious. I will escort her to some of the events. You know she would be delighted to see you."

"Good. I will let you know my arrangements." He stood, and so did Hugh.

"Take care, Ronan. If the king learns the truth about the Glenbrae distiller, it could go poorly for you. Your young lady's father may regret his decision to release you."

"She is not my young lady," he said, earning a keen glance from Cameron. "And I know the risks."

"HERE WE ARE," the seamstress said, carrying a gown of wine-colored satin draped over her arm. A shop girl followed with a second gown in deep blue silk. They laid the dresses out on a sofa, and the girl withdrew. The seamstress, Mrs. Fowler, smiled at Ellison and Sophia. "Lady Strathniven ordered the blue for you, Miss Graham."

"It is beautiful," Ellison breathed, reaching out to touch the blue gown and the wine-colored one as well. The dresses had graceful falls of creamy lace at bodice and sleeves, and lace ruffles in deep rows around the hem.

"And headdresses to match," the woman said, "with nine feathers, just as the viscountess specified." The shop girl returned with the head pieces, one turban-like in black silk with white feathers, the other a narrow blue band with pearls and feathers.

"These are gorgeous!" Ellison was extremely pleased with the blue gown, which was a dreamy confection in deep blue silk with ruffles of plaid silk along the hem. The shop girl added a long swath of matching plaid which could be worn over the shoulder and pinned with a brooch.

"Lady Strathniven asked me to make the blue gown to the same measurements as the mourning dresses we made for you a while ago."

"Thank you, Mrs. Fowler. This is unexpected, and so kind."

"I am glad you can be done with somber colors. They take the roses from your cheeks. The blue suits your complexion well."

Ellison nodded, the silk sliding through her fingers like water. Was she ready to leave mourning colors behind? The blue was a brighter, more joyful color than she had worn for a year and a half.

"It is time, Elly," Sorcha said gently.

"Perhaps." For some reason she thought of Ronan MacGregor. Would he agree?

"The train is very long, the required length for a royal reception," the seamstress explained. "We have been making gowns with these long trains for weeks. There is such excitement over the king's visit! Now, for you, Miss Beaton," the woman continued, turning, "I had a note from Lady Strathniven requesting that you be fitted for a gown as well, to be added to my lady's account."

"Oh, my goodness, what a wonderful gift."

"I have a pale green satin that would complement your hazel eyes. We could combine a green bodice with a creamy white skirt. It would be demure and very pretty for you. Come this way. We can look at trims and laces as well."

While Sorcha went with Mrs. Fowler, Ellison tried on the blue gown with the help of the shop girl. It shaped to her form like perfection, and its elegant long sleeves and neckline flattered her shoulders and slender collarbones. She twirled, spirits soaring. It was wonderful to wear something beautiful after hiding in subdued tones for so long.

She knew she could move on from mourning. She had not only lost her young husband, but had lost herself somehow. Her life had taken a darker turn into loneliness and guilt. The gorgeous blue silk spun as she turned, its susurration exciting. She would wear the gown—and she imagined Ronan MacGregor dressed in Highland finery, tall and handsome, at her side. In an assembly room filled with hundreds, thousands, of others, she would see only him. And he would see only her.

Stop, she told herself. He was to attend one royal event quickly—and then vanish from her life.

Soon, with the gowns wrapped and Sorcha's gown measured and promised, they left the shop with their string-and-paper parcels, spent a little time on other errands, and then walked back to the hotel.

Her heartbeat quickened when she saw Ronan standing with Mr. MacNie. He turned to see her, and his smile emerged like a sunbeam, warmth enveloping her.

She smiled shyly, filled with a sudden certainty. He cared for her. She saw it in that moment. And suddenly she wanted to be in his arms, divinely alone, just the two of them, just the moment and the future—

Of all her unlikely dreams, that was the most improbable.

"MAMA FEARS THE city will be so crowded during the king's visit that she dare not go to Edinburgh." Sorcha set down her tea cup to lean toward Ellison, across from MacGregor in the tea room of the hotel. "She is disappointed, but it is for the best."

"With her delicate health, she should stay home," Ellison said.

"I promised to regale her with the gossip when I return," Sorcha said. "Do you think I could stay in the city with my aunt? I did not ask."

"I am sure of it. I will ask for you."

"Thank you." Sorcha smiled. "Lord Darrach, will you stay in the city as well?"

"Hmm? Oh, aye." He sounded distracted. Ellison stole a glance toward him. For several minutes he had looked around the dining room as if on guard.

"What delicious tea," Sorcha said. "I love a Bohea blend with just a hint of orange flavor to it. Mama prefers Chinese green, though I find it bitter. Which do you prefer, Lord Darrach, black or green?"

"Tea? I, uh, usually black tea."

Ellison spread strawberry jam on a scone as Sorcha chattered on, and glanced toward Ronan. He nodded politely yet did not seem to listen closely, his head half-turned as if very distracted.

Noticing two young men seated in a corner who also glanced their way, she frowned, feeling a bit alarmed. She patted the packages that sat on the empty chair beside her. "Shall we leave, sir?"

"Soon. You bought something pretty, I trust? You came back looking pleased."

"Gowns for the ladies' reception in Edinburgh."

"Ah." His gaze touched hers, blue as the silk of her gown. He lifted his cup and sipped, again glancing toward the men in the corner.

"Do you know them?" she asked quietly.

"Aye." He rose to his feet. "Ladies, forgive me. I see friends and must greet them. Enjoy your tea and cakes. I will be back shortly."

WHAT BROUGHT ALECK and Geordie Muir to the hotel's tearoom? This was not a usual stop for them. Had something happened? Crossing the room, Ronan resisted the urge to look back. Of course Ellison was safe, he told himself. These lads were not scoundrels, though that sort might be around, unnoticed. He felt wary, prickly with it.

"Sir." Geordie glanced past Ronan. "You keep gentle company today."

"I do. Good to see you both. We can talk outside." He led them out and through the yard in the afternoon sun, pausing under the shade and privacy of beech trees.

"I saw your grandfather," he said.

"He told us you came to the distillery," Geordie replied.

"We came to Kinross today for supplies and saw Mr. Cameron in the street," Aleck added. "He said we could find you at the hotel."

"Is there news?" Ronan sensed tension. Rabbie Muir was loyal as old oak, but these young lads had to make their own way and take care of a mother and sisters. They might do whatever was necessary. Pitlinnie could tempt young lads like these two to do smuggling and underhanded deeds if funds were needed. "You can be honest with me."

"Good news, and some not so good," Aleck said. "Geordie will take over the work of the farm from Grandda. Our lad will be married soon." He clapped his brother on the shoulder. "Mary MacGillie down the way."

Geordie nodded. "She works at Strathniven House."

"I met the lass. Cheerful and capable, and just as ginger-haired as you. We may expect bonny ginger bairns someday." He grinned. "I wish you both well."

"We would be honored if you would come to our wedding in the autumn."

"I will do my best. What other news?" He saw Geordie glance at Aleck.

"We would like to open our own distillery," Aleck said. "Did Grandda say?"

"He did not. But it is a good plan." Ronan waited, expecting more.

"Have you seen Pitlinnie?" Geordie asked briskly.

"I have not had the pleasure," Ronan drawled. "Something I should know?"

"He makes more profit than ever moving goods, and no one is the wiser. Those who know keep quiet about it."

"Safety is a good reason."

"Sir, we could earn extra money with him," Aleck said.

"If you truly want to work with that rascal, go ahead."

"Some of our cousins are doing so, but they are not as discreet as Pitlinnie thinks," Geordie said. "They tell us what they know."

"So we heard Pitlinnie says he wanted you and your friends out of the way, and so it was done," Aleck said.

"The arrest? Did Pitlinnie put the excise on us?" Ronan asked sharply.

"He might have arranged it."

Ronan thought of Dawson, the excise officer who had led the ambush and arrest in Culross. He was not to be trusted. "What else?"

"Pitlinnie tells his men you are more than you seem, and dangerous. He says you will inherit Darrach and claim the credit and profit for whisky-making in these glens. Says all whisky-men in this region should beware Glenbrae once he becomes Darrach."

"I see," Ronan said. "All lies. Let me know what more you find out."

"He said you are a wolf among sheep."

"You two are hardly sheep. Keep quiet and stay smart. It will protect you."

Geordie nodded. "Sir, we saw him recently near Invermorie. He saw Aleck and me and told us you are ruined. Told us we can earn good coin by joining his lot. Aleck refused straightaway. But I—I am thinking about it."

"Soon you will be a married man, and someday have a family to support. So you want to build a life. It is understandable."

"But I am loyal to you, sir."

"I appreciate it."

"Sir, if we ever need an advocate in court, would you stand up for us?" he asked.

"If you go with Pitlinnie, lad, you may well need me one day," Ronan drawled.

"I do not want to go over to him," Geordie said. "But his runs are profitable."

"They are. Tell me, how does Pitlinnie know anything about me?"

"From your sister-in-law, Mairi Brodie," Aleck said. "He visits as a neighbor and treats her well. He makes himself useful and is wooing her."

"He wants to marry her?" Ronan narrowed his eyes.

"If she would agree," Aleck said. "What he wants is all of Glenbrae, including Invermorie. Mairi Brodie is a way to get that." He swept an arm northward.

Marrying Will's widow would level a direct blow against Ronan. "That cannot happen."

"We hope not. Do you have work for us, sir?" Aleck asked. "We have not moved Glenbrae whisky over the hills since you and your lads got locked away. We sell through the shops in Kinross and Perth. Legitimate but slow to put coin in our pockets."

"Best keep a low profile for now. When the tax laws change next year, there will be little profit from illicit trade, and harsher penalties. You will make more legitimately."

"What is harsher than hanging?" Geordie asked. "Or being pistol-shot on a hillside, like your brother and cousin?" He spit on the ground.

Ronan felt a muscle pump in his cheek. "The laws will help legal distilleries." He was loath to scare them, so promoted the tax laws as promising, even if they were not.

"Is the free trade done?" Geordie asked.

"Nearly."

"Just as well." Aleck echoed Ronan's tone like a lad after his father. At times, Ronan had felt like an older brother, even a father, to these two.

"Lads, keep an eye on our goods. Let me know what Pitlinnie does."

"If I went over to Pitlinnie's crew, I could learn more," Geordie said.

"I would never send you into the fire. If your cousins will share information, take no more risk than that. And watch their backs as well as your own. Kin are kin." Geordie and Aleck nodded, looking relieved.

"We will check the goods stored near Darrach Castle soon as we can," Aleck said.

"Good. I will need your help to move them and arrange shipment to Edinburgh. It must arrive in time for the king's arrival."

"The king!" Aleck said.

"A gift from the Scots." Succinct was best. "The king enjoys Highland whisky."

"That is good for us!" Geordie grinned. "Though any Highland peat-reek the king drinks surely came to London through smuggling. And that's a fine joke."

Ronan chuckled. "Indeed. You can find me at Strathniven House for now."

"Auld Rabbie told us. You have fine friends, sir," Aleck said.

"Aye." Ronan stepped back, raised a hand.

"Glenbrae," Geordie said, "watch your back."

"I will." He crossed the yard toward the hotel.

ELLISON SIPPED THE last of her tea, listening to Sorcha, and trying to quell a thread of fear. The young Highlanders who had gone outside with MacGregor had a rough look to them. He had not returned. What if he met with trouble?

What if he was not trustworthy after all, as Papa and Corbie predicted? What if he ran and was never seen again? Yet he had asked her to trust him. She wanted to.

Suddenly he was there at the table, so close she felt the solid warmth of him. She glanced up. He looked grim, cheek muscle jumping, eyes shadowed and somber. She felt the urge to reach out, offer hope, be his remedy.

The moment was not the flash of lightning she might have expected. Nor was it flowery or romantic. Rather it was tender, a gentle, certain flow of realization. She felt an expansion within, and longed to reach out and touch his hand. Love filled her.

His gaze met hers like a caress. She glanced away before he could read her feelings, clear as bells and stars in her eyes.

"Miss Graham, Miss Beaton. Are you ready to depart? The bill is satisfied and MacNie waits with the carriage. Let me help." He picked up the wrapped packages, drew out Sorcha's chair, then Ellison's.

As they walked out, he touched her elbow lightly. The sensation lingered as she walked ahead, climbed into the carriage, and sat.

She was glad her bonnet shadowed her eyes, so that he would not see the revelation she felt within. So he would not know her silly, smitten heart.

They rode northward while Sorcha chattered about shops, dresses, tea and cakes, and plans for Edinburgh. Ronan murmured politely. His voice sank through her like hot whisky, honey, spice.

"You are quiet, Ellison," Sorcha said.

She caught Ronan's gaze, a searing blue flame. "I am tired. Just that."

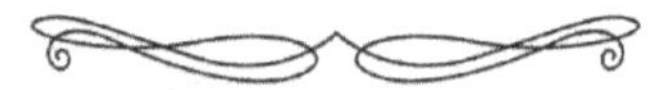

Chapter Fourteen

I HAVE A *secret—*

"Lord Darrach," said a soft, beautiful voice, "shall we—"

"I have a secret to disclose to you," said he, "which cannot be divulged—"

"Lord Darrach," Ellison repeated, "shall we discuss protocols for the royal visit?"

Ronan looked up from reading Jane Porter's novel, *Scottish Chiefs*. He had secrets too. He smiled at her while rain tapped against the windows.

"Miss Graham." Setting the book aside, he stood.

"Are you enjoying Miss Porter's book?" she asked.

"I am sure Ellison Graham writes just as well, just as brilliantly."

"Thank you." She smiled, a tiny dimple emerging. "You have not read my work."

"Someday I hope to. Is it time for our lesson?"

"Aye, we must review the protocols for the royal visit." He saw she held a copy of Scott's leather-bound booklet.

"Of course. Ah, Miss Beaton," he said, as Sorcha entered the parlor carrying a basket of stitchery work, ready to act the gentle chaperone.

"Sorcha, do join us. Reviewing the guidelines for the royal visit will help all of us."

"I am happy to, Elly," Sorcha said as she sat beside Ellison on a sofa near the window. Ronan felt reluctant to sit on the thing himself, for its delicately curved legs gave him pause. He preferred more solid furniture. Sorcha resumed her needlework and Ellison opened the book. He chose a sturdy chair covered in red tartan cloth.

"Studying etiquette is a suitably dull task for a rainy day," he said. "Proceed."

Sorcha giggled, but his pretty tutor gave him a scathing look. "We have work to do," Ellison said primly.

"I did want to ride out later, regardless of the rain." He could not stay cooped up inside for long, after months in a dungeon cell. Besides, a Highlander was accustomed to being out in any sort of weather. Today he wore trousers and coat again, but at least they were his own; Donal had fetched them along with the rest of his Highland kit.

"Will you tour your Darrach estate, sir? I would love to see it," Sorcha said.

"It is a distance from here. He may be too busy." Ellison arrowed a look that warned him not to take the viscount ruse too far. He needed no reminder.

"If you would both like to tour the countryside, I will show you a pretty loch not far from here. Perhaps Donal would come with us." He noticed Sorcha brighten at the mention of Donal, a handsome, engaging lad near her own age. "We could go fishing."

"Could we do that tomorrow?" Sorcha asked eagerly.

"Perhaps," Ellison clipped out. For some reason, she was not pleased with him. Did she worry he might indulge in a bit of smuggling if left to wander outside? He twisted his mouth sourly.

"We can catch fish," he said.

"I do not want to catch fish," Ellison replied, wrinkling her nose.

"I will show you the Highland method of fishing. It's just the sort of thing one might read about in a book," he added teasingly.

As he suspected, her eyes sparkled at the prospect of research.

"Perhaps."

"Tomorrow, then, if the weather suits."

"Wonderful!" Sorcha, who easily radiated enthusiasm, beamed.

"Then it is settled. I will speak to Donal Brodie."

"Perhaps Mrs. Barrow will pack a luncheon basket." Ellison opened the book. "Now, let us discuss what is expected once the king arrives. Let me see." She traced a finger over one page, the next. "Here. The Lord Provost and magistrates, with the sheriff and other officials, will meet the royal party when the king disembarks at Leith Harbor. The ancient keys of the city will be presented to King George, and the Edinburgh cavalry will lead the progress from Leith to Holyrood Palace . . . Darrach, are you listening?"

"Aye, madam," he drawled, opening one eye. Sorcha laughed.

"Gentlemen are expected to wear a blue coat, white waist-coat, and white or nankeen pantaloons. This can be got up handsomely for an inconsiderable cost, it says."

"I may have to miss this momentous occasion," he remarked.

"You would look fine in that outfit."

"I doubt anyone would look well in that. Besides, I am not expected to attend that part of the festivities."

"True," Ellison agreed. "My father will be there, but we can stay away."

"There will be a large assembly of Highlanders in full regalia," Sorcha said. "Will you join your clan, Lord Darrach?"

"If MacGregor of Clan Gregor summons me, I must answer." He doubted it.

"In plaid, bonnet, feathers and all?" Sorcha smiled. "So romantic! Ellison, do you not agree Lord Darrach would be the grandest fellow there?"

"Grand indeed," Ellison said, pink rising in her cheeks. "Some may elect to wear Highland dress, but Papa and other gentlemen will wear formal black and white."

"We must comply, I suspect," he said.

"Highland gear is a display of the pride and dignity of Scotland," she said. "But I wonder if King George can appreciate the pride and tradition in the Scottish character."

"He might try," Ronan allowed.

Ellison still looked prim, a curious mood for her, he thought. "Back to the protocols," she said, turning a page.

"Fire away, Miss Graham. Lord Darrach is fascinated," Ronan drawled. Sorcha giggled again, but their petite and earnest teacher sent him a withering look.

He must stop teasing her, he thought. The ruse distressed her, from her role as tutor to his as viscount, her father's involvement, and Ronan's casual air too. But it could not be helped now. And since humor could make her eyes sparkle, he would try.

"Very few Scots have met the king or any royalty, unless they have attended court in London," Ellison said.

"Then tell us, what fancy steps and phrases must we backward Scots learn?"

"Sir," she warned gently, "do take this seriously."

"Madam, I do." He met her eyes directly.

"Papa says notable gentlemen will be invited to a levee at Holyrood Palace the day after the king arrives. You will receive an invitation, sir. It will come to Papa's office, and you and Mr. Corbie will be in his party to attend the gentlemen's levee."

"Mr. Corbie too. How exciting," he murmured.

Sorcha, stitching away, looked up. "Will ladies be invited to this as well?"

"A separate assembly will be held for ladies, with gentlemen escorting them. An evening ball is also planned for another evening."

"It truly is exciting!" Sorcha said. "Darrach, will you attend the ladies' assembly?"

"My invitation may only be to the gentlemen's levee."

"Surely you will be asked, as a Highland viscount!"

"Papa will make the arrangements for Darrach," Ellison said. "You will be introduced there, and Papa will do that. Guests can only be introduced to the king by someone who has previously met him. Papa will be introduced to him when he arrives," she went on. "Or you could give your card to the Lord-in-Waiting, who can present you."

"My card?"

"You will need a few. Mr. Corbie is having some printed up for you."

"Very helpful. Ah, Balor, come to join us!" Glad of the interruption, Ronan patted his knee as the little terrier trotted into the room and came straight to him.

"Will Lady Strathniven introduce us, Ellison?" Sorcha asked.

"I believe so. She will be introduced before we will. When a person is introduced," Ellison went on, consulting the booklet, "they approach the royal dais between the lines of dignitaries, attendants, cabinet ministers, and so on. A lady must curtsy deeply to the king. A gentleman will drop the right knee and kiss the king's hand."

"What then?" Ronan stroked the dog's warm, silky coat, feeling the rapid little heartbeats under his hand. He needed to know what to expect after the introduction.

"The crowd will be so great that each person must move forward. But guests must never turn their backs to the king when departing."

"And this takes but a few moments?"

"Sir Walter says here that introductions take less than a minute."

"And then it is done."

"Aye," she replied softly, watching him.

"And Lord Darrach will wear full Highland dress," Sorcha reminded them.

Ellison nodded. "Gentlemen must wear full dress. Those who have an officer's rank may wear their uniform, and Highland gentleman may wear their regalia."

"Lord Darrach, do you have an officer's rank, by chance?" Sorcha asked.

"Actually I do." He felt Ellison's quick, curious gaze. He had never mentioned it, nor was it in any of the documents Sir Hector had regarding him.

"Do you!" Ellison's lips formed a sweet, bewildered moue. He wanted to kiss that mouth, but pulled his attention back to the moment.

"I do, but prefer Highland gear, and have a choice," he said simply.

"This says," she went on, cheeks pink, "any gentleman with the right to Highland costume as a chief or chieftain must wear proper Highland gear."

"How does Scott define it?" Ronan ruffled the dog's ears.

"Highland gentlemen may wear feathers in their bonnets— three eagle feathers for a clan chief, two for a chieftain, one for a Highland laird."

"A single black feather suits if one carries a grudge," Ronan added.

"I would not advise that," she said crisply.

"Some might be tempted. Go on."

"Full Highland costume, bonnet, sporran—and weapons. Those who wear Highland dress can also be armed in proper Highland fashion. That means steel pistols, broadsword, and dirk." She made a wry face.

Ronan cocked a brow. "Armed in the king's presence?"

Sorcha looked horrified. "How savage!"

"Anyone carrying weapons will be very cautious," Ronan said.

"I hope so," Ellison said curtly. "And Highland chiefs and chieftains will attend 'with their tail on'—that is, attended by their followers."

"Is the chief of Clan Gregor your kinsman, Lord Darrach?" Sorcha asked.

"A cousin, Miss Beaton."

"Papa said the MacGregor chief will lead the entire Highland procession when the Honors of Scotland are moved from Edinburgh Castle to Holyroodhouse to be kept there during the royal visit," Ellison said.

"How exciting this will all be!" Sorcha said.

"Very," Ronan murmured. He doubted Sir Evan would welcome him in his tail of MacGregors. He rubbed the dog's head thoughtfully.

"Balor is very attached to you," Ellison said. "It will break his heart when you go."

"Mine too," he murmured.

She stood suddenly, hems falling softly around her feet. Ronan set the dog down and stood too.

"Sorcha," Ellison said, "we should discuss the protocol for the ladies' assembly."

"We will. And I cannot wait to see my silk gown and feather headdress."

"Ladies, I will leave you to talk of feathers and silks. Thank you for the advice, Miss Graham. I am the better gentleman for it."

Ellison turned. Those eyes, those lips, that look of candor and something more. He felt the power of it push through him, heart and soul.

He spun for the door, terrier at his heels.

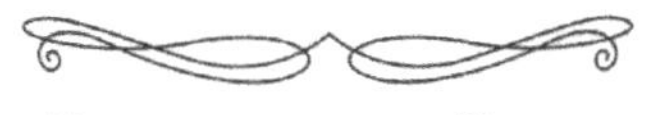

Chapter Fifteen

"IT IS A lovely morning." Ellison surveyed the blue haze of the sky arching over heather-purple hills, and smiled at Ronan as he strolled beside her.

"Beautiful," he agreed, looking only at her. A breeze stirred his wrapped plaid and bared shirtsleeves. The simple Highland costume suited a day of fishing.

She smiled shyly, staying close though his arm bumped hers as he carried the fishing poles over his shoulder. "Yesterday's rain seems to have washed the heat from the air," she said.

"Washed the midges away as well, if we are lucky."

"You were right about today," she admitted.

"The weather, the fishing, or the midges?"

"All of it."

"I hope my tutor is pleased with me, then." He smiled. Her heart leaped.

She laughed and stepped ahead, skirts swishing, to pick her way across the shale rocks that formed a natural pathway along the riverbank. Glancing over her shoulder, she saw the cart pulled by two sturdy Highland ponies, which Donal drove along an earthen track. Sorcha sat beside him, steadying the luncheon basket Mrs. Barrow had provided when they headed out that morning in Lady Strathniven's dogcart-like vehicle, which seated four on benches. The cart had enough room for fishing gear and baskets, and Donal was a competent driver, following over the hills and alongside the stream.

Now they went onward toward a tributary of water beyond a hill. Ellison had wanted to walk for a bit, tired of bumping along in the cart, and Ronan came with her.

Negotiating a rocky incline slippery with spray, she was glad of her plain gray muslin dress. Under the chemise, she had added pantelettes at Sorcha's suggestion, who had gone fishing before; the pantelettes could save modesty when stepping in the water. Ellison was also glad of the wide straw bonnet that gave her shade in the sunshine, and her leather boots and plaid shawl were practical and comfortable.

She had no intention of falling into the water that day, having done that recently to her embarrassment. Instead, she planned to sketch and read while the others splashed about. Just being outside on a glorious day, enjoying fresh air and sunshine and a sense of freedom was enough. Being near Ronan was enough too, for now.

"I can teach you to fish today," he said. "You might prefer the pole, but the Highland manner is more effective and enjoyable."

"They jump into the water to grab fish! I would rather watch you do that while I sketch." She threw out an arm for balance as she walked over the damp rocks. On one shoulder, she carried a linen rucksack with sketchbook, journal, and graphite pencils.

"I might enjoy seeing you jump in after a fish," Ronan said.

"I would be wet all day if I did that."

She saw the twinkle in his glance. "Wet, but happy. If I teach you properly, you will not get too wet."

She waved an arm. "I am enjoying freedom right now, as are you. Oh dear, I am sorry. I did not mean—"

"Free from prison?" He reached out to offer a steadying hand. "I am grateful for it, lass. And glad for a respite from lessons with my strict teacher."

"I should end your lessons entirely," she retorted. "Your English is perfect and your manners would hold up under anyone's scrutiny."

"See how much I have learned from you." He supported her elbow as she followed a descending stack of rocks. The rush of the river kept their conversation private, and the brace of his fingers felt good. Too good.

"Donal can fish with you. I will sit in the shade. Sorcha might fish though." She waited as Donal drew the vehicle along the track near where they walked.

"Miss Beaton, would you rather fish or sketch?" Ronan called.

"Fish!" Sorcha returned. "My father taught me how."

"If you would rather read," he told Ellison, "stay nearby." He shot her a quick concerned look and pointed toward a grove of trees ahead. Near the trees, a branch of the river diverted into a peaceful stream. "We can stop here."

Donal drove the cart toward the trees and helped Sorcha out of the vehicle as Ronan and Ellison caught up to them. Then Donal led the ponies into the cover of the trees and situated them, released their harnesses, and tied them securely to graze.

"Over there," Donal said, pointing toward the water, "the fishing is very good."

Entering the grove of birch trees, Ellison found a place to sit to watch the tributary that cut through banks feathered with trees and grasses. Beyond the water, wide flowery meadows met blue-misted hills far in the distance.

"Ronan," she said as he came near. "Could there be danger out here? Do smugglers come through those hills?"

"Sometimes, but usually at night. It is not so common as you fear."

"The men you met in Kinross the other day looked used to rough business."

"They are Rabbie Muir's grandsons. Good lads."

"Your business with them seemed important."

"Sir Hector wants a good deal of whisky delivered for the king's visit. It is not easy to arrange transport. I must have help."

"Does it involve a smuggling route?" A gust of wind blew past and she put a hand to her bonnet.

"If free trade proves the fastest way to do this, so be it. The king will have his whisky, and your father his moment of glory."

"Papa is not doing this for royal attention. And I only asked because I fear harm might come to you."

"Do not worry about me, lass," he murmured.

She lifted her chin. "But I do."

He gazed down at her, calm and strong, and said nothing.

"I just do not want trouble for you—or any of us," she continued.

"It will be fine. Look, those two are down in the water already and will have all the fish. Are you sure you want to stay here?"

She nodded. "Go ahead. I will be fine."

He hesitated, then murmured assent and went down to the water. Ellison settled with the sketchbook, looking up as Sorcha called out laughing and Donal splashed into the water, kilted and bare-legged, to grab after a fish, nearly falling into the water. Ronan's laughter boomed out, and Ellison watched, then returned to her drawings.

But hearing their laughter, seeing the sunlight sparkle on the water, she watched, her sketch less interesting than the three laughing and playing a stone's throw from where she sat.

Taking up her pencil again, she sketched the burn, flowing between banks softened by grasses and wildflowers, and added three figures in the water. Smudging the graphite with a finger, she captured the textures and was pleased. But again her attention was drawn to the others.

"Hush it, or you two will scare all fish away," Ronan called.

Snapping the sketchbook closed, Ellison stood and went down to the water's edge. Donal waved and Sorcha turned. "Ellison! Come into the water!"

Standing apart, shin-deep in the burn, Ronan gestured to her. She wanted to be near him—but hesitated, feeling that she should keep her distance.

More and more, she was aware of her attraction to him, and

how much she liked his company and wanted to know more about him. More and more, she knew she was falling in love, and that, above all else, made her hold back. What she wanted simply could not be. What she felt was a fantasy; she must not fall foolishly in love again.

She shook her head. He shrugged, stepping through the clear water, the current spilling around his bare, muscular legs. She watched, yearned, glanced away.

At the pebbly shore, Ronan took up a fishing pole and waded deeper. When the taut curve of the fishing rod showed something on the string, he pulled back sharply and a fish flew upward, then wriggled free, splashing into the water. Tossing the pole aside, he bent forward, hunched still as a statue.

Curious, Ellison moved forward. He stood focused, water swirling around his sturdy calves, and bent slowly, cupping his hands over the water. A ripple of golden-brown flashed beneath the surface, and Ronan dipped his hands quickly, then straightened with a floundering fish in his grasp. He tossed it toward the bank, and it landed just at Ellison's feet.

Leaping away, she stumbled, ankle rolling so that she stepped inadvertently into the water, sinking to one knee with a surge and a splash. Quickly Ronan reached her, fingers strong on her arm to keep her upright. "Here, lass, come up! Good?"

"Good, thank you." Standing full in the water now, her gown's hem swirling around her legs, she lifted the soggy hem of her dress a bit and raised one foot, her boot drenched and dripping. "Oh, dear."

"Sit down over here." He guided her to the grassy bank.

"I must take off my boots," she said, sitting, gown sopping around her.

"And stockings. Let them dry in the sun."

Unlacing her boots, she paused, unwilling to remove her high stockings while he stood there.

"If you will go barefoot like a Highland lass, you can learn the way of true Highland fishing."

"I just saw you demonstrate that." She laughed.

"Try it for yourself. For your story, aye? Take off the stockings and such and I will look away." He turned.

Hearing peals of laughter downstream, Ellison glanced to see Donal, knee-deep in the stream, grab at a fish, miss it, and fall into the water with a shout. Laughing, Sorcha surged forward to help and stumbled knee-deep too. Ronan laughed to see them.

Suddenly Ellison felt hesitation fade. She pulled off her shoes, drew off her wet stockings, and set them on the grass to dry. Her father was not here to criticize her, nor would anyone here make her feel less for what she did. Standing, she walked past Ronan and stepped barefoot into the water, shivering at the chill. Lifting her drenched hem, she moved through the burbling flow. The water was cool and soft, the rocks smooth and mossy underfoot.

"Good lass," Ronan said behind her.

"It feels wonderful," she admitted. He chuckled, touched her arm briefly, a friendly, affectionate brush of his fingers.

Then Sorcha stumbled and Donal helped her up, both laughing freely. Ronan shaded his eyes and laughed to see them. That warm sound won her over entirely.

"Very well, Ronan MacGregor. Show me how to catch a Highland fish."

ONCE AGAIN, RONAN glanced toward the hills beyond the trees along the bank. Though he had made light of the threat of smugglers, he remained vigilant. He knew too well what could happen out here.

"Now I understand why Highland men wear the plaid and go barelegged into the water to fish," Ellison said.

"Aye so," he agreed. "Careful now, the rocks are slippery." He extended a hand behind her, ready to catch her if she stumbled.

"When I stand to wait for the fish, my dress gets in the way, and the fish go by without me even seeing them." She bunched her skirts in one hand, fabric trailing and floating around her.

"Highland women hitch their skirts high." He mimicked a wrapping gesture.

"Like this?" Leaning down, she pulled the back of her skirt forward between her legs, then drew it up and over the front to tuck the damp fabric into her ribbon belt. Her lacy-edged pantaloons, he saw, exposed her neatly shaped calves, ankles, and slim feet. Her small toes were darling somehow, flexing under the clear water. He smiled.

"Aye, just like that," he said, as his mind conjured images best not pursued.

Her straw bonnet tipped forward, damp golden curls tumbling over her shoulder. She straightened, straw brim partly hiding her face. "How is this?"

He lifted the brim with a finger. "Without the bonnet you will see more fish."

She undid those ribbons, and Ronan took the hat to fling it toward the bank. Ellison bent forward and waved her hands about above the water.

"Those fish had best look out for me now," she muttered.

He laughed with delight. "You are enjoying this."

She giggled, then went still, her gaze trained on the rippling water. "So this is how they fished in ancient Scotland?"

"Then and now, though other ways are more common."

"I like the old ways. And I like Highland fashion." She pulled at the wet, tucked skirt. "It is like the loose trousers that ladies in harems wear. I have seen illustrations."

"You would be an enticing sultana, swathed in silks and jewels."

"There's freedom in it. I would like that."

He would like it, too. Here and now, barefoot and drenched, curls loose, sun already pinkening her nose, she was utterly beautiful to him. Whimsical and joyful, too, when she allowed herself to be. He felt his spirit lift, and felt the urge to kiss her, love her, share easy days like this with her. He understood the way she enjoyed this taste for freedom. He yearned for it too, the sort of freedom that could lead to genuine happiness.

"Here comes one," she said softly.

"Hush," he whispered.

As she surged through the water, bending, missing, laughing, persistent, Ronan walked behind her. He held a hand out protectively, though she did not see. He would not let her stumble or fall. He wanted to be there for her, until the day he could not be.

LATER, HE GLANCED up when something caught his attention on the nearest hill. Did something move up there? Ronan narrowed his eyes, watching. Perhaps it was just wind blowing through the pine trees climbing the slope, and rocking the purple froth of heather. Earlier he had seen sheep grazing all along that hill. But whatever moved up there now was not a large, slow sheep. He frowned.

Time to return to Strathniven, he thought. They had been out most of the day, had fished, picnicked in the shade, fished again. The sun had reached its zenith and was sinking. Right, then. "Ellison."

She was splashing through the water, hands out to grapple with a fish bigger than any they had taken so far. A trout, by its rainbow flash. Ronan sloshed toward her.

"Elly, that rascal will pull you in—let me help—"

"*Ach!* Gone! I nearly had him!" She slapped the water and straightened.

"Is this the lass who would not fish today?" He laughed, but his glance strayed toward the hill even then.

"I like fishing better than I thought. Do you see something up there?"

"Naught. Have you had your fill of the fishing? We should leave."

"Must we?"

"You have become adept and give the fish no quarter. You outfished even Donal."

"We have had a wonderful day!" Holding her soggy skirts, she came toward him, neat little knees pushing through the flow.

"So we have. Donal! Here!" He waved, and his nephew waved back as he helped Sorcha up the bank to gather the fish they had caught and tossed to the bank. Ronan and Ellison did the same, putting fish in the baskets. Then, like Sorcha, Ellison let down her wet, tucked skirts and sat to put on her stockings and shoes.

"I am fair wet, but it is warm in the sun," she said.

"You will soon feel the chill. Here." Ronan picked up her plaid shawl from the grass and wrapped it about her shoulders. Thanking him, she pulled on her stockings.

"MacGregor, look away," she admonished.

"I have seen your limbs all day under the water," he said, but turned around. Plucking up her bonnet, he handed it to her when she stood, and she tied its ribbons. The straw's weave cast a golden glow over her lightly sunburned nose and cheeks.

"Your nose is pink. A lovely color," he said, thinking she looked joyful and beautiful. "You needed some sun."

She smiled, securing the bow under her chin. "I wish we could stay."

"Another time." He was reluctant to leave too, savoring this time with her. July had already slipped into August. Soon their days together would end.

Donal carried a basket in each hand as he trudged toward the grove where the ponies waited placidly. Once there, Ronan and Donal harnessed the animals to the cart while Sorcha and Ellison settled the baskets inside and climbed up to the seats.

Ellison paused, shaded her eyes, looked up the hill. "Something moved up there. Did you hear that sound?"

Frowning, Ronan studied the slope where he had seen something moving earlier. "Perhaps a small animal. We should go."

She hurried past him. "I will just see."

"Stay here," Ronan told Donal and Sorcha, and turned to follow Ellison up the long slope, parting a sea of heather blooms as they went. She ran ahead, damp skirts flapping, bonnet sliding back, hair loose golden ropes. With his longer stride, he caught up near the top, where she had paused.

Then she cried out and ran, dropping to her knees in a tangle of brush and heather. Following, he heard a bleating sound.

"What's this?" He sank to a knee beside her.

"Look! A lamb—a wee one, caught here." She pushed at a cluster of undergrowth to reveal a small white lamb, trembling, curled, little face poking out.

"Wandered away from your mam, did you?" he murmured as the little creature bleated and struggled to stand. "And fell into heather and gorse, wee rascal. It will take some time to free it," he told Ellison. "The shepherd will be looking for it once he counts his flock, or notices that one of the ewes is upset."

"We cannot leave him here. A wolf could find him."

"Wolves have been gone from Scotland for a hundred years or more, they say." He reached past her to pull carefully at the gorse, its branches ripe with wicked thorns and small yellow flowers.

She pulled, too, freeing thin branches snarled in the lamb's coat, wincing as a thorn pricked her. "There, my dear, we will— *oww!*—have you out soon. Oww! How old is the lamb, Ronan?"

"Perhaps two months," he said, judging the solid little body, its new coat, the shape of its head, the large eyes and small snout. "Be still now," he told the lamb. "This lady wants you free, and we do what she wants, hey. Ah, he is a she," he said, freeing a small leg.

"Sweet lassie! We are nearly done, my darling," Ellison said.

"She is fair calm. She must be used to people." Ronan ran his hand over the animal's head, soothing the ears, patting the little belly.

"She knows we are helping her." Ellison pulled at the thorny, flowery gorse. "Ow!"

"Gorse is pretty, but it has a bite." Finally the branches bounced free, and Ronan scooped up the lamb and stood. Taking off her shawl, Ellison tucked it around the creature.

Glancing down, Ronan saw red streaks on his fingers and drew back the shawl. "She has quite a gash on one hind leg."

"What should we do?" Ellison patted the little head.

He made a quick decision. "Mairi Brodie lives nearby. She treats illness and wounds. I will take the lamb there while you return to Strathniven with the others."

She shook her head. "I want to go with you. Is it far?"

"Three miles or so across the glen. You would be safer going back."

"If you mean smugglers, I would like to meet some—for my book." Her eyes flashed with determination and courage. Though warmed to see that strength in her, he could not risk any harm coming to her. He felt an eerie sense of trouble nearby.

"Trust me, madam, you do not want to meet that sort."

"I met you."

He huffed. "Fair enough. But I am a nicer sort."

"Sometimes. But if you are with me, all will be well. Please," she added.

Her faith in him touched him unexpectedly. She wanted adventure, a challenge to test her mettle, and he would not discourage that. Yet he had a strong urge to protect her from danger. Looking at her big bonny eyes, he sighed.

"Very well. I will at least know you are safe if we all go to-gether."

"Oh my dearie," she cooed sweetly to the lamb. Something melted inside him.

"Come on." He spoke curtly to dispel the feeling and headed down the slope, the lamb shaking like a sapling in his arms, Ellison keeping pace.

"A lamb!" Donal said as they drew near. Ellison explained quickly. "Should we look for the flock?"

"Later," Ronan said. "This one was separated from its mam and injured her leg. She cannot walk, and we cannot leave her prey to a wildcat or some rogue wanting a bit of tender shank for supper. I want to take her to Mairi Brodie," he added.

"She is at Invermorie now, but I could fetch her over to Strathniven," Donal said.

"This wee bit needs attention now. We will hurry to Invermorie."

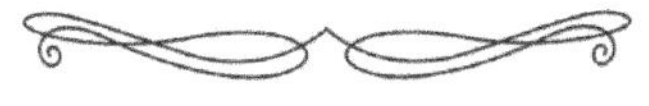

Chapter Sixteen

BUILT OF FIELDSTONE, Invermorie Castle overlooked a hillside thick with heather and gorse to one side, with a precipitous rocky slope to the other. Ellison remembered seeing this castle at a distance and recalled a woman crossing the yard.

"That slope looks a treacherous climb," she said, touching the lamb's little head. "The castle looks quite old."

"And formidable in its day. The eastern incline leads to the gate. We will go that way," he said as Donal guided the cart along.

"Donal's mother lives here, you said. Will she welcome visitors? I know it is Highland custom, but one never knows."

"She will." He spoke quietly. "Mairi is my brother's widow."

Startled, she stared at him. "Your sister-in-law? But that means—Donal is your nephew? You never mentioned."

"He was assigned as my valet. I thought it rather awkward."

"My father need not know," she said quickly. "Mrs. Barrow mentioned Mairi Brodie. A healer, she said, who helps people throughout the glens here."

"She is skilled with herbal remedies and such, aye. And helps animals as well as people. She will know what to do for your lamb."

"Donal and his mother live at Invermorie, which is—your castle, as Glenbrae?"

"Aye." He sounded curt.

"May I hold the lamb?" she asked, and he shifted the blanketed weight into her arms. The creature slept as they rode on. Ellison looked up at the castle and wondered about the laird's family living there when he did not, for he kept a small house at the distillery, as she had learned earlier. What did the widow Mairi Brodie mean to him? She sensed something in his voice, in the way he held back the truth and did not meet her curious glance.

Soon Donal halted the cart before the castle entrance just as an older gentleman came through the arched doorway. He was white-haired, wearing an old patched frock coat of pale blue with saggy knee-breeches, hose, and red slippers. Grinning, he waved.

"Donal!" He waited as Donal handed Sorcha Beaton to the ground and handed the reins to a young boy who ran across the dusty yard to take the horses. "And—is that Glenbrae?"

Ronan stepped down, turning. "Sir Ludo! Good to see you!"

"It is you! Where are my spectacles," Sir Ludo muttered, patting his old-fashioned coat, finding a pair of eyeglasses and perching them on his nose. "This is a surprise! Have you come to stay? And who are these pretty lassies? Is that a child in that plaidie?"

Taking the lamb, Ronan handed Ellison down. "A lamb," Ronan said, drawing back the cloth. "It is injured. We came to see if Mairi could tend to it."

"She will. And here I was thinking ye had a wife and child at last!" He clapped Ronan's shoulder. "You are wet. Did it rain? I thought it was a fine day." He looked up at the sky. "Well, come inside and Mairi will sort you out. First introduce me to these ladies."

"Sir Ludovic Brodie, this is Miss Ellison Graham and Miss Sorcha Beaton. Ladies, this is Donal's grandfather."

"Pleased to meet you, sir," Ellison said, as Sorcha murmured the same.

"And I am pleased to make your acquaintance, ladies," Sir Ludo said, taking each one's hand in turn with a broad smile.

"Welcome. Graham and Beaton! Two fine Scottish names. What part of Scotland are your people from?"

"Sir Ludo is writing a history of Scotland and is keen on family trees," Ronan said.

"Fife, I believe, sir," Sorcha said. "My grandfather said ours was an ancient line."

"The Bethune line, perhaps. And Miss Graham? There are many branches of Grahams. The first to come to Scotland were French. Norman, you see."

"My great-great-grandparents were from Strathearn, sir," Ellison said.

"Who is your father? I know many Grahams. Is he of Strathearn as well?"

"My father is Sir Hector Graham. We live in Edinburgh."

"The Deputy Lord Provost! Glenbrae, we are in fine company indeed. I know the name, but not the man. I must write this down. I keep a record of Highland lines when I can. Where is my journal and my wee pencil too," he muttered, scrabbling in his pockets to extract a notebook and pencil stub.

"Sir Ludo, you will have Miss Graham's heart with your scholarship," Ronan said as the old man led them toward the entrance while Donal ran ahead to open the door.

"Strathniven and now Beatons and Grahams! Excellent! Glenbrae, Donal told us of your circumstances." Sir Ludo cocked a bushy white brow.

"I will tell you the rest, but first we must get this lamb into Mairi's care. We found it in the hills above the Lealtie Burn where we were fishing."

"So that is why you are all damp-like. Did you bring fish for supper?"

"We did, and are happy to share. So Mairi Brodie is at home?"

"This is your home, lad. And of course she is here."

Puzzled, Ellison wondered at Sir Ludo's remark as they went through a second door and entered a foyer.

The castle room was wide, high, and cool, with a tiled floor and wooden staircase to one side, a stone fireplace to the other, and vaulted ceiling over all. Stained glass in tall windows cast rainbows over the floor. Hearing a step, Ellison saw a woman coming down the staircase.

She glided, slim and graceful and beautiful in a plaid green gown and rumpled apron, black braids wrapped around her head. She crossed the foyer, lovely as a medieval Madonna, her brown eyes as warm as her smile.

"Ronan!" She ran to him, arms out. He extended an arm to welcome her into an embrace, holding the bundled lamb close in the other arm.

"Mairi!" He kissed her cheek.

Ellison blinked, feeling the sudden dip of disappointment and bewilderment.

"I did not expect to see you! Donal said you might not have time to visit." Resting a hand on Ronan's chest, she turned to her son, who shrugged shyly. "Wicked, the pair of you, for not telling me you were coming today."

"Sorry, Mother. We did not plan it, but Glenbrae said we must find you when we were down by the Lealtie Burn. The lamb is wounded, you see."

"Oh, poor dear!" Mairi peeked into the blanket as Ronan and Donal explained what had happened. "Of course I will take care of her, you need not even ask."

Watching them, seeing the affection there, Ellison shrank a little, feeling a bit diminished. They were close. They were family. She was glad for Ronan's sake, yet what she sensed between him and Mairi sobered the tiny hope she had been nurturing.

"Will you be here long?" Mairi asked Ronan. "We knew you were—in Edinburgh. But my heart leaps to see you. Now you are home, will you stay?"

Home, Ellison thought. He was home. She was glad for him. Though he had kissed her passionately, truly, the other evening, and though she felt closer to him, he had not mentioned family nearby. He had so many secrets, she thought, and might never let her into his circle. She bit her lip softly.

"I must return to the city soon. We will talk later. Let me introduce my friends, Miss Ellison Graham and Miss Sorcha Beaton."

Friend. Ellison smiled, stepping forward to greet Mairi. "It is good to meet you, Mrs. Brodie."

"Welcome to Invermorie." Mairi took the girls' hands. "Do call me Mairi."

"Ellison," she responded. "And Sorcha."

"Miss Graham is the daughter of the deputy lord provost," Sir Ludovic said proudly. "And Miss Beaton is related to the Bethunes of Fife. We are privileged in our guests today."

"It is an honor. But your clothes are damp! We must let you get dry and rest a little. Will you have tea? Donal," she directed, "carry the lamb into my workroom and I will be right there." She turned back. "Miss Graham, Miss Beaton, come sit by the hearth, and we shall fetch blankets and tea. Glenbrae, you too."

As Donal left the room with the lamb, Mairi took a few moments to make sure they were cozy by the hearth. She built it up with kindling on top of the peat bricks to coax warmth more quickly, and handed blankets around despite the summer day. Ellison sighed in the comfort, feeling her things begin to dry even as she wore them.

Watching Mairi, she felt surprised to learn that the beautiful young woman was old enough to be Donal's mother, and was, like herself, a widow. Mairi was special to Ronan—that was clear—and Ellison liked her immediately. Yet she could not shake a twinge of jealousy even as she wanted to feel grateful.

THE GREAT HALL was just as shabby and antique as he remembered, with heavy leather-seated chairs, stiff old red sofa, worn rugs scattered on planked floors, whitewash peeling in places on stone walls. He loved every drafty, crumbling, threadbare bit of it.

Smiling, Ronan looked around at his childhood home while Sir Ludo chatted with Ellison and Sorcha. Ever congenial, Ludo urged them to take more tea, have a scone, an oatcake, Mairi's rowanberry jam, and tell him all they knew about their family histories. Leaning back, Ronan was content to listen and savor the place and the company. It felt so good to be back.

He had grown up at Invermorie, the castle seat of Glenbrae, had spent countless hours in this room and everywhere in the castle and on the grounds. Every hill and tree and rocky incline were dear to him.

But he had left Invermorie when he had seen his intended, the beautiful young widow Mairi Brodie, kissing his younger brother; he had walked out when he had seen how fervently she returned Will's embrace, realized how desperately they whispered and clung together. Packing his things, he had sent a message to his cousins, the MacGregor chief and his son, that he would join Evan in the military. Then he informed his father of his decision to leave his apprenticeship in the law for a while to seek travel and adventure. He had not really wanted that. He had wanted the law, and a quiet Highland life with Mairi and her wee son, Donal, from her first brief marriage.

He had changed in the time he had been away. Years in the Highland Black Watch and military duties eventually took him from the Continent to India. He changed regiments to follow his cousin, Sir Evan MacGregor, an officer sent to India.

That led to a day he wished he could erase from memory: a savage attack, Sir Evan's severe wounding and rescue as Ronan and others barely managed to escape alive. Returning to Scotland months later to take Evan home, he resumed the practice of law and found himself laird of Glenbrae after his father's death.

All that time, he did his best to avoid his brother and his sister-in-law. Yet he was fond of Mairi's Donal. Had he married her,

Ronan would have adopted the boy as his own. William did so instead, a good husband and father who made Ronan an uncle.

But then Will died on a rocky slope beside their cousin John MacGregor of Darrach, and Ronan had done what he could for Will's widow and son. He had brought them, along with Mairi's aging father, into his home at Invermorie. Then he moved into the cottage at the distillery—and took a path he had never planned—distiller and lawyer, aye, but smuggler too.

He closed off his heart from what was so dear to him, making sure they were fine and keeping his distance, though he was determined to provide whatever was needed.

His arrest then interrupted that obligation. Now he was back.

He looked up as Donal returned to the hall. "The fish are wrapped and cool in a bucket of water, but we must get them to Strathniven," Donal said. "Mrs. Barrow expects to cook fish for supper. We should go soon."

"Best go back with Miss Beaton and Miss Graham. Leave some fish here for their supper too. I will borrow a horse from the stable and follow later."

Nodding, Donal left the room, while Sir Ludo talked with Ellison and Sorcha, hardly taking a breath in his animated discussion of Highland history. While Sorcha listened politely, looking a bit bored, Ellison had a rapt expression. She was fascinated.

Ronan smiled, loath to interrupt. But they should be going. When Mairi entered the hall, he stood to meet her.

"How is the wee beast?"

"No bones broken, but her leg is sore injured. She should stay here for a bit and I will care for her. Donal seems in a rush to leave," she added.

"We must get back to Strathniven."

She nodded, her dark liquid eyes lingering on his. "Do you know which shepherd owns the wee lamb?"

"Donal will find him, but let her recover here. Thank you, Mairi."

"Aye. Ronan—" She touched his arm. "It is so good to see you."

"And you," he said gruffly.

"Is it the same? You are still so distant. I feel we can never quite talk." Her eyes searched his. He saw the glint of tears suddenly. "Will you never forgive me?"

He sighed, emotions tumbling. Behind him, he heard Ellison replying to Sir Ludo. He realized he was ever alert to her voice, her presence, ever wondering what she thought, how she felt. When had that happened? He drew his brows together.

His feelings for Mairi had been passionate, then ravaged by betrayal like a fire consuming him, hurting him deeply. He knew how deeply she had loved his brother. To her, Ronan was like a brother, a friend. Time had tempered his feelings, bringing him to acceptance and true friendship.

Yet only in that moment did he know he could finally let go. What he had begun to feel for Ellison Graham was fulsome and new, not like the frustrated passions of the past. He wondered when that change had occurred. He had not been aware of it, and yet it had happened.

"Ronan?" Mairi asked.

"Aye, forgiven," he murmured, bringing his thoughts back. "Do not fret."

She sighed. "And Donal?"

"I have always loved that lad, always will. He has your intelligence and heart."

"He wants to go to university and study medicine, did he tell you?"

"I hope to help him do that. My freedom is a bit in question as yet."

"But you are home now."

"Some conditions must be met. When all is resolved, I will be back."

"Good. This is your home, Ronan. But what of Linhope and MacInnes?"

"Still held in Edinburgh." He did not want to elaborate. Not yet.

"I hope they are released soon too. Listen, please," she said, her hand on his arm. "I know we hurt you. I hurt you," she clarified.

He shook his head. "It is not necessary now—"

"It is. I never seem to find a chance to tell you, because you spend so little time with me. I understand. But I know I made mistakes and I regret them. I could have been more honest with you. And yet you have always been good to us, despite all."

"You are my family." Now, he searched for a remnant of the wild love he had once felt for Mairi. Searched for the deep wound too. Both were gone, faded like a dream. Over the years he had healed and had not noticed. "It is I should ask forgiveness of you."

"You always had it. You never gave me a chance to tell you."

He nodded, humbled, then glanced at Ellison; she looked toward him, then away.

"You never married," Mairi said, following his glance.

"Not yet." He had never thought if it that way. *Not yet.*

"I like your Miss Graham. I see how you look at her. How she looks at you."

"She is a bright lass. Kind," he murmured. "She has been a friend. I am grateful."

"If you feel more than gratitude, give it a chance, Ronan. Give it time."

He shook his head. "I hold no hope of that."

"Life can surprise us." She drew a breath. "Ronan, you should know—I am thinking of marrying again."

He had heard the rumor from his friends and did not relish hearing the name. "Is it so?"

"I will tell you more when I decide for sure. He asked, and left me to consider it until he returns for my answer." She blushed.

"What will you say?" he asked quietly.

"I am thinking I will accept if he sincerely means it."

"A man does not ask unless he means it." Or sees some advantage for himself, he thought bitterly, knowing Pitlinnie's untrustworthy character.

"Here is Donal." She turned away. "The lamb will stay here for a while," she told her son as he approached them.

"Good. Sir, we should go back before it gets much later. We may not want to be traveling in these hills at such a time."

Ronan nodded, began to speak—and saw Ellison and Sorcha crossing the hall.

"How is the lamb?" Ellison asked, and Mairi quickly filled them in on her condition. "Thank you for taking care of her."

"I hear you deserve thanks for finding her. You saved her life," Mairi said.

"I am not sure, but I know that wee cry in the hills caught at my heartstrings."

"One should always follow their heart." Mairi looked at Ronan, her warm brown eyes telling him to listen. He nodded, wishing he could let his heart lead.

"We are leaving soon," he told Ellison.

"Thank you for your kindness, Mairi," Ellison said. "Oh! I just remembered—I left my things by the burn. When we found the lamb, I forgot. Can we fetch them?"

"Perhaps Donal and Miss Beaton could go on to Strathniven, since you should get that fresh fish to Mrs. Barrow," Mairi suggested. "Glenbrae could borrow our gig and take you to fetch your things." She sent Ronan a twinkling, mischievous look.

"If you like, Miss Graham," he said casually, though his heart quickened.

CALLING TO THE horse, Ronan drew up the reins as the two-seated gig slowed on the earthen drover's track. "You were sitting just down there, under those trees," he said, pointing toward the cluster of birches overlooking the burn where they had fished earlier. Climbing down, he came around to reach up for Ellison.

"Thank you." She slipped her hand into his to step down, and he held her fingers a moment too long as he cast a wary eye toward the hills once more. Only a few goats along the upper ridge, he saw with relief. Yet he remained concerned and watchful.

As he walked with her toward the little grove of trees, he felt protective, alert, tension within like a taut wire. While they had traveled from Invermorie to this spot, the light had faded blue to cloudy gray to lavender, and would deepen later. The night would be clear and moonless, perfect for men to venture across the hills with ponies and loaded carts. Though free traders strived not to be seen, the consequences could be dire if they were. He knew that better than most.

"You were kind to come this way to get my things. It will be dark soon."

"I do not mind. We can still have supper if we hurry. This is summer darkness, with enough light to travel quickly."

"You have been watching the hills again. Do you expect to see something there?"

"Better wary than surprised, lass."

She glanced at him. "Smugglers?"

"Must you sound so pleased? An actual encounter would not be pleasant."

"I encountered you," she pointed out. "So far that has been fairly pleasant."

"Fairly?" He laughed softly. "Madam, I do my best. Go on," he said, gesturing toward the birches. "See if your things are there."

She ran, lithesome and quick, the breeze lifting her hair, skirts. Ronan waited. The evening air was cool and refreshing—but pleasant conditions out here, he knew, could bring trouble. Ellison had vanished among the trees. He looked toward the hills, where stars were beginning to glint in a violet sky.

"Here they are!" she called, emerging from the shadows with a cloth bag over her shoulder. "Just where I left them. It is such a lovely evening," she said, gazing at the sky and hills. "What was it you and Donal called this stream?"

"The Lealtie Burn."

"Loyalty? There must be a story behind that name."

"There is a story at every turn in the Highlands. A vow was made here long ago near this very spot, they say, between a MacGregor man and a MacArthur lass."

"How nice to have local legends about your ancestors. A vow of love?"

"A MacGregor came new to the glen—our clan was tossed out of the west and our name proscribed long ago, only reclaimed more than a century later. This MacGregor, exiled from the west, had very little. He offered to the local MacArthur laird to tend sheep and cattle in exchange for a plot of land near the loch."

"The loch down the way? We passed it this morning."

"The very one. Soon he fell in love with the chief's daughter, and she with him. They made a promise of marriage just here."

"Where we stand? That is so romantic. Did they live happily ever after?"

"They did not. Her father's men killed him, and she threw herself from the old tower beside the loch. Love stories often end sadly." He said it more brusquely than he meant.

"Some do. Not every love story ends in loss."

"So they say. We should go." He touched her elbow.

"Ronan MacGregor, you are not as sour a lad as you like to think. I see through you."

He huffed. "Do you now?"

"I do." She drew a long breath, lifting her face to the twilight. "Have you ever noticed when the light fades at night and the air grows cool, the world smells fresh and sweet?" Drawing another breath, she closed her eyes. "What is that scent?"

He sniffed the air. "Bog myrtle. It grows in the marshy ground between the burn and the loch. The leaves give off a clean and pungent scent."

"Ah, yes. Our housekeeper packs it with the winter things to keep them fresh."

"Ellison." Taking her arm, he drew her along. "We must go. Now."

"What is it?"

"Bog myrtle gives off that strong scent when the leaves are crushed underfoot," he murmured, bending toward her to be heard. "Someone is nearby."

She looked over her shoulder as they hurried. "Here? Now?"

"We will not wait to find out. Come ahead." He tugged her toward the gig, lifted her to the bench, and leaped up to take the reins.

THE GIG ROLLED along at a good pace, Ronan intent on the road, while Ellison looked around. The night was peaceful—she could not imagine danger in these hills, though her companion seemed tense. Seeing a length of water ahead beyond a rocky slope, she spotted a stone tower on its opposite shore. "Stop! Is that it?"

"What?"

"The loch, and the tower you spoke of at the Lealtie Burn?"

"Aye so. Loch Brae, we call this one." He slowed the gig's pace along the track that paralleled the loch.

"Are we still in Glen Brae, then?"

"The loch is named for the glen, aye."

"And you are its laird. Is the loch yours as well?"

"Not any longer. It sits along the border of Glen Brae and Strathniven. Long ago it belonged to my glen and my kin."

"But why is it part of Strathniven now?"

"Things changed over generations."

She had so many questions for him, but felt he would only answer a few. "That wee island in the center—I have not seen it before, though I have been this way."

"It comes and goes, that isle. A fairy spell, so they say."

"What! Is that the one you mentioned? Tell me!"

A half smile, hands on the reins. A bump along the track sent her leaning against him, a welcome, solid warmth. "There is an old legend about that wee isle."

"You know I want to hear it. Can we stop?"

He sighed. "Briefly—I want to get you back soon." When he drew the gig to the side of the track, she fairly jumped out, running down to the lochside.

"A legend about a loch and a fairy isle so near, and you made me wait to hear it?" She smiled up at him as he joined her.

"If I told you all the legends around these glens, it would take a long time."

"Then we must find the time. I have been coming to Strathniven most of my life and did not know of this until you mentioned it. And on Strathniven lands!"

"Perhaps Lord and Lady Strathniven never heard the legends about their property either."

"MacNie and Mrs. Barrow would know, but I never thought to ask. Tell me!"

"Aye then." Seeing a twinkle in his eyes, she was glad. He had been somber ever since leaving Invermorie. She wanted to know his troubles, wanted to ease his mind, but was not sure it was her place. And she worried that his thoughts were not on smugglers, but on his feelings for Mairi Brodie. Part of her did not want to know that.

"Can we go over to the island? A wee rowing boat is tucked just there, see? Then we could visit the tower on the other shore."

"Another day, perhaps. That old ruin is in poor condition. It dates to the time of Saint Columba, they say. Come to the shore now." He reached for her hand, folding his fingers over hers as they crossed rocks and bracken toward the water's edge.

Ellison never wanted to let go of his hand, loving the sense of belonging, of rightness between them. But he let go, and Ellison clenched her hand, missing his.

He pointed toward the small, flat, green isle in the middle of the narrow loch. "A local legend claims that the island vanishes at times."

"Do you mean in fog or darkness? But it would still be there."

"For a romantic idealist, you are a pragmatic lass. They say you will see it one moment, and the next, it is completely gone."

"Do you believe it?" She gazed at the thin little isle, a green crescent with a hillock or two and a spread of wildflowers tossed along its length like colored stars.

"Likely it is an illusion. But the older name is Eilean à Cheo." *Ee-len-a-kyo,* he said in rapid Gaelic.

"Isle of Mist? The fog comes over the water often here, I suppose."

"Whether fog or fairy mist, the island disappears, they say, because of a spell cast long ago." At her eager glance, he smiled. "My mother was a MacArthur, and her kin told this tale when I was a lad. A long time ago, a MacArthur met and married a fairy."

"I love it already!" She wrapped her arms around herself, thrilled.

"The fairy queen—or perhaps it was a princess—fell in love with the human, a fine MacArthur warrior, and they married. But he could not keep her for long. It is the nature of fairies to be free, is it not? After a while she left him. But he looked for her every day, mourning his missing bride, always hoping she would return."

"True love," she said, and sighed. Ronan looked down at her for such a long moment that she glanced up. He smiled and continued.

"I suppose. They had a wee son in the care of the father's kin. Then one day the fairy bride came back to see her son, and her husband brought his child to the shore, near where we stand, perhaps, to let her see him. But when his beautiful wife appeared on the island, he set the child in its grandmother's arms, and swam out to the isle."

"And then?"

"It disappeared within moments. He was never seen again, even when the isle reappeared in the water."

"Gone in blissful happiness with his bride," she said.

"Well," he drawled, "they say he drowned. Though it could have been fairy magic. Either way, the fellow left his wee son, which is sad."

"There is that." She frowned. "But love and magic together is a reckoning force."

"I suppose so," said Ronan MacGregor.

"And the tower? Is there a legend about that as well?"

"Remember the bride I mentioned back at the Lealtie Burn? On the day her husband was murdered by her kinsmen on this shore, they say, she rowed out to the isle, perhaps hoping for that magic you speak of. That love. But it was too late. Her kinsmen came after her to bring her back. But she vanished before their eyes on the little island. They could not find her and left. Later, they discovered that she had thrown herself from the tower."

"That is so tragic!"

"She also left a wee son in the care of kin. Both legends are part of my kin's old legacy, as it happens. They say those of our blood can see the isle even when it disappears for others. A kind of magic doorway, they say."

"This is fascinating!" She wished he would go on talking about it. She loved not just the tale, but his deep warm voice, and his elegant profile in the gathering luminous darkness.

"A good tale. But stuff and nonsense, my lass."

She touched his arm. "A fairy spell on Strathniven lands, and you with the blood of a fairy prince in your veins. Lovely," she said.

"That blood is fair dilute by now, I would think."

"I can see fairy blood in you," she said softly. "Like a prince."

"Like a lowly smuggler." He smiled, quick and light.

"Not you," she said. Her heart lifted, soared, with the slightest smile, glance, touch. She was falling for a man who might never be welcome in her father's house. Or was she falling for the idea of a romantic hero like the one in her manuscript?

"So, you have your fairy legend, Miss Graham." He took her arm to turn her away from the loch and guide her toward the drover's track.

"Ellison," she reminded him. "Your legend is enchanting."

"It is," he murmured, as he helped her step up into the gig.

IN THE GLOW of a violet sky, he saw the men approaching, heads and then shoulders first, then forms striding forward as they crested a hillock and moved over turf and meadow; three, then six, eight. Three led ponies bearing panniers; others carried lanterns gleaming gold in the twilight.

He knew the big, broad man in the lead. Slowing the gig, he narrowed his eyes.

Neill Pitlinnie—Sir Neill, as the man preferred, for he had a knighthood that rumor said was obtained with a generous gift to the Turnpike Trust to help fund the work of Telford and McAdam in Scotland. The building of roads would benefit all, including the free trade. However his title had originated, Pitlinnie liked it well and no one questioned it.

But what the devil was Pitlinnie doing out here with men, ponies, and goods? The man rarely did the work of transport, hiring others to take those risks.

Ronan glanced at Ellison, who had lifted a hand to her straw bonnet as she watched in the distance. The open gig offered scant protection, Ronan realized, and the old horse from Invermorie was not in much of a hurry.

"Do you know them?" Ellison asked quietly.

"Some. They are not fellows we want to talk to." More lanterns were swinging now, bright dots all along the ridge of one slope and across the meadow.

"Whisky smugglers?" she asked.

She was astute—or hopeful—and he would not worry her. "Possibly. Do not fret."

In answer, she slipped a hand into the crook of his elbow. "I am not afraid for myself. I fear for you, meeting them."

"Worried I might run off and revert to my true ways?"

She bounced on the seat as they hit a rut in the road. "I fear they might hurt you, if they have heard that the king intends to honor Glenbrae whisky. They might want that honor for themselves instead." The next divot in the road threw her hard against him. Shifting the reins to one hand, he put an arm around her to steady her.

"They would not know about that, nor care. They only want profit."

"I want you to be safe, if they recognize you."

"I want both of us safe, lass, so we will avoid them."

But the cart lurched in another dip in the road, and he heard a crack. The vehicle pitched sideways, and Ellison slid against him. Ronan grabbed for her as the gig tilted.

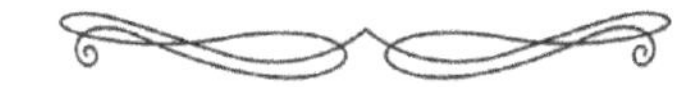

Chapter Seventeen

C AUGHT IN HIS arms, cheek pressed to his chest, Ellison groaned, tried to sit up. His arms supported her.

"Elly, are you hurt?" His voice was close in her ear, and his jaw, its slight growth of beard like warm sand, pressed against her cheek.

"Fine," she breathed. "You?"

"Right enough. Come up." He extricated himself from the tilted vehicle and reached to help her out with strong, certain hands. As she tugged on the hem of her skirt where the fabric caught on an iron fitting, he set it free, then straightened.

"Lean there and get your breath. I must see to the horse." He stepped away to murmur gently to the beast as he checked its legs and haunches. Turning, he checked the vehicle and came back to Ellison's side. "The horse is unhurt. But one of the wheels is bent. These old tracks need attention now and again, but have had none since—well, that's as it may be," he said, squatting to examine the wheel.

"Since when?" she asked.

"Since my great-grandfather was laird." He was on the ground tugging at the wheel.

"He was laird here, on Strathniven lands?"

"Just our luck," he muttered without answering her question. "The wood is cracked. Here is the trouble, see." He knocked at the wheel rim. "The wood is split at one of the felloes"—he indicated the wooden rim between two spokes—"and the steel tire bolted here has come away. If I can fix the band back in place, it may hold long enough." He stood, brushed his hands. "But this will take a few minutes."

"Can I help?"

"Keep an eye out, lass. But stay near, do."

She turned, feeling protective, determined, a helpmate, as if she had learned a new skill from his trust in her, his capable calm. Squaring her shoulders, she stepped forward to look around the curve in the road, back toward the meadow. Seeing only landscape and no men, she ventured ahead a few steps to look past the meadows toward the loch to one side, the hills to the other, beneath the indigo sky. She folded her arms and turned, a watchful sentinel while Ronan worked. After a few minutes, she ran forward a little farther, leaving the steep hill, the drover's track, the man crouched in the road wrestling with a steel strip.

Then she heard the chink and jangle of harness, the thud of boots and hooves. Spinning, she saw men, ponies, glowing lanterns, rising from a dip in the field not far from where she stood. She whirled, aware that she was exposed on a stretch of meadow, too far from Ronan, too close to these strangers.

One of the men ran toward her. She spun away, but he grabbed her arm roughly, tugging her toward him. As she stumbled to a knee, he dragged her to her feet.

"Who are *you,* lassie, hey?"

SWEARING UNDER HIS breath, Ronan pried and pulled at the steel band, trying to fix it in place along the cracked wheel rim. Pulling the small dirk from his stocking, he used that under the metal band. When it popped suddenly into place, he crowed in victory and sat up. And did not see Ellison nearby. He got to his feet, dirk in hand.

Then in the distance, he saw her—a graceful form, billowing skirt, rosy-gold hair flying out as she turned to run from the men surging over the meadow. One fellow was racing toward her. He knew the man.

"Pitlinnie!" he shouted, striding, then running.

"Ronan!" Ellison gasped, hauled close against her captor. Several other men gathered, some holding pony leads, crowding around in a half circle.

"Neill Pitlinnie," Ronan shouted, coming near. "Let her go."

Pitlinnie said something to his men, and Ronan saw the gleam of weapons, dirk handles, pistol butts, half-hidden beneath draped plaids and jackets. He slowed, cautious for Ellison's sake, his heart pounding in anger, but moved resolutely forward.

"Hey, Glenbrae." Pitlinnie kept a firm hold of the girl. "Stop there, aye."

"Let the lass go," Ronan growled.

"What brings you out here this evening?" Pitlinnie held the girl's forearm in a strong grip; she winced when she tried to twist away. Knowing that any threatening movement would bring weapons out in force, Ronan stood still, watching, calculating distances, still too far to reach Ellison and put her behind him.

"Broken wheel," Ronan explained with a shrug. Pitlinnie looked past him.

"I see. I heard you were freed. But why are you here instead of in Edinburgh awaiting trial, I ask? Whisky Rogues, caught at last, I thought." Pitlinnie snorted.

"I am free on good reason. Let go of the lass."

"This wee bonny bit is safe with me. Hey, what is your name, Miss? You canna trust that rascal to help you with yon cart." Pitlinnie leaned toward her. "I will see you safely home. Where do you live? I have not seen you hereabouts, I would remember."

"Pitlinnie," Ronan growled. One of the men stepped forward, fingers clenching the bone handle of a dirk. Ronan had a dirk, too, tucked up his sleeve, ready to hand.

"Let go of me," Ellison said, pulling on her trapped arm.

"You want to go with him, that rascal? Are you sure?"

"Aye. He is my fiancé," she said, yanking in his grip again.

Startled, Ronan met her glance, raised a brow. "Aye," he

agreed. "Betrothed."

"Huh, Glenbrae to be married? Go on!" With a harsh laugh, Pitlinnie released Ellison, who rushed toward Ronan. He swept her behind him. "Who would believe that, after—"

"What do you want," Ronan growled.

"We are passing this way, and do not need your leave for that. These are Strathniven lands, not Glenbrae territory."

"Then you need my leave," Ellison said, "on behalf of my close friend, Lady Strathniven."

Ronan frowned. Less said the better, but at least Ellison was in his keeping now. Her impulsive announcement of a betrothal might help. Even Pitlinnie had his limits.

"Strathniven! Glenbrae, is it true what they say? You are a peer now? Lord Darrach! Begging your pardon, sir," Pitlinnie said with a mocking little bow.

"Darrach? But would he know—" Ellison began.

"Hush." Ronan offered his elbow and she tucked her hand there, pressing close to his side as he slipped his hand over hers. Playing her protective fiancé might help.

"Whatever you heard is just rumor," Ronan said. "There is no truth to it."

"Are you sure? I heard the property might go to you, but for your arrest. Whisky Rogues," he said again, and spit into the grass. "We know the truth of that, do we not? I hoped we might be rid of you when you were taken. Does she know about it?" he barked.

"Of course," Ronan murmured. He felt Ellison's gaze on him. No help for it now, he thought. He would have to tell her soon. "I only came here to see to the distillery."

"All fine and according to law, eh?" Pitlinnie looked smug. "So the new Viscount Darrach follows the rules while his lads move goods by devious means."

"You are one to talk about devious," Ronan said, tipping his head toward the men, the horses, the panniers holding goods.

"Oh, are you Sir Neill Pitlinnie?" Ellison asked. "Lady Strathniven has spoken of you. She enjoys your whisky. My father Sir Hector is quite fond of it too."

The man's eyes flickered toward her. "Graham . . . the deputy lord provost's lass? Lady Strathniven's nephew—that is Corbie, aye? Precious company you keep now, Glenbrae. Or Darrach. Odd that I heard nothing of your engagement."

"Why would you?"

"From your sister-in-law. I saw her only days ago. But she never mentioned you. Did you know we are courting, Mairi Brodie and me?"

Ronan went cold, squeezing Ellison's fingers in his without thinking. "I heard."

"We hope for your approval as her kinsman."

"Mairi Brodie is twice widowed. You need her permission, not mine."

"I hope for it soon. Then we would be kinsmen, hey. We could work together."

"Ah," Ronan said.

"A benefit to both of us." Pitlinnie smiled. "So. You have Graham's daughter and the claim to Darrach lands too. Well done, sir. It is no surprise you escaped trouble with the law. Clever lad to find a father-in-law to fix that problem for you."

"It is not your concern," Ellison said, "but my father did not arrange Ronan's pardon."

Good Lord, she was outright lying for him, Ronan thought, and standing up to a disreputable fiend. She had no true idea of the risk, but he was deeply touched by her loyalty and courage. He blew out a breath.

"Enough," he growled under his breath, hoping to stop her from elaborating.

"Glenbrae is a criminal, Miss Graham. You would be wise to remember that."

"It appears that you are the criminal here, sir." She pointed to the men and ponies behind him. "What are you transporting across my lady's lands?"

"My dear, best we go," Ronan said. He had to get her away before she said more.

"Delivering whisky to some respected customers," Pitlinnie said. "Lady Strathniven is a loyal client. Love thy neighbor, brother. You understand."

"Give us Strathniven's lot," Ronan said. "We will bring it there since you are out doing your good deeds."

"Should I trust you? I think not." Pitlinnie chuckled. "Unless you want to come away with us, lad. There is good money in it if we work together."

"Move on," Ronan said.

"Certainly, Lord Darrach. Miss Graham. We will be on our way." Pitlinnie waved his men forward, pony harnesses jingling, glinting in the twilight.

Ronan stepped back with Ellison as Pitlinnie led his men along the drover's track in the opposite direction of Strathniven.

"Ronan," Ellison said.

"Back to the gig," he said grimly, taking her with him. Turning to help her in, he climbed up to sit beside her, taking the reins.

"Ronan," she said. He looked down at her, saw her lip quivering. "I am sorry."

"What the devil? Why?"

She turned teary eyes to him. "This is all my doing—"

He put his arm around her, drew her into his embrace, easily, naturally. "Hush. You did naught wrong, and had a terrible fright."

"If I had not left my things behind, we would not have come this way, and would never have seen those men—and—" She caught back a sob.

"This was not your doing." He rested his cheek against her head. "I was in too much haste to get you home. The speed caused the wheel to break. If not for that, we would have missed those fellows. No apologies." He stroked her shoulder.

"And then I said we were betrothed. I am sorry."

He chuckled. "It was a good thought. He stepped away, did

you see? It gave him pause and gave us the upper hand at the right time."

"If he tells others, what then?"

"I doubt he will tell anyone. But if he does, we need only deny it. Another rumor."

"For a moment, I feared you might go with them."

"Hardly," he said, and pulled her close. "No fear of that, lass."

"He offered you money—"

"I keep clear of him and his lot. I know him too well."

She hesitated. "It puzzles me, your past. I do not understand enough of it. I trust you," she added. "I do. But Papa and Mr. Corbie cautioned me against you, and they would remind me of it if I need to explain any trouble."

"What a parcel of trouble, having to tell them that rascal MacGregor ran off in pursuit of profit and crime as soon as he had the chance."

"But you stayed."

"I gave you a promise. You agreed to make me into a gentleman. I agreed to let you try."

"You made it easy. Were you tempted to go back to smuggling?" She searched his face, his gaze.

He realized then that his ruse, and the ruse now assigned to him, were still in conflict. She truly did not know if he was a rogue or a hero. That was his fault. He had kept secrets and skirted honesty in favor of protection and silence.

"Who said I was a smuggler? Has it been proven?"

"I suppose not, but I thought—"

"Whatever I am, I would not have left you there." He touched her chin, lifted it.

She lifted her face, waited, invited. He leaned down, nudged her nose with his, pushed her bonnet away, skimmed fingers through the softness of her hair. Then he kissed her, the warm cushion of her lips under his willing, inviting. He felt her breath catch, felt his heart pounding.

The feeling he had denied for too long swept over him,

through him, like the rushing water not far away. As if his soul was a fish glimmering in a stream, going with the current of his life, he followed his heart, kissed her again, whispered reassurance.

He had wondered, once, if he would ever find this again. But here it was, more full, more meaningful. Kissing her, he felt sure suddenly that all this was meant to be somehow. Felt that he could lay at her feet all the truths and mistruths of his life. Kissing her, life made sense in the moment. He was just where he should be, with her, here, now.

Yet a cold rational sense surged through him, breaking that spell. He pulled away. No, he told himself. Not yet. Silence and secrets must be kept if he was to protect her, and protect his friends behind bars on Calton Hill.

"Beg pardon," he whispered. "I did not mean—"

"You did. And I meant it too." She stretched to kiss his cheek, the corner of his lip, and when he leaned in, unable to resist, she pulled away. "But we must go."

"Aye." And he would keep a wary eye until they reached there.

THE GIG CREAKED, bumped slowly along. The sky turned dusky purple. Ellison pondered, curious, heart thumping. "Ronan," she began.

"More questions?"

"Just one. Pitlinnie asked if I knew who you are. Do I?"

He was silent, letting the horse push faster, wheel rattling. "I am a MacGregor to my bones."

"One with many secrets."

"Some must be kept for the good of others."

"But why smuggle whisky and risk going against the law?"

"So many questions." He shook his head. "Strathniven's rooftops are just there, see, beyond that hill."

"You will not give me all the truth?"

"Not yet. Just trust me."

"I do. But I fear some secret you hold could undo all our plans."

"What plans do we have?" He glanced at her.

"The king's visit."

"Oh, that. I thought you meant our betrothal," he drawled. "Lass, just know that I do what I believe is best. Even if it goes against the law."

"What I know is that I need the truth."

"Soon, Miss Graham," he murmured, "you and I will lay out all our truths between us, hey? You have secrets too."

"None of mine would endanger you."

"Nor will mine. Ellison," he added, "I am still a prisoner, in a way. And that needs caution." Chucking to the horse, he leaned to the side to look down. "The wheel is holding, just barely. We need to go carefully."

"Carefully in all things?"

"As you say."

They moved ahead, the gig swaying awkwardly. Ellison rode, silent, grasping the wooden bench rather than Ronan's arm. Breathing in the cool night air, she thought about freedom, and realized neither of them felt free.

She was a prisoner too, of her life, her heart, trapped by her father's expectations, by guilt. One day she might tell him more of that. And one day he would tell her more of himself. She trusted him in that, and much else.

Did he want what she wanted, to feel free, to have love and a home, a family?

Just then he glanced down at her, nudged his shoulder against hers. Just that. And something melted within her, wrapped around her, through her like an intangible embrace, a quiet joy in his steady presence. Love, she thought. Yet the feeling was different than she had known before—this was generous, nurturing, exciting, intimate. And vast somehow.

After a moment, she slipped her hand inside the bend of his elbow and rested her head on his shoulder.

"Almost home," he whispered.

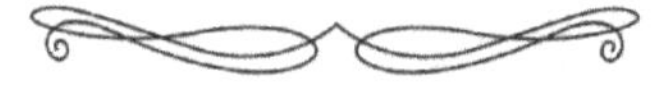

Chapter Eighteen

"WILL THAT BE all, sir, and Miss Ellison?" The housekeeper set a bowl of strawberries and a plate of oatcakes, steam rising from the stack, on the dining table between Ronan and Ellison.

"Thank you, Mrs. Barrow, this is more than enough," Ellison said, looking at the generous breakfast spread. "You were thoughtful to prepare a late breakfast."

"And kind to leave supper trays for us last night," Ronan said.

"We did return rather late, but it could not be helped," Ellison said.

"Aye, Miss Beaton was worried for your safety last night, but we all assured her you would be fine, even if we were not sure," the woman emphasized. "But we thought you might be hungry when you finally arrived. It was a relief to hear MacNie say this morning it was just a wheel needing repair, and no harm done."

"None at all. These cakes are delicious, Mrs. Barrow. You are a treasure," Ronan said. The housekeeper beamed as she left the room.

"Nicely done, sir," Ellison murmured. "You have quite charmed her. Sorcha, good morning!" she continued, looking up as the girl entered the dining room then. "I wondered why you had not come down to breakfast yet, but we are all a bit weary after yesterday, I think. Would you like some tea?"

Clutching an embroidered handkerchief to her nose, Sorcha

took a chair at the far end of the table and sneezed. "Thank you," she mumbled.

"Oh dear, are you poorly?" Ellison poured tea into a cup and handed it to her.

"A bit. I may have caught a summer cold when we were out yesterday."

"Perhaps you should go back to bed and let me bring a tray up. And I could read to you if you like."

"That would be so nice, thank you. I only came down to tell you the news."

"Oh?" Her stomach gave an anxious flip.

Ronan leaned forward. "I hope you feel better soon, Miss Beaton. News?"

Drawing envelopes from her pocket, Sorcha set them on the table. "While we were out yesterday, Mr. MacNie fetched the post in Kinross, and a messenger arrived from Duncraig as well. But first, can I ask if all is well? You returned so late last night."

"Just a mishap with a wheel. Nothing to be concerned about," Ronan said.

"I am glad it was not worse. But sorry you missed the excitement." Sorcha held up the creamy envelopes. "One for you, Elly, and one for me—well, the news is for all of us." She handed one letter to Ellison.

Miss E. Graham, Strathniven House, Perthshire, read the envelope in Sir Hector's spiking, impatient scrawl. She felt a sudden dread. "Tell us your news first, dear," she said.

"Mine is from Mama. She enclosed a note for me, and an invitation to all of us! She has decided to hold a country supper and dance at Duncraig. My lady aunt persuaded her. And Lord Darrach, you are invited too. Mama insists upon it, having heard all about you from Lady Strathniven."

"Indeed? How kind." Despite his smile, Ellison thought he paled beneath the shadow of his clean-shaven jaw.

"The dance is to be a *cèilidh* in the Highland style," Sorcha said. "Though it is often a celebration after harvest or for a housewarming or something similar, Mama and Aunt Strathniven think it will suit their friends who are summering in the Highlands just now with plans to depart for Edinburgh soon. There will be Scottish dancing and a late supper."

"How nice! When will it be?" While uncertain if Ronan—or she—felt ready for a social event for Lord Darrach, Ellison knew it was inevitable.

"At the end of the week. It is not much notice, but it will be informal as cèilidhs are, with locals and gentry mingling together. Mama hopes Lord Darrach will be free to attend."

"He would be honored," Ronan murmured with a tilt of his head.

"It will be a wonderful evening, I am sure," Ellison said.

"Mama says this will give people a chance to gather intimately before the large assemblies in the city. Besides, my lady aunt has a birthday, part of the celebration."

"August, yes! I nearly forgot," Ellison said.

"Mama also invited her good friend Lady Elizabeth Murray and her husband." She dabbed at her nose to suppress a sneeze. "Oh! Excuse me. He is Sir Evan Murray-MacGregor, who is the new chief of the MacGregors. Do you know them, Lord Darrach?"

"He is a cousin." Ellison raised an eyebrow, hearing that, but cousins abounded in any clan. "He will be very busy during the royal visit, I understand."

"I hope they can come. I am looking forward to having a cèilidh dance," Sorcha said, and then began to cough behind her handkerchief.

"If you are to recover by next week, you must rest," Ellison said.

"I will go up in a moment. Did your father send good news, Elly?"

"I hope so." Opening the letter, Ellison read her father's brief note, written in his usual terse tone. Her stomach sank after a moment, but she looked up with a smile.

"He says the city is already crowded with people arriving from all over. And the king is expected in less than two weeks." She paused. "He also says—Adam Corbie is coming up here. We can expect him Thursday. MacNie is to meet the coach in Kinross that afternoon."

Sorcha stifled another sneeze. "Wonderful," she said thickly. "We must invite Mr. Corbie to come with us to Duncraig. I will write to Mama this afternoon."

"Thursday," Ronan said, looking at Ellison.

"Three days," she murmured, her gaze touching his.

"THE LESSONS MUST continue," Ellison said, when Ronan joined her in the library later, "considering what is coming all too soon."

"Corbie?" At his skeptical look, his prim tutor pressed her lips together.

"You will soon be introduced to the king, but your lessons are not done." Standing by the library table, she set down the books she held and faced him.

"My dear Miss Graham, I can conduct myself impeccably when necessary, whether at a king's ball or a cèilidh. We do not need more lessons, and you have no cause for concern."

Her hands, her graceful fingers that he so wanted to hold, to kiss, flexed anxiously. "What concerns me is that you will be under scrutiny from my father and Corbie, who expect to see perfection."

"I will give it to them for your sake."

"Thank you—but you do not want more lessons?"

"I will miss them dearly," he said in a wry tone. "But you would have more time to write, and I could attend to some matters."

"Such as shipping the whisky?"

"Finding the whisky," he clarified. "The Muir lads will count what we have, and then it will be transported."

"Even so, we still have time for lessons."

He tipped his head, curious. "Do you want to continue?"

"I enjoy our time together." She looked down, tracing the pattern in the oak.

"So do I. But must we devote time to stodgy old books on manners?"

"Perhaps not." She laughed softly. "It will be useful to introduce you at Mrs. Beaton's cèilidh first. You would have some acquaintances at the royal event."

"This wee cèilidh is a risk, lass. The MacGregor chief, Atholl, Huntly, and others may question my introduction as Darrach."

"Pitlinnie did not question it. He seemed impressed."

"He is easily impressed."

"I am a bit nervous that he might mention our betrothal." She twisted her mouth.

"He might. But it may serve as a distraction if we go forward with this ruse."

"If?" She frowned. "You cannot change your mind now."

Ronan blew out a breath. Her question hit the heart of the matter. At first, he had resisted the idea, then reluctantly saw its advantages. It was only one day, he told himself. But his introduction at a local gathering was more of a problem. He sighed. He was in the thick of it for his friends. For Ellison. He could not back down now; she was right in that.

"I did give my word."

"Let us finish our tutoring, Darrach," she murmured. "There is not much time."

"Three days. What next, Miss Graham? I have absorbed all I can from the books."

She tapped a fingertip on her chin. "We could practice some dancing."

"Dancing?" He shrugged. "If you like." He came around the table toward her.

"Have you done much dancing?"

"A little." He held out his arms, right arm crooked, left arm out, an invitation.

"Waltz! I doubt we would see that at a cèilidh, and it is probably still frowned upon at royal assemblies. It still is in Scotland, I think. Better that we practice steps for a Strathspey or a reel."

"I will say that a waltz with a beautiful woman in candlelight is a fine thing. Though I am familiar with some Scotch dances."

She tipped her head. "You waltzed with a beautiful woman in candlelight?"

"Not as lovely as the lass I am looking at in daylight, but aye."

Her cheeks went pink. "Did you dance it in England, perhaps, or France?"

He owed her some of the truth. "Both, aye, as an officer."

"The Black Watch?" She seemed more interested in his past than in dancing.

"For three years, aye. Then I exchanged to the Dragoons to accompany my cousin to India. Sir Evan," he added.

"I remember Papa saying that Sir Evan MacGregor was sorely injured in India and showed much courage there, as did the men who were with him. You were there?"

"I was. Many were with him at the Talnar ambush. Four years ago, that was, and in the past. Shall we practice strathspey steps?" He stepped back as if to face her in a dancing line. "Though with one couple and no fiddle, we may not accomplish much."

She stepped forward, back, lightly hopped to the side. "Cast off left, then right?"

"Aye so." He reached out, took her hands in his, and turned with her in a circle. Moving with him, she began to hum a tune, the notes clear and sweetly sung.

"You have a hidden talent, Miss Graham," he said, guiding her around.

She laughed. "My music tutor did not think so. And one, two, three," she counted as they broke apart, turned, linked arms, spun, parted, faced to clasp hands again.

"There," he said, moving closer. "We could try a waltz."

"In case the king thinks it appropriate for the great ball being planned?"

"Aye, just in case"—he drew her close, sliding his right hand to the small of her back, extending his left arm with her hand still in his—"I am invited to that ball."

"My father says you may only be invited to the gentlemen's levee for a quick introduction."

"Then this may be my last waltz," he murmured, pulling her closer, so that she rested her hand on his right shoulder. When she angled her head to the side, he leaned close to her ear. "I just want to waltz with you. Have you danced this before?"

"Aye," she said as he began to turn her, gliding, swirling around. "But not like this." She was breathless, soft, warm, so close.

A sharp knock sounded on the door, and the girl in his arms startled and jerked away as if he were made of fire. Ronan looked up as Mrs. Barrow peeked in the door.

"Oh, excuse me, Miss! Sir!"

"What is it, Barrow?" Ellison smoothed her skirts and looked flushed.

"A Mr. Cameron is here to see MacGregor. Darrach," she added with a frown.

"Thank you," he said, realizing Mrs. Barrow was not easily won over.

"Do show him in here," Ellison said, and Mrs. Barrow withdrew. "I will look in on Sorcha to see if she feels better. Isn't Mr. Cameron the solicitor in Kinross?"

"Aye. He is doing some work for me."

"Perhaps he brings good news." She swept toward the door.

His heart was pounding and his thoughts were still with her when Hugh Cameron came into the library moments later.

"Good to see you," Ronan said.

"And you. What a fine place," Hugh said, glancing around. "I have seen Strathniven from a distance but have never visited. I met your Miss Graham in the corridor. Lovely."

"She is. Is there news? Sit, please." Ronan indicated two damask-covered chairs beside the fireplace, where peat bricks glowed blue and comforting on the cloudy day.

"I do have news, and thought to bring it quickly. A letter from Sir Evan." Hugh extracted an envelope from the pocket of his dark blue jacket, and removed two sheets of paper covered in brown ink. Ronan recognized Evan's distinctive script, the letters stiffly formed; losing the use of his right hand at Talnar, he relied on his left now.

Ronan read the letter quickly.

Ronan, Sir Evan wrote. *I trust you are well and in better circumstances than recently. Though we have not met for a few years, I have heard of your exploits and situation from Mr. Cameron. I am pleased to learn that you are free of the burden of charges. You are not one to commit felonies, and a clearing of charges seems merited.*

I have studied the status of the Darrach inheritance, including properties, environs, means, and heritable title. The Courts of Session and Lyon Court had the matter, but entrusted it to me to decide as Chief of the Gregorach in my father's stead. While the courts will finalize the decision, my opinion will guide their declaration.

Ronan turned to the second page, read through to the end, and glanced up, stunned and relieved. "He will recommend that the courts grant Darrach to me."

"Lock, stock, and barrel. You will be—and essentially *are*—Viscount Darrach."

Shaking his head slowly, trying to take it in after so much doubt, Ronan read on. "He says he will ensure that I am declared legitimate heir to Darrach through close kinship. He will recommend that I be awarded the estate, including Darrach Castle and its grounds and lands to its north, south, east, and west boundaries, including villages, crofts, and tenanted properties."

He felt almost dizzy, as if the world had tilted and was righting again.

Hugh nodded. "He submitted his decision in signed documents to the Session and Lyon Courts. We must await the letters patent, but Evan made their task simple."

"My God," Ronan breathed. "I did not expect this." Relief washed through him. Now the ruse was unnecessary. He could be presented to the king and to anyone as a legitimate member of the peerage.

And the risk to Ellison was lifted. He blew out a breath, rubbed his neck.

"It is not quite as perfect as it appears," Hugh said. "There is a condition."

Ronan narrowed his eyes. He should have known not to fully believe in luck.

"Sir Evan wrote to me separately. His father, the late chief, favored you as the heir to Darrach, but without your cousin's will, it needed to be reviewed by the Court of Session and the Lyon Court. Then Sir Evan had to review clan matters anew. All this you know."

Ronan nodded. "Go on."

"Your, ah, legal difficulties gave Evan pause. But rest assured that Ronan MacGregor, accused smuggler, is not named in the inheritance documents. Only John Ronan MacGregor of Glenbrae, lawyer, nearest kin of the deceased, is mentioned."

"My legal name. Good."

"You should also know that Sir Evan took pains to keep it separate."

Ronan felt his throat tighten. "I am grateful."

"The courts had tossed the decision to the clan chief, but when Evan heard of your pardon, he was keen to review it carefully."

"I am not convinced that the charges have been cleared entirely. I do not trust Sit Hector—or his secretary Corbie."

"Nor do I. We will sort that out. Now to the condition."

Hugh sat forward. "Sir Evan has decided that Glenbrae must be sold."

Ronan stared, dumbfounded. "What do you mean?"

"The inquiry into the Darrach estate revealed considerable debt, the result of poor decisions and expenditures over two generations. Nothing you knew about."

"I had no idea. My cousin John never said during the time he held Darrach. Go on." Lose Glenbrae! He felt cold and numb.

"The debt on the estate must be cleared to avoid forfeiture, especially as it is attached to a peerage title. Sir Evan feels that selling Glenbrae is the solution. There has been an offer."

"I see." He suspected from whom, and it sat like a stone in his chest. Suddenly other things made sense. He recalled his father and his uncle, the elder Darrach, arguing about luxuries and expenses. When Ronan's cousin John had inherited the Darrach estate, he had insisted that Ronan make Glenbrae whisky the finest it could be and move it as fast as possible to fetch the highest price.

Risks were taken too often. Ronan, Will, and young Darrach had argued, and soon the notorious Whisky Rogues—Will and John only—emerged to be chased, hunted, and finally killed. To protect their reputations and that of the whisky, Ronan had taken on all of the work—and the smuggling plan—with help from the Muirs and Linhope and MacInnes too.

But he had not known about the burden of debt on the Darrach estate.

"I see," he repeated. "What becomes of Glenbrae now?"

"You will have the rank and title of Viscount Darrach and keep the Darrach lands. But you must relinquish Glenbrae, Invermorie, and any related properties to be sold. I am sorry, Ronan."

"My glen." Ronan gripped the arm of the chair. "The tenanted farms. The castle where my family lives. The distillery?"

"All of it."

"Sold to whom?"

"He did not say."

"But we can guess." Ronan stood, hands fisted as he paced back and forth. "We have to stop this from going forward."

"We could if there was another way to absolve the debts."

"What if I find a way? We can convince Evan to delay the sale. Buy time."

"Perhaps we could, given the royal madness overtaking the city. I will ask Sir Evan to wait until after the royal visit. Courts and banks will not operate normally for a little while anyway." Hugh stood. "That might give us until September."

"Fine. Keep me informed."

"For now, accept the grant and title that are offered, and wait on the rest."

"If I accept the condition, then I am agreeing to give up Glenbrae. I do not agree."

"For now, do it. You have never been afraid of a challenge. We will find a way."

AFTER HUGH HAD departed south for Kinross, Ronan saddled a horse and rode north for Glen Brae. Reining in, he sat for a long while looking at that familiar profile of hills, watching the golden rim of the sun sink below the cloud cover and vanish behind that distant, beloved blue ridge.

He could never give up Glen Brae.

Going back to Strathniven, he stabled his mount and stepped into the house just as an inky gloom overtook the sky. In the hallway, Ellison and Sorcha were walking out of the dining room and he greeted them, though his smile was flat. As Sorcha took the stairs, Ellison paused, eyes wide as she considered him.

"You rode out. Is something wrong?"

"I had an errand. I apologize if I missed supper."

"Mrs. Barrow is keeping a plate warm for you in the kitchen. Sorcha feels a bit better, we thought to go to the parlor to read together. Will you come?"

"I will leave you to it." When she nodded and took a step, he touched her elbow.

"Ellison. We must talk," he murmured low.

She blinked, nodded. "When?"

"Tower library," he whispered. "Late."

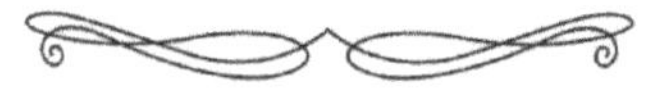

Chapter Nineteen

"WHAT IS IT?" Speaking in a whisper when Ronan finally appeared at the tower library door, Ellison stood back for him to enter. The hour was very late, the room glowing with candlelight, the house, the world, filled with a deep hush. She stifled impatience, pushed away worry as best she could. Impatient to see him, unable to concentrate on her writing, she wondered what he wanted to talk about.

She had read her father's letter so often that she still held it creased in her hand. "You have news?"

"I thought we could talk here for some privacy. It is a delicate matter."

"Sit, please," she urged, but he stood, and so did she. "What is the trouble?"

"Not trouble, exactly." He looked down at the letter clutched in her hand. "I think you have something on your mind too. You are nearly shredding that envelope. Was there more in your father's letter than you did not mention?"

She drew a breath, then sat in a chair by the window. Ronan sat as well, settled, folded his hands. His patient gesture, his willingness to listen touched her deeply and suddenly. "Papa is sending Mr. Corbie here. You know that."

"He wants to be sure the frog has become enough of a prince to pass muster."

"Perhaps. But Corbie's other intention," she said, "is to bring me back to Edinburgh with him. Papa declares it here." She waved the envelope. "I did not tell you before, but I am to return within days. Papa will send a guard for you. But we promised to attend the cèilidh."

"Send Corbie back alone or with the guard. I will take you to Edinburgh myself."

"I thought you came here tonight to refuse to be part of the introduction."

He shrugged. "Circumstances have changed."

"The country dance gives us a reason to stay longer." She met his eyes.

"You should do what you want, not what Corbie and your father want." He tapped his fingers on the arm of the chair. She felt his tension, sensed a hint of anger directed at Corbie. "You know you need not follow their demands."

"I know." She looked away. "We should go to the cèilidh. I want to. But I know you are not anxious to be introduced as Lord Darrach. And Mr. Corbie coming up here to evaluate you as a gentleman just makes me so—so crabbit!" she burst out.

Ronan huffed a laugh. "Makes you what?"

"Something my granny used to say. Crabbit. His arrogance makes me angry, but if I tell him so, Papa will soon hear of it in a way that twists whatever I do."

"Someone else needs to learn his manners," he drawled, then sat forward. "Ellison, listen now. You have a gentle soul and a forthright nature, but you need not suppress one in favor of the other. Let them know your strong opinion. And that is my own opinion on your behalf." He sat back.

"Do you think so?"

"It hardly matters what I think. What matters is what you think."

She blinked. "Lady Strathniven tells me the same."

"She is a wise lady. I apologize if I overstepped, but I am—protective of you. You have a fire in your soul, but you do not let it shine often enough."

She felt her cheeks heat, felt a swell of pleasure. "If Corbie heard you incite rebellion in me, sir, we would have even more trouble."

"I quake in my boots."

"They have taken advantage of you for their own ends, Ronan."

"More, I have taken advantage of them." He spread his hands. "I am free."

"But if this should go wrong, they will let you take the blame and claim you lied to them." She stood, began to pace. "Oh, this horrible ruse! I hate it so!"

He stood. "But it is not a lie."

She whirled. "I cannot blame you if you decide to disown us all, though I would worry about you, and your friends still in the jail. We can find a way. We must!"

"Ellison." He stepped closer, his voice husky. "It is not a lie. I am Lord Darrach."

She stared. "You—what?"

He took her hands, faced her as if they were about to dance a wild reel, and drew her toward him. "Hugh Cameron brought word. I am to be named Darrach's heir."

"But—how can that be?" She looked up at him, her fingers tightening in his.

"Darrach was my first cousin. He left no will. It went to the courts."

"I knew that, but Papa said it would be delayed for months. Is it decided?"

"The court sent it to the clan chief. Another cousin. Under Scots law, a chief has the authority to absorb a title and lands into the chiefship, or he can recommend an heir. He decided in my favor."

"So it is yours now?" Her head was spinning, his grip her anchor.

"The letters patent require the nearest blood kin to be named heir. I am that man. Sir Evan weighed the situation and recommended my name. I am to be confirmed."

"Then what Sir Neill Pitlinnie said about your inheritance is true."

"It was not true then, but it is now. This is good news, at least in part."

"So you need no pretense."

"None." His smile was touched with sadness.

"Did you know this might happen? You never mentioned it."

"I knew it was possible, but had to keep it secret. The ruse that I am Darrach was ironic all along. But I did not expect it entirely, and not so soon."

"So we can truly call you Darrach and Glenbrae." She smiled brightly.

He squeezed her hand, then sighed, his dark hair falling over his brow, blue eyes twilight indigo in the candlelight. "In Scotland, only one title may be held at a time. A little detail imposed by English law. Sir Evan has decided to take Glenbrae away from the Darrach estate award."

"Glenbrae?" Her brow furrowed as she realized the loss. "Oh, Ronan. But all these week, I have wished for you to be free, and for something good to come of all this. If you are Darrach, it is like a dream come true—your freedom is assured. That is what I want for you. Though this is like discovering you are a prince who has passed his ordeal and cast aside his disguise, like in a fairy tale. I suppose it sounds foolish."

He smiled wanly, listening, tall and strong, all quiet power. "Not foolish."

"But you are Darrach in truth, and Mr. Corbie will choke over it. And I like that."

He huffed a little. "True, there is nothing he can do to change it."

"One day he will inherit Strathniven, and petition for the title of Viscount Strathniven as well. It is not attached to the property or the heir, since it was awarded to Lady Strathniven's husband singularly."

"Corbie would have a good chance of claiming it if it begins a tradition."

"But I know how much Glenbrae means to you. I am very sorry."

His fingers flexed, gripped hers tightly for a moment and did not reply.

"I know how important your home and your distillery are to you. But you will have the distillery as Darrach, is that true?"

Ronan nodded. Then he let go of her hands, cupped her shoulders, drew her toward him. "There is something even more important, now that I think about it."

"What is that?" she whispered. Her heart, her body, pulsed, so near to him.

"Not what. Who." He leaned down, and Ellison felt her knees go weak, while his hands on her shoulders felt solid. Safe. She tilted her face upward.

Footsteps, a knock, sudden and sharp, on the door. She leaped away from Ronan, bumped the table beside her, and set a hand to her heart.

Mrs. Barrow poked her head in the doorway.

"Oh! Again!" Ellison burst out.

"Glenbrae," the housekeeper said, "there you be! We have been looking high and low for you all over. There is a man at the door. He says it is very urgent."

"Did Mr. Cameron return? Is there trouble?" He approached the door.

"Not him, sir, a young man. Aleck Muir is his name. He says he must speak with you. We nearly toppled the house looking for you, and here you are in the old tower, while most of us were asleep." She pinched her mouth. "And some of us are awake."

"Did you invite Mr. Muir in out of the rain?" Ellison asked.

"I did. He is dripping wet in the front hall. What should I tell him, sir?"

"I will come directly. Miss Graham, please excuse me. Mrs. Barrow, will you send for Donal Brodie to meet us at the door?"

"Aye, sir." The housekeeper stepped back as Ronan rushed past her. "Miss Ellison," Mrs. Barrow said then, "will you be needing anything?"

"Nothing, thank you. I will stay here to finish my correspondence and then to bed. I did not realize how late it was."

"Indeed. Miss Ellison." The housekeeper paused, hand on the door. "If you wish to meet with the man alone at night, I will turn a blind eye. You may do as you like here. It is always Lady Strathniven's wish for you."

"Thank you, Mrs. Barrow. Rest assured Lord Darrach is every bit the gentleman."

"I am not surprised, I will say that."

"And he is Lord Darrach, so you may call him that."

"Nor does that surprise me either." She studied Ellison for a moment. "I suppose he is a good man, if the Muir lads trust him. They are a good lot, them."

"He is a very good man, Mrs. Barrow."

"GLENBRAE," ALECK SAID, breathing hard. In a damp plaid, hair slicked with rain, he radiated urgency. "We need your help. Now."

Alarmed, Ronan gestured to Donal, rushing toward them. "Bring the lad a dram. Then saddle horses. We will need them. Aleck, what happened?"

"Geordie," Aleck went on breathlessly, "wounded sore. We went to Darrach Castle to the caves there. But he was attacked. We took him to Invermorie and I rode here for you fast as I could." He took the dram from Donal with a nod of thanks.

"Who attacked him?"

"I am not sure. So much blood." He touched his head. "Mairi Brodie is with him."

"Is it mortal? I will come straight away."

"I do not know, but you must come, aye. There is another problem."

"What else? You went to Darrach to check the caves?"

"Aye, to count the whisky cache we keep there by the waterfall."

"I know." Last year, Ronan and the Muirs had moved twenty kegs and a dozen casks of whisky to the Darrach caves, where they were sure to be safe.

"We found nothing there."

"Nothing? No whisky?"

"Gone. We thought we were mistaken in the dark, as the caves are numerous, so we split up, west and east, to be sure."

"There is a honeycomb of caves there. Easy to get confused. Did you find it?"

"We had the cave, but found it empty." Aleck swallowed the last of the dram. "We could not find it. Just a few crockery jugs and broken wood from the crates. And footprints all around."

Ronan sucked in a breath. "What happened to Geordie?"

"He had not come to meet me, so I went out and walked about, called, and then heard some sounds. I ran, and saw him lying there, wounded."

"Shot?"

"Stabbed, it seems, and clubbed on the head. I ran for Grandda. He was waiting for us with the cart. We did not want him to risk the climb, see."

"Aye. And you and Rabbie took your brother to Mairi? Good."

"First we put him in the cart, then I ran for Tam Comrie, the groundskeeper at Darrach. He and his wife are still there, even without a laird there now. Rabbie wanted to know if Tam had seen anyone. Tam came to Invermorie with us. But the whisky is gone, sir." Aleck breathed hard, rubbed his wet, dirty face. "I am sorry!"

"Not your fault. We must find it, though. When was the last time the whisky was seen there?"

"Grandda gave it a count not a month ago. But there were footprints about, and dragging marks. Someone else was there tonight."

"Then it has not been gone long, and has not gone far. Can you ride?"

"Now? Aye."

Ronan stepped outside into a light rain under a darkling sky. Donal came running, leading three fresh saddled horses with the help of a groom, who led Aleck's horse back to the stables.

"Geordie may have seen the men tonight," Aleck said. "He may be able to tell us more."

"Aye, then. We ride for Invermorie," Ronan said.

TAPPING HER FINGERS rhythmically on the old, scarred table, Ellison caught the faint scent of the lemon and oil polish that one of the maids had used recently. The scent stirred her out of thoughts and worries and back to the too-quiet tower library and her unwritten letters. What had brought Aleck Muir here so late? By the chime of the clock set in the bookshelf, it was past eleven at night. Had something gone wrong at the distillery?

Frowning, she dipped her pen in ink again and set it to paper to answer her father's letter but blotted the next line she wrote. Truly, she only wanted to tell him not to send Adam Corbie here. But it would be too late—Corbie would reach Strathniven before her letter would reach the Edinburgh New Town. With a resigned sigh, she stood and went to the window, where rain had begun to sweep down from a sky gone eerie gray-green.

A new rhythm merged with the patter of the rain, and Ellison leaned forward to see three horses and their riders pounding over the earthen drive that fronted the house, riding toward the open road. The man in the lead was deeply familiar to her now, his long, lean silhouette swathed in cloak and plaid against the rain.

The others, she realized, must be Donal and Aleck. Where were they heading with such urgency, in such weather?

Worry swept through her, but she took a breath against its force, spreading her fingers on the cool window glass, rain sliding down the other side of the glass. Taking a deep breath, she felt something strong and certain begin to emerge within her. She need not give in to fretful uncertainty. She could rise above it, she knew that now. Facing smugglers by the Lealtie Burn had shown her that. Being with Ronan MacGregor had shown her that she need not hide behind extended mourning and meekness any longer.

Straightening her shoulders, taking another breath of resolve, she left the room. However late the hour, she must try to rest. Ronan would be back soon, and safe. She trusted him, and now must trust that all would be well.

"IN MAY I think it was," Aleck said, "when Pitlinnie took a half dozen kegs of Glenbrae with his own load over the hills to Culross to ship out."

"Aye, that is the claim Dawson used against us, though we had done naught." Ronan sat with Aleck, Donal, Sir Ludo, Rabbie, and Tam Comrie in the great hall at Invermorie. They had a dram each, or more, and Ludo had scrabbled together cheese and oatcakes. The rain pounded the roof and windows, and they spoke quietly, while Mairi sat with Geordie above stairs.

Upon arriving, Mairi had allowed them to talk to Geordie for only a few minutes. The lad was bruised and swollen, bandaged and made more comfortable, but he was tired and mildly confused. Someone had leaped on him in the dark—two men, he thought, one in Highland dress, one not; both spoke English. He fought back, blacked out, and could remember no more. When Mairi returned with a poultice and a potion, she ushered them out of the room. Geordie, she said, would heal, but had taken a hard knock to his head, had a broken rib or two, a broken hand as well.

"The lad gave as good as he got, I think. And I hope they are sore hurting. I will watch over him for a while."

Now, Rabbie shook his head. "The last of our lot that went out with Pitlinnie," he said. "But for the new casks at Glenbrae, the rest of our store was in the Darrach caves. We have not shipped anything out but for that sold in shops in the towns and in Perth."

"What went out from Culross marked the last of my brother's and Darrach's agreement with Sir Neill," Ronan went on. "He made a good profit with us, but he cannot move a drop of ours without my consent. And I have been away," he added wryly. "Not only that, we swore off such deals. Done with the free trade."

"Done?" Aleck asked. Ronan answered with a curt and final nod.

"So they decided to steal it outright," Rabbie said.

"If them, why now?" Aleck asked.

"Who else? And how did they find it?" Donal added.

Ronan shook his head. "It is a fair wealth of whisky, worth searching out. With me away and you lads distracted with the work at the distillery and all, it may have seemed the right time to look for our store."

"And finding it, take it," Tam Comrie said. Tough and gray, the grizzled fellow had been groundskeeper at Darrach estate since Ronan's uncle had been there and had stayed when John inherited and stayed even since, he and wife alone at the castle, awaiting news of the new lord. Ronan very much wanted to tell Tam, knew he would be pleased, but this was no time to share his news. Far more important matters were to hand this night.

"But you came back to the glen," Sir Ludo said. "Pitlinnie knew he must act."

"You surprised all of us, returning to fetch whisky for the

"king," Rabbie said.

"The king!" Sir Ludo brightened like a lamp at that. "What do you mean?"

"A supply of Glenbrae whisky is promised for the royal visit," Ronan said succinctly, for he had not mentioned the situation to Sir Ludo. "I will explain later."

"I want to hear it," Ludo said.

"The whisky in those caves was there not long ago," Tam said. "Rabbie and I saw it but a month past. That lot did not walk away on its own."

"I told you all I know and all we saw, truly," Aleck said, and Ronan nodded.

"I hear," Tam said, "that Glen Brae and all that the glen holds has been sold. I hear the distillery belongs to another now, and its whisky too. Or soon will."

"What did you hear?" Ronan asked.

"My wife had it from the kitchen maid at Darrach, who had it from her mother, who had it from an old man down the glen. The rumor is going about that Pitlinnie owns Glen Brae now."

"He does not," Ronan said curtly.

"Good. We want our own Glenbrae in charge. You, lad," Tam told him.

"Would you sell it, ever?" Donal asked, distress cracking his young voice.

"Never. And tonight I just need to know who beat Geordie Muir, who took our stock of whisky, and where it is."

"I also heard," Tam said, "or me wife heard, that Pitlinnie was asking if the laird of Glenbrae has been named Viscount Darrach."

"You have been waiting on the news, Uncle Ronan."

Ronan drew a breath. "I have had promising news. But we will save that for later." The men grinned but did not ask more, and he appreciated their focus.

"For now, all roads lead to Pitlinnie," Rabbie muttered.

"Though he is a scoundrel," Ronan said then, "he is no low

thief, nor is he desperate for goods. Some of this does not make sense."

"He has plenty whisky of his own to move," Tam agreed.

"But he wants the Glenbrae distillery," Rabbie said. "And he thought Ronan MacGregor would hang, so he has been planning to take over the business."

"Good sirs and fair lads, we cannot solve this now," Sir Ludo said in his grand and archaic manner. "What is important is to find the whisky. The king's wish must be served."

"Just so," Ronan said, and swallowed the last, a mellow burn down his throat.

SHE WOKE IN the dark, startling out of a noisy tilt of a dream into a dim and rainy dawn. The dream clung as she pulled on a dressing gown and slippers, still in the thrall of climbing a steep hill in strong winds, seeing Ronan MacGregor far ahead amid a cluster of strangers. She struggled to reach him, calling out, slipping, sliding, but he did not see her. At last reaching the top, she found herself at the edge of a cliff and, in the way of dreams, Ronan even farther away, still beyond reach. The ground where she stood crumbled away beneath her feet then, and suddenly she was falling—and had to fly or perish. Somehow, she soared and tried to swoop toward Ronan. Seeing her, he reached out—and then she woke, still feeling an odd sense of floating that quickly dissipated as she sat up.

Had Ronan returned in the night? She had slept fitfully until the desperate dream had taken over. Pulling her dressing gown over her nightgown, she heard the dull rumble of thunder as she went downstairs. The house was dark and silent, the kitchen deserted but for Balor, asleep by the warm hearth. He raised his head to greet her with a low woof, then went back to dozing as she built up the fire in the grate, warmed the kettle, and prepared a pot of tea. Minutes later, she sat sipping a cup at the well-scrubbed table, listening to the whip of rain and the grumble of thunder.

Then she heard a sound over the predawn storm—horse hooves, shouts, and a distant voice, so familiar now that she gasped in relief. Going to the kitchen door, she angled to listen and to look toward the stables, just visible to her left.

She could hardly run outside in her dressing gown. Instead, she hurried to the hob to add more hot water to the teapot, then searched for scones, rolls, jam, butter.

Bringing a tray to Ronan's tower room was something she could do now, an offer of plain before breakfast was prepared for the household. If she could see him for a moment, she would feel reassured that he was safe and well.

Soon she carried the tray along the connecting corridor to the old tower and headed for the stone steps, going carefully up the old, worn steps. A few of the treads bore wet prints just visible in the dim light from the narrow stairwell window. Ronan had come this way ahead of her.

At his bedchamber door, she hesitated, suddenly wishing she had written a note to leave with the tray—*Dearest Ronan*, she would have written. She bent to leave the tray outside the door, about to give a quick knock and flee. But the silver tray scraped over stone and the teapot clinked against the cup as she knelt on the floor.

The door swung open. She stared at two large bare feet, tracing her gaze upward past bare calves dusted with dark hair, past the folds of a dark kilt wrapped and belted over a loose linen shirt open at chest and throat to reveal a mat of dark hair. She looked up at his face, his dear face and scruff-bearded jaw, his dark hair wet and curling, his wide shoulders, all haloed by candlelight.

"Why, Ellison," he said, and reached down to her.

Blushing like fire, she set her hand in his as he brought her to her feet.

Chapter Twenty

S HE LOOKED FLUSTERED, delectable, sleepy, and the most welcome sight he could have imagined. He just wanted to pull her into his arms and bury his soul and troubles in her gentle, whimsical, comforting nature. But he let go.

"I did not mean to disturb you," she said. "It is good to see you safe, and home."

Home. That word, from her, was everything. Bending, he picked up the tray and brought it to the table, then gestured toward his bare feet and shirtsleeves in apology. "Pardon me. I had a wash and was dressing. It has been a long night."

"I only brought tea, thinking you might be hungry. But you must be tired. I should go." She turned.

"Stay." Reaching over her head, he shut the door. "Will you stay?"

"I could pour."

"Please pour, my lass."

She went to the table. Her dark blue dressing gown, prim, plain, poufy, enveloped her throat to foot, its hem dragging as she moved. Pouring tea, she added cream. Her hair fell in a tousled golden mass, her cheeks were pale, purple shadowed her eyes, and she had made tea for him before dawn. His heart warmed.

"You have not slept." His fingers brushed hers as he took the cup.

"I was worried." Her lashes lifted, her eyes the color of the clouds crowding the sky. "But I am glad you are home now."

"I left in a hurry last night. I apologize." He sipped. The tea was hot, good.

She shook her head. "MacNie said you rode to Invermorie with Aleck Muir and Donal. It must have been important."

"It was." If he wanted her in his life—Lord, he did—he owed her more honesty. "Aleck came to say that Geordie had been hurt. They were looking for the whisky we had stored away, but it was missing. And someone attacked the lad."

She gasped. "Is he hurt badly?"

"He will recover. Mairi is taking care of him."

"Who did this? Did they also take the whisky?"

"Possibly."

She nodded, brow creased with concern. Dear God, Ronan thought—she was so lovely, standing beside him here in a closed bedroom, as if it was no breach of protocol at all. As if she belonged here, a natural part of his life.

"You mean to go out again," she said.

"The store must be found." Taking a deeper sip, revived, he set down the cup.

"This is Thursday," she reminded him. "Corbie will be here later."

The name sullied the air. "I had forgotten."

"MacNie will fetch him this afternoon." She began to butter-fly her fingers in that way she had, delicate knuckles pale, fingers weaving. He realized she had stopped doing that lately. She had been calmer, more certain, these weeks. Now the anxiousness had returned.

For that reason alone, disturbing his lass, he had a grudge to settle with Corbie.

"He and Papa will want to know if we did what was asked. We have no time left."

"No more time to ensure the gentleman passes muster?" he drawled.

"To be together." She took a step toward him.

He opened his arms as if that, too, was a natural thing to do here in his bed chamber. He pulled her close, wrapping her in warmth better than any voluminous gown could do. Pressing his cheek to her hair, he held her. Just that.

But when she lifted her head, he sensed the invitation, touched his lips to hers gently at first—*you are safe*, he wanted to tell her, saying it instead with his lips, his embrace. *You are loved.* He so wanted to say it, his heart surging, body surging with each kiss. *So loved.* Yet he could not say it, was not sure he had the right to, not yet.

Then she looped her arms around his neck with a soft little cry, pressing closer, matching kisses with fervor, inviting, exploring. Morning thunder boomed again outside the window, a fresh torrent of rain driving against the glass panes. Ronan felt a storm break within him, yet still he held back.

"I was going to leave a note," she whispered against his lips. "With the tea. But I had no paper or pencil. And you opened the door."

"I did," he murmured, and kissed the corner of her lip, her soft cheek, her lips again. "What would you have written?"

"Dearest Ronan, here is your tea," she whispered against his mouth.

He half laughed. "Dearest girl," he murmured, lips on hers, now tracing along to the delicate curl of her ear, "thank you for the tea."

"Welcome," but the word was lost in a kiss that shook him to his core, and her body, her hips, pushed against him, so that he had to move away or have no secrets.

Just then the squat little clock on the mantel chimed out—one, two—four times. So late, yet so early. The sound made him pause, cleared the fog from his thinking.

He drew back. "Ellison, this is not how I would want to treat you. Not—"

She leaned to kiss and silence him, and he surrendered, hungry, then gathered himself again. "Not gentlemanly."

She looked at him. "We have no time for lessons. We just have part of the day."

"Lessons be damned, then." Snugging her small waist in his hands, feeling her hips against him, so willing, he felt too the deep pulse in her body and in his.

"You need no lessons from me. You never did."

"I did," he said, tipping his head to take her mouth in a deep, rich kiss that plunged through him body and soul. "I am learning—that I have a heart after all."

"What do you mean?"

"This," he said, dipping his head to kiss her so thoroughly that he tasted her soft groan, felt her sink a little in his arms. Lifting her against him, he leaned back so that her feet cleared the floor, her body planed softly to his. "If you like."

Pressing her cheek to his, she put her lips to his ear. "The household is asleep," she said. "I do not need to go back just yet."

He shifted to carry her full in his arms. "Sure?"

"Oh aye," she whispered. "I think we did claim to be betrothed."

"Oh well, then," he breathed, and set her on the bed. As she shoved the coverlet aside, he leaned over her, keeping his weight on his hands as he kissed her.

Stormy darkness filled the room, the single candle burning like a bright star. Thunder rolled in the distance. Under the canopy of the stout old bed, rounded mattress sinking under his weight, he lay beside her, curving a hand along her jaw, then letting his fingers seek the buttons at the ruffled throat of the shapeless dressing gown. Her trembling fingers went ahead of his hands to find others, to open the folds. Just a night-rail beneath, he found, all gauze and lace, the veil of it sliding away beneath his hands and hers together.

"Sure, now?" he asked again.

She gave a soft laugh and pulled him down to recline in the cool, deep nest of pillows and linens beside her. He rolled to his side and she turned too, allowing him to sweep his hand down along her bared arm, the skin supple, warm as he kissed her, as she returned it, pulling him toward her, over her. His fingers found her breast, cupped, and he caught his breath as his heart pounded, body swelled for her.

Nuzzling her ear, then the line of her throat, he sank down until his lips found the pearling center of her breast. He heard her gasp, felt her fingers slip through the thickness of his hair, still damp from the washing in the moments before she came into his life in this profound way, a way he had not expected nor dared dream.

He tasted her, felt her pull in a breath of deepest pleasure, and she arched to invite him further. She knew where this could lead—he knew that, and as her hands found the wooly fabric of his plaid, sliding upward, he knew she was not surprised, that she had more courage in the moment, helping him to breach and break whatever was reserved and formal between them. Nothing, now, would be the same, all for the better.

Sliding a hand along the smoothness of her thigh, the light shift gathering like flower petals under his hand, he shaped her hip, followed the sweet curve of her abdomen, the delicate mound that made her gasp anew against his lips on hers. Every part of her was exquisite, warm, welcoming, soft and slippery as his fingertips found her, rocked her, took her little cries into his lips, her breath and his breath, in and out again. Then her fingers seeking, shaping him, deft and then soft and bold again, until he pulsed for her, his body echoing his heart, wanting, yearning, the sweet power of her touch shuddering through him. She was soft, golden, lush in his hands, all grace and satin where he was taut and hard with need. Her touch had mischief in it, easing him along as he eased her, until he could hold back no longer. Now the thunder was the pounding of his heart and hers together.

Breaths, and resting together, but too soon she rose, kissed him, and whispered something. Thanks? Love? He thought he heard that soft, wonderful word. It was time.

"My love," he murmured. Fatigue swamped him, and so

truth prevailed. He could no longer hold up falseness like a curtain between them. *"Tha gaol agam ort,"* he whispered in Gaelic. My love is upon you; I love you.

"Mo graidh," she said. *My love.* She kissed him. Before the door closed behind her, he slept.

LONG INTO THE day, she saw him at last, her heart near bounding out of her breast when he stepped out of the larger library just as she walked through the passage. She had thought to be discreet upon seeing him, yet a hot blush spilled into her cheeks with the sweet memory of the hour before dawn. He had been gone much of the day, riding out with Donal, so she did not know until now that he had returned.

As he emerged and saw her, he tipped his head, and gave a crooked, almost wicked smile. "Come in here," he said low, holding the door open.

"It is nearly tea time." She paused, trying to hide her smile. "Come up to the parlor. You have been out all day and must be hungry."

"That is the least of what I feel just now. Come here." He took her hand, pulled her inside, shut the door.

Setting her hand on his shoulder, she leaned in expecting to share a kiss while they had privacy. Instead, he put a hand to her waist, and, standing tall, stretched her right hand out with his left arm. "Miss Graham, will you dance with me?"

She laughed. "You need no lessons. We established that."

"I have just enough dancing to get by at a cèilidh or a ball. But it is not the dancing. It is having the afternoon to ourselves to practice—whatever we want to practice." He swayed with her in his arms, turned with her.

"Well, Sorcha is resting in her room, Mrs. Barrow is preparing tea, and the housemaids are busy getting our things ready."

"For Edinburgh?"

"For the dance and supper tomorrow evening. And MacNie has gone to Kinross."

"I did not want a reminder of that errand." As he stepped forward, she stepped back and then to the side, turning with him in the pattern until they spun on dancing feet, the hem of her gown filling out as she turned. She laughed with the dizziness and the delight of it.

"So you learned this in London? Do not tell me you have already met the king. Though I would not be surprised, you with your secrets."

"Never met the gentleman." He twirled her, pulled her close, leaned his cheek against her head. "I was there for a few weeks before India."

She tilted back to look at him, and they whirled toward the other end of the wide room with soaring, turning steps. No music, just the natural rhythm of shared steps and breaths, as if they had always done this. "There is much I do not know about you."

"You know more than most."

"With no time to learn more." She spun with him, captured in his steady formal embrace, as her spirit soared, feeling that strength and the grace of shared movement.

"This is not over," he said, bringing her slowly to a stop. He tipped her chin up with a finger. "It is just beginning."

"I wish it were so." She drew a breath. "We both have secrets, and trust comes hard. But truth will out, so I should confess. What would you think if you discovered my secret was a disappointment to you?"

"You," he said, "are a guileless and lovely creature. Whatever you may have done in the past does not worry me now."

"You might think otherwise if you knew."

"Would I? Who am I to judge another? Listen now." Fully serious, he met her gaze. "I know your innocence and your naivete, your trust in people. I know your temper and your backbone, your secret about writing. I believe you understand more about life and sadness, loyalty and love, than most at your age. You have a strong will and you are not perfect. That is enough for me."

"If there was something to forgive, could you?"

"Surely you did what you had to do. Lass, you have lived like a mouse in your father's home, being meek, following orders, pleasing others instead of taking care of yourself. You were married and widowed and that was not easy. You would have had to protect yourself. But it is past. I see you changing, growing stronger every day."

"Because of you."

"Then we are in each other's debt, and a support for each other. Whatever you did needs no one's forgiveness. Least of all mine."

"Others do not share that opinion."

"That does not surprise me." He sounded almost angry.

"My father never approved of Colin Leslie," she said. "He was a poet, the son of a viscount whose title was not heritable. He had very little money of his own, but for a house and some valuables. My father thought him a useless lad—so he called him. A useless lad. But Colin was a good man, intelligent and kind, but did not know how to please my father. Mr. Corbie was very disapproving too, told me it would all come to naught and I should come to my senses and marry at my own level."

"He wanted you for himself," Ronan said, letting go of her to lean back against the library table, folding his arms as he listened.

"Perhaps. Lady Strathniven rather liked him, thought he was pleasant, but was convinced he would eventually make me unhappy. But—I loved him or thought I did. I was in love with the idea of love. And so," she said, "I eloped."

He waited, said nothing.

"It caused a terrible rift, embarrassed my father terribly, nearly cost him his position, or so he said, though he was appointed deputy lord provost regardless of what had happened. And my mother—" She paused.

"You rarely mention her. What did she think?"

"She was gone by then. My father made it clear she would

have disapproved and been ill over it. But I rather think she would have applauded—any decision that chose love. But my father would not speak to me for a long time. But then—Colin died. An accident, fell from his horse when out riding with his friends. Reckless, he could be, but in good spirits, in fun. The shock—was awful. My father was good to me after that, invited me back to the house. I did not want to stay—where I had lived with Colin. But then," she said, "Papa insisted that I must live quietly, take no more chances, do what was appropriate in all things. For my happiness, he said. For my safety."

"For his own peace of mind."

"He cares, in his way. I felt responsible because he was un-happy, you see. He changed so after Mama died. I felt responsible for—" She drew a breath, shook her head. "I just needed a little forgiveness, parent to a child. Lessons," she said. "Always lessons from Papa, to improve me, more so than either of my sisters."

"Lessons!" He gave a wry little huff. "I have not heard much about your sisters, but later for that. Ellison, nothing needs forgiveness here that I can see. Perhaps you need only to forgive yourself, stop judging yourself harshly. At the time, you needed their understanding. But I think Sir Hector can be unfeeling, even when he believes he is being fair. As for Corbie—what you do is simply not his business."

"Papa thinks I should marry Mr. Corbie, says he will go far in the Scottish government one day. Says Corbie is willing to accept my past behavior. And Lady Strathniven would not object, I think, since he is her heir."

"Willing to accept?" He shook his head. "If the lady approves, it is because she knows Corbie must marry a woman with common sense and a heart. But it is too late now."

"Too late?" She caught her breath, not sure what he meant.

"Too late for your Mr. Corbie. You could never marry that cold fish. Besides, I hear you are betrothed to another." He held out his hands. A welcome. A haven.

With a little sob, she ran to him, felt his arms encircle her. He held her, kissed the top of her head. Closing her eyes, she took in the feeling.

"Ronan MacGregor, I think I love you," she said impulsively. "Only weeks, but I feel it is so." Her heart pounded—she held her breath, waiting. Hoping.

"I feel the same." He kissed her brow. "I love you, Ellison Graham. I am only beginning to see how much, I think. Keep your secrets. I am hardly one to judge."

"Nor will I ask about yours. I think it all went away, the doubt, the sense that you were a stranger, on the day we went to Kinross."

"Kinross? When you visited the seamstress?"

She nodded. "That day, you were just strong and sure and it felt so good to be near you. And when you met with the two men—it was only Aleck and Geordie, I know that now—I feared something bad might happen to you. And then I just knew. Later, when we took the wee lamb to Invermorie, you were so gentle and kind, and I saw how much your family means to you, saw how much you had sacrificed for their wellbeing. Keep your secrets, sir. I know you have your reasons. And I am content."

He tilted her face, kissed her. "Here is a secret. I dread meeting the king."

"So do I, for it might be the last day we ever see each other."

"I am thinking all will be well. I cannot say why just yet. Trust me. I only dread meeting the king because it is—not my way, the world of peers and lords and earls and suchlike."

"I do trust you," she said, as it welled up in her. "And I do not care a whit if you are a lord, a laird, a farmer—or a scoundrel. I love you as you are. And if I did not see you again after the king's levee, then I"—she searched for the words—"I would search for you. Wait for you. And feel grateful that we met, and that I know what the deepest sort of love is like."

"I would not leave you to wait. I would find a way." He bent to kiss her again.

"Ronan," she whispered. "I know am too romantic. I know

what may be said about us. But this is no fairytale, and we have no guarantee of a happy ending. But what we have is worth far more. I think we both want—and deserve—the same in life."

He touched her cheek. "Love and freedom."

"Love, aye. And freedom from burdens and threats. Freedom to do what we will."

"We may have to fight for that, my lass. This situation—is not resolved."

"Then we will stand up for each other. I am learning better how to do that."

He laughed, and kissed her, and soon sent her on her way, though she did not want to go. But it was time to return to the main house, the day, the world out there.

"The sunset is brilliant," Sorcha said, pointing toward the window in the parlor that evening. "All rose and gold and purple. What a relief to see the rain clear away."

"It will take the heat from the air in time for your mother's cèilidh tomorrow," Ellison said. "Though Papa mentioned that the heat lingers most unpleasantly in the city. I hope it cools a little before we all go south." She glanced at Ronan, then away.

He knew her thoughts and sensed her reluctance. Sparing a glance for the stunning sunset, he went back to watching the hills where the road curved up from Kinross. Likely Ben MacNie was bringing Corbie along that road by now.

He fisted a hand behind him, not looking forward to that meeting. Ellison, seated with Sorcha, held Balor in her lap, stroking his head as the girls discussed plans for the party. He was not keen on that event either, but there was naught to be done. He must go through with all of it.

"My mother has a knack for arranging flowers and candlelight and such," Sorcha was saying. "The house will look wonderful. And tomorrow we will be dancing! We will have strathspeys and reels!"

She stood, grasping her skirt as she began to hop and spin

about while humming. Ellison laughed as Sorcha sidestepped toward her, and set the little dog down so that she could stand and clasp hands with her friend. They spun about the room, their slippers light on the carpet and their skirts, blue and green, belling like flowers.

Ronan smiled at Ellison, happy for the moment—Sorcha was a bright wee thing who could lift the mood wherever she was. Balor leaped about, barking as if he wanted to join them, and as the girls whirled past, Sorcha reached out to Ronan.

"Don't be such a curmudgeon, Darrach!"

He took her hand, then Ellison's, and circled with them, not quite sharing their elation but willing enough. Soon he could not help but chuckle. He had never in his life done something like this—the spontaneous joy of lightsome girls and an impish dog were new elements to him, a remedy of sorts.

Ellison stumbled over the little terrier underfoot and Ronan caught her swiftly, setting an arm about her for balance. She looped her arms around his neck and urged him to swirl around, while Sorcha picked up the dog and danced with it.

On the last turnabout, Ronan saw a figure in the doorway. He stopped.

Ellison slid out of his arms and stepped back. "Mr. Corbie!"

HEART THUMPING FROM dancing, laughter, and moments of freedom, Ellison went still and silent. Beside her, Ronan seemed to freeze as he faced the newcomer. At her feet, Balor tensed and began to bark in irritation.

"Cousin Adam!" Sorcha ran to Corbie, taking his arm to bring him into the parlor. "We have been waiting for you!" Patting his hand, she smiled at the others. "Here is Ellison. And I think you know Lord Darrach?"

"Miss Ellison. Mr. MacGregor," Corbie said stiffly. Still barking, Balor trotted toward him to stare up, tense and quivering. Ellison hurried forward to pull him away by his collar.

"Balor, here," she said. "Mr. Corbie, welcome."

"Thank you." Corbie said.

Ellison held Balor now, scruffing her fingers on his head as she stood beside Ronan, who briefly touched her elbow in discreet reassurance.

"Mr. Corbie," he said.

Corbie looked sour, tired, and tight-lipped. Rather than feeling angry or resentful, Ellison felt sorry for him. Had he arrived earlier, he would have killed any impulse for merriment. Her heart sank as she hoped her newfound happiness had not abruptly ended with his footstep on the carpet.

"Please have a seat," she said. "I hope you had a pleasant journey."

"Not particularly." Corbie sat beside Sorcha on the narrow sofa, while Ellison took a wing chair, holding the dog. Ronan stood beside her, silent. "Your man MacNie kept me waiting while he finished a pint in the tavern—expecting me to wait for a servant! And just what is going on here?" He looked sternly from one to the other. "My lady aunt is not here at present. Cat's away, mice will play, is that it?"

"Certainly not," Ellison said.

"We were practicing dance steps," Sorcha said. "You came just in time!"

"I have been in a coach for hours on rough roads. I am not in a mood for dancing."

"I meant you are here just in time to join us tomorrow for a cèilidh at Duncraig," Sorcha said. Even she sounded subdued now.

"I heard. My aunt wrote to invite Sir Hector and me as well. He is much too busy to come north, but sent me, as other matters require attention." He lifted a brow to look at Ellison, then Ronan. But there his glance skittered away, as if he could not meet Ronan's steady, searing gaze. "We must discuss why I came up here, and what has been going on at Strathniven."

"Going on, Cousin?" Sorcha looked bewildered. "We are enjoying the summer and looking forward to the royal visit, so we have been practicing for introductions, if we are fortunate enough to be introduced."

"Ah," Corbie said.

"And looking forward to the dance tomorrow," Sorcha added.

"I hope it proves as simple as you imagine, Cousin Sorcha. Just for now I need some rest. Did I miss supper? No one mentioned."

He had given her no chance as yet, Ellison thought. "We had a light supper earlier, but Mrs. Barrow can prepare a tray for you. I will ask her to send it upstairs. You will be in your usual room."

"Good. It has been a long day. Traveling north took longer due to the unusual traffic on the roads. Crowds at every stop, and the roads full of carriages. We will need to return very soon, Miss Ellison. Plan for a long journey due to the number of travelers heading to Edinburgh."

"Very soon?" Ellison asked.

"Your father expects you home as soon as possible."

"I—I thought there was more time," she blurted. Beside her, she saw Ronan rest an arm on the high back of her chair, a simple gesture that made her relax. "What of Lord Darrach?" she asked.

"Expected as well. We will arrange a separate escort."

"No need. I will find my way there," Ronan said flatly.

"I was hoping we would all travel there together," Sorcha said. "Oh, dear, it is getting late. We should all get some extra rest tonight. I am glad you are able to join us, Cousin Adam."

"I have not yet decided," he said, as Sorcha stood. "Good night, Cousin."

"Mr. Corbie," Ellison said when Sorcha left the parlor. "I promised to attend Mrs. Beaton's cèilidh, and I plan to travel south with Lady Strathniven and Sorcha. Lord Darrach can travel with us. I am sorry if you have other plans."

"Miss Ellison, your father is displeased that my aunt left you unchaperoned."

She lifted her chin. "Sorcha is my companion here, since Lady

Strathniven was called away to help her sister."

"Sorcha's mother is healthy enough to host a country dance, apparently. I am disappointed in my lady aunt for leaving you here." He looked pointedly at Ronan.

Though she could not see Ronan's reaction, she felt his ominous silence.

"Miss Ellison, you may not care that your father's reputation rises or falls on the behavior of his family at this crucial time. We will discuss that later, you and I—and MacGregor too," he added.

"You mean Lord Darrach," she corrected.

"I know Sir Evan MacGregor requested that the inheritance go to his cousin. It came to our office for review. The law of succession is not a clear path in this case. We disagree with the decision to grant the title and estate to MacGregor."

"'We?'" Ellison repeated. "Presumptuous, sir."

"I only share your father's opinion as his secretary."

"Yet you and Papa are willing to present him as Darrach to the king."

Corbie's nostrils flared. He stood. "That is different. A temporary necessity."

"For whom?" she asked.

"We all know the answer to that." Ronan spoke at last, his voice reverberating low. "The decision about the title is fortunate, Mr. Corbie. It eliminates a certain risk."

"We are not prepared to accept the decision as final."

"Usually, intestate succession in Scots law," Ronan said, "results in the granting of goods equally among spouse, children, siblings and other kin if agreed by all parties. It has been a stable factor in Scots law. The difficulty comes when there are few relatives. My cousin, the previous Lord Darrach, had no clear inheritors other than myself. As his first cousin and nearest male relative, the title, land, and goods can legally come to me."

"Except that the nearest male relative is a criminal."

"That is not a factor under the law, sir. I have not been convicted, and have been pardoned—as you well know."

"Conditional."

"And innocent of charges unless proven otherwise. What is most unusual here, as you may be aware, is that a peerage title hangs in the balance as well as an estate. Therefore, the court deferred to the clan chief, which is their prerogative and his right. Sir Evan recommended in my favor. And that is that. You and Sir Hector cannot hold sway, as you have no legal claim or authority in the matter."

Corbie gave a scoffing laugh. "Where did all that legal parlance come from? Pretending to be a lawyer as well as a peer?"

"I am a lawyer," Ronan said calmly. Corbie stared.

"Sorry, did no one mention?" Ellison smiled, cool and quick. "He read for the law and is a very fine lawyer who practices in Perth and Edinburgh." The smug satisfaction she felt seemed almost evil.

"That cannot be! He is a small laird, a smuggling thief, and an imposter."

"I am an advocate for the defense, as it happens," Ronan said.

"Outrageous," Corbie sputtered. "You should have said so."

"You never asked," he drawled.

"If you advocate for criminals, how did you end up in a dungeon?"

"A question I intend to solve," Ronan said.

"I am going to bed," Corbie snapped, and turned on his heel for the door.

When he was gone, Ellison stood, and Ronan came around the chair, tipping a brow at her. "A very fine lawyer, is it?"

"I have every faith in the incomparable Lord Darrach."

"Miss Graham," he murmured, pulling her toward him to kiss her cheek, her ear, her lips, so that her melty knees nearly gave way. "You had best hurry away before I think of something two people could do in this room, all alone."

She sighed. "I cannot feel alone anywhere now that he is here."

"Aye so. Off with you, lass. Tomorrow will be a busy day indeed."

Chapter Twenty-One

"SUCH A GLORIOUS day!" Sorcha said as she sat beside Ellison on the leather seat of the big black barouche. "I am so excited! Thank you for suggesting I wear my pink gown. And you look lovely in your gray-blue satin. How nice that we can go to Duncraig a bit early to help Mama and Aunt Strathniven."

Ellison smiled, sobering quickly when Corbie stepped inside the carriage to take the opposite seat.

"You must be looking forward to seeing our lady aunt, Cousin," Sorcha said.

"She should have been here, not at Duncraig," Corbie said.

He had been especially disagreeable ever since his arrival, Ellison thought, and wondered if Corbie noticed a closeness between her and Ronan and resented it. But she would not ask. As the vehicle rolled down the earthen lane, she glanced out the window.

Near the stables, she saw Ronan mounted on a bay stallion, with Donal beside him on a roan mare. Both men wore Highland gear, with dark jackets and waistcoats over wrapped plaids in the tartan that MacGregors favored, a handsome pattern of dark red crisscrossed with forest green. She swelled with pride to see them, both so handsome, with the singular dignity of Highlanders.

Earlier, Ronan had told her they planned to arrive at Duncraig later in the day, after a visit to Invermorie. The Muirs were still searching for the missing whisky and he wanted to talk to them, and see how Geordie Muir was faring. She suspected he had no desire to ride in an enclosed space with Corbie, nor could she blame him.

"Lord Darrach knows the dance begins at seven o' clock?" Sorcha asked.

"He does. He means to visit kin first, and he and Donal Brodie will come later."

"At least he is taking his valet with him," Corbie said.

"Donal has been a help," Ellison said. "In truth he is Darrach's nephew."

Corbie shook his head and waved a hand in a futile gesture. "There is so much we do not know about this man."

"We know that he is an educated and well-mannered gentleman who will be a credit to Scotland—and your party, sir—in Edinburgh."

"Let us hope so."

"You do not seem to like Darrach much, Cousin Adam. You just need a chance to know him better," Sorcha said. "He is a most excellent gentleman, and a handsome, congenial bachelor. Mama will be so pleased to have him there this evening. Though I must say he seems quite fond of Ellison."

"Does he," Corbie drawled. "I hope you have not become infatuated, Miss Ellison. Such attachments rarely end well."

She said nothing, gazing out the window.

"Even if Elly is not infatuated, I am," Sorcha said brightly into the silence.

DUNCRAIG HOUSE WAS a small castle out of a fairytale, with round towers and conical roofs, set prettily against a heathered hillside topped by green pines. As Ronan and Donal arrived at twilight, a stable boy came forward to take their horses, and they walked toward the entrance. Carriages were still arriving and guests were climbing steps toward the arched entrance, though he and Donal trailed behind the rest. Golden light twinkled in leaded windows and fiddle music drifted outward in the purply dusk.

When Donal slowed, Ronan turned, sensing the lad's hesitation. "You are as welcome here as anyone, Donal."

"Though I am a laird's son, I am just a stable boy and a valet for now at Strathniven."

"That does not matter. Everyone is welcome at a cèilidh. But there is something you should know. You know that I might be given the Darrach title and inheritance." He drew a breath. "Indeed, the courts decided to grant it to me."

Donal began to whoop, but quickly stifled it. "Truly?"

"Which makes you a viscount's nephew—and his heir."

"What!" Donal gaped at him now.

"I have neither wife nor offspring as yet. I mean to secure an inheritance for you."

"One day you will marry and have heirs of the body, surely."

"We cannot know what the years will bring." His future and his freedom, too, were uncertain as yet. But as soon as all was clear, he meant to marry Ellison Graham if she would have him. He thought of it constantly now and saw no other course for him. But he was pragmatic, and would to take care of any eventuality. "No matter what happens, you can be assured of an inheritance from me."

"Uncle, I am honored."

Ronan clapped his shoulder. "Go inside with your head high, lad. You are a young man with a certain future. You have integrity and intelligence, and you will have an education and an inheritance. And you are not bad to look at, you rascal, for you take after your mother. Listen. One day you will ask a lass for her hand. But be sure that both of you know what a privilege it is to have someone's heart, more than anything else."

"Aye, sir. I am grateful. We are not blood kin, I know."

"You are like a son to me. I will honor that all my life."

These short weeks had taught him, more than any other stretch of time had, that love mattered most—family, friends, the love of one's life. Nothing else sufficed.

Ronan walked beside Donal toward the warmth of lights,

music, chatter, and merriment—and the promise of the lass who waited for him.

THE VAST INTERIOR twinkled with candlelight and lamplight sparkling over chandeliers, wine glasses, dishes, and glittered over jewels and silks. Under a high ceiling, walls were festooned with swaths of greenery and flowers. Guests clustered about, women in bright frocks, men in tartan or coats and trousers. The crowd was colorful and busy, some talking, some swaying, some already dancing to the music of fiddles and drums wafting through rooms open for the occasion.

Ellison tapped a foot, standing with Sorcha, Lady Strathniven, and Sorcha's mother. Everywhere she looked, she saw smiles and lively exchanges. But she did not see Ronan MacGregor.

A filament of worry went through her and she hoped nothing had gone wrong. But she knew that if she could join her life to his, she might have to accept an element of danger in what he did and who he knew. He never seemed to mind it much, and she wanted to understand better the calm and confidence that fueled him, even gain some herself.

Turning as she glanced about, she caught her breath and ducked her head, but was too late to avoid Adam Corbie's glance as he waved and saw the group of ladies.

"Miss Ellison, a moment please. I must speak with you."

"Mr. Corbie, perhaps this is not the time."

"I will not keep you for long. I have a message from your father. I have just been through the library—a handsome room that you will want to see. Let me show you."

Lady Strathniven waved at them. "Ellison, if Adam has a message from Sir Hector, it must be important. We will wait here for you."

Dread spun like a wheel inside her as she walked with Corbie, who took her elbow to guide her through the crowded room. Entering the library, a beautiful room that she could scarcely take in for her anxiousness, she turned.

"What is it?"

He sighed. "I am concerned about you and this MacGregor fellow."

She bristled. "No need. We did what was expected of us, and he is ready to meet the king. He will represent Scotland admirably. His manners are impeccable, and he knows just what to do and say. He is very—presentable."

He waved all that away. "He fooled us, especially you. Now he claims to be heir to a title—and a lawyer as well, which he never mentioned before. If it is true, he has kept a great deal from us—and you."

"The important thing is that he can be introduced, and my father can sponsor him without a falsehood about his identity. What word did Papa send for me?"

"I will inform him that there is improvement in the rogue's demeanor and appearance." He stepped closer. "But I have a greater concern."

She moved back. "What is that?"

"You are clearly infatuated with him, and you have had too much freedom at Strathniven, too susceptible to his influence."

"He is more a gentleman than anyone I know, I assure you."

"Truly? We suspect he plans to move illicit goods through the Highlands, which he arranged while he has been up here at our expense and hospitality."

"Is that all? He is preparing to send whisky to Edinburgh for the king. Papa requested it. That is hardly smuggling."

"I fear you have been naïve and easily led. Thank God I can look after you now."

"What you can do is go back to the city and tell Papa that Lord Darrach can be presented, so you both can earn whatever accolade you expect. Just remember that you owe your success to Ronan, Lord Darrach. His title makes this process so much easier for you. Am I correct in assuming Papa gave you no message for me? Then we are done here."

"Sir Hector will be greatly disappointed in you."

"That is not surprising. I would like to go back to the party." She turned.

"One more question." He took her gloved forearm in a tight grip so that she could not step away. "Have you gone entirely mad, Ellison?"

Dumbstruck, she pulled against his hand. "What do you mean?"

"I heard you are engaged to MacGregor now. What possessed you? Come this way. We might be interrupted here." He dragged her toward the French doors that led to the terraced gardens.

HEARING HIS NAME, Ronan looked around to see Lady Strathniven waving. She stood with a smaller, younger version of herself, clearly her sister, as Sorcha stood with them. Then Ellison would be nearby; he had been looking for her ever since he entered.

"Darrach! Let me introduce my sister, Mrs. Beaton," she said. "Viscount Darrach is our guest at Strathniven."

"Madam, good to meet you. Thank you for the invitation. And Miss Beaton, good to see you again." He smiled as Sorcha returned a sweet, happy grin.

"Look over there, sir," Lady Strathniven said, pointing. "That is the Earl of Huntly and his lady, and just there is the Duke of Atholl. There are so many I would like you to meet. They will welcome a newly inherited peer." She looked proud as a peacock. "Your cousin, Sir Evan MacGregor, and his wife could not attend, as they have already gone to Edinburgh."

Ronan nodded, feeling a surge of relief. He did not relish that reunion.

Lady Strathniven pointed out guests to him, rattling off names, many familiar. Some he had encountered in the Scottish parliament; others had recognizable names and titles, including clan chiefs—MacDonald, Stewart, MacIntosh, Fraser, and more. As the fiddle music soared and chatter filled the room like the roar of the sea, he looked for Ellison and did not see her.

"An excellent turnout, Mrs. Beaton. You must be pleased," he said.

"We are fortunate, my lord, that many were in the Highlands for the summer and had not yet left for the festivities in Edinburgh. You will go south as well, I think?"

"I will, madam. May I ask if any of you have seen Miss Graham?"

"She went with Cousin Adam to look at the library," Sorcha said. "You know her penchant for books."

"Aye. Thank you. I have—a message for her." He turned just as Lady Strathniven tapped his arm with her fan.

"Someone you must meet, Darrach. Sir Neill Pitlinnie. He is the one who gifts us with a supply of his whisky."

"Ah." Glancing that way, he saw Neill Pitlinnie in deep conversation with a Highland man he did not recognize. "He makes excellent whisky. Give him my compliments."

"He is a friend of my nephew Adam as well," Lady Strathniven went on. "They met in the Edinburgh High School. Boyhood friends, you see. So we are treated to a supply of whisky. Sir Neill is very good to us."

"Is he," Ronan murmured.

"Sissy dear, the dancing will begin formally soon," Mrs. Beaton told her sister. "The principals will dance first. The highest ranking, you know," she clarified for Ronan.

"That would be the Duke of Atholl and his lady, and the Duke and Duchess of Gordon, whom we are very pleased are here," Lady Strathniven said.

"You may dance too, Sissy, as hostess. We will need a fourth couple for a foursome. Sir Evan is not here, and besides, he is lame now." Mrs. Beaton had her sister's forthright manner, Ronan noted.

"Perhaps Corbie will be my partner. Darrach, would you dance as the fourth peer with the principals? Perhaps Miss Graham would be your partner." Her eyes twinkled.

"It would be an honor. First I must find her—and your nephew." Inclining his head, he made his way across the crowded room, his earlier anticipation transforming to concern.

"Betrothal?" Ellison pulled against Corbie's grip. She wanted to cross the terrace and escape into the house, but he held fast. "What do you mean?"

"Do not try to deny it. I was told of it almost as soon as we arrived."

Her stomach sank. "Who—"

"Neill Pitlinnie told me. Does Sir Hector know?"

Her heart pounded fiercely. "Pitlinnie! I did not realize you knew him."

"Since school days. He said he had the news straight from you when he saw you with MacGregor out in the hills at night. Why?"

"We were out for the day. That is not your concern."

"If you foolishly promised to marry him, it is very much my concern. I genuinely care for you and would give you the life you deserve. Is it true?"

She did not answer that, pulling against his hold. "Do not listen to rumors."

"I will if it means you are in the thrall of another rascal who will bring ruin to your family. Your father must hear of this before someone else tells him the news."

"I will tell him the truth when I see him."

"So you did promise?" He yanked her close and she stubbed the toe of her slipper on a stone, stumbling into him. "Then someone must save you from disgrace again."

"I do not need saving. Let go," she said between her teeth, twisting her arm.

"This will ruin your father. He is poised to take the Lord Provost's position."

"Lord Provost!"

"When Lord Arbuthnot steps down in a year or two, your father could be appointed, especially if he succeeds with the royal visit. He could be granted a title as well as promotion. You cannot destroy what he has worked for!" His grip was bruising.

"I would never do that."

"We can fix your grave error. I have a solution."

"You worry over nothing. You will get what you want. Lord Darrach will only bring credit to my father—especially if he lets him go free afterward."

"MacGregor wants to benefit, so he coerced you into marriage, is that it?"

"He did not, because he—"

"Loves you?" Corbie laughed bitterly. "Is that what you think? He sees the advantage of a father-in-law who is chief of the constabulary so he can keep out of prison despite his criminal actions."

She stopped struggling, breath heaving. His cruel words felt like a visceral blow. She had brought scandal to her family once. But Ronan would never deceive her.

"We cannot risk bringing him to the king, especially if he is still smuggling up here. He will be arrested as soon he reaches the city."

"He did everything you asked. You cannot betray him. His title is legitimate and he is innocent of the other charges."

"And you believe that! Poor lass." He shook his head. "But you can still save your father's reputation and yours too." He moved closer, bending her arm to press it between them. "Sir Hector could lose all. Now listen. This is how we will fix it. We will announce our engagement," he went on. "That will erase the rumors and protect you. MacGregor will be forgotten after the royal visit."

She felt dread rise like bile. "I would never marry you."

"Sir Hector and my aunt have hoped for our union since we were young. Surely you knew that. It will make them happy."

"No," she said firmly.

"You were coerced—threatened—by a reprobate, and came to me for help. So romantic, just as you like. We will mend any harm to your father. Solved, you see."

"Not solved. You need my consent."

"If you want Darrach and his friends safe, you will agree. Save all of them from hanging and let them be banished. Be the heroine in our story, my dear."

She felt cold all over. Numb. She had known he could be vile, but not like this. "You could not harm them!"

"Not me. The law will do it. MacGregor's actions will bring about his hanging and that of his friends. His lands will be lost. His family will be evicted. Marry me instead, and we will do what we can to lessen their sentences."

"Stop," she moaned, as tears stung her eyes. "You cannot mean this."

"I only care about you. I only want to help you." He released his fierce hold to take her hand. She froze as he raised it to kiss her knuckles through her glove.

"No," she whispered. "Leave us alone. I will tell Papa what you have said."

"I could not stop your first ill-fated marriage, but I can help you escape this one. We will be happy together, you and I. You will forget your infatuation when you see how proud your father will be. We will be content and elevated in life. You will be Lady Strathniven."

She gasped, realizing that his hope of inheriting Strathniven rested on her. "Elevated?" She grasped the word. "Your aunt will learn the truth."

"But will she believe it? Think of your father. He could be Lord Provost someday. And I might become Deputy Provost in his place."

If she agreed to this, she knew Corbie would make sure Ronan suffered more than her father ever would. Corbie would ruin him utterly. Ronan's life and their happiness together stood in the balance here and now.

But if she refused, if she relied on newfound strength and determination, she might only destroy what she loved most in the world.

She felt the fight drain out of her. "Let me think about it."

Corbie pulled her to him, leaned to kiss her. She angled her head away and his lips smeared her cheek. "Make the right decision, Ellison."

She could not betray Ronan's love and trust in her. Yet that could save his life, and if it did—he could never learn the truth.

Corbie leaned to attempt another kiss, but she torqued away. "Later, you will be glad you did this," he said, lips eager even as she avoided him.

"Stop! Let me think."

From the corner of her eye, she saw a tall shadow stride across the terrace. An arm reached out swiftly out to shove Corbie aside.

"Leave her be," Ronan snarled.

Corbie stumbled. "How dare you interrupt a private conversation?"

"Am I unwelcome?" Ronan demanded, turning to Ellison. She set a trembling hand to her chest above the lace at her bodice.

"Not at all," she said breathlessly.

Taking her arm, Ronan turned to face Corbie. "The lady does not wish your company, sir."

"We were discussing matters that are none of your concern."

"Miss Graham?" Ronan asked.

Lifting her chin, she stood close to Ronan, relieved to feel his steadiness and calm, and the banked power he radiated. He was all she could ever dream of and all she could ever want. Yet she might have to distance herself, detach her heart from his, else Corbie would ruin him.

As she looked from one to the other, she felt a well of strength rise in her. *Take the risk*, a voice within seemed to say.

"The rumor of my betrothal to Lord Darrach," she said, "is true."

"My God, woman, you are a fool. You will regret this!"

Ronan bristled beside her, squared his shoulders. She saw the pulse in his jaw, the blue flash in his eyes. She set a hand on his sleeve.

"Miss Graham," he said in a hard voice, "explain it to the

gentleman."

He was leaving it to her, though the very air thickened between the two men. And she was about to add fuel to fire.

"It is true," she repeated. "I will marry Lord Darrach, if he is still amenable."

"He is amenable," Ronan said.

Love warmed all through her, strengthened her further. His resolve made her certain, his composure fed calmness into her. She straightened her spine. "We will be married as soon as it can be arranged."

"You will come to disaster over this. Think carefully, Ellison. The price of your stubbornness is too high," Corbie snarled.

Ronan stepped forward. Ellison tapped his arm. "No," she said. "Mr. Corbie, perhaps you would return to Strathniven now in the carriage. I will find a ride later."

"I will do better than that. I will go straight to Edinburgh." Corbie glared at Ronan. "We gave you every privilege, and you preyed on a vulnerable widow. It will not go well for you now. What did you think to gain?"

Ronan's arm tightened under her hand. "Nothing you could comprehend, sir."

"I only wanted to protect her from such a scoundrel as you. I only wanted to guarantee her safety so her father will know she kept her honor with you."

"I will tell Papa what he needs to know. Best leave now, Adam."

"Enough," Ronan barked. "Leave now if you wish, sir. But Lady Strathniven expects you to partner her in the first dance. Go tell her what you have decided. Go on, before I show you the door."

He pointed toward the French doors. Corbie stomped away. "This is not finished!" he snapped as he yanked open the door and went inside.

"I have never wanted to kill a man so much in my life," Ronan growled.

Ellison gave a half-laugh, half-sob. "I am glad you controlled the urge."

"Barely." He took her hand. "Are you all right, lass?"

She nodded as a wave of relief and love rinsed through her, rocking her nearly to her knees. She leaned her head against his chest, and he held her.

"I am fine now. Thank you for ending that."

"You ended it, love, and far more nicely than I would have. But I have a feeling this is not over. What did he really want?"

"To complain about my poor judgment. And demand that I marry him."

He swore softly. "Small-minded man. He wants something more, but what? With luck he will be gone soon. But in Edinburgh, be sure to keep your distance from him."

"He thinks I should obey what Papa wants. But Corbie wants it more."

"That troubles me about him. Do you feel ready to go back inside?"

Nodding, she walked beside him, but her legs and hands trembled, and she could not shake the awful sense of dread that turned her stomach. So much of this bad situation was her doing, and hers to fix. She had gambled that Corbie's threats were empty, but now she was not certain. He was bitter and angry, and would cause a rift with her father and trouble for Ronan if he could. And she felt responsible.

In these past weeks, she had begun to feel a deep desire for happiness, dreams she had given up. She desperately wanted love and contentment and freedom with Ronan, and had begun to believe it was possible. But now all that had changed.

"Ronan." She stopped in the center of the silent, beautiful library. "What now?"

"Why, Miss Graham," he murmured, "I am thinking we should marry, and soon."

Her heart thumped, thrilled, wishing it could be so. "But—"

He leaned down to kiss her gently, sinking a new feeling

through her knees. She clutched at his lapels. He drew back to look down at her. "But?"

"Perhaps we should keep it to ourselves."

"I should speak to your father first. Widows do not need permission—but in this case, it is better for you if I go to him."

"If Corbie does not poison the waters first, aye. But I can undo whatever he tells Papa, I think. But can we keep our plans to ourselves for a little while?"

"If that is what you want, let them wonder. Is Miss Graham is engaged? And is he a rogue or a viscount?"

She smiled. "A frog or a prince?"

Chapter Twenty-Two

THE FIDDLERS SWEPT their bows over the strings in unison as Ronan led Ellison through the slow beat of the strathspey, following the patterns and rhythms as the couples moved in alternating loops. He smiled, seeing Ellison's grace as she flowed through the movements of the dance. Corbie, who had stayed for his aunt, clomped along while Lady Strathniven proved a lively dancer, hopping about with enthusiasm.

Ellison circled with Corbie in turn, turning away before he could speak to her, which Ronan was glad to see. He wanted to remove the man brusquely, but the urge passed when he saw Ellison's lightsome beauty and felt the pull of love within him.

The principals' dance ended and other couples took the floor as the fiddlers struck up a fast reel. Soon the dancers were stepping right, left, hopping, whirling, and laughing as they kept up with the rhythms. Ronan led Ellison into the fray, wanting to keep her dancing, keep her merry and breathless as she whirled in his arms.

Later, in the supper room among the crowd, he roamed past tables groaning with food—roast mutton, fowl, beef, haggis; steaming vegetables in sauces; plates of oatcakes and bannocks with butter and cheese. Another table held puddings, pies, cakes, bowls of fruity ices, while bowls of whisky punch and decanters of sherry wine filled another table, along with coffee and port. Finally, as servants cleared away dishes, couples took chairs to rest and visit, and then in pairs, resumed dancing.

Watching Ellison, Ronan was glad to see that she glowed with happiness in the moment. But he kept watch, alert for anything that might disturb the mood and the camaraderie. Too soon, he was proved right.

Though the fellow should have departed, Corbie stood in a shadowy corner engaged in earnest conversation with Pitlinnie and a bearded Highlander. As Corbie gestured, Pitlinnie shook his head and the third man hunched his shoulders, listening.

What the devil was this? Ronan crossed the room, determined to interrupt, but the trio separated. A few dancers whirled through, so that Ronan paused, and when the path cleared, the three men were gone. He hoped Corbie had finally left, but he felt a distinct unease.

"Lord Darrach!" Hearing Sorcha's voice, he turned to see her with a tall, thin man who looked deucedly familiar. He had seen the fellow in Edinburgh's Parliament House. On a bench. In a wig and the dark red robes of a lord justice.

Sorcha's brother, The Honorable Lord Justice. His heart sank. Sorcha called again, and Ronan approached reluctantly.

"Lord Darrach, let me introduce The Honorable Lord Justice Beaton. My brother," she added, smiling.

"My lord." Ronan took the man's extended hand. "Pleased to meet you, sir."

Justice Beaton. Ronan had passed the judge often enough in the halls of the Scottish parliament in Edinburgh, had even argued before his bench a few times.

"I was just telling my little sister how familiar you look. Then it occurred to me. Sir John MacGregor, one of our most capable advocates. Now Viscount Darrach, by God! Excellent."

Nothing for it but to own it. "Thank you, sir. I am occasionally in Edinburgh, though most often I practice in Perth."

"Which explains why I have not seen you of late," Beaton added, and his eyes narrowed. The man was no fool, and might know more about John Ronan MacGregor than was comfortable.

If so, the judge did not allude to it.

Hearing Ellison's greeting, Ronan felt relief and tension both. She greeted the Beaton siblings, whom she knew well, and stood beside Ronan, not close enough to draw attention, yet close enough that he felt buoyed up.

"I understand your cousin is the new chief of the Mac-Gregors," Beaton said.

"Sir Evan MacGregor, aye."

"He was invited tonight," Sorcha said, "but he and his lady have gone to Edinburgh already."

"Sir Evan owes his life to Darrach," Beaton told the others. "Saved his cousin's life in India. Sir Evan suffered terrible injuries. But Darrach here pulled him out of the fray in a brutal ambush. Sir Evan is hearty today because of it."

"Many fought alongside Sir Evan that day. He was the very soul of courage," Ronan said. He disliked talking about it. "His brother was lost in the battle. We all helped each other survive that day."

"Must have been hellish." Beaton shook his head. "Sir Evan owes you. Indeed, the entire clan is in your debt."

Ronan was uncomfortably aware of how intently the others listened. He had told Ellison little of that part of his life. Yet now he felt her warmth and faith like a blanket.

"Thank you, my lord," he said simply.

"Anything you need, sir. Anything at all," Beaton said. "Miss Graham, I nearly forgot. I have some news for you from Mr. Cameron. There was an issue with a house on Castle Street, I think?"

She lifted her brows. "North Castle, aye. Mr. Cameron brought it to you?"

"It came to me and was decided. The previous tenants are gone," he said tactfully. "A new tenant already offered to rent it for a generous sum. Rental fees are exorbitant in Edinburgh this summer, which is fortunate for you! Mr. Cameron has the papers."

"Thank you! It is a lovely house and I hope the new tenants will be happy there."

"It is a very desirable location," Lady Strathniven said, having joined them.

Silent, Ronan only smiled, hoping for a chance to step away before Beaton remembered more.

"Oh, there is the Duke of Gordon," Beaton said. "I must speak with him about the procession planned in the city. We are both on Scott's Celtic committee. Scott is a grand fellow," he confided, "but his precious project, representing what he calls Celtified Scotland, has required a great deal of effort. Please excuse me." He departed the group.

"Ellison, it is good to know the problem with the house is solved. And a paying tenant as well, excellent! You must stay with me if you ever tire of your dear Papa. And Darrach," she added, startling him. "You saved Sir Evan! I had no idea!"

"A testament to Darrach's humility, for none of us knew." Ellison looked up at him, her eyes limpid gray, searching. Someday he would tell her all of it and more. Suddenly it occurred to him, standing with Lady Strathniven, Sorcha, and his lady love, that he owed all of them affection and gratitude for helping him these last weeks.

"I am glad you three found out," he murmured, his gaze touching Ellison's. "But keep it to yourselves, aye?"

"Darrach does like his secrets," Ellison said with a light laugh.

MUCH LATER, ELLISON stood outside watching the line of carriages crawl past Duncraig's entrance and down the drive to the main road. Drawing her paisley shawl closer in the light chill of the late summer evening, she looked around for Sorcha or Lady Strathniven among the clusters of guests chatting as they waited. Stifling a yawn, she realized how very weary she was, almost swaying on her feet. All she could think of was getting home to Strathniven, to her bed and pillows and dreams.

And to the last chance to see Ronan there before they all left for Edinburgh and the commotion—and risks—of the king's visit.

Earlier, Ronan had reminded her that he and Donal had ridden to Duncraig and would head out on horseback to return to Strathniven. When he asked if she wanted him to follow as she rode in a carriage with the other women, she shook her head.

"We will only slow you down," she said. "Lady Strathniven planned to ask her sister to lend a carriage, since Mr. Corbie left in our barouche. I regret giving him the idea, as there is a great scramble for carriages this evening."

"Better that you do not ride back with him. But if you wish to wait for Lady Strathniven and Sorcha, I will go back with Donal and see you at the house." He had briefly touched her shoulder before leaving. She had felt his caring and her own rush of desire. But it did not matter if they were seen. She did not care what the rumors were.

Hearing Sorcha, she turned. "Mama wants us to stay the night," she said. "So far all the carriages are in use, and she would like us to stay and leave tomorrow. I am to ask what you prefer."

"I would rather ride back to Strathniven if a vehicle is available. I so want to be home after such an exhausting—and lovely— night. But I have found no carriage yet. And Lord Darrach already left with Donal on horseback. I may have to stay."

"Wait here, and I will see what can be done." Sorcha hurried away.

Gathering her shawl around her, Ellison stood watching, glancing up at the stars, delicate against the indigo sky. Hearing a step as someone approached, she turned.

"Miss Graham." Neill Pitlinnie stood behind her. "I overheard your conversation. Mr. Corbie has taken your carriage? I wonder if I could offer mine."

Startled, she shook her head. "I will stay if I can find no other way back."

"You would not be riding with me," he said. "I am happy to loan you my barouche, which is not being used. I mean to ride back, as I brought a horse here as well, as friends needed transportation. I—owe you an apology, Miss Graham."

That surprised her. "You owe me nothing, sir." She looked about for Sorcha.

"I realize that I shared news that was not mine to tell. Accept my congratulations and my apologies. Let me direct my driver to take you home."

She had not expected that, but perhaps he had a moment of conscience. Ronan would not be happy about it, but she was so very tired, and could explain later. "A kind offer," she said.

"Here is my driver now. Go on. I will tell Lady Strathniven your plans."

The carriage pulled up, a sleek black barouche with seats of cushioned red velvet. She relented, seeing that temptation. She wanted to meet Ronan at Strathniven. If Lady Strathniven and Sorcha stayed here, and Corbie had gone on to Edinburgh, or at least the inn at Kinross as he had threatened, she would be alone with Ronan. It could be their last night together before returning to the city and the unknown.

"Thank you, sir," she said, smiling up at the bearded driver.

"To Strathniven, and hurry, for the lady is weary," Pitlinnie told the man. He opened the door. "Miss Graham, I hope you will forgive me. Enjoy your journey."

"I am grateful, sir." She mounted the lowered step, accepting the support of his hand, sitting and sat as he shut the door and tapped the carriage roof.

Sinking onto the cushioned bench, she leaned back as the carriage lumbered away to join the long line of vehicles rolling down the road. Seeing a plaid folded on the seat, she drew it over lap and sighed, lulled by the swaying motion and the darkness.

Somewhat later, she woke, noticing that the rocking motion of the carriage had stopped. Strathniven already? Rousing herself, gathering her shawl, she felt the vehicle lurch as the driver dismounted and came around to open the door.

"Miss," he said, "out now." Before she could answer, he reached in to grab her. Shocked, she pulled away, and saw another man standing behind the driver.

"I do not understand—"

"Out. Now!" The driver grabbed for her again. Standing, she exited, trembling.

"What is this? Where are we?" She looked around. In the darkness, she did not see Strathniven House—just a wide stretch of bleak, dark moorland, hills to one side, a gleam of water elsewhere.

"Come along. And dinna try to get away." The bearded man clutched at her then, pulling her toward him, while the second man looped a rope around her hands. Roughly shoved, she fell to her knees in mucky grass, unable to stop herself with her hands tied.

As they took her arms to haul her to her feet, she took a breath, lifted her head, and screamed with all the fervor she could muster, hearing the sound travel over moor and water before a brutish hand clapped over her mouth.

The driver grabbed her shawl and she heard a ripping sound. Then a wad of cloth was forcibly tied around her jaw, gagging her.

"Now she will be quiet," he growled. "We should hae done that first. Come along. 'Tisna far to walk. I wouldna drag a wee lassie aboot, see, but it canna be helped. Come."

She could not form words, could only concentrate on walking forward, keeping her balance, breathing, as they pulled her between them along the edge of the water toward the tower in the distance.

Looking around, she saw a small island in the water, and glancing further, began to recognize where they were walking. They were walking beside the narrow stretch of Loch Brae, where the fairy isle sat in the middle. Ahead of them, yards away, she saw the massive ruin of a tower—the ancient ruin that she had wanted to visit.

Nearby would be the birch grove where a fast-flowing burn cut through moor and meadow, where she and Ronan had fished.

They had met Pitlinnie near the meadowland. And he had lent her the use of his carriage that evening.

Not so kindly as she had thought. She had been naïve to trust him. But why would he lure her deliberately?

Then she knew. He meant to use her to lure and harm Ronan.

"WHAT WAS THAT?" Donal halted his horse and looked at Ronan. "Did you hear it?"

"Aye." Ronan stopped too, looking about. The sound, oddly familiar, sent a chill down his back.

"Fox, most like. They can shriek something fierce." Donal gathered the reins.

"Huh," Ronan agreed, but instinct told him otherwise. That was no fox. He looked around in the darkness. "I saw a coach heading that way not long ago. Odd."

"I saw too, but dozens of coaches left Duncraig tonight. It would be one of those just heading home."

"But this one took drover's track in that direction. There are no houses or villages that way, and it is too dark for a carriage to take such a rough track." The uneasy feeling plunged through him again. He stopped, and Donal did the same.

"What is it?" the lad asked.

"That way lies the Lealtie Burn and Loch Brae, and a crumbling old ruin. Nothing else for miles. It is a bit late for fishing, but not too late for free traders to be about."

"They might go that way, but it is not the best route through this part of the glen."

"I saw Pitlinnie and his lot come this way one evening, and I wondered why for that very reason. The only thing out here is—" Quick as a falling star, he knew.

"What?" Donal asked.

"The old broch tower. Have you been there recently?"

"Not since I was a boy. Too dangerous. The walls are near to collapsing. No one goes there. But—" He whistled. "No one goes there."

"Exactly. I wonder if we might find our whisky there. Come on!"

As he rode, he searched in the moonlight for any trace that would tell him a vehicle had come this way. He stopped once or twice, noting wheel marks, and then saw footprints and mashed grasses. Those subtle marks led eastward toward the loch.

Something compelled him this way, a strong pull in gut and heart. If Pitlinnie and his men intended to hide a quantity of whisky in casks and kegs, the deserted old broch would be ideal. Why had he not thought of it before? Logic simply said the place was ruinous, useless. But that might not be the case.

Few ventured to the ancient ruin due to the danger of stones that might collapse, ancient ghosts that might appear, and the risk of injury or worse. Yet it was an excellent spot to hide a stock of stolen whisky for a while, though it was sure to be guarded.

"Donal." He stopped the horse. "Ride to Invermorie and get Aleck if he is still there. If we are correct, we will also need a cart to move our brew out of there."

Waving a hand, Donal turned his horse and rode off to take the military road, the fastest and safest route to Invermorie.

Urging his horse forward, Ronan followed the drover's track until it faded into a grassy hillside. Desperate to see his instinct through, he cantered forward as the loch came into sight.

At last, they were gone.

Tilting her head in the darkness, Ellison waited, hands bound, holding her breath as she listened. Not long ago, she had heard the men's voices fade. They must be heading back to the carriage they had left on the moor. Now the silence inside the old broch felt safer. She heard the shush of wind through trees, midnight birdsong, and nearby, water lapping softly. She sighed, releasing fear with a long exhale.

Uncertain how much time had passed, she knew she had to find an escape before they returned. She struggled against the dry, choking grip of the gag in her mouth, and pulled at the rope binding her wrists in front of her. Her hair shook down in loose tendrils, obscuring her vision. There must be some way to get free of the ropes. If she could do that, she could run out of the broch, and find her way back to the road, and Strathniven.

She scooted along the floor, just earth and some flat stones overgrown with moss and grass. They had left her leaning against a stone wall with the smell of stone and earth strong around her. But somewhere above, she sensed fresh night air coming from somewhere. Looking up, she glimpsed the night sky and a sprinkling of stars.

The structure was an ancient round tower, its roof gone, so that the massive cylindrical walls opened like an upright tunnel. The rooms of such a fortified keep were usually built inside the wide hollow walls, she knew from reading about ancient architecture one summer. A honeycomb of chambers could be separated by dividing walls. But she was in the central area, and had to locate an exit.

Scuttling along, resting, moving again, she paused to breathe and listen. Silence continued. Frowning, she thought back to what the men had said, looking for any hint that would help her understand what had happened and what they wanted.

A scrap of conversation between her captors came back. "He should be here," one man had said to the other. "Should have met us by now."

"He will be here. He wants this. He will pay well."

"What of the other one?"

"If he finds the place, then pity the man, for he will step into a trap."

She froze with dread at the memory. A trap—for Ronan. Surely they referred to him. The other man they spoke of had to be Pitlinnie.

She had to get free, find Ronan and warn him.

Something else came back to her. "We must leave the lass here. We canna wait longer. Have to find him."

"Keep her bound. She will go nowhere. When this is done, we will have gold in our pockets."

"We'd earn more if we took what's hidden here, hey." They laughed as they left.

Moving again, scooching awkwardly, her hand struck something hard, and she heard the dull thunk of wood. In the darkness, she could just see a wooden chest of some kind.

Along its edge, the wood had split, and a large nail stuck out. Wondering if it was sharp enough to cut rope, she maneuvered until the rope caught on the metal edge. Shifting, rocking her hands, she sawed the rope against the metal piece. After a while, shoulders aching unmercifully, she nearly gave up. But she felt the fibers weaken a little. Pulling and sawing anew, she kept at it.

The wooden chest was heavy, hardly shifting as she worked the rope over the edge of the large nail. Her movements created a chinking sound. What was in there? China or pottery? How odd to store such in this ancient place.

Whisky, she thought then. Whisky in glass bottles or pottery jugs. It must be.

Then the fibers collapsed around her wrists and she pulled her hands free. Wincing, she eased her stiff arms, rubbed her hands, tore off the gag, and got to her feet. Shaking out her muddied satin gown and sagging shawl, she looked around.

Standing on the earthen level of the broch, she could make out broken walls and jumbled stones in the moonlight, but did not see an exit immediately. She remembered stumbling over a maze of stones when the men led her inside. She knew there was a narrow opening somewhere in the tumble of broken stones.

She peered again at the wooden box, which was a crate built of rough wood, its lid broken and split. The contents had made a chinking sound. Poking a hand inside, she felt straw packed around the shoulders of crockery jugs, the sort used for ale or liquor.

She knelt, snatched up a small flat stone, and pried the rest of the lid away. Reaching inside, she pulled out a squat crockery vessel plugged with wax. A pale paper label was glued to the shoulders. She rotated the jug in a moonbeam.

Glenbrae Distillery, Perthshire, Scotland. An ink drawing showed the profile of Invermorie Castle.

She had to find Ronan quickly.

She made her way around the broch, hands skimming mossy walls, feet careful on cracked and tumbled stones. As she went, she listened for hoofbeats and voices, praying she could get away before her captors returned.

The men were expecting at least one more man, likely Pitlinnie. No one else would steal and hide a stock of Glenbrae whisky. Perhaps Sir Neill had heard it would be sent to the king. But why would that even matter to him?

The broch was widest at its base, and enormous cracks in the old stones revealed the double stone walls where interior rooms had once existed, now filled with rubble and risk. Moonlight picked out uneven shapes and shadows.

Yet she could see regular shapes in some of the niches. Those had to be crates and kegs. Moving cautiously, she went toward them and gasped.

As clouds shifted overhead, cool moonbeams brightened the space to show stacks of casks, kegs, and crates.

Heart pounding, she knew she had to get out—and find Ronan. Whirling, she ran, stumbled, her knee hitting stone. She rose up and ran on. A line of light appeared in the shadows, an opening in the immense and partially collapsed retaining wall.

Then her dancing slippers met a wooden ramp and she was outside in the night air. Overhead, a canopy of stars sprinkled across an amethyst sky and a bright blur of the moon. Down the hill, mist floated over the dark loch like a cloud.

Recalling which direction led to Invermorie, she ran through the grass keeping the narrow loch to her right, the broch behind her, and miles of meadow ahead.

Hearing shouts and the thud of horse hooves, she stopped short. As she stood there exposed in moonlight, the splash of oars sounded in the water. Someone was crossing the loch toward the hillside bank where she stood.

Spinning, she hurried back to the broch. Her best chance was to hide in a shadowy niche and hope the thugs would think she had escaped the ancient tower.

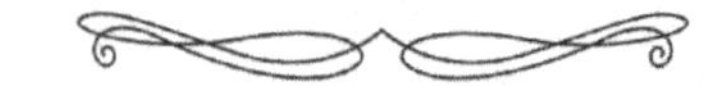

Chapter Twenty-Three

SECURING HIS HORSE under trees in the moonlight, Ronan patted the steadfast bay and headed toward the loch. Donal and Aleck would soon return with a cart, but he wanted to explore to see if the whisky was hidden in the tower despite its precarious state. Instinct had drawn him here like a lodestone, and he had to know why.

Hearing hoofbeats, he stepped back under the dark and leafy canopy, then eased out to see two men ride across the moorland toward the loch. When he realized they were not Donal and Aleck, he drew back.

The riders dismounted, leaving their horses to graze, and walked toward the water. Their voices floated back in the quiet.

"There should be a wee boat here—" said one.

"Further down," said the other.

"We left that lass too long. Something might have happened."

"That scrap of a lassie is tied snug and fears for her life. She will be there."

"The reward for this better be worth the trouble," the first one complained.

Ronan felt his heart sink, then anger flame. *Ellison.* He had to do something quickly. If he could distract them, he could get to the boat and cross the loch shielded by the mist on its surface. Slipping out of the grove of trees, he ran to the grazing horses, released their pegged leads, slapped their hindquarters, and sent them whickering and cantering in an opposite direction.

Shouting, the men frantically chased after the escaping horses. Fast and silent, Ronan went down to the lochside to find a small rowboat nudged among the reeds. Fog swirled thick over the water as he pushed it free and set off over the smooth, quiet water.

The loch was a narrow stretch here, and soon he passed the little island, hardly seeing it through the mist. Reaching the shore in the darkness, he berthed the boat among reeds and stepped to the bank. Cautious, glancing about, he climbed the slope to the broch's curving foundation, looking for the old entrance, wary of falling stones.

A crude wooden ramp creaked beneath his boots. As he edged through the tumble of stones in the entrance, his footsteps crunching over pebbles and earth, he glanced about in utter darkness. The only light came from far above as moonbeams filtered into the center depths. Just to his left, he glimpsed the movement of a pale shadow.

"Ellison?" he whispered.

Just as he spoke, a missile flew toward him. He ducked barely in time as a stone crashed into the wall behind him. Another followed swiftly. Ronan put up an arm to protect his head from falling debris as he sidestepped the onslaught.

A wraith flew out of the shadows, a fairy bit of a girl in a pale gown with pale hair, arms out now as she ran toward him, sobbing. He pulled her into his arms, every fiber in him infused with gratitude, relief, love. "Ellison!"

"You came for me, you are here, oh, Ronan," she sobbed against his chest.

"I am here," he whispered, kissing her hair, her brow, her lips, cupping her face in his hands. "What happened? How did you get here? Did those bastards—"

"They did not hurt me. They only tied my hands and took me in here. Gagged me, too, when I screamed—"

"Was that you I heard out on the moor? I did not know it was you—but that shriek brought me here. Who took you? You were at Duncraig when I saw you last."

"Pitlinnie," she said breathlessly. "He loaned me his carriage, and was so polite. He apologized and I believed him. I am such a fool. I am sorry. His men took me here, but they left and I got free. And now you are here, and oh, Ronan, I must show you!"

He cupped her shoulders. "If anyone touched you, I will kill him—"

"Only to bind me up. One of them was at the dance. I think the other was with Pitlinnie the night we saw them out on the moor. Ronan, the whisky, it's here! Come look!"

"Is it? I wondered." He glanced toward the entrance. "We need to get out of here before they come back. Where is it?"

"Inside the walls." She took his hand to tug him along, and he stepped ahead of her to make sure the going was safe. High overhead, visible in the wide ruined opening at the top of the tower, the moon slid out from behind clouds to spill more light into the wreckage of stone that filled the old floor of the structure.

"Over there, in that section, do you see?"

He did. Round casks, small kegs, stout wooden boxes. "My God," he growled. He moved forward, ducking between broken chamber walls, and reached out to touch and examine the wooden containers.

"Is it all there?" she asked.

"Possibly. Come here." He handed her toward him and pulled her to him to hug her closely, kiss her swiftly, then let go. "My dear lass, what tremendous luck to find this, though I am sorry for what you had to go through! I had a feeling we might find the whisky here, so I sent Donal to fetch Aleck with a cart so we can move the stuff. But I want to get you out of here." He took her hand to guide her over rubble and debris toward the entrance.

"I can help move the whisky," she said.

"No need, the lads and I will take care of it. But I will take you to Invermorie first." He led her through the opening and into fresh, misty, moonlit air. "Down the slope and over the water. My horse is on the other side."

"Ah—aye," she said, and he heard the shivering in her voice.

Noticing then that all she wore was her thin, lacy, muddy dancing gown and a torn shawl, he took off his jacket and draped it over her shoulders as they walked down the wet grassy slope.

"I am s-sorry—"

"Hush now. You, my love, have a warrior's heart even if you do not know it. Into the boat with you."

She stepped in readily, and he loved her even more for her pragmatism as she reached for an oar. He bade her sit, took both oars, and pulled out onto the loch.

Months ago when he first met her, she had seemed such a delicate and anxious creature, yet even then he had glimpsed courage in her. She had an ability to accept whatever came without complaint and press ahead. In mere weeks, he had watched her discover her strength, test her voice, find her wings like a kestrel perched on the edge of the nest. Now she was finding her freedom and the strength to fly out on her own.

But tonight above all, he wanted her safety. Pulling on the oars, he glanced about, looking for any movement, listening for any sound.

Darkness and mist obscured his view as the boat slipped over the water toward the center of the loch. Above, the moon was a soft blur, its light barely touching the ripples. He headed for the opposite shore on instinct, having rowed over this loch many times as boy and young man. Then he heard noises—shouts, horses neighing.

"They are back," Ellison murmured.

He slowed, stilled the oars. Torchlight glowed like a golden blur through the fog. Shouts echoed over the water. He did not hear Donal or Aleck calling. Pitlinnie's scoundrels, then.

Picking up the oars, he pulled hard and quiet. But the motion felt odd, slow, as if the boat went through syrup rather than water. With a soft thunk, the prow hit something, and the craft shuddered to a stop. Reaching out, he touched earth and something mossy rather than water. Had they hit the little island in the middle of the black water, or had they reached shore already?

He pulled backward, but the boat did not move, and the oar's paddles thumped solid earth. He swore low. "We are hung up on something."

"Ronan—is this the fairy isle?" Ellison whispered.

"The what?" He pushed, pulled, but the boat seemed stuck.

"The fairy isle. The one that appears in the mist."

"It feels like a sand bar, but it might be the wee island. In this fog, I am not sure. Damn it," he muttered as a thick blanket of mist swirled and settled all around. He could hardly see the boat or the oars, and Ellison, sitting across from him, had a curious glow around her, as if a strand of moonlight had threaded through to find her.

"Remember the legend? The isle that appears and disappears?" she whispered.

"Hush. They are shouting," he said low. They quieted, waiting, listening as men yelled, their voices echoing over the water.

"Ellison Graham! Where are you, lass?"

"She cannae ha' gone far," another said.

"Perhaps she escaped and swam the loch!"

"If she drowns in this murk, we are done for. Ellison Graham!"

"Lads! The wee boat is gone! There is another down this way. Hurry!"

Ronan heard splashing, swearing, and then oars moving through the water.

"We can get out on the island," Ellison whispered. "Come on." Without waiting, she stepped quickly out of the boat, rocking it. Ronan dug an oar into earth to stabilize it—solid earth. He stood and reached for her, though she all but vanished in the mist.

"Ellison Graham!" The voice echoed over the water. "Your father wants you back! Your betrothed is looking for you!"

"Betrothed! But you found me." Her whisper was disembodied, and her hand came out of the fog to beckon to Ronan. "Come this way." Her voice was soft, a hiss.

He stepped out of the boat. The ground underfoot rocked gently but held. It could not be, and yet it was so. There was no solid island in this loch, just a bar of sand and grass and water plants. Yet he stood on firm earth. Ellison took his hand.

ELLISON CLUNG TO Ronan's hand, warm and strong in hers, while water licked at her shoes and her limbs trembled like the earth beneath her feet. She could hear voices calling through the mist, hooting her name, threats that chilled her. Ronan's fingers pressed hers, real and safe.

Mist swirled and poured around them, a cloud-ring that surrounded them, shielded them, even covering the rowboat beached on the narrow shore. She stood silently beside Ronan while the fog enveloped them like an embrace.

Shouts echoed again over the water. She heard the splash and creak of oars as her captors—she knew their voices—glided nearer. She could hear the lap and surge of the water, heard one of the men swear in a low tone. Any moment now, they would strike the mossy bank where Ellison and Ronan stood.

Now the soft blanket of mist erased the water, the isle, the boat, all but what was nearest her—Ronan's sleeve and shoulder as he held her hand.

"Cannae see a damn thing," a man groused. "Where the devil are we?"

"Go back to shore. We darena go through this soup. 'Tisna like anything I've ever seen. Turn back!"

"What about the lass?"

"If she escaped, she either drowned in this accursed loch or she's out in the hills. We cannae go on—must come back later to look for her."

"Nor has that other fool shown up," the man said. "This is an accursed night! Why did we agree to this madness?"

"Coin, that is why!"

"But there are tales about this loch and the auld tower—bad tales. Best get away quick before this water takes us doon, lad."

Ellison heard the long swish of oars as the boat rounded in its path through the water. Breathing out in relief, she stood with Ronan in silence long after the sounds of the boat, then the voices, faded.

Ronan pulled her close. "They could easily have seen us standing here, yet they did not. What luck the mist came in so thick and fast just then."

"The Fey protect their own."

He huffed. "The Fey, is it?"

"You said it yourself once. The island is here and then gone, and no one knows why. But it was here for us when we needed protection. The isle, and the Fey, saved us."

"It is just a legend, love, and a small spit of land that is hardly noticeable."

"It appeared for us when we needed it. I am sure of it. And you carry fairy ancestry in your blood."

"So they say." He kissed her head. "You have an imagination, love. The hour is late, and this has been quite the night."

"The Fey protect their own, and you are one of them."

"A lovely tale for you to write into your story. Watch your step into the boat." He guided her and she sat, the boat rocking. "Let us hope this magical mass of vegetation lets go of us."

"You do not believe me," she said.

He chuckled as he took up the oars and pulled hard to disengage from the land bar. Looking over her shoulder, Ellison saw the mist thin to a vapor. The little isle was revealed in the moonlight—a narrow, shallow hump of earth and scrub that was hardly visible on the glittering water surface.

"Ronan, look. It is all but gone now. Surely the fairies

watched over their own."

"And over my love too, who believes in fairies, much to their delight."

She smiled, weary, chilled, and so glad he was with her. When they reached the shoreline, he nudged the vessel in among the reeds, then Ronan lifted a hand to wait.

"They are gone," he said finally. "Do you see them far off, riding away? They are not heading for Invermorie, but into the hills."

They left the boat and went toward the grove of trees. He stayed in front, an arm out protectively. Then he stopped, and she bumped into him in the dark. Hearing the thud of hooves and creak-creak of wheels, she peered around his arm.

"Is that Donal riding? And Aleck in the cart?"

"So it is. Good lads. Come ahead, my girl."

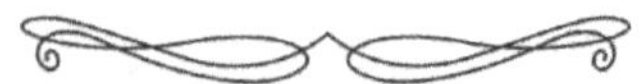

Chapter Twenty-Four

INVERMORIE'S GREAT HALL, warm and shabby, was bathed in candlelight in the hour before dawn. Ronan sat back, a cup of hot tea nestled in his hands, and gazed at the others there—Mairi, Ludo, Donal, Aleck, Rabbie, and the love of his life beside him, nibbling at buttered toast.

The table was scattered with dishes nearly empty now of scrambled eggs, sausages, toast, fruit, and more, as if this was a normal hour for breakfast. Somehow Mairi had managed to produce simple comforts quickly, and he was grateful.

Even better, Donal and Aleck had just returned, having rescued and moved the whisky casks and crates, lumbering back to Invermorie in the cart.

"So, you had quite the adventure," Mairi said.

"We did," Ronan replied. They had explained what they knew during the meal. "But we should not stay for long."

"Aye, thank you for your hospitality," Ellison said. "At Strathniven they will worry when they find we did not return last night."

"Do stay and rest if you can. We can send the stable boy over to Strathniven to say you are here and safe after—an incident on the road last night. Aleck?"

The young man nodded, rose from the table, and hurried out the door.

"We could stay for just a bit," Ronan agreed, seeing Ellison's look of relief.

"Will you need to leave immediately for Edinburgh when you reach Strathniven?"

"The viscountess wants to leave today. When she returns from Duncraig, she will be eager to take to the road, knowing her."

"All Scotland is in a mad rush to reach Edinburgh this week, I think. I wish we were also leaving for the city," Mairi said.

Sir Ludo shrugged. "I would like to witness the festivities, but every nook and cranny is full, they say. Will you stay in the usual hotel, Ronan?"

"I am generally at the Waterloo when I am in the city, but my friend Hugh Cameron says it is full. Fifty rooms were reserved in July as soon as word was out. Barrie's, The Crown, Davidson's—all the hotels are full by now, he said."

"I hope your friend has a spare bed," Ludo said as he buttered an oatcake.

"I am sure you could stay with Lady Strathniven," Ellison said.

"Mr. Cameron found a room for me, I think," he replied.

"Good." She sipped her tea, but Ronan sensed something troubled her.

"What is it?" he asked quietly.

"I do not want to see Mr. Corbie," she murmured.

"If he is smart, he will not come near us. If I see him, we will have words."

"Ellison, does your family know you and Ronan are betrothed now?" Mairi smiled. "I am so glad to hear it. Thank you for telling us though you wanted to keep it a secret. But you know we will not tell."

"I have not told them yet, though they could have heard a rumor at the dance last night," Ellison answered. "My father will not be happy with me, but I will talk to him."

"Sir Hector would surely think Ronan a fine choice for his daughter," Sir Ludo said. "You have a proud ancestral line that includes the MacGregor chiefs as well as the old line of the earls of—"

"I will talk with Sir Hector," Ronan said quickly, holding up a hand to stop Ludo from saying more about the original earls of Strathniven. He had not yet told Ellison that years ago the land had been forfeited and granted to Lady Strathniven's husband.

"A daughter's happiness should bring a father great pleasure." Mairi smiled at her father. "One day I hope to be as happy."

"I am sure you will be, dear," Ludo said.

"Well." She tilted her head. "Now is as good a time as any. I have something to tell all of you."

Ronan grew still, dreading any news of Pitlinnie. It was hardly the time.

"I had a letter," Mairi said, "from Lord Linhope, from Calton Jail."

"Linhope!" Surprised, he sat forward. "I did not expect that. How is he? And MacInnes? Are they well?"

"Somehow he got a letter out, and said that he and MacInnes are well enough. They did not know where you were taken, and they have been worried about you. When he found a way to send a letter, he wrote to me on the chance I might know something about your fate."

"I have been just as worried about them. But I heard he is able to act as a physician there, which is promising. Did he say anything else?"

"He said their accommodations have improved because of his work there. But there is something else." Mairi looked around at them. "He said he hopes for my favorable answer."

Stunned, remembering what she had told him the last time he was there, Ronan suddenly realized what she meant. He leaned forward. "Mairi—is it Linhope?"

"It is." She smiled. "Who did you think?"

He only smiled. "Well done, my dear. But your father and your son must approve before I say aught." Greatly relieved, he was still concerned about the fate of Linhope and MacInnes. He had yet to find a way to gain their release, if it was even possible.

If he could not save them, Mairi would be heartbroken once more, and he could not live with that. He sat silent while the others congratulated her.

"Lord Linhope is a fine man," Ludo pronounced.

Donal beamed. "Truly, Mama? Linhope is an excellent fellow!"

"Did you answer him?" Ronan asked. Beside him, he saw Ellison looking from one to the other, silent, eyes shining.

"I would tell him aye, a thousand times aye, if I could only see him. I wrote my reply, but have not posted it yet. I fear it will be lost and he would never see it."

"Give it to me. I will take it to him when I go to Edinburgh."

"Oh, Ronan, thank you. And I am so happy that all of you are pleased!"

Ronan smiled and reached over to take Mairi's hand. He knew for certain now that his wounded heart had healed and was coming to life again. He had found love and so had Mairi. He could ask for nothing better than that.

"Linhope," he repeated. "I feared you were considering Pitlinnie's proposal."

"Pitlinnie!" Mairi looked horrified.

"We all thought so, Mairi Brodie." Rabbie Muir had come in late to the discussion, having been sitting with his grandson Geordie, recovering upstairs. He was finishing his breakfast, and sat back. "That Pitlinnie made no secret of courting you for marriage. We feared you might fall for him."

"*An amadan sin!* That fool!" Mairi gave a bitter laugh. "I always thought he had something to do with Will's death, and the troubles that came to Ronan and Linhope and MacInnes too. So I let him visit in case I could learn something about it."

"Brave and kind," Ronan said. "And I beg your pardon for thinking you gave a moment of thought to Pitlinnie. I am more than proud to welcome Linhope to the family. And we will welcome Ellison too, if she will have us just as we are."

"I will," Ellison said, her impish smile glowing. Ronan took her hand.

In a moment of clarity, he knew she was part of his life now, heart and soul, and part of his family. He was grateful she had agreed to marry him so quickly, but if she needed time to think on it, he could wait. He would wait for her forever.

"What I want to know about Pitlinnie," Ludo said, "is why he arranged to have Ellison taken, and what can be done about it?"

"I have my suspicions," Ronan said, "but we must go carefully. We cannot accuse a man without evidence. It will not stick."

"Says the lawyer," Ludo remarked with a wise nod.

"And how is Mr. Corbie involved?" Donal asked.

"I might know something about that," Rabbie Muir said. "Last night I went to the distillery. I wanted to make a good count of the kegs and bottles there, since we had not yet found the whisky store."

"Aye. What happened?" Ronan asked.

"A man came to the yard, very late. He said he needed some whisky and would I sell him some. Said if I gave it to him for free, he might remember where the lost Glenbrae whisky was. I had a bad feeling, since only the thieves would know that. But I agreed, see, and then a second fellow came in and they took three kegs."

"Did they tell you where the other lot was?" Ronan asked.

He shook his head. "They said the whisky was for a wedding celebration, and that I would learn about the missing whisky if I came with them."

Ellison sat forward. "Came with them! Oh, Rabbie Muir, how dangerous."

"But I am a careful fellow. They asked if Ronan MacGregor was about. Then they showed a pistol. I had no choice but to go with them."

"Where did they take you?" Ronan asked. "Thank God you are safe."

"They said we would go to a wedding. I was puzzled. But now, hearing you lot, it is clear to me. The marriage, see."

Ronan frowned. "Whose marriage?"

"They said they needed whisky for the wedding and they needed me."

"Why? As a witness?" Ellison asked.

"No, Miss Graham. They wanted me to perform a marriage."

"Perform?" Ronan sat straighter. "Why you?"

"Rabbie Muir was a pastor when he was a young man," Sir Ludo said.

"I did not know that." Ronan blinked in surprise.

"I was ordained as a young man and had a parish north of here," Rabbie said. "Well before you were born, lad. But the clearing agents came through that glen and put my home and church to the torch. I had to protect my family, my young wife, and my aging parents, see. Your father, Ronan, bless him, was laird of Glen Brae then. He took us in and made me his factor, even gave me land in the glen."

"I knew you were my father's factor," Ronan said. "I did not know the rest."

"No reason to tell it. But know there no one more grateful and loyal to your kin than Auld Rabbie Muir." He thumped his chest.

"I know you were a great friend of my father and grandfather too. How did these men know about you? Did you make the marriage?"

"Nah. But it was some lad marrying his ladylove quick-like."

Sir Ludo looked at Ronan. "You? And Miss Graham?"

"No," Ronan said.

"I heard a name." Rabbie pursed his mouth. "They said Corbie was to marry his lady love."

"Corbie!" Ellison cupped her hands over her mouth.

"I did not know the name. But now I am thinking those who wanted the whisky stole Miss Graham last night."

"Devil take the man," Ronan growled. "Was Corbie there?"

"He was to meet them but never showed. Nor did the lass."

"Indeed," Ronan drawled. "How did you get away?"

"They took me near Loch Brae. That made no sense to me, for there is only that cursed water and that rotten old tower. They left me waiting in the cart," Rabbie explained. "But then horses got loose, and the idiots went chasing after them. And me sitting with the whisky in a cart. So I left and came here." He shrugged.

Ronan laughed, shook his head. "We are glad you did."

"If they looked for find me, they did not think to come here. And now we have our whisky back. All of it." Rabbie looked smug and satisfied.

"So Corbie meant to force Ellison into marriage," Ronan said.

"I fear so," Rabbie said.

Ellison looked at Ronan. "They mentioned others. Perhaps they meant Pitlinnie."

He nodded. "Corbie and Pitlinnie must have schemed this at the cèilidh after we told him we were engaged. I saw them deep in discussion later."

"But why would they bother to stage a marriage?" she asked.

"He wants to prevent our marriage, and thought this would do it."

"How did they know you could marry them, Rabbie Muir?" Mairi asked.

"Some in the glen know about it. I am muckle glad his plan was ruined."

"So am I," Ellison said.

"Likely he is on his way to Edinburgh," Ronan said. "And I mean to find him." He fisted a hand on the table, taut whitened knuckles containing his anger.

"Miss Graham may still be in danger if he was that desperate to marry her," Sir Ludo said. "What does the fellow really want?"

"I wish I knew." Ronan glanced at Ellison, who began to reply.

"He wants Strathniven," she said. "He is Lady Strathniven's heir, but she insists that he find a practical wife if he expects to inherit."

"He wants your father's approval and favor very badly too," Ronan murmured.

"He does. With a good marriage and a peer's title, he could rise high in a civil office. And if he sees Papa before I do, he could convince him that he should marry me. Papa relies on him. Favors him."

"We must get to the city before he does any more damage." Ronan flexed his hand, anger simmering. Ellison rested a gentle hand on his forearm. He relaxed, feeling the care in her touch.

"What if we could ensure that Mr. Corbie cannot marry our Ellison?" Mairi asked. Ronan and the others looked her way.

Our Ellison. He drew in a breath. "What do you mean?"

"Mr. Muir, what do you think?" Mairi smiled at Rabbie, sitting beside her.

He tipped his head. "I would be honored to perform marriage for those two."

"Now?" Ronan glanced at Ellison. He immediately saw the sense in it. And he knew how much he wanted it. But he tipped a brow toward her in silent question.

Ellison stared up him, eyes wide. "Married, now?"

"If it is agreeable." His heart thumped. "I would agree. But it is up to you."

"It is—very sudden." She looked a little stunned.

Mairi stood and beckoned to the others. "Come. They need to talk alone."

"Now or later, I can do a marriage any time," Rabbie offered as he left. "But this one should happen quick if you want to outwit Mr. Corbie."

"He is right," Ronan murmured as Mairi shut the door. Ellison stood as he did. Her fingers began to twist, anxious and uncertain.

"You truly think Corbie is a threat?" she asked.

"Very much, if he arranged to abduct you for marriage."

"Last night no one mentioned a wedding. But I heard them talk about setting a trap for someone. I knew they meant you."

"We are both fine now, and we will stay that way, I promise. But if we do this now—it could keep you safe from anything else Corbie might plan."

"It would infuriate him. He would turn on us with vengeance, and convince my father that you should be arrested or worse. He will find a way to hurt you."

"If you do not want to do this, we will not." He waited.

She looked away, breathed out. Finally she nodded. "We did promise to marry." Fluttering her fingers together. "But I did want to talk to my father first."

He reached for her hands to still them and calm her. "I may not be your father's choice for you. But I have something to recommend me now—the title, the estate, a good income from that one day. But there are legal matters that need resolution."

"He will also respect that you are an educated gentleman and a lawyer. But it does not matter what Papa wants." She lifted her head. "It is my decision."

"It is." He still held her hands, glad she seemed content with that.

"He may never approve. But it is time he knew that I have the right to be independent. And time he knew what sort of man Adam Corbie really is. But—what if we did not marry now, what then?"

He sighed. "Your father might pressure you to marry Corbie."

"I would refuse. I would," she insisted, when he cocked a brow. "I have been coddled and far too meek. I have been trapped," she said. "When I tried to be independent before, it was disastrous. That first marriage—" She sighed.

"Whatever you want to do, lass, you have my heart. You always will."

She squeezed his hands. "Ronan, when I promised to marry you, I meant it. If I marry again, it must be for love. True love. Not infatuation or a wish to escape my life."

He waited.

"I will," she said. "Let us do this now."

He cupped her cheek. "As you wish, Lady Darrach."

"I HAVENA DONE a wedding for a while," Rabbie Muir began, "but a pastor never forgets the words that bind two souls together in happiness."

Ellison glanced at the others gathered nearby as she and Ronan stood with Rabbie Muir in front of the hall's large ancient fireplace. Ronan looked fine in his wrapped plaid, a jacket pulled over his rumpled shirt. Smoothing her gown, muddied and torn, she was grateful for the soft, clean plaid shawl that Mairi had draped over her shoulders.

"Good, then," Rabbie began. "We have all we need—two hearts what love one another." He looked up as Mairi came near. "And wee flowers," he added, as she handed Ellison a small bouquet of flowers tucked together in a sweet tangle tied with ribbon.

Ellison sniffed the gently scented cluster of wild dog-roses, pink-purple heather, and sweetly aromatic bog myrtle, tucked together with purple thistle and strands of mountain laurel and tiny young pine branches.

"Pine and laurel for MacGregor and Graham," Mairi whispered. "The rest is for love and luck." She slipped back to join the others.

"Good. Now take her hands, John Ronan MacGregor, and take his, Ellison Sophia Graham. Then listen and agree."

Rabbie cleared his throat and proceeded without a stumble, though he had not uttered the words for years. Ellison felt her heart soar as he spoke. She felt strength flow through her in Ronan's hands over hers, in the love shining in his eyes, deep as the bluest loch. And she knew this simple, impromptu wedding was all she could ever want.

"I pronounce thee man and wife. And no man may put thee asunder." Rabbie smiled. "We will write up a document for all to witness and sign."

Then a tender kiss, Ronan's lips upon hers, his hands at her waist. Kisses were not the usual at weddings, she knew but this little wedding felt different, truly so. Tears slid down her cheeks as she smiled up at him, feeling the devotion in her heart, seeing its match in his eyes.

"It is done, love," Ronan whispered.

Within the half-hour, mounted on horses from the Invermorie stable, she cantered beside her husband toward what lay ahead.

Chapter Twenty-Five

"Oh my heavens, Ellison, we heard a rumor at the dance last night. But we shall get to that," Lady Strathniven said, seated on the carriage's leather bench opposite Ellison and Sorcha. "Tell us more about what happened last night. We were in such a rush to depart this morning that I hardly took it in."

"Just an unfortunate incident on the road," Ellison said, as the barouche rumbled through the glen. "Pitlinnie's carriage—had a problem. Luckily Darrach came by and took me to Invermorie, as it was close," she added. "Mairi Brodie and Sir Ludo kindly took us in for the night. We had a lovely breakfast with them this morning."

She blushed fiercely and hoped they would not notice. Very soon she would confide in them about her marriage. She thought of her parting with Ronan that morning when he left to meet Hugh Cameron and arrange for the shipment of the whisky to Edinburgh, and smiled to herself at the memory.

"I will see you in Edinburgh," he had murmured only two hours ago, standing with her in Strathniven's foyer. "As soon as possible."

"Do that, Darrach," she had said, tapping his chest. "You can find me at my father's house." As she rose on her toes to kiss him, he had pulled her into his arms for a stirring kiss that melted through her, head to toe.

"Wife," he had growled, "we need to be alone together very soon."

"Aye, but I cannot spend my wedding night in my father's house."

"Hugh Cameron secured me a place. I will take you there."

"Wonderful," she had whispered, pressing close.

Then she had entered a whirlwind of packing and hurrying about. Lady Strathniven had insisted that they travel that very morning, and had orchestrated a caravan of two carriages, the ladies in one, and her maid Jeannie and another servant maid riding in the other with trunks and bags. To Ellison's great relief, Adam Corbie had already left in something of a hurry, as Sorcha had reported.

"Oh, these awful roads!" the viscountess said now. "I order repairs on my lands, but other landholders must do the same to keep the old glen roads in good condition. The Crown is only interested in their military roads, straight as arrows through the hills and not very picturesque. Scottish peers must be the custodians of the Highland legacy."

"I agree," Ellison said, petting Balor, who slept in her lap. She stroked his head and shoulders and watched the road and hills fly past. Wondering where Ronan was now, she hoped he would not cross paths with Corbie at any point.

"Oh dear, it is raining again," Sorcha said, looking out the window.

"Mr. MacNie expects to keep a good pace so we can reach the ferry over the firth on time," Lady Strathniven said. "We will also have to stop for tea along the way. Even with so many carriages on the roads heading for Edinburgh, MacNie thinks we will reach the city by this evening."

"It is so exciting," Sorcha said. "They said at the dance last night that the king's ship is already anchored offshore at Leith, but must stay beyond the rough waters until the storms pass and they have clear sailing into the harbor."

"The Duke of Atholl himself said that the storms have been simply awful in Edinburgh all summer." The viscountess looked at Ellison. "Was Darrach able to arrange for Glenbrae whisky to be delivered to Holyroodhouse for the king's visit?"

"He is arranging that this morning. He and Mr. Cameron will travel by steam packet with the shipment so that they can be sure the whisky arrives safely in Leith, where it can be taken into the city."

"Excellent!" Lady Strathniven smiled. "This will be a great feather in Darrach's cap now that his inheritance is confirmed. He is such a good man, and such a good friend. We are fortunate this has turned out so well. Do you not agree, Ellison?"

The hot blush rose again, and she twined her gloved hands nervously. "Very fortunate, my lady. And—well, Darrach and I have some news." In her lap, Balor lifted his head to look at her, tipping his head quizzically, even as Sorcha and Lady Strathniven raised their eyebrows in quick interest.

"Good news?" The lady's eyes sparkled. "Does it have to do with a certain rumor that we heard last night?"

"We did hear a rumor!" Sorcha beamed. "Tell us!"

Her smile was tremulous. Tugging at her gloves, she deliberately stilled her hands. Be calm, she told herself.

"Lord Darrach and I were married this morning."

Silence for a moment. Balor gave a little yelp, as if he understood. Lady Strathniven gasped and set a hand to her bosom, and Sorcha squealed in delight.

"Oh, my dear girl, married! I did not expect that!" Lady Strathniven leaned forward to take Ellison's hand. "And to such a lovely gentleman!"

"Thank you. I was not sure how you would feel about it." She gave a shy smile.

"I could not be more pleased," the lady said with a knowing look. "Truly."

"This is wonderful!" Sorcha hugged her. "So you are Lady Darrach now!"

"I suppose so." Ellison laughed a little.

"This morning? We had no idea—though I thought you two were just marvelous together," the lady said.

"Aye, early this morning. An impromptu decision because Mr. Muir, Darrach's friend, was there. He was a pastor in his younger days, and we had agreed to marry—and his family were all there. It seemed better to fix the marriage now, before we stepped into the madness in the city. Arranging a wedding in Edinburgh would take such a very long time these days with all the commotion. And we were very happy to have a simple ceremony." She hoped the explanation made sense.

"It is such a Highland thing to do, simple and straightforward," the viscountess said. "No fuss. I like it."

"Oh, Ellison! You fell in love with a handsome Highlander and promised to be together always, and had a small Highland wedding." Sorcha sighed. "It is so romantic!"

"I wonder," the viscountess mused, "if you felt compromised last night when you were stranded in your carriage and had to be rescued in the middle of night. Darrach is a perfect gentleman and a wonderful man. He would not want you to endure any scandal."

"There is something to that," Ellison admitted.

"A man like Darrach has the integrity and strength of character to admit responsibility," the viscountess continued with a nod.

"Compromise? Oh, Auntie!" Sorcha giggled.

"It seemed the right thing to do," Ellison said.

"From the day you first saw him, I thought there was something there," the lady said. "I think you have found someone who suits you well. He is strong and calm and intelligent and he clearly respects and cares about you. One would have to be blind to miss it. Yes, very romantic, despite all."

"Despite all?" Sorcha asked.

"My lady means the uncertainty about the inheritance. That is all," Ellison said.

"Yes, that," the lady agreed.

"He is a true catch," Sorcha agreed. "My mother said so last night. And I said, but Mama, that handsome man only has eyes for Ellison Graham."

"I did not think anyone noticed." Ellison blushed. "It all happened so quickly, the decision to go ahead and marry. I have the certificate to show Papa," she said, patting her reticule.

"He may fuss about it, but it is done," Lady Strathniven said. "I will speak to him if he proves difficult. You have made a good choice, my dear. I am convinced."

"Thank you, my lady." She sighed in deep relief, glad to have shared the news.

"You had a little wedding, my dear, but we will plan a proper wedding reception for you as soon as this royal visit is over and done. We shall hold it at Strathniven or in the city, as you like."

"That would be lovely," Ellison replied, grateful, yet still wary of what lay ahead.

"You will want to talk with your father as soon as you arrive," the lady urged. "Though I fear Adam will be heartbroken. He is so fond of you, Ellison, and had hopes himself. But he will soon recover from it."

"I do hope so," Ellison murmured.

THE MANTEL CLOCK chimed ten times as Ellison stepped into her father's house. Lewison, the butler, hid his surprise as he opened the door at such a late hour, and the housekeeper, delighted to see her, wanted to make sure Ellison was tucked up in bed with hot tea and scones to help revive her after the long journey. The room was ready with a hearth fire and a hip bath, and though she wanted to sink down and then sleep, she had to do something first. "Is Papa here?" she asked.

"Sir Hector is not at home presently," Lewison said. "He is at dinner with Sir Walter Scott and the fellows of the Celtic Society. This is a busy time, as you know, Miss Ellison. But he will be pleased to know you are safely home. I shall tell him as soon as he returns. Mr. Corbie was here not long ago inquiring after him also."

"Is he gone?" She set a hand to her chest. She desperately wanted to see her father before Corbie had the chance.

"Aye, Miss. He indicated he would return in the morning or else meet Sir Hector at Parliament House tomorrow. That is my understanding."

"Thank you, Lewison. It is good to be home." And a relief, she thought, to have a chance to rest and gather her thoughts before she saw either of them. Climbing the stairs to her room, she ate a little, bathed, and snuggled into bed, exhausted.

She wondered if Ronan was in the city yet, and where he might be. As hope winged upward—she was in love, she was married, she would talk to her father in the morning, and all would be well—she drifted to sleep.

GRAY SKIES PROMISED more rain as Ellison came downstairs that morning. She went toward her father's study when Lewison emerged from the library carrying a silver tray with an empty cup and saucer. She knew it signified that that her father might have already left for the day.

"Good morning, Lewison. Is Papa still here?"

"Sorry, Miss, he left for breakfast with the Lord Provost. He came in late last night but insisted that you should not be disturbed. He asked me to tell you that he will see you this evening. Ah, a note arrived for you." Setting down the tray, he handed her a small envelope. "Lady Strathniven sent a message over early this morning."

Cracking the wax seal, Ellison read quickly. "I am invited to breakfast on Charlotte Square. It is not far, I can walk. If Papa should come home while I am out, do tell him where I have gone. Will you have someone look after Balor until I return?"

After rushing to her room for a bonnet and spencer against the light drizzle, she was soon on her way up the street. Lady Strathniven's home on Charlotte Square was two blocks from her father's house on George Street. Crossing Castle Street, she glanced toward her narrow townhouse, situated in the middle of a row on the hilly street.

Thanks to Mr. Cameron and Justice Beaton, the previous

occupants had been sent away and the house was rented. She need not worry about that any longer. She owed thanks to Ronan, too, who had asked his friend Mr. Cameron to see to the situation. It was another thing off her shoulders, and another good thing that Ronan MacGregor had brought to her life.

Hope soared, but she could not shake the uneasy feeling that lingered beneath it. Once she had spoken with her father, and once the king's visit was done, finally all would be well. It had to be.

Love and happiness must prevail. She could not let the shadows win.

"HEATHER SPRIGS," LADY Strathniven said as she sat with Ellison and Sorcha at the dining table, "for our bonnets and headdresses. I had Jeannie pick an armful before we left the Highlands. The Edinburgh Ladies' Silver Cross Society will give them out to the ladies at the royal events, and Mrs. Siddons will add heather to the bonnets she is making in her hat shop. During the king's visit, we ladies can tuck a bit of heather in our bonnets or in our hair to show our pride in Scotland."

"A lovely thought," Ellison said.

"Indeed. Will the gentlemen have to wear heather too?" a man asked.

Ellison whirled to see Adam Corbie in the doorway. Suddenly the rainy day seemed gloomier. He looked at her and a tight, mocking smile.

"Adam!" His aunt sounded delighted. "You are here in time for breakfast."

"Thank you, but I breakfasted already with the Lord Provost and Sir Hector."

Ellison sucked in a breath. Had Corbie told Papa about the betrothal this morning? He would be sure to twist the tale in his favor. At least he did not know about her marriage and could not spread that news.

"Well, we are glad to see you," his aunt said. "Will you stay here this week? You are welcome to, but you left Strathniven so hastily that we had no time to chat."

"No, my lady aunt. I will keep to my rooms on Princes Street. There is much to be done and I would not want to disturb your household with my comings and goings."

"We are busy as well. We were just going to do some shopping."

"I would like a word with Miss Ellison before you leave." As he came closer, Ellison leaned back in her chair as if to escape.

"It is a very busy day," she began in protest.

"He only needs a moment, Ellison," Lady Strathniven said blithely. "Come, Sorcha, we will wait for the carriage in the foyer." She rose, as did Sorcha, who turned.

"Shall I stay?" she asked Ellison, her gaze sympathetic. She seemed to sense Ellison's discomfort. "Cousin Adam, I have not had a chance to ask how you enjoyed the dance at my mother's house."

"Very much. You may go, Cousin. I want a quick private word with Miss Ellison."

Ellison nodded. This had to be done. "I will see you in a moment, dear."

When Sorcha left the room, Corbie took her arm firmly and drew her away from the door. As he began to close it, Ellison pulled her arm out of his grasp and faced him.

"Leave it open," she said.

"I did not think propriety was that important to you." He took her elbow in a fierce hold and pulled her toward a window niche where they could not be heard.

"And I thought acting the gentleman was important to you," she returned.

"I have been considering for hours," he began, "what to do about your betrothal."

She raised a brow. "Did you tell Papa about—my engagement to Lord Darrach?"

"Not yet, but I will. I want to give you a chance to rectify the situation first."

"It cannot be rectified." Squaring her shoulders, she had to take the risk. The truth might save her, and save Ronan. "We are married now."

"What in blazes! Married? I just saw you. When were you married?"

"Yesterday morning." She drew a breath. "I met Darrach at the ancient tower near Loch Brae. You know the place." She gave him a cold stare.

He went pale, small dark eyes narrowing. "What tower?"

"You know where it is. Darrach found me there. We met with his family and old Mr. Muir. Did you know he was once a pastor? No?" She paused, watched him swallow hard. "Mr. Muir offered to marry us, and a quiet, quick ceremony seemed just perfect at the time."

"Impossible. This cannot be!" He stepped back as if stunned, shaking his head, pulling at his neckcloth as if it choked him. Warily, she moved back a step.

"It is true."

"I feared that rascal would undo our good work," he said in a low, threatening voice. "But this is far worse."

"It seemed a better solution than your suggestion at the cèilidh."

"You little fool—this man has manipulated you to his advantage. But if he is caught smuggling again, this time he will hang, and so will his friends."

"He is not smuggling."

"Trust that I can find the evidence."

"You cannot be trusted for much, Mr. Corbie." A strong feeling warned her to say nothing about his scheme to force her into marriage.

"We cannot risk introducing him to the king," he went on. "He will likely be arrested as soon as he arrives in Edinburgh."

"He did all you asked and more."

"Oh, much more," he said in a cruel tone. "Betrothal is one

thing. Marriage quite another. Once again you have made a poor choice. This puts your father in an untenable position. The scandal could undo him."

"Do not be so dramatic, Mr. Corbie. I married a viscount and a clan chieftain, the cousin of the clan chief who will lead the procession in the city. Papa will be proud."

"I told you," Corbie said, "MacGregor intends to transport whisky by sea, so my sources claim. Moving it by sea can be considered smuggling. The excise officers will be interested in that."

Even now, Ronan might be coming into Leith harbor. "You would not do that."

"I would. Since I had word of it, I am obligated to report it to Sir Hector, since he serves as chief of the constabulary."

"You are despicable, Adam Corbie." She took a step backward. Another.

"But I have a solution. Here is what we will do." He moved toward her, grabbed her wrist. "Listen to me."

"I listened before. It did not go well. Let me go."

"Sir Hector, and my aunt too, will have to hear the truth. But you and I can fix this before they are shocked and disappointed in you."

"The truth, sir, is that I am married, and you do not like it. But it is done."

"And can be undone. You must apply for an annulment immediately. Your father will need to know so he can press to have it reversed with urgency."

"No." She pulled away, and he pulled her back.

"You will save your father's future."

"His future is not threatened. You invented that for your own interests."

"Did I? Your father cannot advance if his son-in-law is a criminal, or worse, executed for his crimes. Sir Hector will lose all. But you can prevent it, and I will make sure your—groom—has a better chance."

"You would leave him be?" Her heart pounded, her stomach knotted.

"After the annulment, he might still be arrested and sentenced. I cannot change that course. But we will announce our engagement and marry quickly, and others will understand it is meant to protect you and help you recover from harrowing events."

"I do not want an annulment. I refused you the other night. It still stands."

"From what I recall, you accepted me, but you were coerced—perhaps forced—to marry this reprobate. We will mend it."

She grasped at a straw. "Did you forget that Papa must present Darrach at the royal levee, by the king's request?"

"We can find someone else to represent the whisky." He waved a hand.

"No one knows Glenbrae whisky as well as—" She stopped. "Pitlinnie!"

"I will say that Sir Neill has promised Sir Evan MacGregor that he will purchase Glen Brae and its distillery to absolve the debts attached to the Darrach estate. Sir Neill can be introduced as Glenbrae's owner. It is simple. It only needs a signature. Yours, on the annulment decree."

"Why are you so intent on punishing Ronan?"

"My dear, he stands between me and all that I should have. Punish? I mean to eliminate him from your life."

"You have kept your true character well hidden," she said.

"Have I? Am I as tough as your rogue? As desirable?" Snarling the words, he pulled her against him with surprising strength. Then he kissed her roughly, hurting her mouth, while she twisted away. She broke free and slapped him.

"He is a rogue. You are a wretch," she snapped.

"You know what to do," he said, rubbing his jaw. "Do it today. All the ways you have hurt your father can be mended. It is your choice." Spinning away, he strode out of the room.

Sorcha rushed in moments later. "I heard raised voices. Cousin Adam seemed very upset as he left."

"Just upset with me," Ellison reassured her. She clasped her shaking hands. She had to think, had to find a way to stop Corbie. "Sorcha, I must—I have an errand. After we visit the hat shop, will you accompany me?"

A short time later, riding in the carriage with Sorcha and the chattering viscountess, her mind and her heart raced. She would never betray Ronan, but he could not learn the truth of what happened with Corbie—or her father's secretary would not survive the day.

But she had to do something. Her idea was risky, but could solve this.

Chapter Twenty-Six

L EITH HARBOR WAS busier than Ronan had ever seen, with sailing ships and steamships arriving ahead of the royal party. He stepped aside as a group of English gentlemen passed with barely a glance for the kilted Highlander standing beside a stack of kegs and crates. He waved to see Hugh Cameron coming toward him.

"A madhouse," Hugh said over the cacophony on the quay. "But I managed to hire a cart to deliver the whisky lot to Holyroodhouse, and I found a hackney to take us into Edinburgh. Once the whisky reaches the palace, your obligation ends."

"Not quite. There is still the king's levee and the introduction. But before that, I need to see that a legal issue is properly cleared."

"I know which one you mean. We had best get to that today if you will meet me at Parliament House this afternoon. First, I must see my mother, who expects me today. Will you come along? She would be very glad to see you."

"I have a pressing errand. But open one of the crates and bring her a jug of Glenbrae with my compliments. Hugh, listen." Ronan shrugged. "When all this is over, I want to build a new distillery on Darrach property and devote time to creating an even better brew someday." The notion that he would lose his glen and the distillery of Glenbrae hurt deeply.

"Does your bride know you want to stay in the north?"

"I am sure she will want to be in the city near her father, but I will also continue practicing law here. We can travel back and forth as I have always done."

"I am sure our firm would be able to give you plenty of cases."

"Thank you."

"I was surprised but very glad to hear about your marriage. You could not find a finer lady than Ellison Graham. Nor could she find a better man."

Ronan smiled. "There is still the dragon to confront in his den."

"Sir Hector? He will see reason. He is more bluster than malice, in my experience. The real threat is from his secretary, it seems."

"A matter I intend to address. Ah, here is our cart."

Later, as they rode the short distance to the city, Ronan thought of the last time he had been in a hackney on the same streets. He had been baffled and weary, in need of a bath and burdened with participating in an unsavory scheme. Yet fate placed him in the hands of an angel.

He felt he was a changed man now, more firm of purpose, certainly lighter of heart, walking a path that had appeared unexpectedly. Ellison Graham was a gift in his life, and he was grateful. Whatever she needed, he would provide; whatever she wanted, he would give. He wanted her to feel more cherished, loved, and valued than she had ever known.

As the hackney drew up along the Canongate, Hugh turned. "I will leave you here, lad. Are you sure you will not join us? My mother has invited nearly every relative we have, I think."

Ronan laughed. "I am off to my rented place, then straight to the dragon's den. I will see you later at Parliament House."

"You will find the key under an urn and the place in good repair. By the way, the judicial courts are open today but closed tomorrow for the royal procession, and will likely stay closed for a few days. Today is your best chance to put things right."

"I will do my best. Look at that crowd," Ronan said, watching the throngs that filled the streets. "I have never seen so many Highlanders in full, fierce gear. The gathering of the clans has surely come to Edinburgh."

"Sir Evan expects you to be part of the procession, you know, as one of his chieftains, helping to display and promote the strength of the clans of Scotland."

"He stated that in his letter, aye, so I brought my gear along. Let the grand Celtic spectacle begin as we show the English what authentic Scotland is all about."

"Which His Majesty will miss if his ship does not dock soon. Either way, he is about to experience some miserably authentic Scottish weather."

Laughing, Ronan bid him good day, and the driver progressed up the hill through the center of town. The streets were densely crowded as people moved in a noisy mass of color and bright tartan patterns. Bagpipes skirled somewhere as Highland units practiced for the procession, and above the other sounds, the bells of Saint Giles' cathedral rang out the hour.

He reached into a jacket pocket to pull out one of the visiting cards that Corbie had delivered at Strathniven. *John MacGregor, 6th Viscount Darrach,* it read, *of Darrach Castle in Glen Darrach, Perthshire.* A printed image depicted the crest of Clan Gregor, a crowned lion, a buckled belt, and the motto *S'rioghal mo dhream"*—royal is my blood. The Gregorach, a proud clan, went far back in time.

"Driver," he called. "George Street, if you please."

The ride through crowded streets took longer than usual. Once the carriage stopped, Ronan asked the driver to wait, then went to the Graham house to knock.

The butler studied his card. "Lord Darrach. We understood you might call."

"I would like to see Miss Graham if she has returned to the city."

"Miss Graham has returned but is not home at present."

"I see. May I ask if Sir Hector is available?"

"The Deputy Lord Provost has gone to his offices for the day. It is a busy time."

"Of course."

He returned to the carriage, disappointed to have missed Ellison and Sir Hector both. He wanted to resolve the situation—and he longed to hold his bride in his arms.

Next the driver stopped on the cobbled slope of North Castle Street in front of the house he was renting. Narrow yet elegant, its stone façade was set with a bow-curved window and a tall red door. Tucked beneath a stone urn filled with flowers, he found the key. He let himself into Ellison's house.

Inside, the hallway divided a parlor to the right and a dining room to the left, with the kitchen at the back. Upstairs, he found two bedrooms and a bathing room. On the uppermost floor were three small empty rooms. It was a simple but handsome house, freshly painted, repaired, and scrubbed, and would be the perfect home for a newly married couple, and someday a family.

Just now the place was scarcely furnished, with a chair and table in the parlor, a chair and table in the kitchen, and a bed and small furnishings in an upstairs room.

Later Ellison could furnish it however she liked. They could live here, or rent it out, or sell it altogether. He would leave that up to her. In the Highlands, they would have Darrach Castle and perhaps other properties once all was sorted. Whatever she wanted, he meant to see she had.

He changed quickly from his plaidie and jacket to frock coat, trousers, waistcoat, and the lot. Downstairs, he stood looking out the wide bowed window in the parlor, with its view of Edinburgh Castle in the distance, high on a dark cliff overlooking the city. Rainclouds gathered overhead.

An odd feeling swirled through him. He frowned, trying to define it. Not weariness, though he was tired after the journey and a few trying days. Not dread, for he knew he and Ellison had made the right choice. Hurdles lay ahead, but he had hope.

Happiness, he realized. That was it. For the first time in years, he felt content.

He left the house to walk toward the bridge and up the High Street. The city teemed with people, with the tantalizing smells of food cooking, bread baking, with the pandemonium of merchants and visitors, soldiers and errand-boys, flags and tartan and heather wherever he looked. The sound of bagpipes and drums filled the air.

Scottish pride had overtaken the city. Sir Walter and his Celtic Society's design of a magnificent, exhilarating spectacle infused every corner, every sound, the very air.

Walking along, shouldering here, begging pardon there, Ronan enjoyed the anonymity and the freedom. He was just another tall gentleman, another lawyer, another husband, just another Scotsman heading up the High Street. He smiled as he went.

"DO STOP, ELLISON, I nearly lost my slipper," Sorcha said. "You are in such a hurry!"

Ellison slowed as she walked beside Sorcha up the High Street. They were surrounded by pedestrians bumping, pushing, edging past each other. Bells pealed overhead, and the haunting skirl of bagpipes filled the air.

"Such a warm day, despite the rain. Look, Saint Giles!" Sorcha pointed to the high spires of the cathedral on the High Street. "Let's go inside. It will be cooler there."

"Not yet. I have to do something," Ellison said. She locked elbows with Sorcha as they crossed the wide earthen street, avoiding calamity with other pedestrians and a constant stream of carts and horses. Walking past the cathedral, she led the way toward the wide square formed by the cathedral and the massive Scottish Parliament building behind it that held courts, offices, a law library, and more. Papa would be in his office there, but she had another purpose in mind here.

She adjusted the heather sprig in her bonnet and the fat blue bow under her chin, then smoothed her dark blue skirt and tugged at her spencer jacket of blue-and-green tartan. The elegant outfit would lend her the look of a lady of merit. She would need that today.

"Now to gird the lion in its den," she told Sorcha. "Thank you for coming with me. I did not want to do this alone."

"After what you told me after we left the hat shop, I would not miss this for the world! What a kerfuffle!"

"I hope it will not take long." Ellison pushed through the doors to enter the bright, high-ceilinged hall of Parliament House. Sorcha stopped to read a brass plaque. "Court of Session, this way. Court of Justiciary, over there."

"Justiciary," Ellison said, and marched toward a huge polished door to push through. Inside a waiting area with a large desk and some chairs, she approached the young clerk behind the desk.

"Yes, Miss—?"

"Miss Graham. I wish to file a complaint."

"Then you want the constable's office. I can direct you."

"I have spoken to the chief of the constabulary." Partly true, for she had not yet seen her father that day. "I wish to see a lord justice regarding a legal matter."

"I could refer you to an advocate to discuss it. It is not necessary to see one of the justices."

"But I am in such a hurry, Mr. Robertson." She smiled sweetly, reading the name plaque on his desk. "And quite desperate. If you please, I must see a justice."

"Well—first, provide your name and address and the reason for your visit." He handed her a paper. "There is an inkstand on that table. But those who are still here will likely refuse to see you. We are closing early today. May I ask the nature of your legal matter?"

"I wish to report a kidnapping," she said.

WALKING ACROSS THE enormous entrance of Parliament Hall, with its marble floors and soaring walls, Ronan strode toward wide oak doors trimmed in brass. Hugh was beside him as they passed several men strolling through or gathered in conversation. He pushed through the doors leading to Court of Justiciary.

"Let us hope it is still open," Hugh said.

"We have a little time yet." As a nearby door opened, a few men came through deep in discussion. Ronan paused.

"Blast it," Hugh muttered. "Of all the luck."

Steeling his spine, Ronan waited as Sir Hector, Adam Corbie, and Sir Neill Pitlinnie crossed the vast hallway. Neither of the men, at first, looked around.

When at last they did, Ronan would have given any amount for a sketch of Corbie's expression in that moment. The man looked stunned, then alarmed, then frightened. He stumbled back as Sir Hector and Pitlinnie looked around too.

"Lord Darrach!" Sir Hector said in a booming voice.

Ronan inclined his head as all three came closer. "Sir Hector," he said. "Good to see you. Mr. Corbie. And Sir Neill. What a surprise."

"MacGregor," Pitlinnie muttered. Corbie gaped like a fish.

"I believe you know my solicitor, Mr. Cameron," Ronan said, as Hugh nodded.

"What brings you here?" Sir Hector asked.

"A judiciary matter," Ronan said. "As it happens, I am an advocate."

"I heard that recently," Sir Hector said. "Wish I had known earlier. Mr. Corbie has filled me in on some events of the past weeks. You have been—perseverant, sir," he added, with a pinch of the lips that Ronan could not quite decipher.

"I hope so," Ronan drawled. "Has Mr. Corbie told you what he and Pitlinnie were up to in the Highlands last week?"

"This is not the time, MacGregor," Corbie muttered.

"Darrach," Ronan corrected, fixing a searing gaze on him.

"Sir Hector, we have some business to complete," Corbie said. "We must hurry. Sir Neill has documents to sign." He gave Ronan a smug smile. "Speaking of Glenbrae."

"That can wait," Sir Hector said. "What exactly is your business today, Darrach?"

"Mr. Cameron and I intend to submit a warrant for the release of two individuals in Calton Jail."

"Impossible," Corbie said.

"On what grounds?" Sir Hector asked.

"We cannot disclose that here in a public space," Hugh said. "You understand."

"Sir, you are welcome to accompany us if you wish to know more," Ronan said.

"I do want to hear this," Sir Hector growled, gesturing for Ronan to open the door to the judiciary area. As the deputy lord provost went inside, followed by Hugh, Ronan shut the door firmly before Corbie and Pitlinnie could enter.

"Go easy, man," Hugh warned.

"I will," Ronan clipped out.

Entering the judiciary office area, Ronan hardly glanced at the people in the room—a few men, two women. Approaching the clerk, he began to speak when Sir Hector stepped up beside him.

"Mr. Robertson, which justices are still here?" he demanded.

"Sir, Jameson and Beaton are here, I believe. We close soon."

"I am aware. This way," Sir Hector told Ronan as he cut around the clerk's desk and left the waiting area with hardly a glance around. Ronan and Hugh followed.

ELLISON GASPED TO see Ronan and her father on the far side of the room. She rushed toward the desk, Sorcha hurrying after her. "Ellison, what is it?"

"I do not know," Ellison said. Then she caught her breath, seeing another man walk toward the same desk. "Mr. Corbie!"

"Why, Miss Graham," he purred. "You cannot go back there without authority. What brings you to Parliament Hall today?"

"I am submitting papers," she said, folding the papers she had just completed and sliding them quickly into her mesh reticule.

"Just as I suggested. Good. You remember Sir Neill Pitlinnie," he continued.

"Aye," she said stiffly, glancing past them to the door where Ronan and her father had gone. "Why is Papa with Darrach?"

"I do not know, but Sir Hector will likely see to Darrach quickly," he drawled.

"What have you done, Mr. Corbie? And why are you and Pitlinnie here?"

"Just signing papers. And looking forward to the celebration in the city."

"Come, Sorcha, we will find out what is going on." She took Sorcha's arm and rushed past the desk as the clerk sprang up.

"Miss Graham! You cannot go back there!"

"Sir Hector is my father. I must see him."

"Your father? Still, I should not—"

"And I am Lord Beaton's sister," Sorcha said. "This is urgent!" She pushed Ellison through the doorway as the clerk sputtered in protest.

"Mr. Robertson, I will see to this," Corbie said, and followed them.

Ellison hurried beside Sorcha looking at brass plaques on the doors. Finding "The Rt. Honorable Justice E. Jameson" and hearing muffled voices behind the door, she raised a gloved fist to rap.

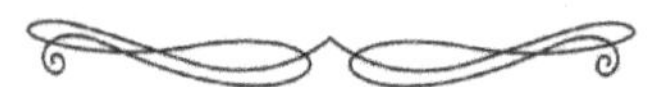

Chapter Twenty-Seven

"THIS HAD BETTER be important, Sir Hector. Mr. Cameron, I know you." Seated behind a tall mahogany desk, Jameson peered at the men standing before him. Scowling over his spectacles, he offered no one a chair. He peered at Ronan.

"You look familiar, sir."

"My lord, this is John Ronan MacGregor, an advocate," Hugh explained. "Recently named Lord Darrach."

"Ah! Heard about that. What do you want? It is late. I am only allowing this because you are with the deputy lord provost. Even so, I want my tea, so be quick."

"Lord Jameson, thank you for seeing us," Sir Hector said. "Darrach has a matter to submit to the court. If you please, perhaps you could hear a preliminary discussion."

"Is this in your bailiwick, Sir Hector?" he demanded.

"It appears to be a matter of the constabulary, sir."

"Lord Justice," Ronan began, "Mr. Cameron and I intend to submit an application for warrant of liberation."

"For whom? Now that I think of it, I have heard of you, sir. Something about Edinburgh dungeons. But you look liberated to me." Jameson scowled at him.

"My lord, Darrach was incarcerated briefly," Sir Hector said. "And pardoned several weeks ago. I oversaw the matter. It is documented and approved."

"A misunderstanding, was it? Tell me why I should listen to

any of you. We are all busy at the moment."

"Aye, my lord. I do not know what Darrach and Cameron have in mind. I will vouch for them, if not for the matter of concern, which I have not heard in full."

Ronan regarded him in surprise and murmured his thanks.

"An interesting recommendation. Someone explain it," Jameson said.

Hugh produced a packet of papers from his pocket and set it on the desk. "My lord, here is a warrant of liberation under the Habeas Corpus Act of Scotland of 1701."

"Who do you want to liberate and why?" Jameson asked as he opened the packet.

"Arthur Stewart, Lord Linhope, and Sir Iain MacInnes," Ronan answered. "They were arrested under irregular circumstances and are being held in Calton Jail."

"Then you are petitioning for two writs of habeas corpus."

"Aye, my lord," Ronan said.

"Why should we release them? This could be a ploy of one cohort to free the others." Jameson turned the pages, then glanced up as a knock sounded on the door. "What is it now!" he bellowed.

Ronan looked around as the door opened and a young man peered inside. "Pardon, my lord. These people insist on seeing you."

"I have already been disturbed once! Not again!"

"Uh, my lord, this gentleman says he is Sir Hector's secretary. This young lady says she is Sir Hector's daughter, and the other says she is Justice Beaton's sister. Sir, they are quite insistent."

"Damned circus," Jameson muttered. "Damned gypsy fair, the whole blasted city. Let them in. Let them all in! Open the windows and let the whole noisy horse fair in here! Bring the damned pipers in too!"

"Sir, sorry, sir." The clerk stood back to let others file into the room.

What the devil? Ronan stared as Ellison entered, followed by

Sorcha, Corbie, and then Pitlinnie. He glanced at Hugh, who shook his head, frowning. Sir Hector turned an interesting shade of purple.

"Do you know these people, Sir Hector?" Jameson demanded.

"Yes, my lord. This is my daughter, Miss Ellison Graham, and her friend, who is indeed Justice Beaton's sister. That gentleman is my secretary, Adam Corbie, with Sir Neill Pitlinnie, who has been a generous donor to our civil expenses."

"Sit over there and be quiet," Jameson ordered, sending the newcomers to chairs in the back of the room.

Ronan caught Ellison's eye and frowned. She glanced away, shaking her head slightly. Beautiful in blue and plaid, she looked delicate yet determined, lifting his pride—but he narrowed his eyes as Corbie sat beside her.

Outside, the noise of the crowded streets mingled with the peal of the bronze bells of Saint Giles, the melody followed by three booming strikes for the hour.

"Three already! I see I will have no blasted tea today," Jameson said. "Go on, Darrach. We do this fast or not at all."

ELLISON LEANED AWAY from Adam Corbie, who sat all too near, as she strived to hear Ronan at the justice's desk.

"Your Honor, we are petitioning due to the length of time these two men have been incarcerated without trial," he said.

"Sixty days?" The justice turned the pages. "Ah. I see. Since the first of May?" He looked up. "When was the sixtieth day?"

"The twenty-ninth of June. Weeks ago, my lord. A letter of intimation was issued as required the day after the initial arrest," Hugh explained. "I notified the Court of Justiciary and the prisoners were brought to Edinburgh. The indictment was preliminary, but as there was no murder involved, it did not go to the high court from the sheriff court. But the final papers were not signed, as the petition notes."

Jameson glanced up sharply. "You are certain of this?"

"Yes, my lord, as detailed in our petition."

"The law requires indictment or trial within sixty days. That was the twenty-ninth of June," Jameson said.

"A trial should have been set within forty days," Ronan said. "The time expired without a trial date on eight August, as you see there. Today is eleven August. One hundred and three days, my lord."

"Huh," Jameson grunted as he read. "No signature on the original indictment?"

"None, my lord," Hugh said. "It appears to be missing. Done in a rush."

"Huh," Jameson said again.

"The Scottish Habeas Corpus Act of 1701 expanded a law established in 1695 and has not been altered under English rule," Ronan said. "It allows any prisoner incarcerated in Scotland for one hundred days without trial to apply for a warrant of liberation."

"You act on behalf of your fellow prisoners?" Jameson rustled through the pages.

"Mr. Cameron and myself, my lord."

Listening rapt, Ellison was thrilled as she comprehended what Ronan intended here—and had been intending all along. She recalled how he had pored over law volumes at Strathnive, keeping late hours, taking notes. All that time, he had been researching old laws, counting the days, and shoring up his argument. He had taken that those facts to Hugh Cameron in Kinross.

All this time, he had never forgotten the plight of his friends. Bringing the matter before a justice was a risk that could expose him to scrutiny. He stood here now arguing for their freedom at the risk of his.

Corbie leaned toward her. "There's falsity in this somewhere."

She rolled her eyes. "Be quiet."

"Issued in Culross," Jameson was saying, studying another

page. "Sir Hector, as chief of the constabulary, what do you know of this?"

"My lord." Graham cleared his throat. "This case came through my office as a routine case of accused smuggling."

"Hardly routine. These were the Whisky Rogues—the notorious fellows whose capture caused a spectacle. Annoying! Crowds clamoring to see them. And now we have another spectacle on our streets," he added. "Go on, Graham. What else?"

"My lord, if there was a lapse in dates or if a process was missed, it was never brought to my attention."

"Why not?" Jameson barked.

"Such things are handled by my secretary and are stamped and approved routinely. They are passed along as necessary. The men were sent to the dungeon and the Lord Provost decided to—ah—"

"Make a little coin by renting them out for view," Jameson grumbled. He examined another page. "So in July, MacGregor—Darrach—was conditionally pardoned, and the other two were moved to Calton weeks ago."

"Aye, my lord," Hugh said. "One hundred and three days have passed since the initial arrest."

"Sir Hector, how was this missed?" Jameson boomed.

Sir Hector blustered. "I, ah, I cannot explain it, my lord. So many matters of immediate importance have come through my office this summer that—ah, something may have slipped."

Listening, Ellison held her breath. Beside her, Corbie went still and silent. What had he done, she wondered. Had it been a mistake—or deliberate for some reason?

Jameson set down the papers, folded his hands, tapped his fingers. The men standing before him waited in silence. *Tap, tap, tap,* then *thud* as the judge slapped a hand flat on the papers.

"We have all been sorely burdened with nonsense from the Crown," he said. "Our offices have been inundated with requests and tasks far beyond the norm. The royal visit was confirmed only months ago, giving our civil and legal offices little time to prepare."

"Very true, my lord," Sir Hector said.

Tap, tap. Justice Jameson studied their faces, one by one.

Ellison watched intently, feeling proud of Ronan for following his staunch principles despite the risk. Yet she feared he would face unfair examination, especially with Corbie determined to take him down however he could.

She slid a glance at Corbie. The gleam in his narrowed eyes made her feel ill. He was set on destroying Ronan; he would turn this bid for justice sour if he could. Even knowing him much of her life, she had not seen the hidden darkness in his character. Perhaps she had not wanted to see it.

"Well," Jameson said, "I do not have my red silks and my wig here today. I am making no decisions. This will need to go through the proper steps. I will take time to read the petition and study the question."

"If I may, Your Honor," Hugh said, "the law of 1701 states that a warrant of liberation must be granted within twenty-four hours of a petition for freedom."

"I know damn well what the law states, Mr. Cameron!" he thundered. "But this court is closed tomorrow. The courts are also closed on Saturdays and Sundays. Any day the court is closed means an extension of a day. This royal visit has thrown the courts and all else into confusion. You will have an answer. Word will be sent to your office. Return when it is appropriate!"

"My lord," Hugh said.

"Thank you, Lord Justice," Sir Hector said.

"My lord," Ronan said, nodding slightly.

"Darrach, remind me of your status. Explain your arrest and pardon."

As the judge spoke, Ellison felt her heart sink. But Corbie gave a dry chuckle.

"Now it will be known," he purred. She wanted to kick him.

"My lord," Ronan said, "my friends and I were arrested at a tavern in Culross where we met one evening. Excise officers took us by force and accused us of something we did not do. I sent word to Hugh Cameron before we were taken to Edinburgh."

"I have copies of all the papers in case of any questions." Hugh handed a second packet to Jameson, who ripped it open to sift through the contents.

"The prisoners were displayed like animals. It was a decision of the Provost carried out by the Captain of the Castle. Not the courts. All for revenue."

"It provided a goodly sum for the city to host the royal visit," Sir Hector said.

The room went silent as the justice studied more pages. After a moment, Sir Hector looked over his shoulder at Ellison. He smiled.

Surprised, even startled by that tentative, almost apologetic, show of affection, she nodded to her father. She had not had a chance to see him since arriving last night. That little smile felt almost like a hug. Almost. Sir Hector was not given to such.

"Darrach, it is not noted in these papers that you are an advocate," Jameson said.

"My friends and I kept our identities private in matters pertaining to whisky."

"You gave false information?" Jameson snapped.

"No, my lord. We use our birth names. Certain other details are just not relevant."

"Arrested for a crime and being an advocate is irrelevant? Hah!" Jameson shook his head. "And the others? Lawyers too as well as—distillers?"

"Sir, Lord Linhope is a physician. MacInnes is a civil engineer."

"Then why in hell," Jameson growled, "were you smuggling whisky?"

"If they were, sir," Hugh said. "That has not been established nor proven."

"Then why in hell were you possibly doing it? This nonsense about Whisky Rogues belongs to you, after all."

Seeing the judge's frustration, Ellison clenched her gloved

hands. She saw that Sorcha looked equally distressed. To her other side, Corbie huffed in amusement.

Ronan was silent for a moment, then cleared his throat. "If my explanation will save two men who do not deserve to be jailed, I will tell you."

"No promises!" Jameson barked.

"My compatriots and I were never the ones that were called Whisky Rogues."

Ellison gasped. Not a Whisky Rogue? He had never mentioned that detail. She saw Hugh Cameron's furtive, knowing glance at Ronan.

"Sir, you are not under oath here in this room, but you are well advised to tell the truth."

"My lord, my brother, William MacGregor, and our cousin, John MacGregor, Viscount Darrach, were labeled Whisky Rogues in the news journals. I believe Sir Walter Scott said it first. They moved whisky out of the Highlands simply because selling for profit has become one of the few ways to help Highland folk. The clearing of the glens over the last two generations has devastated many Scottish regions, ours included. My kinsmen did what they had to do."

"Smuggling is a crime, even if there is a noble reason," Jameson said.

"True. And that is a dilemma for many Highland families, my lord, as you are no doubt aware. Land is sold, tenants are evicted or their livelihoods are reduced. Severe limits and high taxes are imposed on whisky. That leaves few means of income for glen folk. Highland whisky is a valuable product, much in demand, but taxation erases profit for those who make it."

"Did you help your kinsmen build this enterprise while they earned notoriety?"

"I was in India much of that time, sir, part of Sir Evan MacGregor's regiment. When I returned, I set up a distillery legally and my brother operated it while I practiced law in Perth and Edinburgh. But I have a hand in running the distillery."

"Were you also part of the smuggling transport?"

"He was not, my lord," Hugh Cameron said. "That was arranged and run by others. This was established by witnesses but overlooked by the excise."

"I have seen you in these halls and before my bench. Remind me what you do."

"Most often I defend Highlanders accused of smuggling, or those charged with violence due to circumstances such as eviction or attack."

"Would you say you are a Whisky Rogue?"

Ronan hesitated. "For the most part, no my lord. After my brother's death, I did finish some business in his name."

"What the devil! I am losing patience. I am missing high tea."

"Sir, my brother and my cousin were killed by excise officers. My brother left a widow, a son, and tenants in need. Agreements were left unmet. To protect families against ruin and threat, we felt those obligations had to be fulfilled."

"Obligations to whom?"

"I prefer not to say, my lord," Ronan said.

"So you saved Highland hides instead of your own, is that it?"

"He did, my lord," Cameron said.

"I knew my kinfolk might be threatened or killed. I knew innocent people would suffer and our legitimate distillery would be destroyed by rivals."

"I see. Well. In my experience, Highland whisky tends to be far superior to other kinds, especially English grain whiskies. Many would go to great lengths to protect it."

"Lord Justice," Sir Hector said, "Darrach will not bring attention to it, but you should know that King George favors Glenbrae whisky so much that he personally requested to meet its distiller. Lord Darrach will be introduced this week."

"Interesting." Jameson tapped the pages again, loudly and slowly.

Ellison flattened a hand over her chest, waiting in the silence. She did not know some of what Ronan had explained, but she knew his actions had stemmed from integrity, courage, and love. He was not driven by greed and had no disdain for the law. He was not the rogue others made him out to be.

She glanced around the room at those she loved dearly, and two she mistrusted. They were all motionless, somber, hanging on the moment. But Jameson continued to seem annoyed.

Tap, tap, tap. "When were you named Viscount Darrach?"

"My lord, Sir Evan Murray-MacGregor, chief of Clan Gregor, awarded the title with the approval of the Lyon Court," Hugh explained.

Thud. Jameson slapped the desk, folded the papers, crammed them into a drawer and slammed it shut. "Mr. Cameron, Darrach, return here when I am ready to discuss these matters further. You, in the back! What did you want to bring to my attention? May as well hear it."

Corbie stood and spoke before Ellison had the chance to move. "My lord! I believe the charge of smuggling must be revisited. MacGregor, who calls himself Darrach, recently transported illicit whisky by sea. Yesterday he arrived in Leith with goods smuggled out of Perthshire." He walked forward. "I ask the court to renew the charges against MacGregor."

"Darrach comes by his title decently, and you will respect that. Who are you again?"

"Adam Corbie, secretary to the Deputy Lord Provost."

"You bring a serious allegation, Mr. Corbie. Darrach! Is this true?"

"I brought Glenbrae whisky into Leith Harbor, aye. Five casks, seven kegs, and three crates of crockery jugs."

"A good deal more than is allowed for personal use, sir."

"Some was delivered to Holyroodhouse yesterday. The rest went elsewhere."

"Sold? If you sold it, you endanger yourself."

"The rest was taken up to the Castle as a donation to the Highland contingency. Thousands of Highlanders are in Edinburgh now to march in parades and act as honor guards for the royal party. The cost of provisions for them is considerable. The whisky went to the attention of Sir Evan MacGregor and Sir Walter Scott to be dispersed among the clans."

Jameson looked at Sir Hector. "Did you know about this?"

"I did not. Darrach is to be thanked for a generous gift."

"Indeed. But why send so much to the king?" Jameson swiveled toward Ronan. "He will be in Scotland a fortnight at most."

"My lord, he can take it back to England for his personal use."

Jameson nodded, chuckled—then guffawed. He laughed so heartily, smacking the desk, that others smiled uncertainly. "Ha ha! If the king ships that lot home to England—that could make him a smuggler in the letter of the law."

"It could, Your Honor." Ronan smiled.

"A good lawyer would not miss that detail." Ronan shrugged a shoulder in answer and Jameson guffawed again. Then he beckoned to Corbie. "You! The secretary!"

"Adam Corbie, my lord," he reminded Jameson.

"Your request is denied. Foolish and spiteful. Darrach will not be charged. But the king as a smuggler—aye, that fits the regrettable spectacle out there."

A knock at the door interrupted him. As it opened, the clerk looked in. "My lord, you asked to be notified when Lord Beaton was available. He is here now." He stepped aside.

Archibald Beaton entered the room, lifted a hand toward Jameson, and turned to his young sister, taking her hands. "I heard you were here. What a surprise."

Then he went toward Jameson, leaning to confer. "I see. I see," he repeated. "Astonishing. Interesting," Jameson said. He rose to his feet and Beaton took his place.

"I leave you in good hands," Jameson said. "My tea grows cold. The Honorable Lord Justice Beaton will hear this final request. Miss Graham, come up."

She walked forward, feeling a sudden fluttering doubt. "Thank you, sir." Facing Beaton, although she knew Sorcha's oldest brother, she had never seen him in this role. She quailed.

But then caught Ronan's steady glance. He did not know what she intended here, but she nodded, then turned back. "Sir, I wish to submit a petition and a letter."

"Bring your papers here, Miss Graham."

Watched by all, sensing Ronan's concern and feeling Corbie's piercing glare like a knife blade, she handed the pages to Lord Beaton. She did not want to explain the matter before the company here. But this step was imperative. She knew that. But she began to twist her fingers.

Reading the pages, Beaton cocked a brow, then looked up. "Most of you wait outside. Only Miss Graham and her father will remain. Robertson! Show them to the foyer."

"Ellison," Ronan murmured, as he left. He looked puzzled. Her heart galloped, her hands shook with uncertainty.

But she was determined to present her claim to the court— and speak to her father about her marriage. These last weeks with Ronan had taught her greater confidence, but her nature would always be to doubt herself. That demon resurfaced with claws as her father approached.

"Ellison, what is this about?"

"You will see, Papa."

"Darrach, wait," Sir Hector called. Ronan turned at the door. "We must talk. Where can you be found?"

"I am a renting a house on North Castle Street. But I can come to you." He glanced at Ellison.

She set at hand to her upper chest. Her tenant was Ronan? Neither he nor Cameron had mentioned it. Perhaps it was meant to be a surprise. She smiled a little, and he nodded slightly.

"Come to my home tomorrow," Sir Hector said. With a nod, Ronan left, but the flash of concern in his blue eyes went straight through Ellison's heart. Soon she would tell him what she had done here. There had simply been no chance to explain.

"Lord Beaton, I wish a word with my daughter."

"Take a moment, then. I need to consider this petition."

Sir Hector took her elbow and led her to a corner by windows overlooking the square.

"Papa, what did Mr. Corbie tell you?" She looked into his gray eyes, so like her own.

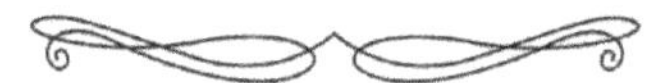

Chapter Twenty-Eight

ONAN WATCHED HIGH rainclouds through the tall windows in the Parliament House foyer. The bells of the cathedral rang again, drowning other noises, but he could hear the skirl of pipes and beating drums as Highland regiments practiced for tomorrow's procession. He ought to be there, he thought, with them, with Sir Evan, who had sent word to invite him.

But he would stay here while Ellison did whatever she had come to do. Had she told her father of the marriage yet? Had Corbie done something to pressure her? Staving off worry, he waited silently beside Hugh and Sorcha, while Corbie and Pitlinnie stood apart, looking annoyed. Lord Jameson crossed to the entrance while speaking with Robertson, his clerk.

"Darrach." Corbie approached. Ronan turned stiffly. "You can go on your way. Miss Graham has important business to discuss with Justice Beaton and Sir Hectory."

"I can wait," Ronan said in a flat tone.

"Take my advice." Corbie lifted his chin high. He was not tall, but had a way of radiating arrogance. "Leave the girl be."

Ronan pulsed a muscle in his jaw, took a breath. Two. The hall was nearly empty, for the place was closing down. Three regimental soldiers stood a few yards away. Jameson was near the door. He gauged his options as thunderclouds rumbled in echo of his rising temper. But this was not the time to heave Corbie by his coat tails, much as he ached to do it.

"What do you mean, sir?" he finally asked.

"The paper Miss Graham is delivering today is an application for annulment."

Ronan flared his nostrils. "How would you know that?"

"She confided in me. Quite upset, feeling she had made a mistake, that she was coerced. I consoled and counseled her."

"Ah." Ronan turned away, sucking in a breath. Then he rounded back, hand clamped in a hard ball, reared back, and slammed Corbie's jaw.

Thrown back, Corbie stumbled into Pitlinnie, who roared at Ronan. The regimental soldiers came running. Ronan opened his fist, balled it again, and hit Pitlinnie with bullish force, knocking both men down like dominoes on the marble floor.

He spun on his heel and walked away. Two soldiers veered after him, with Hugh and Sorcha in their wake along the length of the enormous hall.

Jameson stepped in his path. "Darrach!"

Ronan stopped mid-stride. "Sir," he growled, still simmering. Let them arrest him. He hardly cared.

"I read your bride's petition," the justice said. "To be honest, I might have done the same to those bastards. Guards!" he called. "Leave this man to me. Take those two and hold them for Lord Beaton's decision. It will come shortly."

"My lord, thank you—but I do not understand." Ronan shook his head in confusion, wondering why the girl's petition for annulment made Jameson sympathetic to him.

"Take a walk. Cool your head. Then find her."

"My lord," Ronan said, and shoved through the doors into a light rain. Hugh and Sorcha hurried after him.

"Ronan! What in blazes was that?" Hugh asked.

"What they deserved." He turned. "Miss Beaton, my apologies. Can we take you back to Lady Strathniven's house?"

"I will wait for my brother. Lord Darrach, what you did was just magnificent!"

He flexed his aching hand and gave her a bitter smile. "It did not feel that way."

"Are you coming back inside?"

"I have an important errand. Hugh, are you with me? I am off to Calton Jail. Miss Beaton, your brother will be looking for you soon."

He cleft through the hordes filling the square and strode down the long slope of the High Street. He did not wait for Hugh, knowing he would keep up.

HERE WAS HER chance to explain, Ellison thought. Mustering courage, she straightened her posture and faced her father. She was sure that whatever Corbie had told him was slanted.

"Adam said," growled her father, "that you married this fellow Darrach in a Highland ceremony. Unthinkable! But he explained the circumstances, and assured me that you wisely decided to correct your regrettable impulse. Adam's offer to marry you stands, and he hopes you will agree. You are fortunate." He glowered, but then shook his head. She felt his deep disappointment more than his anger with her.

"I am sorry Mr. Corbie told you first. It was not his place. I tried to find time at home, but you were too busy to listen. I wanted to tell you the whole of it. Corbie left out certain details."

"Best forgotten, I am sure. But he said you were compromised, so at the least, I assume that Darrach recognized his obligation."

"I was not compromised. I owe him my life." *My heart.* "He is not what you think."

"I am usually a good judge of character, and so I was surprised, I admit. MacGregor, er, Darrach, seemed a solid enough fellow once I met him. But you will make amends today, and we will discuss the matter later."

"He is more of a gentleman than many others we know, Papa."

"I did think today that he demonstrated a noble spirit and gentlemanly manners as well. Even so, his actions toward you were wrong and he should pay."

"Papa—"

"Soon this unpleasant situation will be done and we can forget about the Highland spectacle—and the little spectacle of our own making." He shook his head again.

"Papa, listen to me. I am not filing for annulment."

"Corbie said you were submitting the papers. I suppose I am expected to witness them."

"Listen. I submitted a complaint against Mr. Corbie and Pitlinnie."

"Why would do that?" His gray eyebrows snapped together.

"I am accusing them of conspiring to kidnap me and endanger my life."

"What?" He leaned toward her.

"But for Darrach, I do not know what would have happened to me that night. If Corbie had succeeded, I would be married to him now, and would certainly seek an annulment and charges of abuse in addition. Papa, this is why Darrach and I married impulsively—he wanted to protect me and prevent Mr. Corbie's hateful scheme."

Her father scowled down at her. "Ellison, this is madness."

"It is the truth. I am married, aye. And I am happy, Papa. I chose this. I love him," she emphasized. Her hands were shaking, her limbs were shaking. She continued. "You need to know that Adam Corbie is not the good man you think him to be. He and Pitlinnie planned to destroy Ronan MacGregor and take over Glenbrae whisky. And Corbie only wants to marry me so that Lady Strathniven will leave her estate to him. She is undecided. I think she sees more of the truth about Corbie than she wants to admit."

"She has long been of two minds with him." Brow creased, he sighed. "Adam tells this story differently."

"I am sure he does. And I am sorry that you must learn the truth like this."

"How did I miss this if it is true? I saw no indication of such behavior. Is it possible I have not paid attention to what goes on around me?" He spoke half to himself then.

"You are so busy, Papa, with much on your mind, and daughters you have raised alone. You do the best you can."

"Too busy, though. Beaton is calling us over. Let us hear what he has to say. And I must read your account."

Discussing the accusations and documents did not take as long as Ellison thought. Justice Beaton and Sir Hector were quick of shared mind, terse and efficient, and quick to conclude that Ellison's claims were warranted until more was known.

"Sir Hector," Beaton said, "I believe you need to employ a new secretary."

"Whatever the truth is, my lord, I cannot give the man the benefit of the doubt where my daughter is concerned. As for this other fellow, Pitlinnie, I only know he makes a good whisky and is a generous donor to the city."

"He donates to gain favor with the government," Ellison said.

"That could be," Beaton said. "He has some English peers in his pocket, I think. But I cannot guess what he would want with that."

"He wants Glenbrae," Ellison supplied. "He wants credit for the finest whisky to be his, not Darrach's. If Mr. Corbie gains Strathniven and Pitlinnie has Glenbrae, they will combine and make a large profit for themselves. And even rise in the government."

Both men frowned at that. "Interesting," said Beaton. "Your daughter has a keen mind, sir. She might be correct."

"She has a very keen mind, my lord. She is a writer, I wish to add. If her—husband gains the estates of Darrach and Strathniven someday, it might be a good thing for all."

"Well, for now we can only try to resolve this situation. Was there mention of annulment, Miss? Or should I say, Lady Darrach?"

"Not at all, my lord." She folded her hands calmly, fingers still, spirit calm and certain. She felt burdens leaving her shoulders, and thought of Ronan waiting for her outside. All would be resolved and they could find their happiness together—if her father ever recovered from the news of her marriage, she thought.

"I may have misjudged Lord Darrach," Sir Hector said then, and she stared up at him.

"Many have been misjudged here," Beaton replied. "The law will rectify it. Lady Darrach, thank you for bringing this to the court's attention. I will pursue it. For now, I think it best to order Corbie and Pitlinnie to be detained until things can be sorted out. Your accusations have some weight."

"Thank you. I did not want to cause trouble, but this had to be brought to light."

"They will have a chance to defend themselves and the outcome remains to be seen."

"Thank you, Lord Justice." Though he was Sorcha's older brother, she had only used his various formal titles.

"I am glad to help, my dear." He stood. "And glad to assist Lord Darrach, knowing of his bravery in India. A worthy man. Now I must find my sister, who is waiting for me."

Walking out beside her father, Ellison glanced around the hall but did not see Ronan. "They must be outside," she said as they left the hall.

"I MUST SAY," her father mused, "I began thinking differently about Darrach today. His willingness to place himself in jeopardy to help others is singular."

"He would do anything for his friends and kin."

"And for you. But what truly has changed my thinking is seeing you today," he said, taking her arm. "You truly love this man. I saw that, and I saw how much he cares for you. He makes you happy—that is what I want for my daughters, though I may not show it. Even more, I saw a difference in you that I hoped to see someday."

"What do you mean, sir?"

"Confidence. I saw you stand up for what you believe in." He smiled ruefully. "I thought discipline might make you stronger and happier. Perhaps that was not the best course. It is not criticism that improves, I think, but love. You have shown me that, my dear. It is a hard lesson, I vow."

"Oh!" Ellison said through tears.

"Sometimes you are more the image of your mother than your sisters. You have her heart and her imagination. You and Darrach will do well together."

"Thank you, Papa." She blinked away tears.

"We will talk further this." He looked around. "I do not see him here."

She whirled about. "I thought he would wait."

"Something must have come up. I will tell my driver to take you home in my carriage. I have some work to do, and I must have dinner with the organizing committee. I will see you tomorrow." He kissed her cheek.

"THE KING, A smuggler? I wish I had been there!" Linhope said.

"Wish we were all there, and out of here," MacInnes said. "By God, it is good to see you, Ronan, and Cameron too."

"Darrach," Linhope reminded him, for Ronan had told them about the inheritance.

"Time we are done with the past, lads," Ronan said. "I do not regret our efforts to finish the work my brother and cousin began. But we are fortunate that a solution has appeared."

Cameron leaned a shoulder against the wall, arms folded. "Lord Darrach here discovered the remedy for this situation. We all owe him our thanks."

"If this warrant for liberation holds, we will be released soon, aye?" MacInnes asked.

"It should hold," Ronan said.

"And then?" Linhope asked.

"My advice to all of you is to behave," Cameron said.

"I plan on it." Iain scratched at his beard. "We need a barber and a tailor before we leave here."

"I will send a barber in tomorrow," Ronan said. "And a tailor too. We have no guarantee from the court as yet, you do understand that. But you should be ready to walk out of here with your heads high. If for some reason this petition is refused, I will find another way. I will not give up."

"Everyone needs a lawyer like you," MacInnes said, and laughed.

"You have both been of service here in Calton," Hugh said. "That will count as well."

"So, we need be Highland heathens no longer?" MacInnes asked.

"No more. Well, MacInnes may always be a roughshod Highlander," Ronan teased.

"I prefer it. And hardly feel like a gentleman now." He scratched his overgrown beard.

"One hundred and three days? You are certain?" Linhope asked.

"By all counts, aye." Hugh said. "Steps in setting up charges and a trial were missed."

"You may want to thank the king for that—the chaos of his visit may have interfered with procedures," Ronan said.

"If you have freedom," Hugh cautioned, "you are done with the free trade."

Ronan laughed. "The laws will change soon, and smuggling will not be as profitable for anyone."

"If things can be resolved quickly, you lads may be able to enjoy part of the festivities around the royal visit," Ronan said. "I want to introduce you to the friends who helped me. Lady Strathniven is one of them. And Miss Graham—you might remember her."

"The angel who visited us in the dungeons? Bonny lass,"

MacInnes said.

"She is Lady Darrach now." Ronan grinned.

"What!" They stood, clapped shoulders, laughed and congratulated him, asking what had happened.

"I will explain later, I promise," he said. "That reminds me, another friend will be very happy to hear of your release, when it comes. Especially you, Linhope."

Linhope looked puzzled, but a smile quirked his lips. "Who might that be?"

"Mairi Brodie."

"Darrach," Linhope said, shoving a hand through his long blond hair, "when you send fresh clothing and gear here for us, remember that the royal Stewart sett is my right and honor as Viscount Linhope. And send a good deal of soap."

Never had Ruari seen a lovelier sight than Lady Isabella standing on the castle parapet in the moonlight. Its light cast a burnishing glow over her and turned the sandstone walls to silver. She sighed. He sighed too, from his post at the wall.

He was her loyal guard and seneschal now, and must protect her. Keep her safe. Love her from a distance. It would have to be enough.

Far off, under the moonlight, he saw the glint of steel among the shadowy trees, and heard the soft thunder of many hoofbeats.

"Lady," he said. "Go inside. Do as I say. They must not see you here." He guided her to the narrow door in a corner tower. "Hurry!"

He turned back, picked up his bow and quiver of arrows. He did not know if he would see the dawn. But if Isabella was safe—

Ellison set down the pen, seated in her candlelit bedroom.

Outside, the purple bloom of summer darkness gathered. She had hoped Ronan would come to the house that evening and she had waited, but he never came.

But she could go to him. He was her husband—and staying in her own house just a block away. Like her father, he might have duties keeping him away this evening, since the procession of the clans was set for the next day. But she could wait for him. She had a key.

Smiling at the thought, she rose, grabbed her jacket and bonnet, and readied herself. Finding courage for the larger things—escaping the ancient tower, standing up to Papa and Corbie—she was finding it in other ways too. She was stronger now, and grateful to Ronan for helping her discover that. Changes might come on their own, wrought by time and necessity, but in mere weeks, she had reclaimed her bolder self, the girl she had been years earlier.

But she was different now, wiser, more sure of herself. She still felt easily worried and anxious, but she was finding ways to push past fear, not shrink away and concede. She knew that she could stand in the face of the storm and know she was loved, and knew how to love in turn.

She wanted to see him desperately and could not wait longer. He was just one street away, and she was his wife now.

Moments later, she slipped out of the quiet house into the darkened street. Gas lamps, newly set throughout the city, twinkled like stars overhead as she hurried along George Street and turned up the slope of North Castle. A lamppost glowed at the corner, gas lines having been laid in the city a couple of years earlier, to light her way.

She hurried over cobblestones through shadows and pools of gaslight. Ahead, she heard a carriage rolling away, saw its shadow pass out of sight.

The curved front window of her own house, she saw, was dim, with just a little light inside. She slowed, wondering if he was home—wondering for a moment if she should turn back to

George Street after all, and wait. No, she told herself. This was what she wanted.

RONAN SAT IN the single chair in the parlor of the empty house, swirling the glass in his hand, watching the amber liquid flash and swirl. He looked up at Hugh Cameron.

"I do not have much food in the house, if you are hungry. All I can offer is an excellent dram of Glenbrae whisky. King's favorite, by the way." He sipped again.

Hugh huffed, leaning a hip against a sturdy table, for there was no other seat. "I suspect you have had a good bit of that fine Glenbrae by now."

"Not enough to erase discovering that my bride is discarding me. But drink is not my wont and I have a headache now. Perhaps I shall finish drowning my sorrows tomorrow." Ronan set the glass on the floor. "I need a maid," he said, glancing around.

"You need more than a maid," Hugh drawled.

His jacket lay on the floor beside his valise and a pile of tartan, his kilt for the next day, topped by a bonnet fixed with the two feathers of a chieftain. He would wear that gear tomorrow as part of Sir Evan's retinue in the procession. "I need a maid and furniture for a maid to dust. And food, and a cook to cook the food."

"Settling in, are we?"

"And I need the wife who has thrown me over because she took advice from a fellow half my worth. Half my size, at least," he groused.

"Not nearly half your worth. Feeling sorry for yourself is useless. You will sort it out."

"She's annulled our wee wedding."

"She will change her mind."

"She changed her mind about the wee wedding, sir. She seemed happy," he added. "I thought we were happy."

"Her father is a powerful influence."

"Rat Corbie is a powerful influence too. More than I thought." He rubbed a hand over his face. "One good thing about this damnable royal visit," he began.

"I am hard-pressed to think of one just now."

"With all the chaos in the city, Corbie forgot to count the number of days we were in prison. Hah!" Ronan said.

"It was brilliant of you to notice it."

"I am a bit fou," Ronan said then, feeling as if his head spun a little.

"Get some rest. My driver is waiting to take me back to my mother's house. Her place is overrun with guests and good cheer."

"Well, this is not a cheerful place for you, so go on. I will see you tomorrow for a very important day, so they say."

"It is an honor for you to ride beside Sir Evan, as he request-ed. Are you up to it?

Ronan waved a hand. "I will be. Until tomorrow, sir."

"Good night. Get to bed." Hugh stepped out and closed the door.

Hearing the vehicle wheels creak, hearing hoofbeats, Ronan leaned forward, arms on his knees. He was not so very drunk, as such things went, but he was very tired. And unhappy. Miserable, he thought. That was the word. Miserable without her.

But with her or without her, he would be fine eventually. If he had to live without Ellison Graham, by God he would. He would try to forget her, or at least make the effort.

For now, bed. He stood, wavered a bit.

Hearing footsteps, a knock, he stopped. He had not yet drawn the latch on the door.

"Come in, Cameron! What did you forget?" he called.

The door opened and a woman, slight and graceful, entered in a sweep of dark skirts. Her delicate face was shadowed by a wide hat fussy with ribbons and heather fronds. She looked around. He saw an angel's face.

"Ah," he drawled. "The wee landlady."

Chapter Twenty-Nine

Pulling off her gloves, heart pounding, hoping for a welcome but realizing otherwise, Ellison stared at Ronan. He was in shirtsleeves, waistcoat, kilt, without cravat, his collar open to his strong throat. His dark hair was curled and mussed, his blue eyes glittered. So very blue, even in candlelight. He did not look glad to see her.

"Are you drunk?"

"A bit. Not much. Do not worry, it is not a usual state for me, my dear. Oh, wait, we will not be residing together after all, will we. What can I do for you?" He swept an arm toward the parlor. "Would you care to sit?"

"There is only one chair." She walked into the room. He followed.

"I am enough of a gentleman to offer it to you."

She whirled. "What is wrong?"

"Perhaps you can tell me."

"I waited. I thought you might call at the house."

"I have been very busy, madam." He spoke with exaggeration, waving an arm at the empty house.

"You did not wait for me at Parliament Hall."

"Should I have?" He leaned in the doorway, looming over her.

Hands folded, she regarded him, and chose not to sit. She noticed a glass upended in a little puddle on the floor. "I thought you might wait."

"But she is independent now," he said, his gaze intent. "She needs no one. Found her backbone, which she needed to do, I will admit. Come here alone, to a man's home. Drove a gig herself?"

"Walked. To find her husband very drunk."

"Not drunk. More—unhappy." He gestured. "Please sit. Or did you come to inspect your property?"

She stifled the sob that came up quickly. His anger was clear and sharp, and she did not understand. "What is wrong?"

"Why are you here without your wee secretary on your heels?"

"Mr. Corbie is in jail with Mr. Pitlinnie."

"Ah, justice will be served. I punched him," he told her. "Both of them."

"Good. I did not know. I came here tonight because I wanted to see you." *So much,* she wanted to add, but his scowl discouraged her words.

"Did you want a signature?"

"For what?"

"For your paperwork, madam."

"Well, if you want to speak as a witness, you may do that."

"That is cold. I would not have credited you with that."

"Ronan, I do not understand." She was confused. They were talking at cross purposes, and he not listening. She drove her fingers together, twisted them. "I am at a loss here."

"I am the one at a loss," he murmured. "You are the one who knows what you want."

"I thought we were—" *In love.* She hesitated. Love was strong and could survive anything. And love was also fragile, and needed careful handling. "I thought you were fond of me."

A bitter laugh. "Fond! Aye, very fond. We shall be fast friends now."

"Ronan." A sob rose again. "Please, Ronan—"

"Shall I call you a hackney to take you home? I can find one."

He pushed away from the doorjamb.

"No! I thought—I might stay here tonight."

He turned back. "Stay? Have your cake, is that it?"

"I am so confused. What has happened?"

"A great deal, apparently. I heard about the annulment. I wish you had warned me."

She felt the blood drain from her head so quickly that she felt dizzy, and set a hand on the back of the empty chair. "Is that it? Who told you that?"

"Corbie said you brought annulment papers to be processed."

"I never—"

"Meant to hurt me? It just slipped your mind?" He was bitter, a ferocious guardian of his anger. And like her father, he was not listening, just plowing ahead.

Her temper gathered like a storm cloud. "You are so wrong. And so drunk."

"I am not so drunk. I am a gentleman. You ought to know that?"

"Not just now."

"A gentleman, a lawyer, a distiller. A viscount. A rogue. Not a smuggler, not exactly." He moved toward her. "I speak perfect English, Gaelic too. I can tie a cravat and polish my boots till they shine like steel. I know the proper fork to use."

"Ronan—"

He took another step. He was steady, and she realized indeed not so drunk, but indignant. If he thought she had annulled the marriage, he had the right.

"Listen to me," she said, but he was still talking.

"Ellison Graham, you listen to me. I would give you every part of me, I would share what others would never see. I would pledge my life to you because I love you beyond life."

"Ronan." Her voice trembled. Tears sprang.

"We both wanted freedom, did we not say that?"

"We did. Now listen. Listen! You are—you can be so beastly!"

He sighed, pushed a hand through his hair. "Best go before I say something else stupid. I do beg your pardon." A wince flashed across his face. "I am cooling now. But best you go, if you have done this.

"Will you listen? I have not done this! Sit and listen!"

"A gentleman does not sit while a lady stands."

"Did you know," she said softly, "even when you are upset and beastly angry, you are still the finest gentleman and the very best man I have ever known? Did you know that?"

Fingers raking through his messy hair, he sent her a sidelong glance. "Whatever you have to say, out with it."

"I did not submit an annulment, you vile beast."

A quick, surprised look. A near smile, sheepish, clear-eyed. "You did not?"

"No! I brought an accusation of kidnapping against Corbie and Pitlinnie. They are in Calton Jail tonight."

He stared. "No annulment."

"None."

"I am a vile beast." He rubbed a hand over his face.

"You are."

"That took courage, if you did that."

"It did. And I learned it from you."

"You had it in you already."

"Why did I ever listen to Mr. Corbie?" she asked.

"I have no idea." He watched her. "You look like an angel."

"And you," she said, coming closer, "you are sometimes the perfect gentleman. You dance beautifully and catch fish in your bare hands. You distill the best whisky in the world, you always choose the right fork, and you defend others with your very life. And you make a lonely lass feel heard and seen and so good—" She drew a ragged breath.

"Ellison," he murmured.

"And I love you with all my heart and soul. Madly so, even now. Beast."

"I am. I am sorry."

"I do not care a whit who you are, what title you have or do not have. I do not care if you live in a cave or a castle. Or in this house." She gestured with a flailing hand. Tears were running down her cheeks. "It—is so clean. You made it so nice. When did you do that?"

"It has a chair. Two. And a bed."

She sobbed a little, caught it behind her hand.

He opened his arms then, and she ran to him, deep into his embrace, knocking into him so that he huffed. She could get enough of his warmth and strength around her as he caught her deep in his arms, set his cheek against her bonnet, crushing it.

"Silly damn thing," he said, and with deft fingers, stripped loose the bow and tore the hat free, tossing it aside. "Fetching creation, though."

She laughed through tears, pressing tightly against him, inhaled his scent, male and musky, laced with whisky. The warmth and power of his body enveloped her. "I do so love you."

"I love you," he whispered. "I was wrong. I was—so upset."

"I was wrong to not tell you what I meant to do. I am sorry Corbie got to you."

"Well done for taking him down. Ellison—have I ever told you that I fell in love with you the moment you walked into that dungeon?"

"You never said that."

"I am telling you now. You were my angel. The one who showed up to change me, change my life." He cupped her cheek, tilted her face up, kissed her so gently she felt as if she melted there in his arms, had to clench her toes to make sure she was whole and standing.

"You did not need changing. I did. I am better for finding you."

"You were perfect already, lass. You just did not know it." He kissed her again, let it linger, pulled her against him, so that she knew his body was strong and awake and ready.

"God, Ronan, oh," she said, sinking against him. "Oh! Another thing."

"Mmm," he murmured, deepening the kiss, rising again.

"My father—I told Papa"—she kissed him—"we were married and happy and he said—"

"No mention of your father now, aye?" He spoke softly, his voice driving downward in her body, his lips pressed to her hair, then tracing along her cheek. Crooking a finger, he tipped her chin up to touch her lips with his. "But I am proud of you." The kiss was deep, exquisite.

She parted for a moment. "He says he was wrong about you."

"Aye, he was." Ronan laughed softly. Ellison renewed the next kiss and the next, each touch and taste hungrier, more fervent, heated and moist, yet her thoughts whirled yet. "I know it does not matter what he thinks, but—"

"It does matter. But hush now, later for that." His lips on hers smothered her reply. Her limbs were dissolving so fast she nearly sagged in his arms. "Shall we go upstairs, darling girl?" He lifted her in his arms as if she weighed nothing and headed for the steps.

"Wait—the lock—"

"The lock." He swung, carrying her as she reached out to latch the door. "Happy now?"

"So very," she whispered against his neck.

"Nothing in the upper rooms," he murmured. "Well. A bed. I can show you that."

"Please."

This time, she realized as she lay with him, they were finally and completely alone; no interruption, no obligation until dawn or beyond. This time, she felt their love, still so new, ripen into a commitment that they need not explain or examine. It simply existed, a deep trust that was full in every moment, with each touch, kiss, caress, each word. Beyond the darkness of this bed, it would last and deepen. His kisses were different now, hers were different too. The world had changed somehow.

This time she felt a freedom unlike any she had ever known—fear abandoned, worries loosening their hold, thoughts dissolving like mist off a fairy loch. As he explored her body with gentle, knowing fingertips, she discovered his with awe for his sinew and firmness, each taut muscle and velvety stretch of skin moving with strength and certainty. When he surged, she arched, when he stretched, she softened, and when his body eased into hers, her body gloved his.

This time, as the old, plain bed dipped and creaked with their rhythms, they laughed and then grew serious, and when the blankets slipped away, he covered and warmed her. She felt stronger, safer than ever before—and she wanted to give him all that he needed too. She wanted him to know he was loved beyond love in the truth of who he was here and now. He was the hero in her life, the man she had dreamed of, the man she allowed into her heart, vital and real and powerful, embodying the warrior she had created on scraps of paper smeared with ink. Ronan MacGregor was her knight, her rogue, her defender, her dearest friend and tender lover, her rock and anchor. She wanted to be all to him too.

"Dawn," he murmured after a while.

"Let it be," she said. "We need not move."

"Just a little," he whispered, sliding his warm, slow, sleepy touch over her shoulder, his curious fingers finding the softest parts of her, his lips finding hers.

"But I am hungry," she admitted.

"You ought to be, Lady Darrach," he said, and she laughed into his shoulder.

RONAN ADJUSTED THE plaid draped over his shoulder, patterned in MacGregor blood red and forest green, tugged at his black coat, and straightened his bonnet with its fir sprig for the Gregorach, and the two feathers of a chieftain. The morning was already warm and humid, and gray skies foretold another bout of the rains that threatened to drench the royal visit. He looped a painted shield over one arm, checked the sheathed sword and pistol that he carried, and patted his horse's neck. He smiled to himself, grateful to his core to be here, to be clear of worries, to be content and happy in the day and his future.

Behind him were fifty Highlanders replete in bright plaids, gleaming weapons, and feathered and sprigged bonnets. Donal Brodie stood proudly with them. The MacGregors would lead the enormous gathering comprised of over a thousand Highlanders that formed part of the procession set to escort the royal regalia, crown and scepter and more, from Edinburgh Castle down to Holyroodhouse at the foot of the High Street.

Beside him, magnificently dressed in the Highland gear of the chief, Sir Evan MacGregor sat his own horse. Between them, riding a pony, was Evan's eldest son, all of twelve and proudly dressed in full Highland kit too.

"Are you ready, sir?" the MacGregor asked Ronan.

"I am. And I thank you for placing me here with you."

"No one more deserving. I mean that." His cousin smiled, his handsome face puckered with the deep scar running from brow to chin. His right arm lay still on the reins, limp fingers protected in a thick leather glove. Sir Evan MacGregor was known for leadership, pragmatism, kindness—and for surviving devastating injuries and returning to lead his clan. He was also famed in social circles for a singular physical beauty undimmed by scarring. The handsomest man in Scotland, they called him. And one of the most respected, Ronan knew.

"No one I would rather have here," Sir Evan said. "I would not be here today if not for your actions in India. You saved my life—and dragged me back to Scotland when I was weak and vulnerable and furious, blaming you for my brother's death on the battlefield behind us. But I was wrong about that, and it is past time I apologized for it."

"Not necessary, Evan."

"I held it against you. But I am alive because of you, and I will not forget that again."

Ronan smiled, accepting the apology and shrugging away the compliment. "The memories are difficult, I know, and hard for me too."

"I owe you more than I can say. I mean it sincerely. And I owe you congratulations as well. The deputy lord provost's daughter, indeed! My wife is eager to meet her, and we would like you both to stay with us for a long visit after this infernal commotion is done in Edinburgh. Now—shall we get this moving?"

"If you are ready, sir, we are all ready."

"Then let us show the king and all of Edinburgh the strength and majesty of the Scottish Highlanders." Riding forward with Ronan and his young son, Sir Evan drew his sword and raised it high, looking over his shoulder.

"*An Griogarach!*" he shouted.

A huge clamor of voices echoed his cry as the Highlanders stepped forward.

Epilogue

ELLISON SAT IN the carriage, twisting her gloves in her hand.

"Do stop, Elly," Sorcha said. "You are so nervous to-day."

"Calm, dear," the viscountess said. "He will do well in there."

"I know. I just wish ladies were allowed to attend the levee too." She looked through the carriage window and across the Holyrood courtyard. Dozens of carriages were parked along the graveled drive fronting the royal palace. In the vehicles, ladies waited for their gentlemen while others strolled up and down the drive, skirts billowing, bonnet ribbons flying on that windy afternoon.

"We are all waiting, including the very Duchess of Atholl and all the rest," Lady Strathniven said. "Darrach will be praised as a perfect gentleman and an asset to Scotland, and this day will lead to good things for both of you. I am sure of it."

Ellison smiled. "I do hope so, my lady."

RONAN STOOD IN front of Sir Hector as they moved ahead slowly in the long, crowded line of gentlemen waiting to be admitted to the room where they would greet and be introduced to King George.

"Not many ahead of us now, and scores of men behind us," Sir Hector told Ronan. "You are well prepared, I think."

"I am, all thanks to your daughter, sir."

Sir Hector gave him a rare smile. "That turned out better than any of us could ever have hoped. I owe you thanks, and an apology."

"Not needed, sir. All is well, especially once this is over and done."

"And once Corbie and Pitlinnie have their comeuppance," Graham muttered. "I owe you and Ellison thanks for that revelation as well. By the way, I wanted to tell you that I had dinner last evening in a small group with the king, and with the Lord Provost and Sir Walter Scott too. Your name was mentioned."

"Mine!" Ronan looked at him in surprise.

"The king had heard of the scandal with my secretary, and as we filled in some of the story, you and my daughter were both named heroes in the matter. The king asked if you were the one responsible for the whisky he so enjoys. I said aye and proudly claimed you as my new son-in-law."

"Thank you, Sir Hector."

"The king is very busy, but wanted to know more. And—oh, we are moving again!"

Ronan peered ahead as the queue edged along in the reception room. At the far end of the vast room, he could see the draped dais and King George, tall and portly, in a kilt and saggy pink stockings, of all things. The king greeted guests in a booming voice and a rapid, abrupt way, which helped move the long line steadily.

"And what, sir?" Ronan asked, curious.

"King George mentioned reviewing a petition this week to restore an old earldom to the current Lord Darrach. He called you 'that whisky lord,' and we confirmed that as well. Then—you do have your calling card, sir? The Lord-in-Waiting is just ahead, taking the calling cards of those who will be introduced."

"I have it. And then?" Ronan prodded.

"The king seems to favor restoring the earldom to the original family. That would be you, sir." Sir Hector moved forward, as did Ronan. "He seems pleased to approve it, not only because he likes your whisky—ah, here we go," Hector said as he surrendered his card, and Ronan did the same. "He also likes being associated with heroic men, and he had heard of your actions. He is impressed."

"Thank you for telling me so, sir. But who petitioned to restore the earldom?"

"Lady Strathniven," he answered. "She does not want to leave the title to her nephew, and she recently discovered—in talking to you—your family history. Your kin were the Earls of Strathniven. So she took it to Lord Lyon to be approved by the Lyon Court, the court of heraldry in Scotland."

"She never said," Ronan replied, astonished. "I am honored."

"She is set on you becoming the legitimate earl. She would push the very king on it if she could, I think." Sir Hector chuckled.

"I will thank her. And Lord Lyon as well."

"You must meet him. A very good fellow—about your age, I think, with a similar background. Sir Alasdair Drummond—Lord Lyon is his official position in the heraldry office. He is here somewhere—there. I will introduce you later."

Ronan followed Graham's pointing finger to see a tall, black-haired young gentleman dressed in full Highland kit, a big handsome Highland man standing well above the others in the circle where he stood chatting. He saw the fellow smile broadly and laugh heartily. That alone made him like the man, aside from his immediate gratitude and curiosity.

"Sir Alasdair's wife is the daughter of a very fine painter. You and Ellison should have your portraits done. I hear she does rather beautiful miniatures if you like that sort of thing."

"Someday, aye," Ronan said.

"Oh, one thing more." Graham was in an unusually cheerful and talkative mood as they shuffled along, Ronan thought. "I told Sir Walter that my daughter is an exceptional writer who is working on a novel. He expressed interest in reading it if she would like."

Ronan grinned. "She would be more than delighted, I am sure. What I have read is coming along very nicely."

"Good. Ah, Mr. Cameron is just there. He is not being introduced, having met the king earlier, but here he is to cheer you on. Cameron!"

Hugh made his way toward them through the dense crowd. "Darrach! Sir Hector! What a day this is! Glad to see you both—have you heard the latest development? Murder is afoot!"

"Murder!" Ronan lifted a brow.

"Corbie is eager to paint Pitlinnie with tar and is blaming him for everything he can. He says Pitlinnie set you up to be arrested, as he wants to be rid of you. And—he says Pitlinnie was behind the murders of your brother and your cousin. According to Pitlinnie, Corbie was the one who thought to take down the Whisky Rogues to begin a takeover of Glenbrae and finally Strathniven. Those two have been plotting something for years."

"Unthinkable, all of it," Sir Hector said.

Ronan shook his head, sad to hear it. "I cannot say I am surprised."

"We need evidence, of course," Sir Hector said. "But it is sobering to realize they were scheming to take others down, and now seem determined to undo each other."

"Corbie feared he would not inherit Strathniven without marrying Ellison," Hugh said. "He admitted it. And Pitlinnie wanted your distillery, and your glen, and went after those."

"What a tangle," Ronan said. "It will take a long while to sort through that unsavory mess."

"Eventually we will see what a jury decides," Hugh said.

"The line is moving again," Sir Hector said. "Sir Willie Collins. He is so rotund that someone mistook him for the king the other day and bowed to him. Got quite the laugh!"

Chuckling at that, Hugh leaned toward Ronan. "You know Pitlinnie wanted to buy Glenbrae. Sir Evan has refused the offer."

Ronan raised an eyebrow. "I thought it was done even before

we were in Jameson's chambers."

"Not fully signed. But Sir Evan refuses to consider Pitlinnie now. He has had another offer for Glenbrae which would absolve the debts on the property."

"Ah." Ronan felt a new twist of grief at the thought of losing Glenbrae.

"I cannot say much, but the offer would dissolve the debts and still give you full rights to the glen and the distillery."

"Me? To run the distillery, perhaps?"

"This party would gift Glenbrae back to the Darrach estate."

Ronan narrowed his eyes. "Lady Strathniven?"

"I did not say that," Hugh teased.

"I am stunned. So grateful. I just heard about the petition for the earldom."

"Aye, to restore the earldom of Strathniven and rejoin it to the estate of Darrach and Glenbrae. Lady Strathniven petitioned the king. She did not want you to know. A surprise, see."

Ronan huffed, still astonished. "She said nothing of any of it."

"Then be surprised when she does, hey? She is very pleased with herself over it. The Crown still needs to approve it, though the Lyon Court will move it along."

"This is beyond my dreams," Ronan said. "I did not dare hope the old estate that belonged to my family would ever come back together."

"Not guaranteed yet, but aye, it could happen. You would have to give up the title of viscount. Scottish peers are not permitted to hold more than one title. But you would be earl."

"Restoring the original estate would be a huge benefit. But what of Lady Strathniven?"

"She confided to me that she would be happy to rent from you."

"I could never take rent from her. I would give it to her for free. Peppercorn rent," he said, remembering the old tradition. "A token. She might like that."

Hugh laughed. "A bunch of heather every summer. We will

write it into her lease."

"She would love that. So much to think about. So many changes. I am a married man, a viscount—it is a lot to take in."

"And a free man," Hugh drawled.

"Most of all, a happy man," Ronan murmured as his friend clapped his shoulder.

"They are calling your name," Sir Hector said, pushing Ronan ahead of him.

"John Ronan MacGregor, Viscount Darrach!" the Lord-in-Waiting called out. "Maker of Glenbrae whisky. Introduced by The Right Honorable Deputy Lord Provost of Edinburgh, Sir Hector Graham."

Ronan stepped forward.

SEEING RONAN WALKING through a fresh downpour to make his way between the waiting carriages, Ellison leaned past Sorcha to open the door. "Darrach!" she called. "Here!"

"It is raining buckets! You will ruin your gown," Lady Strathniven said.

"It will dry!" Ellison stepped out. "Darrach!"

He ran toward her through the rain, holding onto his dark bonnet, plaid flying. Picking her up by the waist, he spun her about, set her down and kissed her. Laughing, Ellison looped her arms around his neck, the next kiss hidden under the brim of her bonnet and his flat cap. As the rain soaked them, she heard applause and giggles from nearby carriages.

"Not very proper behavior, sir," Ellison said, leaning back to regard him.

"Hang proper. Though if you want to tutor me further, I would not object."

"You know more than I do by now. How was it in there? You are in a rare mood!"

He put an arm around her to hurry her toward the carriage in the rain. "I have some excellent news."

"Tell me!"

"Later, lass. You are soaking wet. And some of the news must wait for privacy."

"Can we wait in the Highlands? I am tired of the city."

"We can. First, the king asked me to bring you to the ladies' assembly in a few days to be introduced."

"Truly!" Eyes wide, she smiled up at him.

"It will be just a greeting and a quick kiss from the king—after you wait hours in the crowd and the heat. But," he said, as they reached the carriage, "it might even change your life."

"I have already had that pleasure. I once met a Highland smuggler who changed my life completely."

"His too." He opened the door and helped her up the carriage steps. "Lady Strathniven, Miss Beaton! Good to see you."

"Darrach, you are cheerful," the viscountess said as they sat, brushing away raindrops. "What did the king have to say when you met him?"

"He likes our whisky, my lady." A little quirking smile and his crinkled blue eyes told Ellison he had a secret that pleased him greatly.

"Well, I could have told you that! You are thoroughly wet, both of you, but you look happy as two puppies, I vow."

"Happy? Oh, yes." Ellison smiled at her husband. He kissed her gloved hand, his eyes twinkling with some secret that she wanted to hear once they were deliciously alone.

Ronan wove his fingers in hers. "Shall we go home, ladies, with a stop at the Graham house first for my lady and Miss Beaton? Then my wife and I will go up to North Castle Street."

"I do hope we can leave for the Highlands as soon as the king departs." Ellison leaned her head on his shoulder, while Sorcha giggled and the viscountess beamed. "That is truly our home."

"It is," he said, and kissed her gloved hand. "Tell me, ladies, how has your day been?"

"Not as good as yours, I think!" the viscountess said as they all laughed.

Author's Note

A Rogue in Firelight (originally published as *Laird of Rogues*) introduces a group of heroes and heroines in Regency Scotland whose lives are changed by adventure and unexpected love when they enter the world of Highland whisky smuggling deliberately or inadvertently. I loved writing these stories. Each one blends adventure, romance, and a touch of fairy magic with a fascinating era in Scottish history. I am thrilled to be able to bring the original trilogy to my readers in new, updated Dragonblade editions with gorgeous covers.

Highland whisky was a prized product, made with the finest ingredients unique to Highland locations—the quality of the water, barley, and peat made the result superior to grain-based whiskies distilled in the Lowlands or England. Whisky smuggling was a busy, tricky, and often necessary business in Scotland, especially in the Highlands. People of every rank and lifestyle might be involved—distillers (legal and illegal), crofters, lairds, titled gentlemen and ladies, excise officers, and even poets (Robert Burns was an excise officer). They roamed the Highland hills, smugglers moving and the excise men trying to prevent the transport of valuable Highland whisky and other products to the border or the sea. There were criminals on both sides of the equation, but many Scots smuggled their goods just to provide for their families. In the face of oppressive laws under English rule and also the ongoing clearances of land and livestock, many Highland regions were devastated over generations. They struggled to survive and to protect their homes, livelihoods, and ancient legacies.

Whether I'm writing medieval, Scottish Regency, or another era, I try to stick closely to history in my novels. I love following pathways through chronology and incidents that inspire plot, dilemma, and resolution, and discovering real people who inspire my characters. Often I include actual historical people and weave them in with my fictional characters to add another layer of authenticity.

For this novel, I dove deeply into the research to learn about Regency Scotland and Regency Edinburgh, as well as the whisky trade in the Highlands, and King George's visit to Scotland in 1822. I followed rabbit holes into warrens that held surprising nuggets of information to illuminate the story. Sometimes, because in my heart I'm a historian as well as a writer, it was hard to come up for air!

Aspects of the characters deserve research too. Ronan Mac-Gregor is a laird, a lawyer, a distiller, and a smuggler, so I studied those areas. Ellison Graham is a heroine who feels boxed in by life, guilt, and an overbearing but well-meaning father. She loves books and secretly yearns to write adventure-romance stories like Sir Walter Scott and other novelists then; I love those novels too, so researching her interests was delightful.

Other than whisky production and the complex business of smuggling. I also delved into Scottish customs, Scottish fairy legends, and Scots law (so exciting to find a wee legal twist to resolve a storyline that had me stumped!). And King George's visit to Scotland was great fun to study—a wild spectacle of pageantry and Celtic magnificence with crowds of thousands on the streets of Edinburgh, while enduring intense summer heat and heavy thunderstorms, as described by contemporary Scots.

The king's visit was raucous and elaborate, from crowded events to his love of Highland whisky, his earnestness in connecting, sometimes awkwardly, with the Scots, and his penchant for kissing every Scottish lady who came within reach.

Reading about his visit inspired me to center my Whisky Rogues series on those crazy weeks in 1822, called by one Scotsman "twenty-one daft days." So many stories and possibilities occurred to me that I'm writing a new series of novels set around the same fascinating historical event.

I hope you enjoyed Ronan and Ellison's story, and I hope you'll look for their companions in *A Rogue in Twilight, A Rogue in Moonlight,* a few related novellas, and my upcoming books too. You can find me at www.susanfraserking.com and also at www. wordwenches.com. Happy reading!

About the Author

Susan King is the bestselling, award-winning author of (so far) 28 historical novels and novellas, a hefty nonfiction history, and dozens of magazine and web articles on education and the craft of writing. Her books, including mainstream historicals Lady Macbeth: A Novel and Queen Hereafter: A Novel of Margaret of Scotland, have been published by Penguin, Random House, HarperCollins, Kensington, ePublishingWorks, and Dragonblade. Praised for historical accuracy, lyrical writing, and storytelling quality, she is a USA Today bestselling author with numerous awards, nominations, and career achievement awards as well as starred reviews from Publisher's Weekly, Booklist, and Library Journal. Most of her books are set in Scotland ranging from the 11th to the 19th centuries.

Susan is a former university lecturer in art history, a private school teacher, and a founding member of one of the longest-running author blogs, "Word Wenches" (wordwenches.com). She holds a Bachelor's in studio art and English literature, a Master's in art history, and completed most of her Ph.D. / ABD in medieval art history. Raised in Upstate New York, she lives in Maryland with her husband and three sons in an ever-growing family.

Website – www.susanfraserking.com